The Edentians

THEY HAVE BEEN HERE SINCE THE BEGINNING OF TIME, NOW THEY ARE LEAVING...

THE EDENTIANS

A NOVEL

GISSELE TRUSSELL

NEW YORK

LONDON • NASHVILLE • MELBOURNE • VANCOUVER

The Edentians

A Novel

Published in New York, New York, by Morgan James Publishing. Morgan James is a trademark of Morgan James, LLC. www.MorganJamesPublishing.com

Proudly distributed by Publishers Group West®

ISBN 9781636981468 paperback
ISBN 9781636981475 ebook
Library of Congress Control Number: 2023931672

Cover Design by:
FormattedBooks
www.formattedbooks.com

Interior Design by:
Christopher Kirk
www.GFSstudio.com

To my husband, with love.

LIST OF CHARACTERS

The Edentians

Danielle: Edentian assigned to record the evolution of the human mind. In her present incarnation, she is an archeologist working for the Met and uses her wealth to preserve the finest works of art and literature the world has produced, to attest to man's worthiness.
Robert: senior Edentian officer and global tycoon, who appears to have been seduced by the wave of greed and corruption. The Edentians no longer know whether to trust or fear him.
Kjell: designer and architect who has influenced civilizations, has disappeared. The other Edentians fear the worst.
Lilith: beautiful immortal, who has amassed incredible wealth and power on the planet, she now lives in pursuit of pleasure.
Cirel: head of the *Group* and planetary representative of Satan, promotes the unholy cause of Lucifer and recruits mercenaries for the next galactic war.

The Mortals

Kitzia O'Neil: clinical psychologist, identifies a pattern in the current violence spreading throughout the country.
Christian Goodman: writer, suspense novelist and former FBI agent, finds himself the protagonist of an adventure more incredible than anything his mind could have ever conjured.
Thomas O'Neil: renowned neurosurgeon, unravels a conspiracy of deceit and misinformation aimed at manipulating the minds of the entire human race.
Jean-Christophe Girard: French archeologist excavating ancient Egyptian ruins, finds astonishing clues that provide answers to the riddle of human existence.

Theodore Edwards: evangelist turned politician, fronts for the *Group* in a universal plot to enslave humanity under the name of God.
Jeff Montgomery: young idealist whose obsession with Lilith traps him in a world of deceit and corruption from which he must escape before it is too late.

PROLOGUE

The two terrorists observed the Hoover Dam with keen interest.

"What do you think?" exclaimed the young man in his mid-twenties who could pass for a college student. His light hair and blue eyes made it easy for him to infiltrate terrorist groups in the US. The two men wore casual clothing, and there was nothing to distinguish them from the other visitors touring the power plant, except for the coiled snake tattooed inside both men's palms—the symbol of membership in the Death Brigade, an international terrorist organization with cells in every major city. The older man was half German, half Arab, and tall, with light olive skin and pale amber eyes, a Berkeley educated chemical engineer. Through his binoculars, he assessed the design of the dam. Then, with a heavy Middle Eastern accent, finally murmured, "It can be done."

"I knew it!" The young man whispered with pride, for he had designed the computer program to measure the dam's cubic capacity, determining the correct amount of contaminants.

"So, Mohammed, what stuff and when?"

The Arab smiled coldly. He never liked to discuss plans with members of different cells.

"What's gonna be the fix?"

Anthrax . . . Botulinum, thought the Arab, but he remained silent, annoyed at the young man's impatience. "Not sure," he said bluntly, vexed to see the usual number of guards protecting the two cylinder intake towers had doubled.

Adjusting the distance control, he continued to scan the area, stopping sharply to focus on a tall, Nordic-looking guard standing on the main concrete tower and looking in his direction. Through his binoculars, he met the guard's eyes. Mohammed lowered his binoculars and turned to look out across the horizon.

"The easiest way, man, would be to blow up the whole thing," continued the young man. "Boom! All gone."

"Perhaps," was all the engineer said. He observed the young American with disdain. Mohammed hated to be assigned collaborators like this young, incoherent earthling, obviously high on cocaine—a computer genius but conveniently expendable.

Mohammed Riezk had a mission to accomplish: the destruction of America. That is how he had come in contact with the *Group*, an international organization with the means to back his mission. He could not stop wondering though, what made the young man and others like him turn on their brothers?

The cell phone rang, interrupting Mohammed's thoughts. He answered, and after a few seconds, he simply murmured, "Understood." He turned to his companion. "Let's go. They're expecting you in New York."

The two men started toward the car. Mohammed extracted a photograph from his shirt pocket, and handed it to the young man. "This is your next target."

The young terrorist grinned. The woman was beautiful, with silky red hair and intense green eyes. Guessing what the young man was thinking, Mohammed firmly stated, "No! And they would prefer her alive."

The young man nodded. He stared at the subject of his assignment and the handwritten name at the bottom: Dr. Danielle Peschard.

"One more thing. Do it expediently. She is protected."

On the other tower, the tall Nordic posing as a guard watched the terrorists rejoin a group of tourists and head for the exit. He knew who had sent them and why. He'd known for a long time this moment would arrive. From his shirt pocket he produced a gadget half the size of an iPhone. When the face of the woman with the red hair appeared, he said, "The time has come." After a brief pause, he added, "You're in danger. It's time to meet at the California safe house."

"Understood. I will proceed with the last transmission."

I

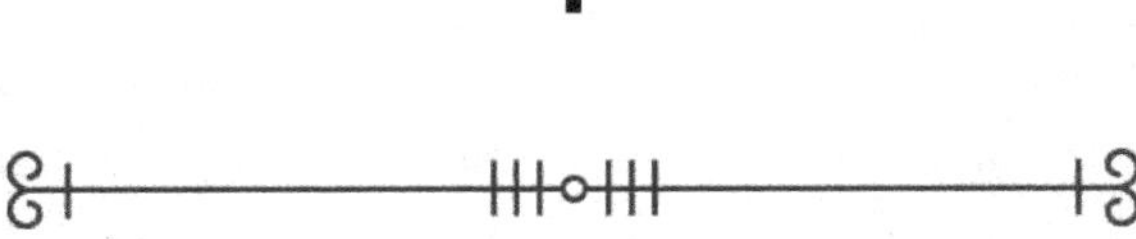

Earth, or Urantia 606 as it was cataloged in the celestial archives, is the farthest and most miniscule of the numerous inhabited worlds in the system of Satania, in one of the 100 major constellations in the local Universe of Nebadon. The constellation's government is situated in a cluster of eleven translucent architectural spheres, of which the brightest and most magnificent is Edentia. (The Urantia Book)

The future of Urantia, also known as Earth, was to be the first point of discussion at the assembly of the Edentian Council.

Here in the constellation's headquarters, the Most High of Edentia and the Mechizedek Council of Three assembled to review all judicial problems related to the administration of the local universe. The Council of Three was empowered to review evidence and formulate verdicts concerning constellation matters.

Machiaventa, chairman of the council, was the first to speak. "Urantia's ongoing calamities are of grave concern. and we must make a final decision." His voice was firm, clear, and beautiful. On Earth, Machiaventa's perfectly proportioned figure and glittering silver hair would have been considered imposing, even breathtaking. On Edentia, his physique did not differ from those of other citizens. It resembled the human body but lacked the density of the pulmonary and circulatory systems. Edentians were created from energy and light.

"It was Urantia's onetime alliance to the universal Luciel insurrection that forced us to impose a quarantine on the planet," added Agath, the second member of the Council of Three.

"They have been isolated, but I'm not sure these souls are redeemable," added Agath. "Man's re-discovery of nuclear power threatens everything we have worked so hard to achieve. The pattern continues to run the same cycle. Earth will sink into darkness and savagery before we take charge again.

"And yet, our Sovereign, Michael, the Creator Son, chose this insignificant, isolated, rebel planet as the rehabilitation ground for fallen angels who repented. We, in the council, have been very supportive of Urantia 606's rehabilitation project and have done everything possible to accelerate the redemption of these souls, as well as uplift the consciousness of their human offspring."

As Machiaventa spoke, a multi-dimensional screen appeared and surrounded the room. It was made of veregonium, an element not yet discovered on Earth. Images of the planet became visible, and the atmosphere displayed a hazy blue-gray, where tropical forests came into focus. Also, where trees fell by the thousands and terrorized birds fled as the rainforests were systematically demolished. The oceans slowly turned a grayish green as the worldwide spillage of oil and nuclear waste progressed, and enormous islands of garbage floated on the water. Horrific images of ongoing earthquakes made obvious the shifting fault lines of the continental plates, resulting from the disturbance created by the worldwide telecommunication industry.

"The planet is still being destroyed faster than we can repair it!" observed Agath, the second council member.

"Yes. We are once again witnessing devastation and annihilation of life." After a thoughtful pause, Machiaventa continued, "Like previous civilizations, Urantia has once again reached its peak, and its inhabitants have once again regressed."

"It is unfortunate that these brutish souls have once again figured out how to split the atom. The time has come to abort the U-606 project." Moriel, the third council member, concluded.

The presentation displayed volcanoes furiously erupting, hurricanes demolishing cities, tidal waves inundating entire islands in the Pacific, and polar icebergs melting.

Machiaventa pointed to the screen, "These events are not the result of global warming. An underground current is being manipulated and wreaking havoc."

The council members exchanged glances of grave concern.

"But our Edentians would not unleash any current without our approval."

"Precisely," affirmed Machiaventa. "I am afraid Arch-rebel Cirel has resurfaced. And look," he said, pointing to the image on the screen. "Other extraterrestrials have joined his cause, forming an allegiance on the planet. They call it the *Group*."

"Then it is imperative that we mobilize our representatives on the planet and prepare the inhabitants," Moriel said emphatically. "Unfortunately, humanity is not ready for the truth."

Agath spoke again. "I agree. The human race has not achieved the rehabilitation objectives we had hoped for. Why should the U-606 experiment be allowed to continue?"

"Because, my brother, our Sovereign wishes it so." In the midst of radiant lavender clouds, the luminous figure of Immanuel materialized. A tone of solemnity filled the chamber. He was Chief Administrator of the universe of Nebadon and was known throughout the galaxies as a Morning Star. He seldom attended the meetings at this level. "My dearest brethren, free will is the sacred gift from our Universal Father. These souls are fallen angels who were once like brothers to us. Remember why they were placed there and who continues to be behind every act of defiance against our Sovereign."

"Illustrious Immanuel, I must remind you that Urantia's time for contrition has run out. The *free-will* legacy is not working," concluded Agath.

Moriel spoke again. "If we allow this project to continue, humankind will join the offense against our Sovereign."

"We are facing universal upheaval," added Machiaventa.

"An evaluation of Urantia is due. RA, the monitoring organic vessel assigned to evaluate Urantia's progress, may not be as sympathetic to the planet's weakness as we are here at the Council. The life carriers aboard RA have reported minimal spiritual progress during the last five thousand years, Earth time. Their job is, after all, the implementation and fostering of life in the universe. They know when a project is in default."

"We could intervene and prevent the re-alliance of Urantia to the Rebellion," said Machiaventa.

"That would certainly abort the leap of consciousness scheduled for Urantia during this millennium," added Immanuel. "A re-evaluation of the planet will take place in 3,600 years—that is, if they survive the coming cataclysms."

The council reconsidered in silence before Agath spoke again. "The cleansing of the planet is inevitable. By the power of Binah, the Edenic currents will rise. RA will direct the wind swipe, cleanse the atmosphere, sink the contaminated continents, and allow new earth masses replenished with minerals to rise. A new chance will be given the planet."

Immanuel interrupted. "Are you advising us to proceed with a drastic world cleansing, a universal pandemic, even another planetary deluge?"

"Is there any other way of revitalizing the planet?" Moriel wanted to know.

Shaking their heads unanimously, a deep silence fell upon the assembly. The images on the screen kept flowing: universal mistreatment of the dark races, young suicide bombers blowing up buses in the Middle East, market and restaurant bombings in Israel, France, and Germany, beheadings in Iraq, human trafficking, especially the enslaving of young women and children. Then back to Manhattan, to the destruction of the twin towers.

"Why have you allowed things to go this far?" Immanuel wanted to know.

"Under the endowment of free will, we cannot interfere. Cirel and his *Group* have found one more way to terrorize and manipulate the masses."

"But this insane Jihad movement is targeting everything that is civilized!" The screen below them showed enormous mosques and multitudes in angry demonstrations on all continents. "And look how fast these followers of the Wahabbism cult multiply!"

"This weak, often cruel race has no idea that portals are about to open, that threatening dark forces await the opportunity to rob their souls. Our universal contract and exclusive domain over Urantia is expiring. Other life orders have acquired the right to come and conduct their experiments. Our only hope was that humankind was ready to take a stand," replied Machiaventa regretfully.

Immanuel did not acquiesce. "Cirel was allowed to remain free and roam the planet to instill the seed of temptation these souls had to overcome. But my Sovereign Brother is finally in agreement that enough time has been given to the rebels to seek salvation. The threat of celestial warfare is eminent since the trial of Lucifer will soon conclude. The rebels' last cry for allegiance will soon be made throughout the galaxies, and we must not interfere. Let the rebels, once and for all, rally with their leader, and let us, who are with the Creator's sons, be prepared."

"The fate of humankind is what we must determine today. We have two options: acknowledge that project U-606 is in default and allow RA's life carriers to decide the fate of these mortals or terminate the 606 experiment, apprehend Cirel, allow the human race to remain in its present state of evolution for another few millennia, and hope for the best." Machiaventa said.

"Why don't we wait for the report from Daniela, our trusted recorder, who has been tracking down the leaders of this insurrection in Urantia, before we make a decision?" suggested Immanuel.

The screen surrounding the room shifted and moved across the waters of the Atlantic Ocean. It came to a halt just above the skyscrapers of New York City.

"Presently, most of the weight of the planet rests here," said Machiaventa. "In this city of steel and glass, much of the brain capacity to sink or carry the world has been focused. It is here, of course, where our nemesis, the *Group* has chosen to establish its base." Machiaventa gestured with his hand and holograms of three members of the Council of Sages of Edentia materialized in the assembly room.

Orsef, ruler of Zones III and IV, stepped forward. His golden hair and bronze skin harmonized with the brilliance of his smile. His garments and the aura around him blended into a single swirl of amber. Behind him, Adam and Eva, onetime planetary rulers of Urantia, entered the council room. Orsef gave a signal of salute and took virtual command of the image presentation. The recorder on Earth, whose transmission would follow, was under his patronage. Therefore, protocol dictated the message be introduced by him. The image of the recorder Daniela, known as Danielle Peschard on the planet, also appeared. Her hair was the color of dark copper, and her eyes blazed a deep emerald green.

Daniela began her planetary transmission from her penthouse in New York City. "My respectful salute to the Council. I hope to bring you more positive images of our advances on the planet. I am convinced the rehabilitation project U-606, though slower than anticipated due to many setbacks, has not failed. It is imperative that you assess the magnitude of our advances in our rehabilitation project. For your consideration: Status of Project U-606."

The screen projected a group of gigantic UNICEF airplanes landing in remote areas, delivering supplies, and workers feeding starving infants in Darfur, teams of Peace Corps youths laying roofs at newly erected schools in Guatemala, and ecologists treading the jungles of Brazil, confronting representatives of powerful corporations and vigorously fighting to preserve the rain forests. Medical doctors were distributing new cures for emerging illnesses and technology displayed immense advances in methods of connecting the world through information and knowledge.

"I believe that balance is being achieved on the planet," she continued as she shifted the images to peaceful demonstrations on behalf of animal treatment and human rights. "Every evil deed, no matter how vast, has been counteracted by another good deed of the same magnitude. For every killer stands a saint, and for every life lost, one has been saved. "Evil seems to prevail, but this belief is erroneous. Evil is self-aggrandizing, while good quietly stands guard." She replayed familiar historical images. Naziism, Communism, Fascism, and every symbol of tyranny collapsed before their eyes. "It is the perpetual desire of the human race to survive tyranny and seek justice. Do not allow the apparent chaos of the planet veil the giant steps humankind has taken."

Orsef interrupted and addressed the council. "Not long ago, we had this same deliberation. In Atlantis, humankind reached a height of technical development, followed by a proclivity for decadence. We were about to report our disillusion to the life carriers, who would have acknowledged the creation error, and humankind would have been added to the list marked for termination.

"But, Michael, Our Creator intervened. He reminded us that because of the quarantine, Earth had not experienced the advantages other planets had. We were reminded to look at humans with deeper compassion and allowed a percentage of the population to survive, and look at how many souls have been rehabilitated!

"Thus, the eternal question prevails: Is humankind—the star seed of those repented souls—evil and corrupt, or is humankind capable of attaining perfection?"

Suddenly, the images disappeared, and absolute darkness fell over the assembly room. A hideous sound—the roaring of a dragon—erupted from a distant vacuum. Within seconds, the light came back, but the images previously surrounding the room had vanished. Controlled fear and evident pain showed in the eyes of the members, although no one spoke. It was not necessary. They all knew what had just transpired.

An angelic face appeared on the screen. It was luminous, white, and beautiful. The seraphim serenely announced, "The vortex has now been closed and secured." Everyone sighed in relief, but Immanuel voiced the thought in all of their minds. "It has already begun."

II

Danielle
Park Avenue, New York City

The recorder, Daniela, identified the signal that disrupted her scheduled transmission. The frightening frequency and intensity of the beams interlocked with the refraction of her message. She had to abort her transmission.

A freezing chill rushed through her veins when she identified its origin. Her hands frantically removed the triangular crystals from the quartz transmitting cube while an agonizing plea escaped her throat. "No!" She had heard these cries before. She had seen and witnessed the horror they announced. The signal had been an interstellar code of allegiance. Its cold resonance was louder and more terrifying than the chilling thunder of Geburah's battle cry. Its howl carried the distant and unmistakable roar of the Dragon.

She knew Earth was vulnerable and defenseless. Its vast accumulation of atomic power and its wide range of nuclear weapons would prove useless against the *others*. She had heard the call—so had the other Edentians stationed on the planet. They had to act fast to prevent any further communication between Earth and the rebel stations outside the galaxy. Only one thing mattered at this moment: to protect the vortex.

Summoning all of her strength, she sent the telepathic alarm signal. *Trebor . . . Kjell!* Daniela held her breath for one instant before she received their response, made manifest in visible streams of luminous violet sparks that shot out of the room and to the sky at the speed of light to form three concentric circles of energy she knew would serve to protect the planet. A moment of total silence followed. All electric currents came to an abrupt standstill.

Once her position was localized, members of the *Group* would be upon her in a matter of minutes. Despite the brevity of the occurrence, she deciphered the code and the message that interconnected with hers during the transmission.

Daniela ran to a wall safe hidden behind a Cezanne landscape painting in the study of her Park Avenue penthouse. The safe shot open in compliance with her mental command. She kept one of the stones in her hand and returned the rest of the quartz to the safe, shutting the door forcefully. When she punched in a code, a red sign flashed, seeking confirmation: Self-destruct?

Yes. She entered

Grabbing her purse, Daniela ran out of the penthouse.

Teterboro Airport, New Jersey

The engines of the Gulf Stream jet had been running for ten minutes when the speeding black car halted next to the plane's boarding stairs. Daniela rushed aboard with unusual agility, tossing strands of red hair away from her face. She was still clutching the crystal, and despite her appearance, her countenance gave no indication of the ferocious physical fight she had engaged in after leaving her Park Avenue building. Three hoodlums, members of the *Group*, had been waiting for her by the back exit of her building. Had it not been for one of her Edentian allies, who appeared on the scene at that moment and helped her fight the attackers, they would have taken her. As soon as Daniela was inside, the plane took off.

Jeffery, the pilot, cast a quick look over his shoulders and caught sight of a second car approaching. There would be trouble, he thought. He was now accustomed to it. Lately, there was much conflict between members of the *Foundation* and those of the *Group*, and he had learned not to question what he saw. Right now, he must think only of carrying out the specific instructions given to him by the *Foundation*. His responsibility was to take Daniela, a.k.a., Dr. Danielle Peschard, to a specific location in California.

Edentia, The Council

The unexpected roar of the Dragon had altered the mood of the Council, but the members knew the matter of Project 606 had to be resolved. Machiaventa paced around the chamber awaiting the images of planet Earth to reappear.

"The present course of events makes our galactic responsibilities and deliberation on this matter much more pressing." Machiaventa informed. "Shall we abort the Urantia 606 project or allow it to reach its conclusion?"

Machiaventa turned to Orsef before anyone had time to reply. "Please continue."

"Thank you, noble Machiaventa. The interception of the transmission is indicative of the urgency of this decision." Everyone focused on the transmission. An image of Daniela reappeared. "I understand it is essential for you to decide at this point if humanity is ready to continue its evolutionary journey. The present conditions in the universe will soon bring it to a crucial point of choice. And you must be wondering, when the inevitable confrontation between the two forces occurs, will humankind be wise enough to differentiate between good and evil? Or will it still be deceived?"

The transmission resumed. On a street in Harlem a woman knelt, whispering something to a man who grasped her hand desperately. The man was frantically clinging to life, of which a narcotic overdose was quickly robbing him.

"She is representative of the souls who have achieved a higher spiritual level," explained Daniela. "These souls are not rushing forward to the next level of consciousness, as would be expected. They are staying behind to help their less enlightened brothers. Therefore, one must conclude that infinite compassion has been achieved by many. I earnestly plead that your decision for humankind be favorable. Protect their endowment of free will. Let's not abandon them now.

"Cirel has come out of hiding. The *Group's* terrorists have been visiting water dams and nuclear facilities. I have deciphered their ultimate goal—a horror of unimaginable proportions. Having been identified as an Edentian, Cirel and his *Group* will track me down, but I cannot leave without accomplishing my mission.

"I hereby request authorization, in the name of all Edentian monitors, to proceed with the scheduled *Formation* and *present* our case to the life carriers.

"I must abort communication. Your faithful recorder: 10010999. Peace be with Michael."

The assembly watched the recorder dismantle her crystals as the stream of light sending her transmission became intertwined with another beam that made use of her access to the vortex to escape into space. They followed the trail of light and saw it attach to the signals of the Luciel alliance.

Orsef's mood was altered, and he tried to refrain from thinking, *How much more can we ask of her? She is offering, single-handedly, to entrap the rebels.* But the tone of his voice did not betray his feelings. "Our recorder's loyalty has been proven repeatedly. She is in grave danger. I will face the Arch-rebel Cirel myself, if necessary, but we must bring her in!"

Machiaventa rose from his seat and paced about the room in deliberation. The Council members remained silent, but before he could utter a word, Immanuel spoke. "If she has indeed discovered what the Cirel Group and the Luciel legions are planning, she will present evidence of what we already suspect. With indisputable proof, Michael will allow us to proceed with our counter-attack. You all know that anything to do with Luciel is still unbearably painful to him.

"The goal of the recorder is noble, and although her assignment is nearing completion, we must allow her to remain there as long as she needs. She will need further protection and the *Foundation* will provide it. We'll also allow the other Edentians—Trebor, Kjell, and Lilith, her soul group—to remain on the planet. However, with the cry of the Luciel allegiance, we must recall most of our agents and all our monitoring vessels back to Edentia. As we issue new orders of surveillance, we'll instruct RA to scrutinize Urantia."

"Have we all reached an agreement as to what to do about U-606?"

They had. Everyone's eyes turned to Machiaventa, who, after a few seconds, announced the unanimous verdict. "Humankind—evolving souls and their offspring—will be given one last chance and be left alone to continue making use of their free will. Daniela may establish contact and present her case to the life carriers. This Council will respect the life carriers' ultimate decision. With the vortex secured, there will now be minimum communication with Terra. Further angelic legions will be dispatched to the planet's orbit to occupy the newly erected stations and detain all souls exiting the planet."

Machiaventa understood Orsef's fears and concern. The fate of his beloved agent, Daniela, remained interlaced with that of the other Edentian agent, Lilith. Before the screen faded, it showed the present manipulation of the underground current. The Council observed a trail of lightning following the path of Daniela.

Turning to Orsef, Machiaventa said, "Our agent needs protection. Let's proceed through the *Foundation*."

Orsef understood.

Arecibo Observatory, Puerto Rico

John Larkin had been sitting in front of his computer for almost twelve hours, implementing a new program to measure obscure lanes of cosmic dust containing organic molecules; some of them included stars in the earliest stages of formation.

The clutter around his desk extended to the floor, where the piles of books and printouts were several feet high.

John was quiet and congenial. His slender body was unusually toned for someone who spent so much time indoors. He had been working at the Arecibo Radio/Radar Observatory in Puerto Rico for a little over two years. The excitement of having been transferred by Cornell University had begun to wear off. He had not been prepared for the absolute isolation to which he had subscribed his life. His two colleagues were constantly out of the office, and there was little interaction with the outside world.

On April 19, overcome with exhaustion, he had dozed off. The sudden beep, emitted by the auxiliary generator as it had attempted to kick on, woke him up. "What the heck?" he exclaimed, jumping up and checking the four computer screens in front of him and the various needles on the metal boxes that monitored the position of the radar disks outside.

The phone rang. "Did you get anything?" his colleague asked with excitement.

"No." Then, looking at the report on one of his screens, he added. "Apparently, the blackout was universal."

"Wow! Keep me posted. I'm heading back."

John hung up and looked again at the report on the screen from Mount Stromlo Observatory in Australia. *April 19. A discharge of electricity hit the Earth's atmosphere. It interrupted all electrical currents for 9 seconds.*

It was past 2:00 a.m. Nothing else was out of the ordinary, when a speck of light and the faint trace of a shadow appeared—so minute and pale, they were almost imperceptible. A residue of something traveling at the speed of light. The weariness and doubt vanished. Something inexplicable was taking place. The tiny speck of light on the tape testified to some kind of interstellar communication. He thought of his friend Danielle, who had asked him to monitor certain areas in the sky and report any disturbances, and became determined to find what had caused the irregularity in the electromagnetic spectrum.

John raked his hands through his heavy, dark hair and leaned back in his chair. *Had this energy accidentally brushed the earth's atmosphere? Had it come from an optical or infrared laser, pulsed neutrinos, modulated gravity waves, or some other source?* He ran the tape to the point of contact. The light beam had definitely interfaced with another one from Earth.

"Impossible!" he exclaimed. "This type of communication is beyond our present capabilities. We are not yet prepared to capture these signals, much less respond to them! Nothing but a coincidence," he told himself. *The interlacing of the two or three lights was a fluke, not a response.*

New York

The Goldsteins witnessed the assault.

The elderly couple rushed breathlessly into the lobby of their building on Park Avenue, hysterically talking over each other. Theodore, the doorman, grabbed the phone and dialed 911. An officer arrived and found Mr. Goldstein shaking so hard that he could hardly understand the old man.

They reported witnessing an attack as they were returning from dinner. Two men jumped out of a car and attacked someone coming out of the back of their building. There was struggling, a flash of light, perhaps a gun had gone off. She fought fiercely and broke loose.

"She?" the officer interrupted with interest.

"Yes. Dr. Peschard of the penthouse. Another car sped by us and crashed into the first one. Two men jumped out to her rescue and took her with them. When we crossed the street, all we could find was that purse." He pointed to the purse in the officer's hand.

Officer Cimino opened the small glittering beaded bag. In it, he found a gold key, and ten crisp one-hundred-dollar bills. The three of them stared at the contents in puzzlement. Robbery could now be ruled out.

Santa Barbara, California

On April 19, the night of the nine-second blackout, a dark fog formed in the center of the park. A dusty haze rose from the earth and enveloped the trees as a ferocious wind ripped through their limbs and tossed them in all directions like discarded feathers. This was followed by a palpable rumbling of the earth. A crack appeared in the ground and widened as it writhed swiftly forward like a wounded snake, uprooting every plant and tree in its path. When it reached the highway, it tore open the pavement. An eyewitness reported fire racing along the fissure. The earth's natural sounds were pierced by the whistling of the storm, followed by the roaring of thunder. When lightning struck, it set everything it touched on fire. Multiple sirens joined the cacophony as fire engines and emergency vehicles headed toward the first blazing homes.

Within minutes, the community was torn and devastated. The earthquake, the lightning, and the uncommon windstorm combined into one raging, terrifying force. Property damage was extensive. Amazingly, there was only one casualty reported. On the outskirts of town, the badly injured body of a young woman was found. Her face was bruised and her flesh showed burns, lacerations, and possibly broken bones. No doubt, she had been tossed around by the wind into sharp rocks and unyielding trees.

The policeman who found her was astonished to see what remained of her attire. The black silk dress was torn. She was barefoot, wore no jewelry, and had no identification. About twenty feet from her, the officer found a broken watch.

The paramedics placed the fragile, broken body on a stretcher, then aboard a helicopter. Because of the severity of her injuries, it was decided to fly her to a hospital in Los Angeles. Despite the pitiful condition of her face and limbs, the officer could see she was a beautiful woman. Officer Jones, who in the past had made it a rule never to get involved in a case past his initial investigation, inexplicably decided to drive to the hospital in Los Angeles and waited patiently for the report from the trauma doctor, which was delivered a few hours after she was brought in.

"She has sustained a head injury," the ER resident explained. "There is evidence she was hit by lightning. It entered the right shoulder, possibly affecting the spinal cord. She has been placed on life support. We are monitoring a blood clot in the brain. A neurosurgeon has been alerted. Have you located her relatives?"

Officer Jones cleared his throat. "She had no identification. I'll see what I can do."

The policeman walked out of the hospital feeling a sense of hopelessness. Somewhere out there was a worried husband, lover, or parent, wondering where she was. The last image of her on the hospital bed, connected to a respirator, caused in him a surge of pity. He would find out who she was.

Jones reached into his pocket for the Bulgari watch he had found and examined it closely. It was the only clue to her identity. He would go to Bulgari in Beverly Hills as soon as it opened. That type of store was solicitous of its clientele and kept meticulous records. The finely inscribed serial number on the back of the timepiece would identify its owner. He had to help this woman with the flaming red hair.

Officer Jones was at Bulgari on Rodeo Drive at 10:00 a.m., sharp. After stating the purpose of his visit, the dapper young manager led him into a private office, where he entered the ID number into the computer. It was obvious the young manager found it fascinating to be a part of the intrigue connected with his clientele.

"The watch was purchased by Robert Powers. You know . . . the Robert Powers." Officer Jones remained unimpressed, and the young man gladly grabbed the opportunity to elaborate. "Mr. Powers is a big tycoon. He is listed by *Forbes* as one of the richest men in the world."

"Yeah, the oil man," Jones suddenly remembered.

"Oil and gas. Powers industries, you name it. Anyway, the watch was purchased at our New York store last spring." Now Officer Jones started paying close attention.

"The watch was given to Dr. Danielle Peschard. A few days later, she brought it in here to have the wristband adjusted." The young man reached into a drawer and produced a private clientele book. He opened it and smiled with satisfaction. "Here it is! That same day, she also brought in one of our most magnificent pieces—the Medusa medallion, with the ancient Roman coin, and baguette diamonds. The odd thing is that she brought in her own coin and had us replace the one in the necklace. Her Roman coin had a beautifully engraved profile—sort of looked like her. Since she is an archeologist, we wanted to know where she got it. She said it was a gift.

"Anyway," continued the young manager, "you must have read that she is a big philanthropist, moves in New York's highest circles, is associated with the Met, and is famous for digging out the oldest statue of Aphrodite."

Jones faintly remembered a front-page story about the discovery a few years back. "What does she look like?"

"Not what you'd expect. She is slim, tall, chic . . . absolutely beautiful! Radiant green eyes, magnificent red hair . . ."

Jones recalled the image of the wounded young woman and suddenly felt sick. "May I have her address?"

The young man turned the clientele book around and offered the officer a writing pad and pen. Jones wrote down Danielle's California address and phone numbers.

When the officer got back to his office, he looked her up on the internet. Within a short time, he had a fairly good composite of who Danielle Peschard was.

Danielle was indeed an archeologist, an ancient cryptologist, and a renowned authenticator of antiquities at the New York Metropolitan Museum. Her career had yielded a series of discoveries that had earned the respect of the international archeological world. Her finds had often made headlines in the media, and her lifestyle made her the subject of various magazine articles and television interviews. Jones learned from more than one source about her discovery of the Temple of Aphrodite in Knidos, Turkey.

Danielle was in her mid-thirties, very wealthy, and served on the board of trustees of almost every major cultural institution in New York—a high-profile woman who moved in New York's upper, close-knit circles. Everyone liked her, yet she was an enigma. She had no husband, no children, and no living relatives. The person to notify in case of an emergency was Dr. Kitzia O'Neil, a clinical psychologist at Lenox Hill Hospital.

After speaking to Linda, Danielle's personal secretary, Jones discovered that despite the report of Danielle's disappearance, no one had any idea that she was in California. The night of April 19, Dr. Peschard attended a charity event and had been in New York until 10:00 p.m., and multiple witnesses could corroborate.

Linda told him it was not unusual for the archeologist and her friends to take off on a private jet after a function. Therefore, it was not unusual for her to be in LA.

Everything checked out up to the moment when Dr. Peschard left the building through the back door. The time discrepancy confused and intrigued Officer Jones. Danielle's body had been found in Santa Barbara less than three hours later. Before making the next call, Jones thought of someone: Christian Goodman.

He had met Christian when both joined the police force. Chris was a great cop: honest, adventurous, and brave. But his sense of adventure had been overshadowed by his even greater sense of curiosity, which led him to a writing career—his first article being an in-depth investigation on the increasing use of assault weapons and terrorism. The article was picked up by a national magazine. Soon after, Chris was writing about crime rather than trying to deter it. His first book was published and did quite well. They had remained friends, and although they seldom saw each other, they kept in touch and came to each other's help when needed. Officer Jones called his friend's number and when his voicemail came on, he simply said, "Chris, give me a call." He then dialed Dr. O'Neil's office, Danielle's emergency contact.

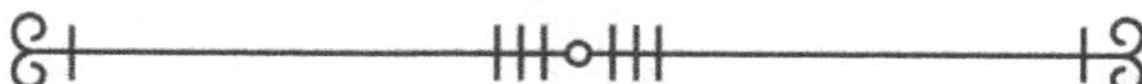

Kitzia

This is not happening. Danielle does not have accidents, thought Kitzia O'Neil, her heart racing as she listened to Officer Jack Jones. Danielle had an almost supernatural ability to detect danger. Kitzia headed immediately for the airport.

A few hours later, she was in LA, on her way to the hospital.

Kit recalled the time when both were young and became trapped on the ski slopes during an avalanche. Within a matter of minutes, they were interred in a tomb, sealed with rock and snow. Danielle made a small opening to allow air to filter in while the avalanche continued. She turned to Kit and touched her cheek, without saying a word. Kit knew then that they would be all right.

Now, twenty years later, whenever she found herself facing any situation that produced anxiety, she flashed on that terrifying moment in the darkness of the cave and Danielle's reassurance. That experience and the composure she witnessed that night had given her the strength to embark on her career as an MD and clinical psychologist.

Kitzia had just turned thirty-five. Her slight frame and bouncy, light brown hair—a couple of shades lighter than her eyes—made her appear much younger. With a successful career, she was financially comfortable. When her marriage of three years had not been a complete success, Danielle told her not to think of it as a failure. Kit had experienced love and grown with it.

Danielle's confidence and altruism inspired Kit to volunteer for every charitable cause she could fit into her schedule. She worked with teenage drug rehabilitation programs and as a forensic psychologist with the police department, helping to locate kidnapped children.

Her many hours of pro-bono social work were balanced with numerous paying clients. Comfortable and secure in her position, even her gift of clairvoyance from childhood was no longer a point of contention.

Los Angeles

Kitzia had never seen anyone who had been hit by lightning. When she first glanced at Danielle's burned and bruised body, she gasped and, for a second, suspected she had arrived too late.

Kitzia quietly let the nurse guide her to Danielle's bedside. She scrutinized the colored, pulsing lines on the life support screen before coming closer. They rose and fell weakly but steadily, attesting to Danielle's body's struggle for life. IVs were hooked to Danielle's left arm; an electroencephalograph machine was monitoring her brain activity and emitting a faint but constant beep.

Some of Danielle's wounds had been cleaned and bandaged, while some of the burns had been left uncovered. They were coated with a yellowish ointment that made Kit think of battle wounds.

Heavy sedation had not reduced the stiffness in her arms. Danielle's fists were tightly closed as if she were clutching something. Kit took a deep breath as she secured her place next to her friend's bed.

Kit hesitated to touch her. She was about to reach out when footsteps from behind made her turn. The doctor's white jacket caught her attention, but before she could say anything, the sight of the imposing man standing behind him gave her such a sense of relief that Kitzia found herself in his arms, unable to control her tears.

"Oh, Robert, how could this have happened?"

He held her while one of his hands stroked her light brown hair as he would that of a child's.

Her eyes suddenly fixed on a couple of cuts on his forehead while the hand that held her displayed a bandage. "What happened to you?"

"It's nothing." He let go of her. It seemed absurd at a time like this to focus the conversation on his minor injuries.

Both of them turned toward the doctor who was checking Danielle's pulse.

"For the moment, her blood pressure is steady." He spoke without looking at them. "Our concern is the clot forming on the left side of the neocortex. Dr. McCutcheon, the neurosurgeon, will be here any minute." Robert Powers took the opportunity to introduce Kitzia. "Dr. Grossman, this is Dr. Kitzia O'Neil."

Kit extended her hand. "I have signed all the releases. Please proceed with whatever is necessary."

"Let's be patient, Kit," Robert's voice interrupted. It was deep and authoritative and underscored his powerful presence. "We'll try to prevent this neuro-intervention. I am having the best neurosurgeon flown here from Switzerland to deliberate before we proceed."

Kitzia came closer to the bed and lightly touched Danielle's hand. Robert and the doctor stepped back, and their conversation fell to almost a whisper.

After taking a deep breath, Kit gently took Danielle's fist in her hand and, closing her eyes, tried to reach Danielle through telepathy, praying Danielle would pick up her thoughts.

Dearest Danielle, you've got to pull through. I don't know what I'd do without you. You have been my best friend, my guide, my . . . An abrupt and direct thought broke through her personal monologue. Danielle's silent communication had streaked straight into her senses. It was a desperate plea.

Help me, Kit! Don't let them touch my brain. Help me get away.

Kit felt a surge of fear as she held Danielle's fist. Then her grip released ever so slightly to allow a small object to pass from Danielle's hand into hers—obviously something valuable, which Danielle was entrusting to her for safekeeping.

She did nothing to attract attention; she didn't even look at the object. It felt like a small rock in her hand. She peered into Danielle's face, which registered no change of expression.

Kit slid her hand into the pocket of her woolen blazer and let the object fall. Turning around slowly, she wondered if the two men had noticed anything. They had not, even absorbed as they were in their discussion. Kit gently reached for Danielle's other fist, anxious to see if it also contained something. It didn't.

The fingers of both of Danielle's hands began to uncurl and relax, and Kit knew that she alone was to know about the object Danielle had given her. Perhaps it held the key to what had happened. Her thoughts returned to their telepathic communication. *How could I justify moving a seriously injured patient? This is a matter of life and death.*

Precisely. It was Danielle's voice again, urging its way into her consciousness. Kit opened her eyes and was horrified to see Danielle's arm turning purple and beginning to swell like a balloon. Kit cried out in alarm, and two nurses began manipulating the monitors, while the doctor again checked Danielle's vital signs.

"Stand back!" yelled Robert from behind them. The doctor waved his hand, urgently instructing the nurses to get to the back of the room.

"As far from the patient as you can!" Robert continued to warn. "It's the lightning," he shouted, aware of what was about to happen.

Kit complied as well. Then it happened. A noise erupted, like a popped balloon, followed by a blinding bolt of lightning that streaked across the room with the force of a thunderclap.

When it was over, the doctor rushed back to Danielle, placing his stethoscope over her heart. Kit moved closer to Robert, who pulled her toward him, and with his arm around her, attentively watched the staff at work.

"Part of the charge of the lightning bolt that hit the patient had been unexplainably trapped in her upper arm and was suddenly released. The force of the emission would have struck anyone in its path," the doctor explained. The staff mumbled in amazement.

Before anyone in the ICU had time to recover from what had just taken place, something just as terrifying happened. Danielle's body shook uncontrollably. The tubes that connected her to the digital boxes vibrated, as if suddenly fed by a surge of energy. Her blood pressure rose, the numbers climbing to an alarming systolic figure of 240 over a diastolic number of 130, at which point the monitor emitted a piercing alarm. Her temperature dropped to eighty-nine, setting off a second alarm, and the oxygen level dropped drastically.

One nurse hurriedly adjusted knobs on the machines; another one turned the handle on the oxygen tank to produce maximum intake. They tried to hold Danielle down. There was a third sudden alarm, indicating the accumulated pressure had produced a malfunction in one of the operating systems. The beeps emitted from the heart monitor became more erratic. A fourth alarm rang. The oxygen tank started to spew. Kit gasped in disbelief at the sudden shrill scream of the flatline indicator.

Danielle became vaguely aware of the weightlessness of her being. She had risen and separated from her physical body. She observed the doctors and the nurses hovering over the hospital bed. She saw and felt the sorrow in Kitzia's heart, and for a second, she thought she could detect despair in Robert's face.

The vision faded almost immediately. She had been in this transitory stage countless times before. She recognized it, and with a sense of relief, peacefully witnessed the disintegration of her past reality. The hospital room, which seconds before had appeared so solid, seemed to break apart. The physical world and all its solid components seemed phased out to reveal the atoms moving within. As her spirit vibrated faster and separated from the physical plane, she regained awareness of the atoms and molecules as basic wave motions. Her mind reorganized itself; her vibration rose and connected with the cosmic consciousness.

She felt a tinge of regret for terminating her life so abruptly; yet, there had been no choice. The *Group* had amassed unbelievable power, and they were closing in on her. Having broken her physical body, they would now try to capture her soul. She had to escape.

The fetters of mortal existence had been terminated when she purposely burst the oxygen tank.

Danielle entered a tunnel, which she identified as the energy helix that connects the material plane with other dimensions. She braced herself for the trip. When the pull came, it tugged at such high speed that movement became unnoticeable. Danielle let herself float in the Dream Sea. What she could see of the Helix tunnel reminded her of a gigantic DNA molecule.

The descent began, and the vortex which would introduce her to her destination opened as she faced the entrance to her next dimension. When the motion stopped and she felt herself stabilize, she looked around but did not recognize the place. This was a state of nothingness, of absolute and complete desolation. There was no up or down, no distance, no atmosphere, no temperature, no color, and no sound or sensation. Danielle never imagined such a place of emptiness existed in the universe.

Danielle's memory bonded to images of times long gone, of dialects now forgotten, of glorious structures of glass and gold now destroyed. She recalled the construction of pyramids of stone. She had witnessed civilizations rise and fall, seen kings and peasants exchange robes in shifts of incarnation. She had observed the corruption and the salvation of man. She had seen it all, and she had recorded it with minute precision for the eternal archives.

She believed in the redemption of humanity and, therefore, had become its most ardent advocate, as the transmission stated. "The Transmission . . ." She suddenly remembered and prayed that it had been received in its entirety, along with her recommendations. Why this sudden despair and feeling of impotence? Where was she, anyway?

Danielle recalled the normal steps in post-mortal existence. Remembering her previous incarnations on the planet, she knew she had bypassed the first of the mansion worlds, where the traveling soul regained the lightness necessary to navigate in the new world of light.

She had not entered the Resurrection Mansions either, where she was to surrender her mortal mind transcripts. Here, evolving souls would consult with the masters and decide whether there was a need to return to Earth and replay life's experiences or resume the spiritual journey.

Something odd struck her. Even if she had bypassed the mansion worlds, a celestial companion would have been assigned to her; yet she was alone. Where were the transition masters?

Something began to take form. It resembled a cloud of dust, and it whirled in a circular motion in front of her. Tiny dots assembled into a shapeless, gaseous cloud. Danielle attempted to move toward it but felt herself repelled by a force that prevented her approach. As it continued to form, she made every attempt to determine what it was, but nothing in her experience could explain it. The configuration of the energy appearing before her . . . the dots of dust . . . were souls. All at once, she had no problem reading their vibrations and translating the code to their recent physical blueprints. They were very young people.

As they brushed past her in the direction of the cloud, Danielle stared at their empty faces. They wore the frightening expression of absolute indifference. Danielle continued to access the blueprints for their identities—the bruises and scars left by heroin needles, piercings, and poorly drawn tattoos of serpents. She recognized the physical and mental abuse, the wishes to escape reality, the drugs, the dark music, the messages of doom, and promises of freedom.

Danielle looked at more youths of Middle Eastern descent, their torsos still showing the imprints of the explosives they had wrapped around their bodies as they departed the world, carrying with them an untold number of innocent victims. The youths continued to pass by, thousands of them. They were being summoned somewhere. They were still following the promise, except they no longer cared.

They were all suicides like her. They had all forfeited their contract with life.

She wanted to tell them they were wrong. Every soul had a mission to fulfill, big or small. It was a component of the total picture of existence. It held reality together. Her purpose had been to record the evolution of the species on Urantia, the acceleration of the mind and its leaps in understanding, and she had also failed, Danielle thought sadly. She had abandoned her post . . . and had let down the Edentian Council.

A strange sensation came over her. It came from nowhere but from everywhere. It surrounded her. It was powerful and vertiginous. The intensity of the emotion was unfamiliar to her—apprehension and excitement mingled in the same sensation. It thrilled her to encounter a new form of energy when she thought she had experienced it all! The sensation continued to grow, and amassed strength as it increased. It was as if all the molecules in the universe were being drawn together by a magnet so forceful as to be unimagined. The more it intensified, the more deeply she understood: This was *God.*

In the presence of the First Source and Center of all things and beings, she recognized the insignificance of her soul. She was in front of the Creator, the Controller and Infinite Upholder, and his presence and magnificence enveloped her.

All the names by which He was known throughout the universes came to her. Father of Universes, Eternal One, Divine Controller . . . but out of myriad names, she had always chosen to address him as Universal Father. She had never seen him, even in Edentia, and knew well that she would not be able to see him now. The Universal Father was not visible because lower groups of spirit beings, including Edentians, could not behold his glory and spiritual brilliance. The fear dissolved. He had come looking for her. Danielle was aware that He was addressing her, that she was hearing His words through her own consciousness.

"Daniela, is this what you really want?" The question echoed in a thousand tones and pressed her for a reply.

"No. No, I don't want to be here." Danielle understood He knew her answer before He asked her. He was omniscient and knew what was in her heart. He had come to ease the confusion from her soul and remove her from the place where she did not belong. This was the place where suicides came, where beings who chose to give up on God ended up. That was not her case.

"My assignment was of enormous consequence, and I was thoroughly accountable. I should have fought harder. When cornered by the enemy, I escaped the only way I knew how—by surrendering my physical body and trying to rescue my spiritual one."

"Is this what you want?" the voice sounded once again within her being. Danielle did not feel He was judging her actions beyond redemption. There was a different meaning to the question. She was being given a choice to terminate her mission if she chose to do so.

"No! If allowed, I would go back and complete my mission." She now felt certain she could rise from her transgression and make it up to the Council.

The transmission. She suddenly recalled the transmission. It had surely gotten through. The Council of Sages would heed her plea and be more lenient with humankind. Danielle's heart addressed the Eternal One in a tone of nostalgia. " Edentia . . ." How she longed to see her home! But she understood it was more important to go back to Urantia.

"If I were only allowed—" Before she finished formulating her pleas, both requests had been answered by the Universal Father.

She felt a sudden force take hold of her, and in seconds, saw herself travel backward through the Helix tunnel of time. Once again, she was hovering above her physical body in the California hospital.

She witnessed the medical team manning a defibrillator to resuscitate her. She saw Kitzia clutching Robert and felt his fear and alarm reach her like a silent prayer; with all his might, he prayed for her to live.

The lifeline reappeared. The resuscitators moved back. The medical team worked to stabilize Danielle with the usual shots of adrenaline, and new solutions were added to the IV bags. A ventilator was pushed to the bed and reconnected. Danielle was again placed on life support.

Kit burst into tears, and Robert took a deep breath. Danielle was back.

Danielle felt she could rest now; slowly, she allowed herself to drift. Though her physical manifestation remained in the hospital bed, she felt her spirit moving independently of her body at thousands of miles per second. She felt herself exit the solar system, headed for the southern sector of Splandon. She rushed past Gallia and Rovandon. She observed the spiral nebulae, the whirling stars, the dark islands of space, and the illumination of the architectural spheres. When she distinguished the triad of sparkling moons at a distance, she recognized her home planet. Edentia, in all its radiance, appeared before her. An exquisite planet whose perfect temperature made for lush displays of beautiful flora, where the color of the ocean reflected the subtle lavender tones of the firmament. There was a prevailing feeling of peace that she had nearly forgotten. This was a place where nature and being came together in perfect, undisturbed harmony.

A familiar female voice greeted her, "Welcome back, Daniela." The woman was sitting on a stone bench in the middle of a garden surrounded by Jacaranda trees. Her feet were bare and rested on a thick, plush chartreuse lawn. The palms of her hands rested over her knees, and her eyes were closed.

The sense of warmth and joy of home that washed over her was incalculable as she gazed at the being that had willed her home. She waited just a moment before materializing before this beautiful being, pausing to take in the vision of Eva, and striving not to miss or forget any detail of this marvelous woman. Eva rose to a height of eight feet and was svelte, with a flawless oval face and features chiseled to perfection. Her pale gold hair fell straight over her shoulders. She wore no adornment, and the simplicity and grace of her white gown served to frame the radiant beauty of her face.

Botticelli's *Venus*, as well as Waterhouse's *Lady of Shallot*, among the scores of paintings inspired by Eva, had never done her justice.

Eva's spirit rose from her body and moved to embrace her dear friend, followed by Adam. Daniela rejoiced at her reunion with the couple who had, at one time, been assigned to Urantia, as biological uplifters and planetary rulers.

Daniela spoke: "I am afraid I have failed miserably. I see that *he* has not come."

"He was not able," Adam assured her. "Orsef has traveled far and must remain where he is because of vortex restrictions." He smiled in such a comforting manner that Daniela felt relieved. "It has been a long time, and I think you have done a good job."

"I shouldn't have left."

"Sooner or later, the *Cirel Group* had to find out who you are." Eva said in a soothing voice.

"But I should have seen it coming. I grew careless; I became too comfortable."

"These are hard times," added Adam.

Because of her friends' reassurance, Daniela stopped her self-reproach. "It is happening all over again. Isn't it?"

Adam and Eva exchanged a sad glance between them before answering. "Yes."

Daniela recalled the interception of the transmission and the momentary blackout that struck the planet. "Did the signal pierce through the universe?"

"We think so." They both knew she was referring to the call for alliance.

Adam pointed in the direction of the distant clouds. "The stations were not able to block the counter-signal. Something else is happening. We can only speculate what the rebels are after, but we cannot be certain."

Daniela fixed her eyes on a distant cloud and recalled the young suicides. "I saw something frightening." She proceeded to tell them about the place where she had been and the massive recruiting in progress.

Adam produced a glass-like sphere and held it between his hands. When he lifted one hand, the ball showed a configuration, which looked like a nebula. Daniela recognized the clouds, which were made up of the young suicides. The floating dots continued to attach themselves to the cloud formation as it pulsated with its increasing numbers.

"That's it!"

Adam and Eva knew where those souls were going, and they recognized the force. Those recruits were on their way to join the Luciel legions in preparation for universal insurrection.

"The transmission?" Daniela wanted to know.

Eva smiled. "It got through. Your recommendation was accepted. This will be the final chance for humankind . . . the Omega. The patience of the Council has expired. But at least for now, Earth is once again free to choose."

Daniela thought for a moment. "But my recommendation as such was sent based on conditions before these dreadful changes in circumstance. Now *everything* has changed. If there is to be warfare on the planet, they are not prepared to oppose the adversary. They are not spiritually ready to take a stand in an open war."

"They might have to do so," concluded Adam in a serious tone.

Danielle became agitated. "What weapons do they have?"

"You . . . and your ability to influence the life carriers." Eva held Daniela's gaze for a moment. "Do you still have them?"

"Yes," replied Daniela in a whisper. "I will have them."

Eva sighed with relief. "Choose wisely. The life carriers will evaluate a strong plea."

Adam stepped forward. "Daniela, we have done everything we possibly can to help the planet; now I believe you should come home." The two women exchanged a meaningful glance. Adam continued, "It was proposed to the Council to bring you back. But your insistence on remaining on Urantia was ultimately accepted."

"This time, I'll follow it to the end."

"Daniela, things have changed. It has become very dangerous. The *Group* will stop at nothing. Your spiritual existence is in danger. Besides, the original setup for contact has been aborted. If RA is to make its scheduled stop, it must be signaled through the *Formation,* and the *Formation* can only occur if the assigned members find one another in time, along with the components to establish connection. Perhaps it would be wiser to let RA pass this one time and . . ."

"No! My job is to ensure that the *Formation* takes place, and it will!"

"We understand your reasons," said Eva, "and what you are trying to do. How we wish we could lift this weight from you and show you it is no longer your responsibility. The vortex may close completely and trap you there for another thousand years!"

"You both know I can't come home now. Trebor was one of us. I must bring him back. You would do no less, Adam."

Adam and Eva exchanged a look of apprehension. Eva spoke tenderly, "Daniela, the most important thing is that you remember—"

Danielle interrupted, "I know there are a lot of memories that I can't access that have to do with Trebor, and even Lilith, but that will not interfere with what I must do."

"Are you even sure of where Trebor stands?" Eva asked.

"Not against us! We will return together."

Adam and Eva looked at each other, and sadness registered on their faces. There was still something beyond Daniela's ken, and she would have to find the answer before she returned home.

Adam took a big breath. "So be it!"

"There are some things I must know," said Daniela. "Is the planet's current atmosphere an indication that we are losing control of the Edenic currents?"

"At least one of them is being manipulated."

Daniela felt a chill as she remembered the storm that had assaulted her—the fire, the fierce winds, the lightning that had struck her, and all the destructive effects that so clearly focused on her annihilation.

"Daniela, we need to find out what Cirel is planning," said Adam.

"And you will! There will be no more desperate attempts to escape. I will conclude my mission. I will bring our brother back. I will find the Cirel *Group's* hiding place. RA will not bypass Earth, and I will not relinquish my post before I have assigned a suitable rememberer."

Daniela's hesitation had been wiped out. She felt renewed strength. Eva advanced and encircled Daniela's head with her hands. "Do take the memories—a souvenir of your Edentia. They will be rest stops in these trying times."

Daniela was gratified beyond words. Spirit beings were usually not allowed to take the memories back. But now Daniela could draw strength from the memory of Edentia, the memory of her love mate, and the bliss of their conjugal life. He was a shining and dazzling soul, a member of the Council, one of the elite masters of Edentia. He had the power to distribute and assure execution of orders from the Most High. He created and uplifted civilizations. He was the Magnificent Orsef, while she was but a celestial recorder with a hands-on assignment on a tiny planet. Yet, because Urantia had been burdened with so many disasters, Daniela had viewed it as a challenge. It was a unique opportunity to record the evolution of humankind, an opportunity to shine in Orsef's eyes and lift herself to his dimension.

Orsef had reluctantly agreed with the decision, and thus, she had departed. Little did she know of the magnitude of the assignment—the years, the centuries, the millennia that would pass before she could return to her life in Edentia.

The three embraced, and the connection broke apart. Daniela cast one last glance at Edentia, drinking in the beauty of the landscape and trying to register in her memory the subtle hues alien to Earth.

IV

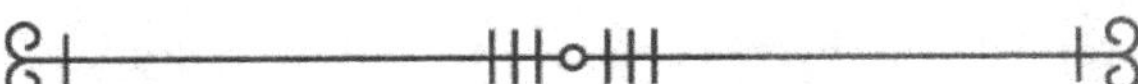

"Kit." Robert's voice startled her awake. She had dozed off. Both Kitzia and Robert had been on watch in a private VIP waiting room for the last twenty-four hours. Or had it been thirty-six? She could hardly remember. The room adjacent to the ICU had been placed at their disposal the moment Robert arrived at the hospital. His presumptive presence allowed him to take control of any given situation.

"Let me take you home," he whispered.

She did not protest. "I've got a rental car." She fumbled through the contents of her bag and produced a parking ticket. Robert took it and phoned the valet.

"I'll walk you out."

As they walked past the ICU, she cast one last look at Danielle's inert body and a woman in pink next to the bed.

"I hired a private-duty nurse," said Robert. "You need some rest."

"What about you?" asked Kit.

"I'm OK," he assured her. "I will see you in the morning."

"Robert, you have my number. Let me know if anything . . ."

He patted her back. "I will."

The glass door slid back, and they exited the lobby. The car was already waiting. They hugged, and she took off, catching a last glimpse of him as he walked back into the building. She could not understand how he could remain so calm, so stoic. She was sure he had not eaten or slept in the last twenty-four hours. His endurance under stress was astonishing. Without Robert there to see to things, she would never have left Danielle's side.

After a short drive, she arrived at the house. The gate was open, and she drove in slowly, hoping the housekeeper would not notice her arrival. There was light coming from the servants' section of the house. She parked the car in front of the main door and entered. She had barely set her things down when the phone rang. She picked up the nearest extension.

"Yes, Maria, it's me. Yes, Ms. Danielle is doing a lot better," she lied. "I'm going to shower and go straight to bed. Please wake me up before eight."

How she loved this house, she thought with every step as she climbed the stairs to her room. Danielle had asked Kit to pick a style and choose an architect. After numerous trips to Normandy in search of period pieces, the result was stunning: an eclectic mix of massive armoires, antique tables, modern plush suede sofas, and hand-carved upholstered chairs. The walls were studded with an impressive collection of Impressionist paintings. In the last three years, the women had escaped here at every opportunity. This was their sanctuary.

Kit stopped at the top of the stairs and admired a recently acquired Picasso—from the private collection of Dora Maar, a mistress of his. She continued toward her bedroom and tossed her clothes over the upholstered chair and stepped into the bathroom. The sensation of warm water coursing down her body felt as soothing as a lover's hand. Kit thought of Tom's hands and sighed deeply. She must not think of her ex-husband. *Not now.*

Stepping out of the shower and wrapping herself in a fluffy terry robe, Kit went into Danielle's room. Her computer was on. There was an email, but Kit noticed a fax that had fallen to the floor. She picked it up and puzzled over its contents, longitude and latitude indicators—coordinates. Other pages in the fax machine were marked *Confidential.* Kit found the origin of the transmission at the bottom of the pages. *John Larkin-Arecibo.* She had not heard that name in years. The date of the transmission was the same as Danielle's accident.

Kit sat at the desk and clicked the email icon. Dots connected by lines formed a diversity of abstract patterns. Scribbled on the left-hand margin of the chart were the words, "Point of intersection."

John Larkin had indicated this to be a computer rendition of the sky as it would appear on the night of April 19. Why would Danielle need this information? Kit realized there was a great deal about Danielle Peschard she didn't know.

Her finger rested on a dot representing a cluster of stars. The words *Point of intersection* flashed again in her mind. What could this mean ? Her eyes moved beyond Hyades and into the next cluster, "The Pleiades, or M45"—the brightest cluster in the sky and the most famous one since antiquity.

The next document was truly beyond her comprehension. She reached for the print icon and clicked *print all.* It appeared to come from a different source and was hand-composed. There were geometric characters resembling the Greek alphabet. No sender was identified.

The next communication was in Italian, from Vatican City. "Foundation meeting confirmed. Departure 4/22 2:30 p.m. Hangar #9." *Why didn't Danielle mention her trip to Italy? Or that she was coming to California?*

Kit studied the strange graphics again as she pulled the paper from the printer. It was definitely a message in a carefully devised secret code. She had actually seen this type of writing before. But where? It frustrated her not to have the faintest recollection. Kit set the papers on top of the nightstand. Suddenly, she remembered the object Danielle had slipped into her hand. She returned to her room and retrieved it from her blazer pocket.

She was puzzled. It was an elongated rock—quartz, maybe. Its configuration told her it had to be part of something significant. Why did Danielle want her to keep it hidden? "Maybe Danielle picked it up from the ground before she was struck by the lightning, and the shock made her clamp it in her fist. Maybe it has no significance at all." But to be safe, Kit placed it in the coin compartment of her wallet and let the purse fall to the side of the bed, slid into the sheets, and reached for the TV remote. She tuned to CNN to catch up on the news of the last couple of days. But before the station even tuned in, she was sound asleep.

The Vatican

Cardinal Gregory Santis walked out of the pope's private chambers, anxious and perplexed by the sudden illness of His Holiness. Just the day before, the pontiff had seemed in good health and was looking forward with great enthusiasm to today's secret *Foundation* meeting, one of major significance. Yet earlier this morning, as he was getting out of bed for his morning prayers, he became weak and disoriented, then fainted. His medical staff urged the pontiff to cancel all scheduled audiences and remain in bed for a few days. His Holiness had reluctantly acquiesced and summoned Santis, the youngest and most energetic of his cardinals, to his bedside with instructions to clear his schedule without letting the outside world know he was not well.

There was, however, one meeting that was imperative not to cancel—the meeting with the *Foundation.* Cardinal Santis would now have to preside over it in the pontiff's place. It was an event of major consequence, one that must be conducted under the utmost secrecy. Members from all over the world would be attending, among them President David Parker of the United States. Cardinal Santis was concerned that "Il Messaggero" had published a notice in this morning's newspaper of the arrival of the US President in Rome. These days, it was hard to keep things under wraps, no matter how hard they tried. Reporters and paparazzi hung about Vatican City like vultures, in hopes of snagging a photo of some dignitary or celebrity. So many precautions had been taken on this particular occasion; it was impossible to imagine how any information had leaked out. Cardinal Santis was determined to get to the bottom of the leak, for he, personally, had been charged with overseeing the arrangements and was mortified and infuriated with the breach of security. He would begin a covert investigation immediately.

This meeting of the *Foundation* was to be treated as if it were a regular Vatican Council Meeting. Although most of those attending were not clergy but individuals from all walks of life, the Vatican was to extend *Foundation* members the same consideration they would grant to visiting world bishops.

All *Foundation* meetings assembled in the Vatican had been carried out under maximum secrecy. To Santis's chagrin, this one would be the exception.

"The *Foundation* Council meetings always close or open a new era," His Holiness had told him. This was to be the twelfth such meeting and the first and only one Santis would get to attend in his lifetime. Although only in his mid-fifties, Cardinal Santis had been a member of the *Foundation* for over twenty years; that was most likely the reason His Holiness had chosen Santis to represent him. The cardinal was not at all sure how many of the 500 Vatican residents were part of the secret organization, but he suspected there were very few; he felt quite privileged to be a part of it.

The *Foundation* was a secret and highly honorable organization. Its members had preserved and secretly passed on, from generation to generation, the knowledge ultimately responsible for maintaining peace on Earth. *Foundation* members who were not members of the governing council were allowed to attend one major Council Meeting at the Vatican. At that meeting, they would be in the presence of one or more Edentians, the original founders of the *Foundation*. The Edentians were referred to as the *Immortals*.

The cardinal had been anticipating this event for years. The compilation of his hard work—gathering, analyzing and cataloging specific information, as instructed by His Holiness—would now be turned over to an Edentian, a recorder of the Decimal Order, for review and proper application. He would finally see the research of a lifetime implemented for the improvement of life on the planet.

There was another reason that excited him. The recorder he was about to meet would, from now on, be his direct contact with the Immortals. *Would this particular Edentian have the answers to all the questions formulated during his entire existence?*

It was 11:15 a.m. when the cardinal walked into his office and verified the time on the gilded clock over the mantelpiece in his lavishly furnished study. On the right hung a fragment of a large Fresco—*The Angel Musician* by Melozzo da Forlì. It had recently been transferred to the Vatican, and Cardinal Santis suspected the transfer had something to do with today's meeting with the *Foundation*. His Holiness had also ordered a detailed inventory of the masterpieces throughout all the 1,400 halls and chapels of Vatican City.

Arranging the documents he was taking into the meeting, the cardinal mentally checked his agenda as he looked through the window and into the grounds of St. Peters. His eyes rested on a carving of the pope's coat of arms, in particular the keys, which represented the pope's power to open the Kingdom of Heaven. Several of the *Encyclicals*, or letters from the pope, which he was about to deliver at the meeting, were marked with the same papal insignia. These were addressed to various bishops who would be at the meeting. The sealed envelopes bore the coat of arms engraved within two concentric blue circles.

It was almost 11:30. He straightened his crimson sash and picked up the envelopes and a stack of files his secretary had placed on his desk just minutes before. The stack was marked "Confidential" and was thicker than he expected. He placed the documents under his arm and headed for the assembly room.

At the doors of the assembly room stood a pair of Swiss Guards in their brightly colored sixteenth-century uniforms. They looked impressive holding their halberds, but since such weapons were only for historical accuracy, Santis had made sure there was sufficient protection around the hall. Several men in black, US Secret Service agents, spoke intensely on cell phones. The Italian police seemed more laid back, despite not being permitted to smoke indoors. The number of security men surrounding the Vatican had been tripled for this occasion.

Everyone rose as Cardinal Santis entered the assembly hall. Earlier concern about his ability to preside over the meeting vanished instantly, just as His Holiness had told him it would. Twenty of the most prominent *Foundation* members stood around a long table in the center of the room, and fifty chairs had been placed around the room's perimeter, to be occupied by members-at-large. As Santis took his place at the head of the table, he made a quick assessment of the room. He was reassured with the presence of President Parker and thanked God he had arrived safely. Then he saw the two chairs at the far end of the table were empty—the two chairs that were supposed to be occupied by the two Edentians stationed on the planet.

He bade everyone sit down, and at that moment, glimpsed something for which he was not prepared. In one of the two empty chairs, as a ray of sunlight shone through the window, the outline of a man came lightly into focus. Just as suddenly, it was gone. He tried not to stare as momentary flashes of a diaphanous silhouette flashed off and on as the sunlight flickered through the window. Santis shook his head to gather his composure but, at the same time, realized the chair did, now indeed, seem to be occupied.

Suddenly, the cardinal understood.

He bowed his head in salute to one of the Constellation Fathers, who was honoring the *Foundation* gathering with his presence.

Behind the honored guest stood another man. Although he appeared to be of flesh and bone, Santis perceived that this, too, was a being of a different order—a messenger, perhaps. His physiognomy was exotic and unusually attractive. He was trim and quite tall, in excess of six feet. His skin was dark, but his features were delicate, though not African. His hair was curly, short, and of a blondish color—most unusual with such mahogany skin. His eyes were piercing, a yellowish green color Santis had never seen. As soon as this man's presence was acknowledged, he stepped back and stationed himself by the window.

After a warm greeting, Santis explained the circumstances preventing the pontiff's attendance. As he spoke, the cardinal determined that the Constellation Father was invisible to the majority. The cardinal's attention returned sadly to the empty seat, that which his Edentian contact should have occupied.

Other minor planetary recorders represented the continents of Europe, Australia, and South America and sat next to their *Foundation* representatives. Everyone at the table displayed concern for the fate of the missing members. No member had ever missed a *Foundation* meeting. Absence from a Council meeting was not something that came about from negligence. Something very serious must have happened.

"This was to be a time of celebration," said Santis. "Instead, we meet in a time of crisis. The electrical outage which took place on the nineteenth of this month, as well as the sudden acceleration in global warming, is an indication of the power the enemy has amassed and dictates that strict measures be taken; for once again, we are under attack.

"His Holiness, as head of the *Foundation*, advises that all members operate under double Code Blue restrictions as you proceed with your individual assignments. With the absence of our two Edentian agents, this meeting cannot take place as originally planned. Our chain of connection has been interrupted."

Santis became aware of a sudden energy vibrating within his brain. He had the impression that his neo-cortex was swelling. He knew at once the Constellation Father was speaking now, making use of the cardinal's voice to communicate to the group. "This was to be the one and only meeting preceding the *Formation,* which is essential to signal the arrival of RA, our organic interstellar planetary vessel. RA is presently in route to our system with an arrival expected on Saturn in October of next year. It will remain invisible unless it receives the signal from the *Formation,* advising that all is well and Earth is ready for planetary dispensation and acceleration in evolutionary consciousness.

"We must now allow the rest of the members assigned to that mission to disperse. The Cirel *Group* successfully intercepted our communication to Edentia.

The Cirel *Group* now has its headquarters somewhere on Earth. Our agent's transmission was a warning of the imminent attack the *Group* is about to launch. Her absence today is indicative that the *Group* has discovered her identity and knows what kind of information she has secured."

The Constellation Father's narrative confirmed to Santis that the missing agent was a female. His heart skipped a beat. He was now certain his premonition had been right. The Edentian agent was Danielle.

"Our alternate members must now step in and make connection if the *Formation* is to take place," the Constellation Father continued. "The second issue we must address today is that of the 'neutrals,' those immortals who chose not to take sides with either the *Foundation* or the Cirel *Group*. We must reconsider their position. Has one of them joined the *Group*? Every immortal roaming the Earth will now have to be accounted for. The dossiers are here. A committee headed by President Parker of the United Sates has been assigned to review each one. This is a most delicate matter because also embedded in these dossiers are the identities of some of our most trusted agents."

Santis moved the pile of dossiers to the center of the table. The file on top of the stack was marked "Powers Enterprises."

"The *Foundation* thanks each one of you for your dedication and loyalty. Because of the absence of His Holiness and our Edentian recorders, the Council meeting of the *Foundation* will be rescheduled. For safety reasons, our planetary recorders will now be dismissed. Our confrontation with the *Group* has begun. Double Code Blue is now in effect."

As the Constellation Father concluded, Cardinal Santis regained his voice and continued to conduct the meeting, wondering how many of the *Foundation* members knew they had just been addressed by the Constellation Father. Santis now understood why the pontiff had given him this daunting task.

"The time has come for each one of you to carry out the specific mission you were assigned. One of the first mandates is to assemble and secure all religious art containing encoded data," explained the cardinal, addressing the bishops. Then turning to the rest of the audience, he said, "Those of you dealing with material concerning current conspiracies in worldwide business and government will at this time turn in your findings to President Parker, who will temporarily act in behalf of the absent Edentians. May the Spirit of the Creator Son be with you."

Everyone rose to go. The apparition of Orsef of Edentia and his dark and mysterious escort vanished in a blink.

The cardinal said to President Parker, "Stay a little longer. I have a word from His Holiness."

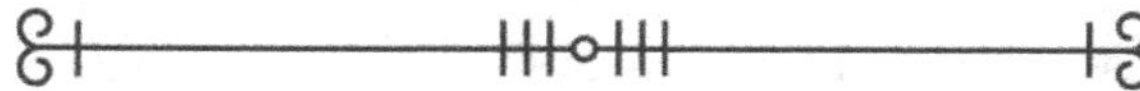

Egypt

"This about does it!" exclaimed the British Egyptologist as he stood up and tried to dust some of the dirt off his worn jeans. The debris in the narrow cave was knee high, and it had become difficult to breathe. "It will be hard to hold them off any longer."

His companion, a tall and slim Frenchman, pretended not to hear him and continued to chip away with his hammer and chisel at a crack in the wall.

"Jean-Christophe! Are you listening? It must be one of us who breaks the news. Despite my strict instructions, one of the workers must have already taken off to spread the news of the find."

Jean-Christophe stopped what he was doing and puffed in his typical French manner. "So? Will they be excited or disappointed?"

"Come on!" The Englishman was trying to sound matter-of-fact, but it was hard to control his excitement. "We'll come back soon with new permits and better equipment. Who is going to deny us a grant now? We have uncovered a mammoth mausoleum!"

Jean-Christophe puffed again. "This particular tomb has been explored and looted for decades, and no one has shown any interest in exploring it further. I really don't think they'll be as excited as you think. So far, all we've found are broken statuettes and jars, but no gold or jewelry. The parking lot they want to build is a more profitable venture."

Dr. Mark Evans couldn't protest; deep down, he suspected the Frenchman was right. He had been excavating in the Valley of Kings, thanks to the American University in Cairo, for six years and had gotten nowhere.

Now, there was pressure from the Cairo government to build parking lots for tourists, to serve the twelve open tombs. Government officials saw no need to excavate new ones. Three months ago, when Dr. Evans was finally ready to quit, this lunatic French archeologist had shown up, ready to assist him. He was independently funded by a wealthy American and had some interesting theories. This man's energy had once more energized Dr. Evans's faith.

He could remember the day the Frenchman had shown up, his nonchalant introduction as Dr. Jean-Christophe Girard, and his urgency to get to work. Dr. Evans was not at all sure he wanted him on the dig but heard him out.

"I know all about what you've been doing," Jean-Christophe had said, tossing a tuft of sun-bleached hair away from his tanned face. "But I'd like to point out where you are going wrong."

"Really?" The Englishman smiled in disbelief.

"Really!" Jean-Christophe produced some drawings and maps and plopped himself atop a large stone amidst the rubble.

"You are assuming that Ramses was no different from any other pharaoh and that his burial site was built just like the others. But he was unique in everything he did throughout his lifetime.

"This uniqueness would manifest in the way he envisioned the afterlife. I'm sure he was more creative in the manner he chose to protect his treasures and the burial sites of his family. Let's not forget that this pharaoh is still referred to as Ramses the Great, despite the pathetic role he is assigned in the book of Exodus.

"He was in his twenties when he ascended to the throne and took over the mediocre constructions that were in shambles. He erected magnificent monuments, like the temple of Osiris at Abydos, expanded the temples at Luxor and Karnak, and worked on the cliff temples at Abu Simbel.

"I am certain we'll discover that the tombs of his children are just as rich and elaborate as King Tut's. It's absolutely incredible what he achieved during the years he occupied the throne."

"True. His empire was huge," the Englishman added.

"From Libya to Iraq in the east," the French doctor threw his arms out dramatically, "and as far north as Turkey and then into Sudan in the south. Didn't he sire over one hundred children?"

"One hundred, sixty-two," Evans added again.

"*D'accord.* What I'm saying is that somewhere underneath this tomb lies the greatest discovery of the century. I am positive that Ramses provided well not only for his sons, but for his wives, concubines, and daughters. Yes, his daughters—a fact everyone has missed. Those undiscovered chambers are right here below us.

"Poor guy! He planned everything so perfectly. According to his calculations, his tombs would have been safe from thieves for all eternity. He just couldn't imagine that in the following millennia, arid Egypt would experience torrential flash rains and floods. Or that his burial site would become a tourist attraction, complete with brutal vibrations from buses, leaky sewer pipes over his tombs, snack bars, and parking lots!" Jean-Christophe laughed heartily. "But we will never find the entrance this way."

"Any suggestions?" Dr. Evans had not minded at all the way Jean-Christophe said "we." He wouldn't be too bad a team partner. He had encountered worse.

"*Oui*, I believe you have gone in a straight line long enough. I suspect the clue is in one of the main pillars. I suggest we go back to the ante-chamber and get grounded again."

And they did. Jean-Christophe showed up at the dig at 5:00 a.m. the next day, and during the next few weeks, both archeologists studied every marking on every wall. They took notes and separated the graffiti scrawled on them from any markings that could be of value.

"I wouldn't be surprised if we leave with a treasure-laden coffin," Jean-Christophe burst out one day.

"Is that what you're hoping for?" Dr. Evans asked incredulously.

"No. Though it wouldn't be so bad." The Frenchman laughed. "We'll find some more tombs, don't worry. Since Napoleon started exploring this place, archeologists have discovered tomb after tomb here. How many had been found by the time your countryman Howard Carter opened the gold rich tomb of Tutankhamen?"

"Sixty-one, I believe."

"I say we haven't even begun! I don't remember who the idiot was that decided there were no more major discoveries to be made in this part of the valley."

Dr. Evans smiled. "I believe it was also one of my countrymen, James Burton, who concluded in 1920 that there was nothing else inside."

"Therefore, your other countryman, Carter, used these halls and entryway as a place to dump debris as he hauled out loot from King Tut's tomb. If that is not the most idiotic thing I ever heard!"

The Englishman, by now, was used to Jean-Christophe's opinionated views.

"To trash a site that lies one hundred feet away from the tomb of Ramses II!" Now Jean-Christophe was getting agitated. "And right here," he pounded on the crypt wall, "and over there, two of the sons of Ramses are mentioned. The names of the daughters are well-hidden but must appear somewhere."

Jean-Christophe noticed Dr. Evans's eyes had opened wide and his jaw had suddenly dropped. As the Frenchman had pounded on the wall, he had accidentally hit a small rock that acted as a switch, allowing an opening to form above their heads. The tiny aperture emitted a narrow shaft of light. As the light bounced over the top of one of the pillars, it cast a pattern over another pillar, which stood in front of them. The men simultaneously understood the configuration of the mausoleum. It actually resembled an octopus, a chamber surrounded by tentacles.

They refigured their calculations based on this new discovery. The room in which they were standing was approximately fifty feet square, divided by sixteen massive columns. Each column would give them a clue to the position of each row of graves. In ancient times, this would have been clear. But now, the room was filled almost to the top with rubble, washed in over the centuries by flash floods.

Dr. Evans had installed a string of lights, but they still had to crawl through a tight passage to get to the other side. It felt claustrophobic, but neither man was intimidated by the tight quarters. The Frenchman crawled back and forth, ignoring the jagged outcropping of rock, which might cave in at any time.

After weeks of effort, they were able to clear enough debris from the passage to move in a line about thirty degrees from the one the Englishman had been excavating for years. At the end of the passage, the archeologists could stand up, and the claustrophobic journey ended as they came upon a wide door. Unable to pry it open, the men had to go back to fetch their excavating team.

On the other side of the door, they found themselves in a spacious corridor and came across several artifacts. Most were damaged or broken, but the two archeologists were, nonetheless, thrilled. They gathered broken pieces of spice jars, urns, miniature figurines, and amulets.

"What is our deal with the Cairo Museum, a fifty-fifty split?" Jean-Christophe asked.

"The norm. They'll be greedy if we find any complete relics."

"By the looks of it, this site had visitors in ancient times. We're getting closer, though. Beyond the next door, we'll find the graves of the children of Ramses."

"Possibly."

They didn't have to search for the next door, for suddenly they encountered the statue of Osiris face-to-face, and it pointed the way. They were sobered by the solemn countenance of the unpolished marble statue of the god of the afterlife, but not intimidated. Some small jars and statuettes lay undisturbed at his feet. Jean- Christophe bent down and picked up one that caught his eye.

"I'm keeping this one," he said as he dusted it off with the sleeve of his shirt. "She reminds me of a friend of mine in the US."

After showing it to Mark, Jean-Christophe put it in his shirt pocket.

They continued along through a series of cubicles and took copious notes as they went in and out of each one. It was evident that the rooms had been ransacked repeatedly over the ages. Jean-Christophe was sure that at some point, there must have been a more accessible entrance through the main entry hall.

That entrance was now hidden, probably damaged by floods and sealed by the earth's shifts.

The doors lining the corridor led to identical ten-by-ten-foot chambers. The openings to each were narrow, no wider than two feet, but the chambers were empty.

"What do you think?" asked Jean-Christophe. "No freaking sarcophagus went in and out of here."

"That's exactly what I am thinking. These are not burial chambers."

"I think these are chapels for funeral offerings, flowers, incense . . . you know. That means the tombs of the daughters must be somewhere below them," said Jean-Christophe. Dr. Evans nodded in agreement. He scrutinized the cracks in the walls. The men returned to the larger chamber and studied the cracks in the four massive pillars. Now they were certain that hollow areas lay beneath them.

"Did you also notice the weird split level design of the tomb?" Jean-Christophe pointed out.

"What do you mean?"

Jean-Christophe walked back to the statue of Osiris. "Look at the ceilings of the corridors to the left and right. They drop abruptly, about three to four feet. That, to me, is evidence of stairways."

They found an opening in an adjacent wall and tried to enter, but the debris was too obtrusive and the jagged rocks and darkness inside the opening made it too dangerous to continue. Dr. Evans knew they could go no further; they were forced to stop. Besides, his permits were about to expire. They returned to the main chamber where Evans produced a flask of whiskey and handed it to Jean-Christophe. "You are a good chap. I am really pleased you came."

Jean-Christophe took a big gulp and said, "Oh, and I'm pleased it was you who was here and not some other schmuck."

"Well, I definitely think we should continue," Mark Evans said. Then added, "September, perhaps."

"I know those bureaucratic *mecs,*" retorted the Frenchman. "It will be at least a year before we get our permits back."

"We have enough evidence to halt the parking lot and convince them we have found the first multiple burial sites of the pharaoh's children. We'll get our permits by July, and we'll continue. The hieroglyphics above the paintings in the burial chambers make it clear that at least three of Pharaoh's sons are buried here," Evans said.

"I have a gut feeling that many of his daughters are here too," Jean-Christophe added. "Perhaps that series of concentric circles on the walls points the way to their resting place."

"Here, and not in the Valley of the Queens?" Evans was still incredulous.

"They are right here. That, my English friend, will be our real find!"

"My suggestion is that we finish now. Let them know what we've found. We can take a short break and return with better equipment, install climate controls, electricity, and the means to better protect the finds."

"*D'accord*, but indulge me in this: Let's work here for one more week. Don't say anything yet. If I haven't found a clue to what I'm after, then I'll compromise and take a rest for the summer."

"What is it that you are after?"

"A special chamber. It is a theory, and I'm being well financed for it," confided Jean-Christophe.

"By?"

"Well, a very wealthy colleague. Her name is Dr. Danielle Peschard, currently with the Met."

"Yes, of course, the one celebrated for finding the statue of Aphrodite in Turkey."

"Right. Tell you what. Let's rest this weekend—I need to call Danielle in New York—then we'll return here for a few days. You do whatever it takes to close the dig during that week, and I'll go back in the tomb with Mousa."

"Ah, Mousa! Mustafa, your faithful assistant . . . I had forgotten about him. Where is he, anyway?"

"Gone back to the hotel. Is it a deal?"

"OK. How many days do you need in here?"

"Monday through Thursday. This weekend, I'll tell you all about Danielle."

Mustafa, who prided himself on being a man of detail, had everything set out for the two archeologists upon their return to the hotel. Appetizers and drinks were ready.

After scrubbing away the dirt from the tomb, the three men met for a late supper at the hotel's main dining room. Mustafa and Jean-Christophe laughed like children or perhaps reunited lovers. Mark Evans missed his family but rejoiced in the fact he would soon be back in London. As promised, Jean-Christophe talked non-stop about Danielle.

"She is intelligent, witty, beautiful, and will most certainly be one of our benefactors upon our return to Egypt," Jean-Christophe told Evans before calling her in the States.

With the first few tries, Jean-Christophe was unable to reach Danielle.

Finally, Linda, Danielle's secretary, returned his calls. "I'm afraid Dr. Peschard is recovering from an accident," she informed him. Jean-Christophe could not get a detailed account of what happened, and after several back-and-forth questions, he realized the young secretary did not know either. All she could tell him was that it had happened during a terrible storm. When Linda couldn't provide more information, he knew he'd never get the story straight until he got back to America, and he considered leaving right away. After thinking it through, he decided to stick with his plan and remain at the dig for a few days longer, realizing that now, more than ever, it was imperative to accomplish his mission for Danielle.

Their find had not been as astonishing to Jean-Christophe as it had been to Mark Evans. Danielle had given Jean-Christophe specific instructions about the direction in which to dig. The various impediments to their progress had eaten up more time than he anticipated, and the clock was ticking on their permit. He had to find the secret chamber. He would re-double his efforts and find Danielle's chamber before returning to the US.

On Monday morning, the archeologists, the assistant Mustafa, and the crew returned to the dig. Jean-Christophe entered the site with renewed determination and began chipping away with brutal energy. Mark and the crew closed and barricaded the tomb. Mark and Mustafa understood Jean-Christophe's concern over his friend's accident and left him alone.

As instructed by Jean-Christophe, Mustafa placed several calls to the States to check on Danielle's condition. The reports were grim, and Mustafa found it kinder to lie, saying he was having trouble getting through. Jean-Christophe's frustration became evident when he could unearth no further clues that would point him to the chamber.

On Thursday, as sunset approached, Mark Evans went back in the tomb and reminded Jean-Christophe of their agreement to abandon the search for now and hold a press conference.

"Are you coming, Jean-Christophe?"

The Frenchman put down his hammer and chisel and wiped the sweat from his brow.

"I know . . . I know. I am quitting today as agreed. But I still have forty-five minutes of light. Why don't you go ahead, dismiss the crew, and set up the conference? I'll make it back in time. Tell Mustafa to wait in the Jeep."

"OK, will do." Mark waved as he headed for the exit. He saw Jean-Christophe disappear in the dark, but the clinking sound of the chisel told him the Frenchman was furiously pounding away.

Danielle! Wherever you are, give me a hint that I am heading in the right direction. . . . I am? . . . If you think so. He continued to chip.

Jean-Christophe stopped as he came upon a relief with a painting of a female wearing a strange headdress, holding two serpents coiled around her arms, and surrounded by carved hieroglyphics. The rock had been badly damaged, and part of it lay in pieces on the ground. The color had faded, and nearly every other symbol in the writing had been damaged. His eye suddenly lit on the eye of a bird, and he wiped it off with his hand. It was not carved out of stone as was the rest of the relief; instead, it was crafted of metal—copper, perhaps. Pulling a small sable brush from his shirt pocket, he dusted it off.

When it was cleaned, Jean-Christophe pushed and pulled it. When he rested his left hand on another character for balance, the archeologist knew he had hit the combination and found what he was looking for. Before he could think, the chamber resounded with a loud, crunching noise, like cellophane being wadded before a live microphone. Jean-Christophe knew then the structure was giving away. He felt the first of the small rocks crumble as they hit his head and shoulders. He looked at the sloping ceilings, which he had previously identified as proof of the secreted stairways.

As the ground beneath him collapsed and the earth swallowed him, the world went black, and he realized he was falling.

"This is it!" he thought as he suspected his life was coming to its conclusion at the age of forty-two. He saw fleeting visions of Mustafa, his devoted companion of the last two years, of Mark Evans, of his friends in Paris, and finally of the incredibly beautiful face of Danielle Peschard, his benefactor and trusted friend.

"Please forgive me. I have let you down," he whispered.

"Jean-Christophe! Jean-Christophe!" Danielle's voice seemed to call to him from beyond. "Jean-Christophe, listen . . . the insignia!"

"What insignia?" He reached for the chain around his neck, the medallion, a silver medal with two concentric gold circles—a gift Danielle had given him years ago for good luck. Jean-Christophe held it and repeated what Danielle had said upon giving it to him.

"May the sign of Michael protect me." At that point, he lost consciousness.

Excruciating pain in his right leg made him open his eyes. He felt soreness and discomfort all over his body. He recalled the sensation of falling and sliding down a smooth ramp with occasional jagged edges. He had no idea how far he had fallen, nor where he had landed. It was damp and dark. After a few minutes, his eyes became accustomed to the darkness, and he could make out shapes. He saw the sharp edges of walls and a distant curve, which was illuminated by a faint ray of light—its origin undefinable.

Jean-Christophe couldn't tell whether he was dreaming or hallucinating. He remembered the ground collapsing under his feet and swallowing him with great speed. Before everything went black, he recalled an image materializing out of nowhere. On a crypt wall, the regal face of a woman had appeared. She wore a gold hairpiece with circular ornaments and interwoven serpents. The archeologist knew then that the image of Pharaoh's daughter would guide him.

He suspected he was at least fifty feet below the surface. He regretted having dismissed the crew but was certain Mustafa had remained behind. After a while, his friend would certainly know that something was wrong and would call for help. As soon as they saw where the dig had caved in, they would know where to search for him. That was probably what they were doing right now, clearing debris and making way to descend.

The utter silence worried him. There was no pounding or any sound that indicated activity above him. He reached inside his shirt pocket for the small flashlight he usually carried and flashed it over his badly scuffed wristwatch. It was almost 11:00 p.m. Several hours had passed since the fall. Despite his excruciating pain, he had to do something to attract attention. It was unlikely he could climb in his condition. He used the flashlight to have a look at his surroundings. The walls were smooth and high and offered no sign of the ramp that had deposited him where he lay.

While searching for a clue, his flashlight washed over an inscription. He focused the light on that area. The beam was too small to see the wall in its entirety, so he moved the light slowly over the writing. He had trouble making out what it said, but it took him no time to realize it was etched on a round stone about seven feet in diameter. He recognized the common Egyptian hieroglyphics: the snakes, the eyes, and the triangles. The archeologist attempted in vain to sit up while he focused on the disk.

He could see it more clearly now. The symbols on the outer rim were not Egyptian at all. To his amazement, they were in Hebrew. He read Aleph, Beth, Gimel . . . the next two rows of inscriptions he could not identify. In the next row, there were more familiar signs, much like those of the Zodiac. Further down, in inner concentric rows, were two lines of Arabic numbers. He followed one row from the outer rim to the center. His flashlight rested first on HEH, the drawing of a window, the sign of Aries, 5, 15. He moved to the next . . . VAU, nails, Taurus, 6, 16 . . . ZAIN, sword, Gemini, 7, 17. He continued until it dawned on him that the rock represented the Wheel of Correspondence.

He tried to ignore the throbbing pain in his leg and ankle and made another attempt to sit up. He could not, so he crawled a little closer to the rock. He pointed the light directly at the center, and there, inside an indentation, he found the representation of the *Otz Chiim*—the Tree of Life.

Jean-Christophe remembered the Tree of Life was the oldest representation of the cosmos in its entirety, and of the soul of man in the microcosm. It had been used by civilizations from time immemorial—much like a mathematician would use a slide rule—to calculate the intricacies of existence. Philosophers had relied on it to explain the invisible composition and depth of the soul. His eyes followed the Ten Holy Sephiroth, that delineated the ten phases of evolution.

This was *it*! The stone was just as Danielle had described it. Here was the entrance to the chamber he was searching for. He cursed his injured leg and wracked his brain, trying to decide what to do.

He became aware of drafts of cold air, which he had not felt before. He circled his light to look for an opening. There was none to be seen. He also realized he was having no trouble breathing; therefore, air had to be coming in from somewhere.

He felt his strength falter and closed his eyes momentarily. When he opened them again, something was different about the chamber. He had the strange feeling he was no longer in the same room. The configuration of the space was different. The use of his small flashlight confirmed his suspicion. He was in a different place.

He located the round stone behind him, which meant he had somehow gone through the door and entered a different chamber. But how? He was sure he had passed out, but he could hardly move. The thought that someone had moved him was too strange to imagine.

It must be a dream. With that in mind, he returned his attention to the inspection of the room, and he quickly identified it as a likely burial chamber. To his surprise, a small amount of light emanated from above. He located four gilded torches evenly spaced on the wall behind him. In contrast to the claustrophobic chambers he and Mark had been exploring, these rooms were tall and spacious. And from what he could see, they were not primitive at all.

The light grew a little brighter, as if someone had operated a dimmer control. Jean-Christophe noticed that what he had thought were torches were not torches at all, but beautifully carved gold sconces, emitting their light in rising, swirling, amorphous vapor that ruled out fire completely. The colors they cast were not the oranges and yellows of flames, but pale violets, cool greens, and blues not indicative of heat. The temperature, the Frenchman noticed, had also changed. To Jean-Christophe's delight, it was no longer cold. There were no more drafts, and he felt a soft fog creeping in.

No longer needing the flashlight, Jean- Christophe's eyes began to see, little by little, more and more of the chamber. The walls were polished to a high black sheen. In the center of the room was a cube about three feet high. It appeared to be carved out of translucent stone, possibly quartz. The next thing he noticed was a low hissing noise. The thought that it might be a snake paralyzed him with fear. To his relief, it grew quiet. A few minutes later, it began again. The Frenchman attempted to tune in, hoping to determine what it was.

After a while, he realized he was hearing voices and that *he* was being discussed. He did not know how he knew; yet he knew. The voices were speaking in a different timbre, uttered in vibrations not compatible with human eardrums. But here, because of the strange silence around him and the rarified atmosphere, something in his consciousness was allowing him to intuit their meaning. He tried hard to concentrate.

Yes, they were definitely talking about him. They did not know who he was or how he had gotten there. The *others* had recently been there and had probably seen him as well.

Jean-Christophe wondered who the others might be but put his question aside so as not to miss the rest of what was being said.

To get rid of him was not a good idea, one of the voices argued in his defense. There would be no elimination there, not in the chamber of Sharah. The mention of Sharah sent goosebumps through his body. He was in the chamber Danielle had sent him to locate! Now, if he could only figure out how to get out! Once again, he wondered if this was all a dream.

The answer came from one of the voices. "No, it is not a dream. You have reached the chamber of Sharah, mistress of the West, keeper of the Treasure and the Truth."

"Who are you?" Jean-Christophe inquired.

"My name is Elan."

"And mine is Ka. We are—"

"Angels?"

The voices erupted into laughter. "No, no, we are not angels. We are creatures like you."

"But you are invisible!"

"No, we are not invisible. You can see us if you try."

Jean-Christophe focused in the direction of the voices and discerned the faint outlines of the two beings. His eyes were only able to capture part of their silhouette. As soon as he moved his eyes from one spot, he was able to pick up a different part of the silhouette, but the previous one would disappear. Therefore, it became impossible to make out the complete outline of either one. Jean-Christophe knew right away they were not of flesh and bone. Their bodies lacked a solid structure and presented an ethereal quality that challenged his senses to confirm their existence.

The archeologist was too baffled to speak, and though still in pain, he tried to get a good look at them, for he suspected it would be important later. Because of their transparency, the two figures resembled holographic images. He guessed them to be approximately four-and-a-half feet tall, and it was hard to determine whether they were male or female. Everything about them was androgynous, from the tone of their voices to their manner of moving. Jean-Christophe continued to study what he could make out of their anatomy, intrigued by their round heads as they resumed conversation among each other.

"He was wearing the sign of protection, so we must treat him as a member of the *Foundation*. He is hurt, and we must help him."

"*Mais, bien sure*!" thought Jean-Christophe. He was afraid the pain would once again render him unconscious.

In awe, Jean-Christophe watched as one of the two beings—Elan, he thought—defied the laws of gravity and went up in the air, then opening what looked like a large drawer in the polished stone wall. The drawer revealed an inner rock marked with thousands of vertical lines. One of the lines popped out, and Elan took in his hand a sheet, which was more visible than his silhouette. The thin metal looked as if it was floating in the air.

"*Incroyable* . . . incredible, " whispered the astounded archeologist. "That is a library, isn't it?"

"Yes. We have all the information here."

"The wisdom of Egypt!" exclaimed Jean-Christophe.

"Oh, it is truly more than that. We have a record of all the information your race has accumulated, plus much that you have yet to discover."

"How long has this been here?"

"From the beginning of time. A copy of everything that has been forwarded to the Celestial Archives is kept here."

"We have done our job peacefully for thousands of years," added Elan. "It is only recently we have been under threat. The *others* have also found us."

"The others—who?"

"Why don't you let us fix your leg, and then we'll answer more of your questions?"

"You can do that?"

"We are not physicians, but we have excellent guidance," said Elan, waving the metal sheet.

Jean-Christophe watched him place the sheet on top of the clear cube and immediately return to him.

"You have fractured your femur and your ankle, torn a ligament, and sprained your wrist. A concussion has produced a slight inflammation in the lower part of your brain. You will probably be dizzy for a few days but will be fine. Your leg will take a few weeks to heal. Now, if you will hold these rocks in your hand, we'll set and repair your bones."

Jean-Christophe attempted to sit up. "Wait, wait, wait. What exactly are you going to do?" With some trepidation, he took the crystalline rocks in his right hand.

"We are going to repair the damage you have done to your body. Just hold on to the rocks. In a few seconds, the pain will subside."

The throbbing and the sharp pain subsided instantly, and Jean-Christophe breathed a deep sigh and lay back. He felt pressure and the manipulation of his bones, but it was not painful. He saw no point in trying to see what the two semi-visibles were doing. Rather than panic, he decided to engage them in conversation if he could.

"Who did you say the others were?"

"The prince's staff."

"The prince? What prince?

"Members of the *Group,* as you call them, and their new alien associates."

"The *Group*? I have no idea what you are talking about."

"Much better that way," added Elan. "They have grown aggressively destructive. They are smashing and crushing everything that crosses their path." He turned to Ka. "I don't know how they found us. But now, we can be sure they will be back."

"We have told them we do not have anything they want." The creatures were once again talking between themselves.

"I don't think they believed us." Elan then turned to Jean-Christophe. "You had better not ask too many questions. So that if they see you again, they will not bother with you. They'll just think you ended up here accidentally."

"But, you see, I was sent to find this chamber."

The transparent beings looked at each other in consternation. "By whom?"

"A friend of mine asked me to verify the existence of this chamber. In return, she agreed to help me locate the tombs of the daughters and concubines of Ramses II."

"Did she give you the medal of protection?"

"Yes." He touched his medal.

"Then she is the one," they whispered between themselves. Their conversation fell to an even lower pitch, and Jean-Christophe could no longer understand them. He waited until they addressed him again.

"We must respect her decision. You may then enter the Chamber of Gida and the other daughters of Ramses. You may retrieve information but must promise not to remove anything from the tombs. The resting places of the selected ones have been ransacked enough. And never divulge its location. Do you promise?"

"I promise." The Frenchman could only agree.

"What your mistress wishes to find is the monolith," said Ka, pointing to the round stone. "It is safe. She will also want to retrieve another important object—the headpiece. Let her know it has never been disturbed."

"Simply give her a message," interrupted Elan. "She will understand. Remember our names—Elan and Ka—and remember these numbers: 3,6,9 00101100 . . .606 . . . 6. Now, I think you must rest and give your leg time to recover." Ka gently removed the rocks from his hands, and the light from the sconces faded. The two figures moved away from him and became lost in the shadows.

No matter how hard Jean-Christophe tried to remain conscious, his eyelids grew heavy, and he closed them, slowly falling into a long, peaceful sleep.

The sound of voices woke Jean-Christophe up. They were not the voices of Elan and Ka but those of Mustafa and Mark Evans. The whiteness around him told him he was no longer in the tomb but in some kind of clinic.

"How did I get here?" were the Frenchman's first words.

"We brought you. You have been here for three days," Mustafa volunteered.

Jean-Christophe sat up. He had a tremendous headache, but otherwise, he had no difficulty moving his body. "Please tell me what happened."

Mark was the one to elaborate. "When you failed to come out of the dig, Mustafa went in looking for you. He did not find you, became alarmed, and phoned me. We returned to the site with some of the other men. It was not until five in the morning when we finally found you. You had apparently fallen, hit your head, wandered around the cave, and finally collapsed."

"But did you go down?"

"Down where?"

"Where the ground collapsed, into the sub-chambers."

Mustafa and Evans looked at each other before responding.

"We saw nothing like that," said Mustafa.

"Right where I fell and broke my leg?"

They all stared at his bandaged ankle. A doctor approached and added, in a thick accent, "I am sure it felt like a fracture, but it's nothing but a sprain."

"I must have dreamed it!" whispered Jean-Christophe, but inside, he did not believe he had.

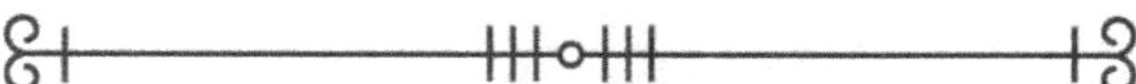

Kitzia woke up when Maria, the housekeeper, opened the plantation shutters and the light filtered through the window. The clock showed 8:05 a.m., and Maria was setting a breakfast tray on the bed while she rambled on about an assassination attempt.

"What are you talking about?" Kit sat up and adjusted the tray over her lap.

"The president! It's on the television! They tried to kill him!"

Kit grabbed the control and raised the volume. CNN was showing a picture of the Vatican behind the American correspondent who was halfway through her report.

"A bomb exploded in hangar number nine at Fiumicino Airport in Rome just minutes before President Parker was to board Air Force One. We still don't know who was behind the attempt on President Parker's life. President Parker arrived in Rome for an audience with the pope. He was to depart at 2:30 p.m., but just prior to boarding, for unknown reasons, the president returned to the waiting room." The camera then switched to the scene of the explosion.

The mention of hangar nine filled Kit with apprehension.

"Terrorists!" Maria exploded. Then she suddenly remembered something. "Ah, Mr. Robert called."

"What did he say?" Kit turned to her.

"He'll see you at ten o'clock at the hospital for a meeting with the doctors."

The reports from Rome were broadcast on every TV monitor Kit passed at the hospital on her way to the ICU. She decided not to get caught up in the hysteria; she was more worried about the meeting with the physicians. She reached the

ICU, but before she could go in, Robert stopped her and led her back into the VIP waiting room.

"Did you get some sleep?" he asked.

Kit nodded. "Danielle?"

"They will extubate her this morning."

Kit's spirits lifted.

"She is breathing and stable for the moment. I've called a meeting with her primary physicians. I will be away for a few days at the OPEC meeting but want to make sure everything is set to meet whatever comes up. She'll be moved to a suite in a couple of days."

At that moment, three doctors walked into the room, still voicing their consternation over the attempt on the president's life. They stopped short and greeted Robert and Kitzia.

Everyone sat down. Kit feared something terrible and waited for the first doctor to speak. Robert took her hand.

"Miss O'Neil . . ." Dr. Erickson corrected himself. "Dr. O'Neil . . ." Kit dismissed the rectification with a smile. "The anomalies in the X-rays," he continued, "suggest a lesion on the lower temporal lobe. The charge of electricity hit and penetrated Danielle's body with such force that it disrupted all neuro-sensory impulses. Some sort of residual impact has concentrated and remains static on the synapses of the brain. We felt it urgent to find out what the lesion was, so we did an MRI early this morning."

"Why wasn't I notified?" She turned to Robert.

"We tried, but there was no answer. There really was no need to have you come running in here at five o'clock in the morning."

She couldn't believe she had forgotten to recharge her cell phone.

"You had signed the releases," added the senior physician. Kit did not like his authoritative tone and calmly inquired, "And what did you find out?"

"We must perform a biopsy to confirm our suspicions, but we believe we are dealing with a Grade IV astrocytoma."

"A glioblastoma multiforme?" Kit asked incredulously. She was familiar with the nature of the aggressive brain tumor. "Do you think the lightning . . ."

"The electrical charge probably created the lesion that provoked necrosis in the surrounding area," said Dr. Erickson. "Or perhaps it only accelerated the expansion of an existing condition."

"What dimensions are we talking about?" Kitzia wanted to follow the thread of the conversation in a professional manner.

"Microscopic, really. Except its location is so delicate that it produces myriad severe effects."

"What can you do?" asked Kit.

"Explorative surgery might be the best course of action, once the risk factors have been considered." The doctor remained silent for a few seconds, awaiting Kit's reaction. She showed none, so he continued. "Then again, while it is in its nascent state, radiation or chemotherapy might be the most advisable option."

A voice seemed to rise again within Kitzia, the all-familiar voice of Danielle's pleading, "Don't let them touch my brain."

"We must proceed with a biopsy as a first step," Dr. Erickson continued.

Kit made an instant decision. "I'm sorry; it's all too fast. I cannot authorize any further intervention until I have time to assess and evaluate this information. I will, therefore, revoke my previous authorizations. Is she stable at the moment?"

"Um, yes. We will extubate her shortly," added Erickson. "Her lungs are strong, but we doubt she will regain consciousness. The decision for treatment should not be delayed too long. You know, Dr. O'Neil, that some forms of glioblastoma double in size every ten days."

"I am familiar with that theory," said Kit.

"Then we must not ignore the possibility."

Kit felt once again that wave of distrust toward the senior physician. He had monopolized the conversation while the other two doctors had remained silent, backing up his decisions with simple nods. She turned to Robert. "What do you think?"

"This is a very delicate matter. For the moment, she must be left alone. I'll be gone for four or five days. When I return, we'll make a final decision."

They all agreed, and the physicians left the room.

Robert put his arm around Kitzia, and together, they walked into the ICU. Danielle looked peaceful. Kitzia kissed her friend lightly on the head before turning to the nurse who stood by the bedside.

"This is Angela," explained Robert. "She will be Danielle's head nurse. I believe you, Kit, or Angela should be by Danielle's side at all times."

"Absolutely!" Kit agreed.

"Angela is used to long shifts, and I trust her completely. So please take your rest as needed. Danielle is in good hands and will be completely safe."

"Yes, she will be safe," repeated Angela. Her eyes met Robert's in a mysterious manner and Kit had not missed the tone of the word *safe.*

Kit looked appraisingly at Angela and felt immediately comfortable with her. So, the suspicious thoughts she had formed a second ago, she set aside.

"I will be working at getting the best specialist down here within days." Robert walked up to the bed and looked intensely at Danielle. He lifted her hand to his lips, then turned to go.

Kit was glad Robert would help her do the right thing. Robert Powers and Danielle had been seeing each other for about eight months. Kit was thankful her friend had found romance. There was something dynamic about this man. He stood six feet, three inches tall; his hair was thick and a rich, gray color, and his eyes were a cool bluish-gray, capable of producing—with a glance—a power both intimidating and demanding. In the past, he had been linked with the world's most beautiful women, including Lilith Keller, the fashion magnate. Financially, there was nothing Robert could offer Danielle that she didn't already have. Therefore, Kit concluded the affection was mutual and genuine.

Robert Powers was chairman of Powers Industries, which was a conglomerate of businesses that included Powers Technologies, Oil and Gas Occidental Investments, Powers Industries . . . the list seemed endless.

Although Robert lived in New York, he was often abroad. Danielle had been traveling extensively for the Met for several years now; therefore, it was impossible for either to make any demands on the other. Kit knew they occasionally met for dinner and also attended benefit functions together. It seemed a perfect match.

There were several messages from Danielle's New York office on Kitzia's answering service. "You finally called!" the voice of Danielle's secretary sounded full of anxiety.

"Linda, I am sorry."

"Is Danielle all right?"

"She is stable for the moment. I promise to keep you better informed."

"Kit, there is something else I need to tell you. Someone broke into Danielle's penthouse."

"What? When?" Kit was truly disturbed.

"I think it was the night of the accident."

"I don't understand. How did they get in?"

"Nobody knows. With everything else going on—the accident, the police inquiry . . . well, nobody thought of checking the penthouse again. When Mai Li went in to clean on Monday, she found the place had been ransacked. I sped over there and absolutely couldn't believe it. Don't know what they took, but the damage is unbelievable!" Linda explained.

Kit's head was spinning. She was desperately trying to find a common denominator for all that was happening around Danielle. There had to be one, and she vowed to find it.

"Kit?" Linda questioned Kit's silence at the news.

"Yes, I'm listening. Did the police find out anything?"

"Not a thing. There is no sign of forced entry. We can't even figure out how they got into the building. It's a real mess! The cushions were torn, the safe was blown up. The odd part is that it didn't look like a robbery. They were more keen on vandalizing."

"Or perhaps they were looking for something in particular," Kit said, thinking aloud.

"Yeah. Whatever it was they were looking for must have been small. They looked in the most inconspicuous places."

Kit suddenly thought of the rock Danielle had given her.

Linda continued, "The saddest part is that three of the paintings were slashed. The Van Dyck portrait of the Bedford Countess in the hall, the Picasso still life in the dining room, and the Matisse in the powder room."

Kit was too shocked to speak. Those were priceless masterpieces. *Who in his right mind would do such a thing?*

"Anyway, we've taken them back to the museum. They're in restoration. They are going to do what they can. I hope you don't mind that I took that upon myself."

Tears slid down Kit's face. She knew how much those paintings meant to her friend. Kit felt helpless against whoever had targeted Danielle. She also realized this was the first time she had been able to shed a tear since it had all begun. Something in her had retained strength and determination to face and fight whatever evil was lurking around Danielle.

"You did the right thing. Has the place been straightened?"

"As much as Mai Li and I could. Of course, the upholstery is damaged almost everywhere. I have called the insurance company."

"Linda, forget the insurance. I want you to put everything back in order. Reorder the fabrics from Fortuny and call Steuben. Repair and replace everything, down to the last broken glass. Get the designers back in there today. OK?"

"OK. One more thing," said Linda. "Jean-Christophe has been calling nonstop. He is still in Egypt, but I know he'll want to come down there."

"Tell him Danielle is out of danger, that she has excellent doctors, and that I will call him very soon. Let him know I am not alone down here, that Robert Powers has been with me."

"That will do it. You know how he feels about Robert," sighed Linda.

Kitzia smiled. "I know. I really don't want Jean-Christophe to drop what he is doing. Danielle would not want him to."

"OK. Kit, I'll let you go back to Danielle. By the way, wasn't it *something* about the attempted assassination?"

Kit did not feel like getting into a political conversation, so she simply said, "Terrible!"

"Really! What was going on in Rome, anyway? Danielle had me make travel arrangements that were very hush, hush. Did you know she was planning to be in Rome?"

Kit didn't, so she said nothing.

"Also, the FBI called, inquiring about Danielle's trip. Apparently, her name was on the list of passengers coming back from Rome on Air Force One. Do you think there might be a connection?"

"I don't see how there could be," Kit interrupted. "Have to run! I'll check with you later."

Kit recalled the fax she'd found, instructing Danielle about the departing time and the hangar number—one more missing piece to the puzzle.

Kit walked out of the VIP waiting room too preoccupied to notice the man observing her through the window. Absentmindedly, she headed for the vending machine in the adjacent room, which had been her main source of nutrition for the past few days. The man followed her.

She slipped her credit card into the vending machine.

"What shall it be, Twinkies or potato chips?" the man's voice broke in to her thoughts.

Kit turned around, a little embarrassed at the realization her recent junk food diet had been observed by others.

"Dr. O'Neil." The man extended his hand. "Chris Goodman."

"I know who you are." She cut him off as she eyed him from head to toe, feeling very sorry she had come out of the ICU.

This was Christian Goodman, mystery writer, ex-reporter, ex-FBI agent, and the one person in the world she despised. He had embarrassed and humiliated her on national TV. He had called her a "fraud." He had publicly derided her unusual psychic abilities. Despite his later retraction, she had become self-conscious of ever displaying, or even acknowledging, her gift in public.

How did I ever think this man was attractive? He was arrogant, closed-minded, and hateful.

It had happened three years earlier. The police department sometimes consulted her on difficult cases. Her insight had been especially helpful in solving a case in which a twenty-two-year-old woman had reported the abduction of her two-year-old daughter from her front yard. When no leads surfaced, Dr. Kitzia O'Neil was asked to appear on a television show and apply her clairvoyance to assist in the investigation.

Christian Goodman, who was being interviewed on a split-screen from Los Angeles, chuckled with sarcasm when the station shifted to him.

Kit swallowed her pride, and when the station switched back to her, continued with more determination than ever. Kit made no more TV appearances. Instead, she met privately with the investigating officer and sadly announced, "The little girl is dead. The mother knows exactly where she is."

The police put pressure on the mother, and the little girl was found thirty-six hours later.

After the mother's confession, Chris tried to phone Kit several times. She never returned his calls. Kitzia also decided never to do interviews again and give her psychic gift a rest.

Chris Goodman wrote a book about the case, and it became a best-seller. In it, he acknowledged Kit's unusual abilities and spoke of her with a high degree of respect. Kitzia recalled seeing the book at a bookstore but would not buy it. She had merely contemplated the photograph of Chris's face and wondered how such an attractive man could be so stupid.

Kitzia O'Neil could not forget the incident.

"I am truly sorry. Will you ever forgive me?" Chris Goodman implored.

"Mr. Goodman, if you're looking for another sensational story, you are not going to find one here. So please leave us alone before I call security."

Chris brought his fist up to his nose tip as if to aid himself in forming his next words. "Dr. O'Neill, that's not why I'm here. Although, I'm afraid your friend's accident has already made the news."

"So what is it you want?" she asked.

"To help you, perhaps," he replied.

"How?"

"A friend of mine, police officer Jack Jones, asked me to come down here. I believe he was the one who tracked you down." Kit nodded as a signal for him to continue. "He knows my fever for investigating, and he thought I might make some connections."

"What kind of connections? Danielle was hit by lightning during a thunderstorm and now suffers from a neurological malfunction. She is semi-comatose. I still do not understand what it is that you can do to help me."

"Well, it's not that simple. A couple that lives in Ms. Peschard's building in New York insists they saw her being attacked. Her penthouse was broken into. All this happened the night she miraculously appeared in California and was hit by lighting." Chris continued, "The FBI wants to know why she was going to meet with the president on his way back from Italy."

"What are you talking about?"

"Well, she couldn't be in New York and in LA simultaneously. Therefore, it's highly logical to assume that someone was impersonating her in New York. Then there was the attempt on the president's life. The fact that she was supposed to be on that plane casts a ray of suspicion on the whole affair."

"I don't like where you are going with this, nor do I see the purpose of continuing this conversation. If you will excuse me." Kit attempted to take a step toward the exit, but he blocked her, albeit gently.

"I see I have offended you again. I'll start my investigation somewhere else. I'll see what I can find out about her assailant."

Now he had Kit's full attention. Her brown eyes widened and could hardly hide their amazement. "Her assailant?"

"You didn't know?"

"No. Tell me."

"I am assuming it was her assailant. A man was seen in the storm, running behind her. He was also hit by the electrical charge. He fell into a ditch but was not found till later. I believe he has also been brought in."

"Who is he?"

"No identification. Did Dr. Peschard have any enemies that you know of?"

Kit took a deep breath. "No. Why would anyone want to hurt her?"

"That is exactly what I am trying to find out."

Kit wondered why Robert had not mentioned any of this. She recalled the bandage on his left hand when he had first come into the hospital.

"I understand Dr. Peschard is a very wealthy woman. Is she involved in politics? All I was able to get from the White House is that the First Lady and Dr. Peschard are social acquaintances, and Mrs. Parker had asked the president to give Dr. Peschard a ride back from Rome."

"She is a political campaign contributor—if you call that political involvement. She was invited to the Inaugural Ball. Other than that, she never mentioned knowing the president personally, or the First Lady."

"Was she going to Rome on business or pleasure?"

"I'm not sure."

"I understand you are close to her."

"Yes."

"Can you tell me exactly what she does for the museum?"

"Dr. Peschard is an archeologist and a cryptologist. She is an authenticator of ancient artifacts and credited for having found the oldest statue of Aphrodite in Knidos, as well as that of the water goddess near the temple tower Ziggurat in Mari." Chris's face registered a blank expression. Kit clarified, "Mari, Tell Hariri, a little northwest of Abu Kemal."

What am I supposed to do now? Kit wondered with annoyance. *I am supposed to give this idiot a lesson on the geography of Mari and Ugarit, the ruined sites in the Near East?* "Danielle has also translated numerous ancient manuscripts for the museum because she is fluent in nine languages, including Latin and Sanskrit."

Kit noticed Chris had produced a small pad and pen from his jacket and was scribbling as fast as she was talking.

"She is a philanthropist. Her personal foundation supports several worthy charities. She feels very strongly about saving the planet."

"Has she ever been married?"

"No."

"Seeing someone?"

Kit hesitated a moment. Perhaps she should not discuss Danielle's personal life. Yet the social section of the papers would give him that much. "Yes. Robert Powers."

"*The* Robert Powers, as in Powers Enterprises?"

"Yes."

"Do they travel together?"

"Sometimes."

"Did he fly her to California?"

"I don't think so."

"Where is he now?"

"At an OPEC meeting."

"Hmm . . ." He closed his notepad and pulled out a business card. "Let me see what I can find out. Here is my card. You can call me anytime." He over-emphasized *anytime* as he handed her the card.

Kit knew she would probably never call. Instead, she would ask Robert to dig around for this presumed assailant.

VII

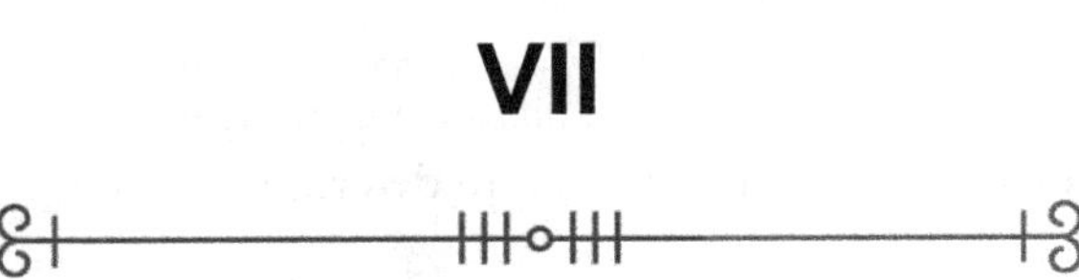

Dr. Erikson hovered over Danielle's bed as the portable X-ray machine was rolled out and away from the ICU. Kit observed the stethoscope positioned over Danielle's heart. Angela kept her eyes fixed on the doctor's movements. Kit sensed something strange happening. She could not put her finger on what it was exactly, but she was sure something had transpired during her brief absence from the room.

The doctor looked up as he withdrew the stethoscope and smiled. It was the coldest smile she had ever seen, gloating and defiant. "Sounds good," he said without erasing the smile.

Kitzia instinctively disliked him. She did not trust this man. When the nurse looked up and exchanged a fleeting glance with the X-ray technicians, Kit was disquieted by what she felt to be an air of complicity among Danielle's supposed caregivers.

"Is something wrong?" Kit wanted to know.

"No, not at all. Quite the contrary," the doctor answered calmly. "Her numbers are great."

Kit's eyes shifted to the monitor and scanned the vital signs. Heart rate 60, blood pressure 120/60, oxygen saturation 99, respiration 26.

"Mr. Powers called while you were out," the doctor continued. "I gave him the update. We'll move Ms. Peschard into a private room as soon as we can wean her from the heart medication drip. The hospital's best suite on the VIP floor has been reserved; I think you will be quite comfortable if you choose to remain with her."

His manner was kind, but she could not shake her uneasiness. At once, she realized what disturbed her about this doctor—his eyes. His expression was not at all in accord with his words. The discrepancy elevated her anxiety.

"I have given her some medication, and she'll sleep," he said as he left the room.

Angela gave her a meaningful look as if she wanted to tell her something, but simply smiled. So Kit pressed her.

"Do you know Dr. Erikson well?"

"Not really."

"Have you worked with him before?"

"No."

Now Kit had an unmistakable suspicion the nurse did not want to be questioned about this doctor and became more determined. "Tell me, what do you think of him?"

"He is considered a very competent doctor." She took a breath before continuing. "The best thing for your friend will be to go home as soon as possible. At home, she can recover."

Kit did not miss the subtlety of the implication. *Is she intimating Danielle is not safe here?*

"How long have you been working for the hospital?"

"I am an agency nurse, not on staff. I get called to do private duty as needed. I took care of Mr. Powers when he injured his leg climbing Mt. Everest a few years ago. That is how he knew to call me. He knows I will take extraordinary care of Ms. Peschard."

Kit believed her, yet something within her made her formulate the next question.

"Was Dr. Erikson alone with Danielle?"

"Just for a couple of minutes. He sent me to get some supplies."

Kit could not get over the feeling that something strange had taken place. "The X-rays that were taken, how long before they are ready?"

"They're probably ready. Radiology is on the second floor. Since you are a doctor, you can see them before they are sent to her attending physicians for evaluation."

"Thanks."

Kit exited the room and headed for the Radiology Department. As she exited the elevator, she saw the two technicians who had taken the X-rays. They walked past her, engrossed in whispered conversation. She was only able to grasp one sentence: "Must implement double Code Blue." When they saw her, they acknowledged her with a nod and stopped talking. *Must implement double Code Blue? What can that mean?*

Before she had a chance to request the X-rays at the reception desk, she caught sight of Dr. Erikson and walked straight to him. He was holding films in his hand. She was sure they were Danielle's.

"Anything new?"

He took two steps toward the wall and switched on the light box. He slapped the four X-rays on the screen, his jerky movements betraying his annoyance at her presence. “The lesion contains a certain degree of necrosis. Therefore, for all practical purposes, the damage to the tissue is similar to that of a glioblastoma. Its damage arises from the tissue that surrounds and supports the nerve cells.”

He ran the point of his pen over the white spot at the thalamus. “The pressure on the left is causing her unconsciousness. As we attempt to alleviate the swelling with the use of steroids, we will pull her out of her coma. We cannot assess the neurological damage that has been done. We will run another CAT scan in the morning.”

Kit’s eyes scanned the transparencies as the doctor spoke. Her eye caught a tiny shadow on the lower part of the skull, away from the lesion. What seemed odd was its geometric regularity.

“What is that?” she inquired as she pointed at the minuscule, square-shaped shadow.

“Nothing really; it looks like a shadow from the machine’s hardware. These high-tech machines are so sensitive. Sometimes, rather than facilitating our work, they make it more confusing.” He smiled and removed the X-rays from the light box. Kit said nothing but was keenly aware of his nervousness. It was obvious he resented her imposing herself into his assessment and treatment of Danielle.

“I prefer no steroids or further medication be given to Ms. Peschard until I get back. I will return shortly,” said Kit, her voice indicating she would brook no dissent.

“All right.” His face muscles became tense again.

“Doctor, what does double Code Blue mean?”

“I have no idea. Where and when did you hear that?”

She was about to tell him about the technicians but decided against it. “I can’t remember.”

He stared at her coldly, letting her know he knew she was lying. “Any other questions?”

“Well, actually, yes. I was wondering if you were also treating the other victim. I heard there was a man hit by lightning at the same time and place and brought here a day later. I was wondering if he was suffering from the same symptoms.”

“I really don’t know. I’ll be glad to look into it.”

“Thanks, I’d appreciate it. I would like to see him if possible.”

“I’ll check into it. Good day, Dr. O’Neil.” With a peremptory bow, he walked away.

Kit decided to call her ex-husband, Dr. Thomas O’Neil. She had avoided calling him in the past for fear he might think she still loved him. She had failed at what mattered most in her life and lost him. She had tried to fill the emptiness he had left with intense dedication to her work: professional accomplishments, awards, social and community recognition, the works. Yet the plaques and trophies had been poor substitutes for the touch of Tom's hands or the smile on his face when he woke up next to her in the mornings.

After the divorce, there had been a series of affairs, all short and meaningless. The only thing of value remaining in her life was her friendship with Danielle. She knew it looked odd, even suspicious to others. Such close relationships between women these days evoked suspicion of lesbianism. Kitzia no longer cared what people thought. She realized with delight that she was absolutely free from such concerns. There had never been anything between them but the strongest and noblest bonds of friendship. The only relevant truth was that she was devastated by Tom's departure and still found it hard to live without him.

Tom probably hasn't heard about the accident, or he would have called. Robert would also understand why I want to get him involved. He is a brilliant neurologist. She reached into her purse for her cell phone.

The traffic on the freeway was backed up more than usual. On the car radio were news updates on the recent fires in the San Jacinto mountains. The rain had stopped, but mud slides and forest fires had followed. Fire after water did not make sense. But this was Southern California.

As she stopped the car in front of the house, Kitzia noted the two main gates were closed—the one at street level and the second, about fifty feet inside the first. She didn't recall ever seeing both gates closed in the last five years.

A vagrant was sitting on the sidewalk by the gate. And there was another man standing across the street, leaning on a tree. He was tall and thin and very unusual-looking. His skin was dark olive and his short, curly hair had a golden taupe tone.

Because it was unusual for men to hang around this area, she was sure they were there to watch her. The same elusive sense of alarm as with the air of complicity in the hospital room struck her.

The gate opened, and she saw Ramon, Maria's nephew, who acted as gardener and chauffeur. She entered slowly, rolling down the window as Ramon walked toward the car. The gate closed behind her before the next one opened.

Ramon asked, "Miss Kit, how is Miss Danielle?"

"Much better."

He shook his head in disbelief. "Nothing ever happened to her before."

"I know what you mean. Ramon, what is going on?" She pointed to the gates.

"Miss Danielle told me that if something weird ever happened to her, I was to immediately activate the double Code Blue."

"Double Code Blue?"

"Yes—activate the alarm system with the buttons that show double blue circles. She specified that both gates should remain closed. All deliveries are to be dropped here." He pointed to the small gatehouse between the gates. "No strangers in the house either—workmen, I mean. I think the phones change frequency too. I also believe there is an electrical charge on the perimeter of the surrounding wall. It is all too technical for me. My job is to make sure the alarm is on until she tells me otherwise."

"She never mentioned any of this to me."

"She said we'd probably never need it. But what happened to her is weird, not to mention all the strange things that have been happening in this part of the country. So I'm following her orders. Oh! She told me to tell you that your voice will activate the gates. Just press the button when you come in and say your name." He handed her a remote control and pointed to a button.

She caught sight of the men in the street through her rearview mirror.

"Who are they?"

Ramon pointed at the vagrant. "I think he is OK. I've seen him before. He comes by from time to time. Miss D. even takes walks with him sometimes. I don't know the other one. He seems harmless, though. He's been here since shortly after the accident. At first, I thought of calling the police, but then I thought he's probably a policeman. He doesn't bother anyone. The alarms are on, so everyone is safe inside."

Safe. What does that word even mean anymore? Kit's mind played the question on repeat.

The sound of fire engines could be heard in the distance. Kit realized that something of great consequence was going on around them, and even the strongest and fittest like Danielle could have their life turned upside down in a matter of seconds. Danielle, who had been the pillar of strength for so many, lay defenseless in a hospital bed. Now it was time for those she had protected for so long to put up their shields and band together to protect her from whatever menace was threatening her well-being. But there was one problem: who or what was the threat?

After giving a brief report on Danielle's condition to the house staff, Kitzia called Tom.

Dr. O'Neil's secretary informed her he was at a convention in Chicago. Kit left a somewhat oblique message on his voicemail, which she hoped would spur him to call her.

She set about prioritizing things that must be done. She had decided to return to her friend's side as soon as possible and remain by her side indefinitely. While Maria packed the clothes Kit had selected to take with her, Kit took a quick shower, then placed a call to her office. She gave her secretary instructions for handling her affairs during her absence. She also checked with Danielle's office in New York, giving them the latest about Danielle's condition. She informed Linda of her decision to take a sabbatical and remain with Danielle as long as needed. Linda listened attentively, but ultimately, unable to contain herself, her excitement burst through.

"It happened, Kit! Jean-Christophe found it! Danielle was right! It will be in the news tomorrow."

Kit broke in. "Wait . . . what happened? What was found?" But before she gave Linda the opportunity to answer, she remembered what the archeologist was searching for and exclaimed, "The tombs? The hidden tombs of Ramses's children!"

"Yes! So tell Danielle her investment paid off."

"Danielle funded the expedition?"

"I would think so. No one here, or anywhere, would give him a grant. The Met must be so angry! They were so sure the tombs had been fully excavated."

"Where is Jean-Christophe now?" Kit felt the sudden urge to congratulate him.

"Still in Egypt. It seems he slipped and hit his head—minor concussion. They are keeping him there a few more days for observation. You know he'll be down there with you as soon as they'll let him."

"Good! Danielle will be in better shape by then. Keep the reviews."

"Will do. Give Danielle our love."

The next calls Kitzia made were to Danielle's other homes in Paris, Cap Ferrat, Aspen, and New York. Everyone she talked to confirmed what Ramon had told her. They had all implemented the double Code Blue alarm, whatever that meant. No one seemed to know.

Obviously, Danielle had foreseen this scenario and had given explicit instructions to all her employees. The alarm changed the frequency of all of her properties' communications, and they activated their own generators to provide electricity. It synchronized all electrical functions and disconnected the units from city and county utility services. It made the properties self-sufficient and impregnable. The infrared beam in the security system became sensitized to metals.

So, at least temporarily, all properties ceased being leisure residences and became fortresses. *What was Danielle protecting herself from?* Kit discovered one more staggering fact when she switched her rental car, per Ramon's instructions, for one of the house automobiles: the entire fleet of automobiles at the Peschard estate was bulletproof.

"Miss Kit, one last thing I forgot to mention. While this semi-quarantine lasts, we are to wear these pins." Ramon extended his hand and offered her a small, circular, silver pin inset with white enamel, upon which were two blue concentric circles. "Here is yours."

Kit took it but saw no need to wear it. She reached inside her blouse for the pendant that hung from a platinum chain—Danielle had given it to her years ago, asking Kit to wear it always, for good luck. Kit loved it and had never taken it off. It was a tiny, round, platinum medal upon which two concentric circles had been inlaid with sapphires. Kitzia suddenly realized she had been wearing the double Code Blue of protection for most of her life.

The hospital suite was overflowing with bountiful arrangements of flowers. Kit knew the Oceana roses had come from Robert, who was still at the OPEC meeting in Europe. The nurses wheeled in Danielle's bed, cheerfully pointing out all the beautiful flowers. Ten days had gone by. The doctors seemed pleased with Danielle's progress and were encouraged by the stability of her vital signs. However, she remained unconscious.

Kit moved about and inspected the suite with satisfaction—a spacious corner suite on the top floor, with big windows that overlooked a park, and only the medical gear distinguished it from a luxury hotel suite. A comfortable bed next to Danielle's hospital bed brought back memories of the years she had roomed with Danielle at boarding school in Switzerland. While the nurses got Danielle situated, Kit moved about the suite, checking the cards on the flowers. Besides Robert's Oceanas, there were arrangements from the staff at the Met, the New York Ballet, the New York Opera, several charity boards, and friends She felt a presence behind her and recognized him even before turning to face her ex-husband, the only man she would forever love. Feeling him near her made her quiver, just as she had the day they had met.

"I'm so sorry. I just heard." He kissed her on the cheek.

"Thanks for coming, Tom."

He walked toward Danielle. The nurses stepped back, except for Angela, who remained standing by the bedside. Dr. Thomas O'Neil felt Danielle's pulse and listened to her heart, then gently lifted her hand and held it in his.

"Beautiful lady, it's time to wake up."

Danielle opened her eyes but closed them immediately, without giving any sign of recognition. Tom O'Neil was pleased.

"She seems to be responding," he added with satisfaction.

"She has started to open her eyes occasionally but doesn't seem to be cognizant."

"She is trying very hard to wake up. We have to be patient."

Tom was holding Danielle's chart, which by now resembled a thick school notebook. He glanced through the many pages without altering his expression, then registered a trace of surprise. Kit knew that face only too well, and no subtle change went by unnoticed.

Does he have any idea how well I know him? Does he know how handsome I think he is? Kit observed him as he continued to scan the dossier. She noticed his jet-black hair had grayed at the temples. She had always loved the subtle shadow that followed the line of his strong jaw, no matter how often or closely he shaved. His thick, long lashes cast shadows on his cheek as he studied the chart. His attitude toward her, however kind, never failed to betray a hint of remorse, which Kit interpreted as a feeling of inadequacy in his inability to return her love in kind.

"Is something wrong?" she asked.

"Too much medication, for one thing."

"I was afraid of that, of an unfavorable interaction."

"Let's see, who is her primary physician? . . . Erikson . . . OK." He continued to flip through the pages.

"I don't like him, Tom."

"Why?"

"I don't know. I can't put my finger on what it is."

"Let me meet with him and see what we can do about the medications." He closed the medical chart.

He kissed her on the cheek and walked out. Kit noticed Angela smiling.

"That was my ex-husband. I trust him completely."

Tom walked to the nurses' station and paged Dr. Erikson, then headed for the physicians' lounge, determined to take a closer look at the dossier. He did not want to worry Kit any further, but there was definitely something strange going on with Danielle's care.

Robert's personal secretary, who seemed to be on call twenty-four hours a day, telephoned Kit about 5:00 a.m. to let her know Mr. Powers's plane would be landing in approximately forty-five minutes and that he would be coming straight to the hospital. With him was Doctor Eric Hansen from the renowned Strauss-Hansen Clinic in Switzerland. Kit was not familiar with the name, but trusted Robert's judgment in bringing the very best specialist the world had to offer.

She slipped into a velour jumpsuit and pulled her hair back into a ponytail. Angela, upon hearing the news, made some calls to obtain all of Danielle's records and then prepared fresh coffee.

Kit tried to call Tom, feeling it was important he be there. She was surprised to find out that he had checked out of his hotel and gone back to San Francisco. That was not like Tom at all. *He must have had an emergency.*

Robert walked into the room just before seven, followed by Dr. Erikson, Dr. Grossman, Dr. McCutcheon, and the eminent physician from Geneva.

Dr. Hansen was of medium build, probably in his fifties, Kit guessed. His penetrating dark blue eyes were even colder than those of Dr. Erikson, and his appearance altogether reminded her of Hitler. After a few formalities, he examined Danielle. Dr. Erikson seemed quite impressed with the Swiss doctor, and for the first time, put his arrogance aside and quietly assisted him. Robert and the two other physicians stepped back and watched attentively. The door opened and someone brought in a tray with cups and saucers and placed it on the coffee table in the sitting area.

Kit realized it was one of the two young men who had taken Danielle's X-rays the other day—the one who had mentioned the double Code Blue. It seemed odd that he would be doing the duties of a nurse's aide. Then she remembered it was only seven o'clock, and shifts were overlapping. She wanted to ask him what he meant by his comment but decided this was not the time. She returned her full attention to Danielle's examination.

After the exam, the Swiss Doctor looked at the X-rays and MRI report and questioned the absence of a PET scan. His thick German accent made it hard for Kit to catch every word, though Dr. Erikson seemed to have no trouble understanding him.

Watching the two of them connect so quickly enhanced her feelings of distrust for both doctors. How she wished Tom were here! She could not believe he had left without saying a word.

The other attending physicians remained respectfully quiet and continued to take notes. Until now, Dr. Hansen had practically ignored Kitzia. Then, as if suddenly remembering she would be the one to authorize any intervention, he turned to her. He mumbled something about the apparent damage done to the basal ganglia, which acts as a control system for movement and cognitive functions.

Forgetting, or perhaps unaware that Kitzia was an MD, he went on to explain the essence of consciousness and how the most minute destruction at any given part of the brain can severely alter the mind in a number of ways and, yet, not destroy it.

Explorative surgery was the next step, he declared emphatically. He could perform it immediately—as soon as the hospital made the necessary arrangements.

Kitzia tactfully explained that she must consult with Dr. Tom O'Neil, who would want to be present during the surgery. Dr. Hansen reminded her of his tight schedule and his urgency to return to his obligations in Switzerland.

Everyone seemed vexed at the prospect of bringing in one more physician. Especially when this god-like neurosurgeon had consented to travel around the world to see this patient. Kitzia hoped she didn't seem unappreciative, thereby offending Robert. Yet, inexplicably, he was the only one who did not seem annoyed.

"If we could just delay the surgery a day or two," she suggested, playing for time.

"All right," said the Swiss Doctor. "Shall we schedule it for the day after tomorrow?" He turned to consult with Dr. Erikson.

Hansen's abrupt, military-like pivot once again evoked visions of Hitler. Angela now stood next to Kitzia, and her expression had tightened. Kit also noticed the technician had never left the room. There was a palpable tension in the crowded hospital suite.

"I think I will accept Mr. Powers's gracious offer to fly me to Carmel," explained Dr. Hansen. "I shall pay a visit to an old colleague of mine." As he concluded his visit, the Swiss Doctor extended his hand to Kitzia, "Fräulein . . ."

Kit shook his hand and made a concerted effort to appear charming. "Thank you for coming, *Herr* Doctor."

"My pleasure."

Robert and the entourage of doctors walked out. Angela and the technician followed them to the door. Kit noticed two other men standing in the hall near Danielle's door. One was the second X-ray technician, apparently waiting for his partner. The two men spoke in whispered tones as they started toward the elevators. The other man was wearing the light blue scrubs of a surgeon, but something in his demeanor suggested he was keeping watch. Shortly, he closed his clipboard, and he, too, started for the elevators. He was tall and thin. With his curly, oddly colored hair, he could he have been the man she saw on the street outside Danielle's house.

No. It can't possibly be him, she told herself and walked back into the suite.

The elevator doors opened, but before the men entered, the Swiss doctor turned to encounter the fixed stare of the surgeon in scrubs. For a long moment, their eyes remained fixed on each other. Dr. Hansen was the first to avert his eyes as he turned to enter the elevator. The man in scrubs headed for the stairs.

Angela and the technicians witnessed the exchange. It was the eye-lock of two enemies, ready to engage in deadly combat.

Kitzia walked down the hall, hoping to catch the technicians.

"Excuse me . . ."

They turned and started toward her.

"I couldn't help overhearing your conversation the other day. You mentioned something about a 'double Code Blue.' What exactly does that mean?"

"Code Blue is an alert. It means there is a life and death situation," said one of the men.

"The patient has stopped breathing," said the other man.

"I know that. But what is a *double* Code Blue?"

Both men shrugged their shoulders in feigned ignorance. "A figure of speech," said one of them.

It was obvious they were not going to tell her. She decided to change the subject.

"I was wondering if you could help me. I understand there is another patient in the hospital who was also hit by lightning. Would you happen to know who he is?"

They looked at each other before answering. Then one spoke. "He is dead."

Kit tried to locate Tom all morning but to no avail. No one in his office seemed to know where he was. She decided to go down to the hospital's administration office to get some information about the dead patient. The staff was friendly and cooperative. They all had been informed that Dr. Peschard was a VIP patient and of her connection to Mr. Powers. Robert Powers was one of the hospital's most generous benefactors.

An employee from the admissions office came and met with Kitzia. He told her what he knew about the case.

"John Doe" had been a man in his mid-thirties, a foreigner. The cause of death had been heart failure—complications resulting from the injury. No relatives had been located. The case, as was the norm, had been delegated to the police department for further investigation. The date and time of expiration on the death certificate made Kit pretty sure that it had been signed shortly after she had questioned Dr. Erikson and asked him to locate the man.

Kitzia insisted on going down to pathology to see the body. The employee found the request irregular but agreed to take her. In pathology, they were informed the body had already been removed.

In this particular case, the usual seventy-two-hour wait before an unclaimed body is removed from the morgue was bypassed. After a few hours, the body had been assigned and sent to the medical school at UCLA. The request had been signed by someone in the neurology department.

Kit spent a couple of hours at the medical library trying to research the peculiar doctor from Switzerland. She found very little. A couple of articles mentioned his name in connection with research in cerebral circuitry.

She had a phone call from Robert Powers. He had flown the Swiss Doctor to Carmel and then continued on to Washington for a meeting with some congressman.

"So what was your impression of Dr. Hansen?" Robert wanted to know.

"Robert, I still would feel better if Tom were here during the surgery. I need to locate him."

"Hansen and I won't be back until Thursday. Tom should be there by then."

VIII

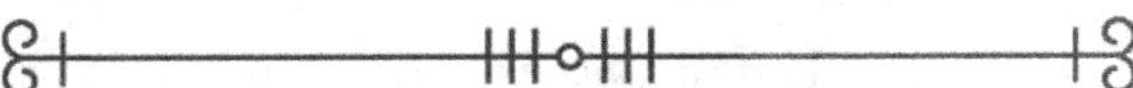

Angela had ventured out during the stormy afternoon to run some errands, and Kit was glad to have the time alone with her friend. She believed it was beneficial for Danielle to hear constant voices, particularly of those she knew and loved. Kit read the news, the financial pages, and when reading materials were exhausted, she would simply chat non-stop.

Leaning back on the armchair next to the Danielle's bed, she continued, "Did my career made Tom and I drift apart? I would have slowed down if he had asked me, but he never did. I just felt him slip away."

After a pause and a deep breath, she continued. "Seeing him again the other day was like opening an old wound. He looks tired, probably overworked, with no one to look after him."

Kit served herself another glass of wine from the bottle she had brought. "I had Tom look at your records. But I haven't heard from him in days."

Danielle opened her eyes momentarily, and Kit, assuming her friend was awake, continued, "I'm worried." Kit took another sip of wine. She hardly noticed she had drunk most of the bottle of Montrachet.

"Danielle, I feel so helpless. I no longer know who to trust." She grabbed Danielle's hand. "Oh! Did I feel a tiny squeeze? Are you trying to let me know that you can hear me?

"Robert went to Switzerland and brought back a surgeon who he claims is the best in the world. I like him even less that Dr. Erikson. He has proposed exploratory surgery. I wish Tom were here to help me make the right decisions.

"I even saw Chris Goodman. He showed up here a few days ago and found out the man who was chasing you ended up here too. But we don't know who he is . . . was. I asked Christian to find out who he was and sent him something to decipher.

"Oh, and John Larkin sent you a message with a star chart. I didn't know you were still in touch. I remember we met him when we graduated from school in Switzerland. You had just come into a big part of your inheritance and leased that yacht, and we went island hopping in the Mediterranean—touring the Aeolian Islands was the most exotic and exciting thing I'd ever experienced.

"It was at Paraneas where we met John. Always so serious, reading for hours on his shady terrace across from ours. When you asked him to dine with us, we discovered he was actually very smart. He joined us when we continued on to Lipari. I am sure it was John Larkin who first got me interested in the stars.

"You invited Father Santis as our chaperon. You two used to be so close. You said he took the place of your parents when they were killed. Weren't you only nine? That must have been so traumatic!"

Kit barely breathed as the memories tumbled from her mouth. "Did you mention Father Santis is now a cardinal at the Vatican? That's why you were going to Rome! I should probably let him know what happened. . . . It was also that summer that we met Jean-Christophe at the Puntazo Tavern, remember? He looked so tan and handsome and was very flirty! I think I had a crush on him. What a let-down when we found out he was gay!" Kit burst out laughing.

"It was Stefano, the bartender he had been flirting with all evening—not us! You thought it was hilarious. I was devastated, and Father Santis was furious at us for staying out so late. I think from that moment on, Jean-Christophe became our big brother. What a wonderful summer! I entered a world I didn't know existed.

"Sending me to Switzerland was a tremendous financial strain on my parents. My mother thought Switzerland would change my life forever—and it did. We became friends and toured the Mediterranean Islands, and you gave me tuition for my college education. Yes, that summer changed the course of our lives. At Stanford Medical School, I met Tom. You made things possible for Jean-Christophe to begin his excavations, and Father Santis built the first of his orphanages in Santorini. You have always been so generous! It was hard for the rest of us to comprehend that such a young woman had access to such an unbelievable fortune.

"Oh, how I fell in love with Capri—those lazy afternoons by the pool at the Hotel. Remember the day that sleazy man, the evangelist, Ted Edwards, tried to pick us up? He was an insurance salesman, wasn't he? Wearing plaid trousers and pink polo shirts. He's now head of the New Era Christian Coalition and goes around with bodyguards in a bulletproof limousine. His corny TV commercials and obnoxious billboards are all over the country. 'Join our congregation. Let us show you the way to salvation.' It's nauseating. You said to never forget him because I was looking at the embodiment of evil."

The door opened and Angela, with several shopping bags in hand, came in. She placed her soaking umbrella behind the door and the bags on the table.

"I brought you dinner. How is Ms. Peschard doing?"

"She squeezed my hand."

"That's wonderful!" said Angela, taking off her raincoat. "It's raining so hard; I'm tempted to start gathering pets in pairs."

Kit laughed. "We shouldn't worry about perishing in a flood. Danielle said that mass destruction would not come from water again—at least, not in our millennium."

"True. It will probably be fire or nuclear war."

"Not if nature does the cleansing. Nature would probably use the element that is ruling. We have entered the Age of Aquarius. We are, therefore, under the influence of air."

"I see you are into astrology."

"Astronomy. But Danielle has unbelievable knowledge and a deep understanding of the forces that rule the universe."

"What else did she say about the Aquarian Age?"

"That it will last 2,150 years. We'll master air travel and will reach far into other galaxies. But, most importantly, it is the age of understanding. There will be great opposition and resistance to change at the beginning, but shifts in perception and vision will reshape the world."

The phone rang, and Kit reached for it. Joy and excitement registered on her face.

"Tom, I have been wondering—"

He did not let her finish. "Kit, I must talk to you."

"Sure, where are you?"

"About two blocks from the hospital."

"Are you coming up?"

"No. I will pick you up. Meet me by the east exit, on the left side of the Emergency Room. Be there in five minutes."

She knew by the tone of Tom's voice that something was wrong.

"I'll be back in a few minutes," Kit said, turning to Angela.

Tom's rental car, a gray Honda, was hard to identify under the heavy rain. She wondered why he had not met her under the covered main entrance.

"Sorry I made you get wet. I didn't want to be seen."

"Why?"

He did not answer. He was attentively watching his rearview mirror and immediately exited the hospital lot.

"I thought they might try to stop me from seeing you."

"Who?"

"Very strange things started happening from the moment I began looking into Danielle's situation."

They were now several blocks away from the hospital, and Tom's voice relaxed. He turned to look at Kitzia's face. The wet hair strand spread across her forehead made her look almost childlike. He offered her his handkerchief.

"Someone ran into me, deliberately. I was assaulted in the parking lot. I might have been killed had it not been for a young doctor and two of his assistants who happened to come out right behind me and jump on the two men."

"Did it happen at this hospital?"

"The attack did. It was the first day I came over."

"The men who helped you, who were they?"

"The doctor was a young man in scrubs, rather unusual looking—tall, dark, light, curly hair. With him were two other young men, big and muscular. I assume by what they were wearing they were physical therapists."

"Technicians," she whispered, knowing exactly which men Tom was referring to.

"The men who tried to mug me ran away. The young doctor said he'd make the police report. I left it at that. I was really in a hurry to make it back to the airport to make my flight.

"I came back to LA the next day. But before coming up to see you, I decided to go back to the lab. The day before, I met with Kirby Smith, a young fellow who had worked for me at Stanford, and who is now doing some research here. He was very helpful in getting me what I was looking for.

"When I went back looking for him, I was told he had taken ill. I placed a call to William DeClaire, the chief physician, who I also happen to know quite well, and asked him if I could work in Kirby's office. Kirby had given me the code and shown me where everything was. When I got there, the copies of the X-rays and the tissue samples were gone. I knew right then that someone did not want me to continue what I was doing. Then I remembered there was a blood sample we had not cataloged, that we had forgotten to take out of the other refrigerator.

"It was still there. I recognized the identifying number. I worked in that lab for about two hours, and all the time, I had the strange sensation I was being watched. I went back to Radiology and requested Danielle's X-rays and MRIs. When I got them, I realized right away there was a discrepancy in them.

"This is mainly the reason I did not want to see you for several days—at least until I was certain about what I was dealing with."

"And?"

"For sure, there is something in those records that someone in the hospital wants—at all costs—to keep confidential. These people are dangerous, Kit, and I am sure they will stop at nothing to reach whatever goal they have. And I am sure there is more than one person involved."

"For goodness' sake, Tom, tell me what you found out!"

"Well, when Danielle was first admitted, CAT scans were made of the area where the electrical charge had been concentrated. Steroids were immediately administered. Shortly after, the area of concern became another part of the brain, much lower. There was a strange object appearing on the subsequent X-rays."

"I remember seeing that. A tiny square on the lower left side?"

"Exactly."

"Erikson said it was probably the shadow of some hardware."

"I hardly think so. The object showed up on several X-rays. Later on, it doesn't show up at all. A shadow in front of it is camouflaged by a liquid. I believe the object could be an implant of some sort."

"An implant?"

"I suspect some kind of experiment is being conducted without your knowledge. I also found out some remarkable things about Danielle's brain. I imagine it was these unusual traits that prompted someone to carry on this secret research. Now, they know that I know something strange is going on. They might even think I have figured out what they are doing and want to stop me from talking."

"I think you should go back with me to the hospital right now and confront the physicians with the records; they have a lot of explaining to do."

"It would be useless. We won't be able to prove anything. The records will look clean and accurate. They have been doctored."

"But we have your testimony and your notes."

"I have nothing. After I left the hospital, I was followed. I thought I'd lose them on the freeway, but before I had a chance, they hit me and were forcing me off the road. Then, miraculously, a van cut in front of their car and cleared the way for me to get away. I know that whoever was in the van saw what was going on and decided to assist me. I was thinking this might have to do with a patent—a pharmaceutical patent. There is usually a lot of money involved in those. If someone came across something resulting from Danielle's condition that can be patented, they will defend it at all costs.

"I was pretty shaken when I got to the airport. I turned in my car and went straight to the gate. My briefcase disappeared at the security check. It never came out of the X-ray belt. While I was talking to the police officer, trying to explain what had happened, I thought I saw, from the corner of my eye, the man from the van."

"The van that helped you?"

"Yes."

"Are you saying that there is a conspiracy in the hospital at Danielle's expense?"

He shrugged his shoulders. "How are Danielle's wounds healing?"

"Extraordinarily well, actually."

"According to my notes, I figure—"

"I thought you lost your notes."

"I did. But it is all here," said Tom, tapping the side of his forehead.

"Then tell me what you found out."

"There is something quite unusual in Danielle's genetic composition. As incredible as it may sound, there is a genetic variance in Danielle's DNA. This would account for her endurance and this superb ability her body has to repair itself."

"Are you serious?"

"I have never seen anything like it. I suspect that when they stumbled upon it, it was confusing. I think they are trying to keep her from waking up. The amount of steroids is excessive and disrupts her electrolyte levels. The shifts in the potassium and sodium levels continue to maintain the unconscious state. Or perhaps it's being done through the implant."

"There has been no type of surgical intervention," Kitzia assured him. "The physicians have been pressing for a biopsy as a preliminary procedure for explorative surgery. But until now, I assure you there has been no surgical intervention."

"There has. Look for a small cut somewhere behind her left ear."

Kit's face lost its color, and Tom wondered if he should continue.

"The other extraordinary thing I discovered about Danielle is that her inferior parietal lobes are approximately twenty percent wider than normal. That explains her superior ability in logical and mathematical reasoning. Furthermore, the sulcus also has a slightly different configuration. It seems to make a more favorable environment for neurons to make connections with one another."

"No wonder the doctors are pushing explorative surgery. They can't wait to see her brain up close. I'm surprised they haven't tried to get rid of me. I've been opposing surgery from the start. By the way, Robert Powers, Danielle's friend, went to Switzerland and brought back Dr. Eric Hindrik Hansen to do the surgery. It is all set for tomorrow. I wanted to run it all by you. But since I couldn't find you, I ended up agreeing. What do you know about this doctor?"

"Not much. Of course, I know the name; he is world-renowned. I am surprised he is still operating. I thought he was getting up there in years."

"I wouldn't say that—early sixties at the most. He's very weird but not really old."

"I must be mistaken. If everything is set for a biopsy, I'll be there to observe everything that goes on. Who is with her now?"

"A nurse Robert hired named Angela. I like her."

"Do you trust her?"

"I don't know. I guess so."

"Your insight is usually right. Watch all the medications administered tonight."

Tom took Kit's hand and held it between his as he continued. "We'll get through this successfully. You are not alone Kit."

Any other time, Kit would have weakened at his touch and tone of voice. Right now, she was too confused to allow any emotion to take hold of her.

"All right. Can you be here by six in the morning to meet with the doctors? I assume they are planning to start early."

People stared at Kit as she walked slowly across the lobby. She hoped it was only because she was wet and not because she had been seen with Tom. She stopped in front of the fountain that dominated the center of the lobby and sat down on the granite steps. She sat quietly for a few minutes, trying to pull her thoughts together. She felt angry with herself. *Aren't I, after all, the psychologist with the remarkable gift? How could this have been going on without my noticing? I sensed something odd from the start. Why didn't I act on it immediately? Was Robert somehow involved in any of it? No. That's ridiculous! Tom would not put his credibility on the line unless he was sure there was something peculiar going on. If Tom is right about this fantastical conspiracy, then this might explain why Danielle was being pursued.*

Kit realized Danielle had been trying hard to regain consciousness, but just as she was about to rouse, her electrolytes would get out of balance, and she'd suffer a relapse. It was as if two teams were at work, one trying to help her and one trying to keep her in the status quo.

When Kitzia returned to the room, Angela looked worried.

"They called to tell us we must start getting Ms. Peschard ready for tomorrow's surgery. They will be coming for her in a few minutes to take her down for another MRI."

Kit walked straight to Danielle. She lifted her hair on the left side and looked behind her ear, where the trace of a cut about one centimeter long was still visible. There was no question in Kit's mind now as to what she had to do.

"Angela, please help me."

The nurse's eyes met Kit's, awaiting instructions.

"I'm taking Danielle out of here."

Angela seemed to welcome the news. "Go get the car," Angela urged, "and I will meet you at the exit on the third floor, the one with wheelchair access. I'll wheel Ms. Peschard out, saying that I am taking her to the MRI room myself. We'll be there by the time you get the car."

Kit grabbed her purse and left. She walked more slowly than usual past the receptionist in the lobby and smiled. The receptionist waved as she got in the elevator, and Kit knew everything looked normal. The parking lot on the third floor was almost empty, and Kit had no trouble securing a place right in front of the exit door. She waited for several minutes and when the door opened, her heart beat quicker in anticipation. But it was a man. Kit recognized the technician. He stood by the door casually and lit a cigarette. Kit's heart sank. *Is he here to prevent us from leaving? Had Angela called him?* She got out of the car to confront him, but the door opened again and Angela emerged, swiftly pushing Danielle's wheelchair. The young man held the door open for them and walked to the car to assist them. He picked up Danielle and placed her on the front seat.

"Go!" he said, looking over his shoulder. Angela jumped in the back seat, and Kit drove off without saying a word. The urgency in his voice told her there was no time for small talk.

After they arrived at the lofty mountaintop retreat that overlooked Los Angeles, the massive iron gates of the estate closed behind them. Kit heard, for the first time in weeks, the voice of her friend. Danielle softly whispered, "Thank you."

"Ms. Peschard seems to be doing extraordinarily well," said Angela as she finished checking Danielle's pulse rate. Maria, the housekeeper, arranging the pillows around the bed and stared lovingly at her employer, who had once again fallen into a deep sleep.

Kitzia turned around and walked out of the room.

What have I done? she thought to herself. *I took Danielle out of the hospital without her physician's dismissal. I didn't even check her medication chart!*

She crossed the den and went into the library, sat behind a massive wooden desk, and stared at the telephone. It had been over two hours since they had left the hospital. *The call will come any second now, and I better have a good reason to justify moving an injured patient.*

Over and over, she reviewed everything Tom had told her. Finally, she had to agree with him; they had no proof of anything, nothing to back up what she had just done. She would think of something when the call came. A nursing agency was the first step to staffing the home.

Kit grabbed a pencil and a notepad and listed the priorities. She had to let Tom know they had come home. Kit flipped open her laptop with determination and searched for a nursing agency, but before she reached the right page, she turned around, feeling the presence of someone in the room.

It was the tall, dark, thin man with the curly, light hair and the strange, pale-green eyes. All at once, she recognized him not only as the young doctor wearing scrubs at the hospital but also as the man who had been standing in front of the house with a magazine under his arm. His presence startled her, although his manner did not frighten her. Perhaps it was because he did not make a move or utter a sound until Kit took the initiative.

"How did you get in?" The anger of the transgression rose inside her.

He remained silent.

She had obviously been wrong about assuming he was a doctor. He didn't look particularly threatening, though, and that worried her even more. He wore jeans, Reeboks, and a simple white T-shirt. Around his neck was a gold-link chain holding some medal that she could not identify, for it was tucked inside his T-shirt.

How did he get past the electric iron gates? She decided she had better keep her cool.

"Whoever you are, you better leave before I call the police."

"You need a chauffeur and a bodyguard."

"I don't need a bodyguard, and we have a chauffeur. I'm calling the police." She reached for the phone while she tried to remember if Danielle kept a gun in the desk. He did not move, only kept his gaze fixed on her. Kit tried to stay calm as she pressed the first digit of 911.

Incomprehensibly, her eyes shifted from him to the garden. The magnolia tree was beginning to bloom. The fuchsia buds were about to open, which only happened once a year, and for a few days. Like everything else in life that mattered, it only lasted briefly. It was precisely the briefness of joy that made it so precious. *Why am I thinking of flowers now?* There was a call she needed to make. Suddenly, she had forgotten.

Her eyes again met those of the man in front of her, and she set the phone back on the desk.

"What did you say your name was?"

"Camiel. You can call me Cam, and I can start right away."

"Fine. I also will be hiring—"

He interrupted her. "You don't need anyone. I am here now."

"Yes, that's right." She smiled with satisfaction. "Now, we must check on our patient."

Still in a trance, Kit walked out of the library and headed in the direction of the guest room, where they had temporarily installed Danielle. Angela was occupied with writing something on a pad—a record of Danielle's vitals. Danielle opened her eyes and looked over Kitzia's shoulder to where Cam was standing behind her. She closed them again, and a peaceful smile registered on her face.

"This is Angela, our private nurse. Cam will be working with us." They all exchanged a nod and a smile. Angela did not give any sign of recognizing Cam.

"Let's go back to the library and discuss your hours, as well as your salary."

He couldn't repress an amused smile and followed her out of the room. Her phone rang and broke the spell. Kit continued to walk toward the library. She resigned herself to facing the questioning that was to follow; it was someone at the hospital calling. She was relieved to hear Robert's voice.

"Is Danielle all right?"

"She is fine. You know, she regained consciousness for a moment and asked me to bring her home. I had to do it."

"I see. Did you get home OK?"

"Yes." She was thankful for his tact. Robert had to know she was lying.

"I was about to phone the hospital and explain; they must be wondering and worried."

"Don't worry about it. I'll explain."

"Everything happened too fast to digest. It must have been a terrible imposition for Dr. Hansen to come down, but I think—"

Robert abruptly changed the subject.

"How much help do you have in the house?"

"Maria, Ramon, Ling, and Eddy. Angela, of course, came with us. Oh, and I have just hired someone who I think will work out fine." We'll also hire some RNs."

"Who is he?"

"How did you know it was a *he*?"

"I don't."

"His name is Cam, Camiel. I can't remember his last name." She did not know much about him, and she realized that it would be advisable to find out immediately.

"Camiel . . ." Robert repeated slowly. "He will be fine. Is everything operating properly? Telephones, security systems, electric gate?"

"I believe so." *Funny that he should ask that,* Kit thought. She had just been wondering how Cam had gotten through. *I better check that. Wonder why I'm not worried about it?*

"Robert, do you think someone is trying to hurt Danielle?"

"Hard to tell. Make sure Cam checks the systems."

When Kit hung up, she had a nagging feeling of uneasiness.

Washington, DC

President David Parker was the first one to receive the message. The envelope, marked confidential, bore a three-digit number inside two concentric circles. The president himself had informed his secretary to consider those circles as top priority mail.

"Ms. Kelly," he said casually, "send a big bouquet of yellow roses—no, make it Oceania roses, to Dr. Danielle Peschard at her California address, with a card wishing her a speedy recovery."

The Vatican

The frail health of His Holiness kept him in bed for several days. Cardinal Santis picked out a select group from the numerous get-well cards and put them on a small round silver tray on the mahogany nightstand. On top of the pile was the card Santis knew would give His Holiness the most pleasure. It bore the engraved concentric circles of the *Foundation* headquarters.

The pope reached for his eyeglasses and picked up the card. Relief registered in his kind face. The elderly man opened the drawer of his nightstand and reached for a pad and pen. On the pad, he wrote a message to Cardinal Santis: "Arrangement of Oceania roses for Dr. Peschard in California—message: Dearest Danielle, May our prayers continue to protect you."

IX

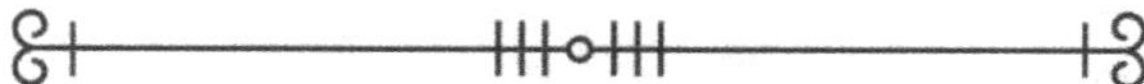

Colorado

"We almost had her!" The man grumbled with disdain. He was standing with his back to Robert Powers and looking through the gigantic windowpanes of the Colorado hunting lodge. Once relieved from the responsibility of posing as the world's greatest brain surgeon, Cirel reverted to his usual mannerisms.

"You never had her," replied Robert. "You saw the kind of protection she had around her. One false move, and *they* would have had *you!*"

"Understood, comrade. As a guest in your territory, I must not abuse your hospitality."

Robert wanted to grimace at the sound of *comrade,* but retained his congenial smile and continued to sip his Napoleon brandy. Cirel continued standing with his back to him and Robert studied the intricate design on the red and black silk robe Cirel wore—the dragons and serpents interwoven with thick strands of gold. On the floor a few feet away lay Cirel's pet, a female cheetah, engrossed in eating something reddish-gray from a crystal bowl. Robert sat his snifter down when he realized what the bowl contained.

"You have grown squeamish, *Caro,*" Cirel said, amused with Robert's reaction to the beast. "Or were you always like that, even in the Coliseum days? I simply cannot remember."

Robert got up and distanced himself from the spectacle. *Cirel will never change,* he thought. He would be forever theatrical, forever perverse.

Cirel snapped his fingers and a young Asian girl dressed in a black leotard appeared and took the feline and the bowl away.

"Sometimes, I feel like we are losing you," Cirel said, serving himself more cognac.

"Why would you say that?"

"Are you with us, Robert? Really with us?"

"The nature of the question insults me gravely."

"Hmm . . . the *Group* is beginning to question your allegiance."

"That is absolutely ridiculous! How could there be the slightest suspicion of my loyalty?"

"Your tolerance for this *Foundation* agent is nonetheless questionable."

"She is well-liked. Why would we compromise our position for the sake of annihilating a small adversary?"

"There is talk that this Danielle Peschard is more than an ordinary agent for the *Foundation*."

"Danielle Peschard is basically harmless. We've got much more to worry about."

"Will you deny she is a transmitter?"

"Yes, she is a transmitter. She transmits useless information—reports on the ecological situation of the planet, the evolution of the species. What harm is that to us?"

"You are right. But just in case, we want to make sure she remains neutralized."

"You have already made certain she stays that way."

"I think I understand. You are enamored with her. Are you not?

Robert didn't answer, so Cirel continued, "And you feel it would be treacherous to take her." He laughed. "The *Group* has worried about you unnecessarily. Take her, and afterward, you won't be so against our exterminating her."

"Thanks for your permission," Robert added sarcastically. "Exactly what was preventing me."

"Do what you want! One thing I am sure of is that she is not the one we are looking for. I was close to her and . . . nothing. I could sense nothing. Now, the friend, the other woman . . . I got very strange vibes from her, even across the room."

"Strange vibes?" Robert laughed. "She thought you looked like Hitler."

"Did she tell you so?" Cirel asked with amusement.

"I picked up her thoughts."

"I see. The kind of vibes I was referring to . . . a type of electric current I have not felt coming from an earthling, not in a long time. Why do you think that happened?"

"How should I know?"

"You don't think she could have *it*, do you?"

"An earthling, a simple woman in possession of something you have been searching for the past millennia? And furthermore, standing just a few feet away from you in a room? Now, I really think your imagination is taking flight!"

"You still think I was wrong before?"

"Wrong? I don't know. Obsessed? Yes! You caused the destruction of six million people. Confiscated their property and smashed all their possessions down to the gold fillings in their teeth. You're searching, always searching, for that elusive, tiny transmitting rock. I would call that obsessive, yes!" Robert assured him.

"They had it then, and they have it now! I'll never give up. Besides, in war, there are always casualties. The Holocaust was only one of our experiments in war tactics—one that works well over and over again. To destroy the enemy, our warriors must be roused to anger and feel certain they will be rewarded. I have always been extremely generous with those who have served me well. Unfortunately, I cannot tempt you with rewards. But there is still something you must want—the agent with the fiery hair, perhaps? I could get the *Group* to back off from her and let you enjoy her."

"That would be nice. In exchange for what?" Robert inquired.

"Nothing really. We would just like to be certain that nothing will divert you from our course. And when the time comes, which I suspect will be rather soon, you will be more active in our pursuit. That you will fight beside us if necessary."

"You still haven't told me what the real objective of your pursuit is. The ultimate goal of the *Group* must be something more than just waging perpetual war on the *Foundation*. In doing so, you are wasting the planet! How will it be of any use to you when it's ruined? This continuous fighting is madness. As Sun Tzu, well put it: 'To fight and conquer in all your battles is not supreme excellence. Excellence consists of breaking the enemies, resistance without fighting.' I really don't understand this obsession with destroying. Wouldn't it be better to take the enemy's territory, in this case the planet, whole and intact?"

Cirel smiled but did not answer. Instead, he shifted the conversation. "Nice place you have here. How do you camouflage it?"

"A shield of veregonium."

"I have always admired your ingenuity. Tell me one more thing: did you get rid of the other agent as we requested?"

"Body and all."

"Good. You know, our manipulation of the currents is almost precise. The way a single bolt of lightning struck them both was superb. It is exactly what I would call a stroke of genius." He laughed. "One more thing before I take leave of you. How is Lilith?" Cirel asked wickedly.

"Doing well under the circumstances. The thought of aging worries her. Will you be seeing her?"

"Not this time." Cirel reached inside the pocket of his silk robe and produced a small glass vial. "Give her this. I think it will relieve her anxiety."

Robert took the vial and stared at the clear liquid. "Oh yes, this will relieve her anxiety."

Los Angeles

It was a charming little restaurant on Sunset Blvd. where Chris Goodman and Kitzia agreed to meet. She spotted him sitting at an outside table, under a Cinzano umbrella, wearing a white T-shirt, a charcoal linen blazer, and sunglasses. Once again, she considered him handsome and was glad she had chosen her favorite white linen dress. It was a simple shift, perfectly cut, and that never failed to make her feel young and pretty in a fresh and casual way. She had also spent time deliberating about wearing her hair up or down. After reminding herself that she actually disliked this man, she opted to pull her hair back and twist a rubber band around it.

When he saw her approach the table, his eyes widened, and it was hard to hide the fact that he thought her lovely. *This is not a date. I'm not here to romance her,* he told himself as he got up from his chair to acknowledge her presence.

This whole thing had gotten off to a bad start from the beginning and probably would never change, he realized. He had been furious when he called her that morning regarding the document she had sent him to decipher. The suspicion that she was playing with him and had sent him on a wild goose chase just to get him out of the way was more than he could tolerate. He had reminded her that he had come to her as a favor to his friend, Officer Jones, and his effort to help her and Danielle was sincere. He failed to see the humor in the whole thing.

"I have wasted days in pursuit of the meaning of the document you sent me, all to realize in the end that it was just a joke!" He had told her in a stormy tone. "Now, the matter of the man at the hospital is bizarre, and I will tell you about it . . . before I leave town."

Kitzia had found once again his tone insulting and, at any other time, would have hung up on him. But too much had happened involving Danielle, and she could no longer ignore any irregularities. She did not know what he was talking about but wanted to hear him out.

"Mr. Goodman, I have no idea what it was that I sent you. If you found out what it means, I'd like to know."

"Oh, I found out all right! Are you a religious person?"

"I . . . think so."

"Then you must be familiar with Enoch? If not, you'd better look up his writings."

She was familiar, and now it was important that he tell her the rest of what he had discovered. The idea of lunch at this little bistro had been an excellent one, and Kit was glad he had suggested it. It was a sunny day and everybody at the restaurant was casually enjoying the day. It seemed like an eternity since Kit had taken a day off and simply relaxed.

"First of all, I want to apologize for my behavior on the phone this morning, and I am glad that you agreed to meet me," said Chris.

"Let's get past that and see what we can figure out together."

The waiter was standing by the table, inquiring about what she would like to drink. Kit looked at what Chris was drinking. "Is that Campari?"

"Campari and soda."

"I'll have the same thing," she said to the waiter.

"How is Ms. Peschard doing?" asked Christian.

"Very well, actually. We have an efficient staff, and Danielle is speaking again and getting around. Her burns have healed, leaving no trace of any scarring. I have not mentioned to her what is going on because it's important that I understand first."

Chris opened a leather folder he had placed on the table and pulled out the document Kit had faxed him along with three other sheets of paper, all bearing the same symbols.

"This type of writing appears in such texts as the three *Great Chronicles of Enoch*, compiled around the second century BC. It is also used with some variations of the Hebrew alphabet, in *La Kabbale Practique*."

"After speaking to you on the phone," said Kit, "I looked at Danielle's files and found a number of such documents. There must be a logical explanation. Now, tell me about the man."

"You were right. The man was brought in shortly after your friend. He had also been hit by lightning. He suffered similar injuries and trauma—burns, cuts, scratches, etc. The nurses on the floor told me he was recovering but then had unexpected complications and expired."

"Were you able to find out his identity and why he was pursuing Danielle?"

"Yes, and no." He waited for the waiter to place Kit's drink down before continuing. "I had very little to go on. But I did manage to find out he was a Scandinavian by the name of Kjell Ullman, who rented an apartment in West Hollywood for the last fifteen years. He traveled constantly. No one knew what he did for a living. He kept to himself . . . bothered no one. Everyone said he was a nice guy."

"You are giving me the perfect portrait of a hired killer."

Chris laughed. "You have seen too many movies. I don't feel he was out to hurt her. It was unfortunate they both were hit by lightning."

"She was trying to get away from someone."

"Yes, but I don't think it was him."

"What makes you so sure?"

"When I was in his apartment, which, by the way, was almost devoid of possessions, I found something that changed my mind."

"What was it?"

"He had pictures of Danielle."

"Isn't that precisely what hired assassins have?"

"No. This was different. He had photographs of Danielle that went back to when she was a child. One in particular caught my attention." He pulled a three-by-five snapshot of Danielle in Paris and handed it to Kit. "I believe that is you in the photograph."

Kit was stunned. She looked at the photograph for a long time before replying. It showed Kit and Danielle in front of the Pont Neuf in Paris—when they were much younger—and Danielle's unmistakable handwriting graced the photo. "My friend Kit" was written underneath a few symbols, the same symbols Chris had identified as Enoch's writing.

"I don't understand."

"Well, it seems this man was not trying to hurt your friend. He was trying to protect her. And wait till you hear the rest of it. But why don't we order first?" he said, realizing the waiter had been standing there, not wanting to interrupt.

Kit ordered the first thing she saw on the menu.

"Make it two," added Chris, without even looking at the menu. "I had no problem obtaining information from the nurses. I said I was there to identify a friend who might have been brought in. They told me the body had been removed—not sure why. A nurse asked if I recognized this medal as belonging to my friend." Chris searched in his pocket for the medal. "I took it because I remembered you wearing a similar one when I saw you the other day.

"I also found out he had a strange blood type, and that presented a problem when a transfusion was needed. However, the proper donor popped up, and that little problem was solved. The nurse also handed me a set of keys along with the medal. Ah, here it is!" He fished it out of his pocket.

Kit recognized the concentric circles. She took it from his hand and held it in hers.

"I tracked the man down. One of the keys was to a postal box in Santa Monica. The box indirectly led me to his address. When I went into his apartment, I had the impression it belonged to someone passing through. He had accumulated hardly any possessions. He had a box of photographs, mostly of Danielle. . . . Among them was one of Danielle and a very fair, Scandinavian-looking man. I should have taken it."

"What happened to it?"

Chris made a sign to let her know he'd get to that part of the story later. "I only took the photograph I've shown you. I decided to go back to the hospital to look at his records, which could not be located. They are gone. I returned to the apartment and found the entire building empty. It looked like it had been vacant for a long time. Everything in the apartment was gone. I mean, everything, even the wooden floors, had been ripped out.

"Well, at that point, I had to question my sanity. Two days earlier, the place looked normal, habitable. The other apartments also looked vacant. Two days before, I had questioned a woman coming out of the building about Mr. Ullman. She described him as a 'quiet sort of fellow, always courteous.' Another man, standing by the door, gave me a similar description.

"Now, the people are gone. How could a building be vacated so fast and made to look neglected? Mr. Ullman's apartment had been shiny and spotless. Suddenly, it looked filthy. It was mind-boggling! The real estate agent that has the listing assured me the building has been unoccupied and on the market for years."

"So what you're saying is that any trace of the man is gone?"

"You got it—as if he never existed. All we have is the medal, and whoever is behind this is always a step ahead of us, making sure we never find him. When the time is right, you must give the medal to your friend. I think she is the only one who might have a clue about his identity."

"Mr. Goodman . . ." she hesitated.

"Call me Chris."

"Chris, I don't know how to say this, but I'd like to hire you."

"You couldn't afford me, baby," said Chris mockingly but immediately regretted it.

Kit ignored the remark. "I am sure we could reach some kind of agreeable arrangement. Something tells me you are the right person to unravel this."

"This is too bizarre, even for my wild imagination! The thing is, I am in the middle of writing a book and have a deadline with my publisher. I really must get back to that unless . . ."

"Unless what?"

"Well, it just occurred to me that I could rent a place down here for a while, and while I'm here writing, I could continue digging."

"That would be just great! I have a small place in Laguna Beach. It is right on the water. We hardly ever go there. I keep it because my parents use it occasionally. You could stay there. I think you will be quite comfortable."

"Sounds good."

"Of course, you can bill me for your time and—"

He stopped her. "We'll talk about that later. Is there any chance I could meet your friend soon? Is she up to it?"

"She is doing quite well, but I don't want to question her or cause any undue stress this soon. I'll have you come over as a friend and nothing more. I'm having a small gathering on the fourteenth. Why don't you come then?"

"Entertaining already?"

"It is a special occasion. A dear friend of ours is returning from Europe. He has been in Egypt working on an archeological dig. He uncovered some remarkable sites. You might have read about it."

"Yeah, the tombs of the pharaoh's children? The two British archeologists?"

"Jean-Christophe is French. But yes, that's the team. Cocktails at six; dinner at seven thirty. May I add your name to the list?"

"That formal?"

"Not really. It has to do with the strict security we have implemented at the house."

Chris nodded with approval. "Please add my name. And by the way—I forgot to mention—you look lovely."

That night, Kitzia had a disturbing dream. Horrific earthquakes and massive explosions in New York, the collapse of skyscrapers, and the crumbling of the city's major monuments. Paintings, sculptures, and books went up in flames, and terrorized people ran through the streets, seeking refuge from a hail of burning refuse.

Kitzia clutched the stone Danielle had given her, which had morphed into a key. Kit knew the key could stop the destruction, but before she could figure out how it worked, Angela woke her up.

The nurse was whispering something about Danielle.

"Perhaps you should come and check on Ms. Peschard. She seems to be agitated."

Kit jumped up from the bed and ran toward Danielle's room.

"I have sedated her, but I thought it might calm her down to see you," Angela was saying as she followed Kit.

Upon seeing Kitzia, Danielle's breathing slowed down. Kit sat on the bed and took Danielle's hand. She looked at her and noticed the streaks of tears flowing down her cheeks. She tenderly placed her arms around Danielle. "It's OK. Darling, you are safe. We are all here."

"I am sorry . . . truly sorry." Danielle sobbed.

Kitza didn't know Danielle was unable to tell her that those horrible images from her dream had come from Danielle's vision of their future."

"What are you sorry about?" Kit whispered back.

"That I have dragged you into this, that I might not be able to protect you from the *others*."

Kit pulled away to give Danielle the opportunity to speak. But the valium took effect, and Danielle's eyes slowly closed. Angela helped Danielle lie down and allowed her to drift back to sleep.

Kit returned to her bed but could not go back to sleep. Danielle's words had interwoven with the images in her dream and produced a sense of impending doom. She took the rock in her hands and stared at the simplicity of its shape and its unremarkable surface. But when she held it against the light, a multitude of colors sparked to the surface, and it took on a degree of translucency. Yet, it was an ordinary geological piece, much like quartz.

It seems Danielle is aware of the charged atmosphere and recent happenings.

Kit turned the light off and tried to fall asleep. After twenty minutes of tossing and turning, rest would not come; nor could she put aside her lunch meeting with Chris Goodman.

The man who had died at the hospital likely knew what was going on, but now he was gone. She was glad Tom had come to their aid, but now, because of what he had discovered, his life had been threatened. The latest X-rays did not show any mass growth in Danielle's brain, and the lesion that had originally shown up was now gone. The matter of the cut behind her ear would remain an enigma.

Tom had inserted a needle to obtain a tiny biopsy of the residual mass and he had retrieved some traces of an unusual protein, but he couldn't find any evidence of the implant. Whatever had been there had dissolved. The skin had completely healed, and the entire matter had been put to rest.

With that thought in mind, Kit finally dozed off.

It seemed to Kit that she had barely closed her eyes when the hum of the household announced it was late morning. She could hear the dogs barking, voices chattering, and even laughter coming from the terrace. Kit got up and looked out.

The dogs were running in circles around a tree, chasing squirrels. Deliveries were still being dropped off at the front gate.

Kit wondered how double Code Blue security was going to work at the upcoming party. Cam had assured her he would handle it all to her satisfaction. Cam was handling everything these days; he had sort of taken over, and she could not really complain. Everything was working fine. He had hired competent personnel, and Danielle improved with each passing day. To some degree, life was returning to normal. What Kit found a little out of the ordinary was the sudden attachment Danielle had taken to Cam. They spent a lot of time together. *What could they possibly talk about?*

The intercom rang. It was Ling from the kitchen, wanting to know if she'd be down for breakfast.

When she came down, Danielle was already sitting at the table and unlike Kit, she looked rested and appeared to be in high spirits. They kissed on both cheeks, and Cam pulled the chair out for Kitzia before walking away to continue helping with the unloading.

"Cam was heaven sent," said Kit to open up the conversation. "And you seem comfortable around him."

"I am."

"Danielle, last night you woke up crying and said something—"

"Another bad dream!" Maria interrupted while pouring the coffee.

Kit stopped talking until the housekeeper walked away.

"You were trying to tell me something. You apologized for—"

"It must have been a dream. I really don't remember."

"OK. But there is something else I've been meaning to ask you. When you were in the hospital, you gave me a—"

Danielle cut her off abruptly. "Look at the beautiful roses Ramon has planted! And over there, to the left, he covered the borders of the stone stairway with a blanket of hairy cap moss. *Polytrichum commune*, I believe it's called."

Kit listened in dismay to Danielle's detailed description of the nature and spectrum of mosses. It was unreal. She had no recollection of what had happened the night before. Kit suspected Danielle was trying to cover up her inability to access her memories.

". . . characterized by the silver hues of *Leucobryum glaucum* to the chartreuse of the *Aulacomnium palustre* . . ." Danielle seemed to be quoting from a horticulture encyclopedia.

Kit recognized the symptoms of transient global amnesia and now understood perfectly why her friend had been avoiding her. Conversing with people who did not know her in the past was less demanding, and that explained why she was so comfortable with Cam.

Kit decided to keep their conversations to a lighter tone.

"The *Plagiomnium cuspidatum* would be an excellent choice to cover the topiaries."

"You know, it will be great to see Jean-Christophe again," Kit said, hoping to get Danielle off the subject of mosses.

"Keep the party small and concentrate on the quality of the food," Danielle said, finally in a normal tone. "You know how fastidious he is about that."

"Don't worry. There will be Beluga, Foi Gras, and plenty of Dom Perignon."

"Jean-Christophe really prefers Perrier-Jouet, Belle Epoque."

"OK. I'll remember that. I left a guest list in your room for you to look at. The only stranger I have invited is Chris Goodman, the writer."

Danielle looked up, a little surprised.

"Do you think perhaps this was not a good time to ask him?"

"On the contrary. He needs to be here."

X

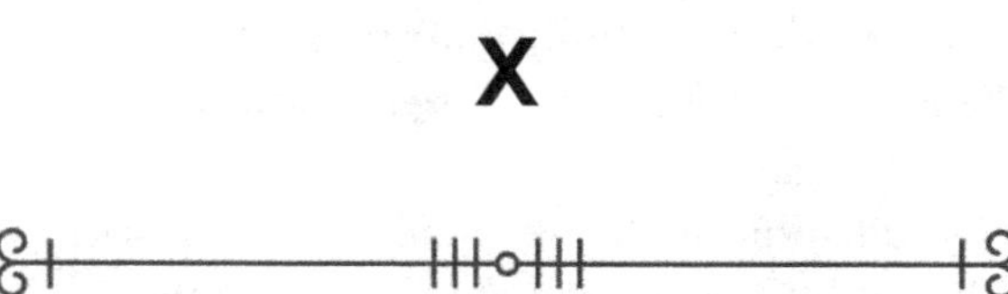

Lilith
New York

Lili Keller DeWinter scrutinized the fine lines forming at the side of her mouth and sighed with annoyance at her reflection in the mirror. The battle to remain young and fresh was becoming more demanding with each passing day. Despite the minor flaws, she was still unbelievably beautiful, she thought to herself with delight, as she continued to practice her various smiles and facial expressions in the mirror. *How old do people guess me to be at first glance,* she wondered with acute interest—forty . . . *thirty-five*? Especially those who didn't know anything about her, and that was precisely why she preferred the company of strangers, why she moved about the world with such frequency.

With the means at her disposal, Lili could pick up and start a new life anywhere, at any time. It still amused her to hop all over Europe, playing up her DeWinter ancestry. From soirees at French chateaux to Italian villas on the Mediterranean, she would suddenly drop out of sight, only to reappear at a hacienda in Buenos Aires or a plantation in South Africa. Yet she liked New York the best and was amazed at how adept she had been at playing the fashion empire magnate.

She tilted her head ever so slightly to admire her face from a new angle as she mused. *It was definitely a good idea to acquire Montaigne Enterprises a few years ago.* Along with the cosmetics and skin care companies, she had gained the European research labs, clinics, and spas in Switzerland and fervently encouraged the development of more advanced anti-aging products. She ran the tips of her perfectly manicured hand lightly over her cheek. *The plasma treatments at the Lucerne clinic were definitely the most beneficial.*

The media had determined she had found the Fountain of Youth. People had no idea how intense her search had been, how obsessive her struggle was to preserve this face and body, and how determined she was to preserve it till the end. It was a never-ending fight . . . myriad surgeries, plasma treatments, peelings, facials, wraps—all just to remain the same.

The beautiful body, at least, had been reasonably easy to maintain. It had always responded to nutrition and vigorous exercise. Yet she could not deny the first warnings of organ deterioration—one more thing to worry about.

Lili cast one final glance at her image in the mirror—the oval face with its perfect features and fair porcelain skin. Thick, silky, black lashes framed her huge cobalt blue eyes, and her black hair was cropped short in a severe style that served to frame, but not interfere with, her lovely face. She knew of no other woman who could display such a tough look and still maintain femininity and grace. Her nose was narrow, in perfect contrast with her sensuously full lips. Her long and graceful neck and her slender frame seemed almost too frail for her height, which was the most striking thing about her. Lili was slightly over six feet tall.

She heard Ted's footsteps but did not move. She watched him walk slowly in her direction as he enjoyed her reflection in the mirror. Theodore Edwards found her to be the most desirable woman in the world and could not seem to get enough of her. His body yearned for hers every instant of the day. When he was away from her, the only thought that comforted him was that of knowing that she was his. Or so he thought.

As he approached her, his own reflection in the mirror pleased him, filling him with a sense of pride. Theodore Edwards was not particularly good-looking, but he had a certain degree of presence. He wore expensive Italian suits and shirts of fine linen. He had come a long way from the days when he dressed in plaid pants and pink polo shirts, as Kitzia O'Neil remembered him. Success and money had come to him easily. He always knew he was a lucky man and that he'd be rich and powerful one day. Luck, in his mind, simply meant waiting for the right opportunity to present itself and not letting it slip by. That opportunity had come with his association with the *Group.*

The *Group,* as it was called, consisted of a select few of the most powerful and influential men in the world. They ran the world from backstage. One of its members had brought Theodore to the attention of the *Group* early in his career, when he was an ardent young preacher, having abandoned the insurance business. The organization had undoubtedly seen his potential and decided to sponsor him. Theodore Edwards knew his deep, rich voice was his most powerful asset, and he orchestrated it to great effect upon his audience. The *Group* had promised that Theodore Edwards was to reach unimaginable heights and groomed him for their future use.

They put him in the hands of linguists, elocution teachers, drama coaches, actors, and image and body language consultants, who reinvented him and taught him to walk, move, and speak with determination and persuasion. All spontaneity had been erased so that now, his every utterance was a performance preordained to suit their needs. Wherever he spoke, Theodore brought his listeners into his thrall. He had learned to manipulate emotions and extract from the audience whatever response he wished. In his early training with the *Group,* he had been under the tutelage of Cirel Hister, a highly placed member in the organization. Although Theodore never understood exactly what Cirel did, what this man taught him had been instrumental in perfecting his role as a spiritual leader. Cirel had taught him the dark art of mass hypnosis.

Theodore would speak at church conferences and rouse the audience to such high levels of emotional motivation that listeners would endorse whatever he suggested. His sermons would move congregations to tears, bring sinners to sudden repentance, and make people dig deeply into their pockets.

Ted reached Lili, and without saying a word, placed his hands loosely around her small waist, sliding them down to lace his fingers over her abdomen. All along, Ted kept staring at their images in the mirror. He absolutely loved seeing the two of them together. He became excited. At that point, Lili released him.

"You are in a hurry. Aren't you, darling?" She smiled wickedly.

"Actually, I am. The plane is waiting at Teterboro." He straightened his tie, trying to return his body to normalcy.

"Are you taking the helicopter?"

"Why . . . do you need it?"

"No. I am staying in the city." She continued to smile maliciously.

"Good! Then I will hurry back." He had not looked away from the mirror and now touched his gray temple as if to straighten his hair.

Lili noticed the new hairstyle. "I like your hair."

"Thanks." He missed the irony in her voice. She never missed the fact that, whatever change he made in his appearance, it was always made to emulate Robert Powers, whom he grudgingly admired.

"Where exactly are you going?"

"Washington. Some members of the *Group* want to meet with me. We are going over some of the new strategies for our campaign. Then I'll have to fly to Atlanta to meet with the representatives of all regional Baptist and evangelical churches to finalize the arrangements for the upcoming national conference. I could fly back between trips so we could spend a little time together."

Lili raised up her hand in dismissal, "Don't bother. I really should take care of some of my business. I have scheduled meetings and social engagements."

Theodore tried to hide his disappointment.

"Why don't you take advantage of the free time and visit the family?" added Lili. "Anna Beth must be lonely. When we get back, I'll make it up to you."

Theodore hated to detect derision in her tone. He was never quite sure of Lili—of what she thought or felt. Perhaps he was crazy about her for that precise reason. Deep down, he hoped her words were rooted in a bit of jealousy. Yet he knew that to be wishful thinking. As much as he tried to keep them from her, Lili knew his inner thoughts. She knew he found his wife plain and dull.

"You must keep up your image, darling."

Yes, I have to keep up the appearance of a happily married man, he thought sadly. The *Group* insisted there were to be no scandals in the life of the revered pastor. When it came to Lili, to his surprise, everyone looked the other way. They all worked in some capacity for the *Group*, so there was a scant risk of a leak to the press.

As far as the country knew, Dr. Theodore Edwards was the role model of the American family man, a respected spiritual leader, seeking to revive the failing hope and faith of the American people. His face stared out from billboards on every major highway across the country. The campaign had been so successful, even Theodore himself had begun to believe the lie.

Still the head of the New Era Christian Coalition Church after twenty-two years, he had stopped considering himself a pastor and was convinced he crossed the threshold into a national leadership role.

Ted took the elevator to the rooftop to board the helicopter, and Lili walked toward a sofa that faced away from the window. She let herself fall on it and rang for her assistant.

A young man in his mid-twenties appeared. He placed a glass of a dark green liquid on the cocktail table in front of her, the special juice Lili drank at mid-morning every day. The young man had always thought the drink looked disgusting, that it was not his place to bring it to her every morning. Others in the penthouse could do such domestic chores, but Lili insisted that he be the one to do it. She enjoyed seeing his beautiful face and had told him that she looked forward each morning to the sight of his body; it was so like that of a Greek god.

Jeff Montgomery had been working for Lili Keller DeWinter for the last three years. His life had taken a sudden detour the moment he had met her. During his last year at Columbia, like many of his friends, he had run into financial difficulties. He wanted to go to law school, but the prospect looked grim. Girls told him he should try modeling while he put himself through school. He interviewed with a modeling agency, which immediately sent his composite to Keller-Montaigne Enterprises. Lili saw his photograph and hired him for a background shot.

She had chosen him for herself and was not going to confuse the issue with promises of a future modeling career. After the initial photographic session, she offered him a permanent part-time job as one of her personal assistants. Jeff had considered this a lucky break and did not imagine for a second that his association with Lili would be the end of his career plans. At first, his responsibilities were those of an errand boy and didn't interfere with his schedule. His employer was gone most of the time, and he had plenty of time to study in this beautiful environment. When Lili started spending more time at the corporate office in New York, she became more demanding. She compensated him well for his time, so Jeff could not complain. But it became increasingly difficult to juggle his classes at Columbia with his work schedule, and he ended up dropping out of school.

Now that he could work full time for Keller-Montaigne, Lili asked that he spend the majority of his time upstairs in the penthouse handling her personal affairs. The penthouse consisted of the top three of the eighty-seven stories of the Keller Building on Park Avenue. The building, belonging to Lili Keller, of course, and housed Montaigne Enterprises, Keller investments, and DeWinter Fashion Group, with its diverse branches of import-export, design, marketing, and distribution. A spa, exercise and yoga rooms, and an Olympic-sized pool were on the eighty-fourth floor—exclusively for Lili's personal use and for her close associates. The rest of the employees used the facilities on the twenty-third floor. The law firm dedicated to the Keller–DeWinter affairs occupied the eightieth and eighty-first floors; the executive offices were located on the eighty-second. Nobody knew exactly what was on the seventy-ninth floor. Its rooms were reserved for special meetings of the board and certain gatherings of the *Group.*

It was a nice place to work, but Jeff's nagging desire to continue with law school caused him to try to resign on several occasions. Lili would not hear of it. Finally, after nearly two years, one day he decided to do it—no matter what. As usual, Lili would not give him the opportunity to speak. He followed her from room to room, answering non-stop questions about her social engagements. "I really must speak to you, Ms. Keller," he had said in a tone unfamiliar to her.

"OK. Do it while I get my massage." She motioned him to follow her and the masseur into the adjacent room, where she let her terry-cloth robe fall to the floor in front of the two young men. Jeff tried to look the other way, but it was difficult. He had never seen such a beautiful and flawless body. He watched her climb onto the massage table and roll onto her stomach. She placed her face in the direction he was standing while the masseur, who had to be about his same age, applied a scented oil to her back and buttocks.

"I am listening."

Jeff began his usual discourse why it was important that he finish school. He was having trouble concentrating on what he was saying. Lili had not moved her eyes from him—and because of the height of the table where she was lying—her eyes were fixed on his crotch. Her gaze and the movement of the masseur's hand were driving him crazy. Those hands were now moving up and down her inner legs in such an erotic fashion that Jeff could not prevent himself from getting aroused.

"Leave if you insist," said Lili, "but not before you talk to Tracy."

Tracy Jackson was one of the company's top attorneys.

"Will you give us a few minutes?" Lili asked the masseur, "and hand me the phone." The masseur handed it to her. She pressed the direct button to the law offices. "Hi, I'm sending Jeff down. He'd like to quit." She abruptly clicked off. Her eyes had never left Jeff's. "Shouldn't we take care of something before you see Tracy?"

When Jeff found himself sitting across the desk from Tracy Jackson, the roguish grin on the attorney's round face all but said that he knew what had just happened upstairs.

"Ms. Keller does not want you to leave. She has asked me to do whatever it takes to retain you."

"But I thought she understood."

"That you want to go to law school? She does. Let me ask you something, Jeff. How much do you think a starting attorney makes in Manhattan?"

"A hundred and twenty grand a year."

"Ninety-five," the attorney corrected. "Now, this is what we are proposing to offer you: one hundred seventy-five thousand a year and a three-year contract. At such time, you will be free to leave and enroll in law school, or you will be given the opportunity to renew or renegotiate your contract. In addition, there will be a yearly bonus equivalent to the amount of your salary. You can take that amount and put it aside to cover the cost of your law school. You will be given stock in both Montaigne and DeWinter Enterprises, an expense account, a car allowance or the use of one of the company vehicles, executive lounge and facilities access, four weeks' vacation, and a number of other benefits. Would you like some time to think about it?"

Jeff had already made up his mind. "And what exactly am I supposed to do? So far, my duties have been no more than those of a gofer."

The plump attorney laughed merrily. "All of our duties are really no more than that. As Ms. Keller's personal assistant, you will continue to oversee her personal affairs. If you would like further responsibilities, we can assign them to you. You could come down here for a few hours during the day and handle them from here. That is, if a law environment is what you miss. However, I must tell you, Ms. Keller is willing to set you up in your personal private office in the penthouse. You can meet with the designers this afternoon and start ordering your furniture."

"Three years?" Jeff mumbled incredulously.

"Three years. It is all right here." He handed Jeff a contract. "If you should accept—"

"Where do I sign?"

"Bottom, fourth page. What I was about to say was that it is imperative you read carefully and understand fully the last paragraph on the contract, the one dealing with confidentiality. We have to make sure you understand what we expect of you, as far as loyalty is concerned."

Jeff looked over the paragraph and did not find the demands and need for secrecy relating to all aspects of the corporations unreasonable.

It had now been almost three years since he had moved into his private office. Jeff knew it was almost time to terminate or renew that contract, but he was in no hurry. He had grown comfortable with his position. Except for the minor tedious chores, like making and serving that nauseating morning juice to Lili, he was actually happy.

Lili was demanding and unscrupulous in her business affairs, but he had also discovered another side of her that pleased him enormously. Lili was pleasure-loving and witty. She loved to laugh and in her presence, one always had a good time. Then there were those rare but terrible times, when she sank into depression and became angry and violent. During those outbursts, everyone knew to steer away from her. He had only witnessed two of those episodes but heard there had been others where she had smashed furniture and even physically hurt her employees. But he had learned to detect when one of those episodes might be coming and warned the others to stay clear.

The penthouse was, for the most part, a fun place. Lili's entourage consisted of several young men and women, all in their twenties, much like himself. They were lively and physically beautiful. He quickly learned that Lili could not stand to be around unattractive people, so her immediate staff looked like it had just stepped out of *Vogue* and *GQ* magazines.

Jeff had long ago abandoned the notion that he was special to her or that she found him particularly desirable. He soon realized her entire personal staff satisfied her in one way or another, although no one ever talked about it. At first, Jeff had suspected her to be a nymphomaniac, but now he knew better. Lili Keller had no needs, only appetites, and a desire to amuse herself.

Lili picked up her green juice and drank it with gusto.

"I have been meaning to ask you what is in that less-than-appetizing drink," asked Jeff.

"You have been making it, darling. You should know."

"Cucumbers and herbs but what is that pungent root and the murky yellowish milk?"

"It's water," she said, stretching her arms above her head.

"What kind of water?"

"From high up in the mountains of Tibet. It comes from beneath the mountain glaciers. It is called glacial milk, but it is water. It is murky because it is full of every colloidal mineral known on this planet. You can only obtain this type of water from mountain villages over ten thousand feet in elevation, those with two percent yearly precipitation. You are aware, aren't you, that the soil in this country is totally depleted of minerals?"

"No, I don't keep up with those things," replied Jeff.

"Well, you should. It is all documented in US Congress Document 264, 74th Congress, Section 200—dated 1936. I really doubt things have changed since. The phosphate, potassium, boron, and vanadium are gone forever.

"The root and leaves come from a plant now virtually extinct on Earth. they provide an inordinate amount of Vitamin K. You should drink it if you want to live forever."

"Who wants to live forever?" Never did he imagine Lili was being serious.

"Unfortunately, I do." Her smile faded. "What is on the morning agenda?"

"Your trainer and masseur are waiting. PR wants to meet with you about the eye cream campaign. *Vanity Fair* wants approval on some shots they took of you at the Guggenheim, and Robert Powers phoned. He would like to see you today."

"Yes to Mr. Powers. Lunch at Pierre Savoy's, 12:30. Get the corner table. You can OK pictures. PR, not today." She watched him mark off things from the list. "You really hate all this petty stuff, don't you?"

"No, but it doesn't exactly boost my ego. I am capable of handling other things for you."

"You know I make a rule of never giving anybody further responsibilities until I am convinced I can trust them fully."

"I didn't know I was still on trial."

"You've passed. When I get back, we'll talk again. I've got something in mind for you."

"Where are you going?"

"To California for a party."

"I haven't seen the invitation."

"This is one that I will sort of crash. I am sure you've done that at some point in your life?"

Jeff smiled, reminiscing while he thought, *What party would not be thrilled to have you?*

"This one. But I have to do it. You see, we all have to do something for someone else."

Jeff had no idea what she was talking about. But he was conscious that, once again, she had picked up his thoughts. But he was getting used to it by now.

"What did you find out about our little archeologist?"

"She has been gone from the Met for about eight weeks. She is supposed to be recovering. Nobody knows when she will be back."

"Must have been quite an accident!"

"I believe it was."

Lili stood up and ran her fingernails slowly around his neck. "Now, tell me, you mentioned having a friend who knew her."

"Yes, Ricardo Duran. His girlfriend, Linda, is Danielle Peschard's assistant. He has been working for Donna Karan but is dying for the opportunity to launch his own line."

"I do remember now. When I get back, let's look at your friend's portfolio."

"Thanks."

"Now, please tell Tiffany to come in for a facial. We'll skip the exercise and massage this morning. I want to look radiant at lunch."

Wearing a gray silk pantsuit and pewter flats, Lili casually strolled into the restaurant. She was a regular at Savoy's, and the entire staff greeted her at once. All heads turned to look at her, as happened wherever she went. She never failed to intimidate women and make men gasp at the sight of her lithe, tall, good looks and lovely face. Robert arrived a few seconds behind her. After a brief greeting, they proceeded to their corner table. A bottle of Dom Perignon, Lili's favorite, was iced and in place.

"You look superb, as always," said Robert.

Lili smiled faintly. "It is so good to see you, Robert. It has been so long."

"I have been unbelievably busy. We are in the process of another merger acquisition—"

"That is not what I was referring to. It seems like you have been devoting all your free time to your little archeologist. Did I hear someplace that she has been indisposed?"

Robert concentrated on straightening the napkin on his lap, making it apparent he did not want to discuss Danielle.

"She has recovered."

"Oh, yes. I heard that too. She is even having a soiree. Tell me something. Does it bother her to read about us in the media? It is amazing how the press seems to always get a snapshot of us when we are together."

"How could they miss it when they are on your payroll?"

"Come on, you don't really think so?"

"I know so. I don't know how she feels. She has never mentioned it."

"Then she probably doesn't care. I think you should take me to her party."

Robert frowned in consternation. "Now, why should I do that?"

"To convince her that we are no more than friends."

"I don't think I need to convince her of that."

"You really care for her?"

Robert's impatience was beginning to show.

"Robert . . . I'd like us three to be friends."

"The answer is no. I am not taking you to California."

"Pity." She sipped her champagne. "Then tell me the reason for our lunch."

"I wanted to do something for you, for old time's sake."

"I am already touched," she smiled faintly.

"I would have preferred a more private place, but considering your enjoyment of notoriety, this will have to do."

Lili, feeling all eyes on her, smiled with satisfaction.

Robert looked around. "Does it really matter that much, the admiration, the adulation?" He did not give her the opportunity to answer. "This couldn't last forever, and you always knew that."

"Was not that why we decided to remain neutral?"

"But have we Lili?"

"We can't complain. We have amassed all that could be had of the material wealth of the realm."

"And forgotten that it is all an illusion! Lili, I'm deep into this, but you don't have to be. You can still—"

"Are you mad? We haven't stolen anything. We've given the race so much!"

"Lili, listen to me and listen carefully. There is going to be war."

"I am used to it. We have been under that threat from the moment we decided to settle here and become part of the plan."

He reached into his pocket and produced what looked like a credit card. The card was not plastic but made from a paper-thin metal, smooth on one side and engraved with tiny dots on the other, much like Braille. Likewise, Lili reached into her Chanel bag and took out a small rectangular compact. She inserted Robert's card into a thin slot at the bottom and snapped it open. Its mirror became a multicolor screen, across which raced a series of symbols at a speed almost incomprehensible to the naked eye. The whole scanning process took less than ten seconds. The waiter, who was refilling their champagne flutes, noticed nothing, but Lili briefly checking her make-up. After she put the compact away, she remained silent for a moment, as did Robert, allowing her to digest the information he had given her.

"I should have known the blackout was caused by an interception of communications," she said, finally. "But I didn't have any idea the hurricanes and droughts had been engineered by the *Group*. I am sure, however, that after the glitches, we'll have control of the atmosphere."

"You couldn't possibly believe that! The *Group's* manipulation of the Edenic currents is not to produce a higher quality of life for its members."

"Why not? The *Group* has provided us with the highest standard of existence possible. It has given us the opportunity to experience all possible forms of emotion, to experience what true humanity is about. As an Edentian, I would have never understood the ways of this backward race."

Robert watched attentively as she spoke. The lightness of her comments told him she was still processing the magnitude of the information he had passed on to her. He knew it would not be easy for her to face the fact that the days of carefree existence were over, that the *Group* would now be recruiting them to take their posts and face the adversary.

"Now, wouldn't *The Group* be a little upset if they knew what you've just done? I mean, wouldn't that be considered disloyalty?"

"Yes, they would. I did say this was for old time's sake. You don't have to be part of it. You could still get away."

For the first time, Lili lost her composure. She lowered her voice and hissed through her teeth, "And what is it exactly that you propose I do? You know perfectly well I cannot exit. I'd be detained at the vortex. We are, my dearest Robert, trapped. Our only hope is for the *Group* to be successful, and we must do whatever is within our power to make sure they—we—succeed.

"As long as you understand what the stakes are," added Robert. "That once you become involved in the actual confrontation, there is no way out."

"Are you fearing the outcome?"

"No, of course not," said Robert. "I am prepared to fight and win. But it is going to get very messy. Especially now that other life forms have come in."

"Now, that is funny. You are prepared to fight and conquer but would like me to surrender and repent for having once doubted that the Divine Plan would work. Besides, all exits are controlled. I have not even had a message from Cirel; he might have gone back into hiding."

The fear in Lili's voice was genuine, and Robert understood it was hopeless to continue. He reached again into his pocket and took out the vial Cirel had given him. It was half full.

"I have something for you." He handed her the glass vial.

Lili's amazement was written on her face. *My magical liquid!* "Where did you get it?"

"It doesn't matter. Be frugal. This may be the last of it for a very long time."

Lili carefully placed it inside her purse. The clear substance from another galaxy was a powerful element with regenerative powers to detoxify and repair cell damage. Once again, she could stop the clock. Lili felt energetic, no longer afraid.

"Thank you. I am sure whatever you've said today is because you care. I will not forget it. I'll let you in on something about your friend at the Met. I've heard rumors the *Group* suspects she is an agent. They think she might even be Daniela . . . from Edentia.

"They had me trace her background," continued Lili. At only nine years old, she inherited a huge fortune after her parents and their daughter were killed in an automobile accident. It is possible that Daniela's spirit slipped into the body of the dying child, adopted her identity, and is living her life as a human being. Even if this is so, I found nothing threatening about her, and I told them so. I think they backed off from her. But something is still not right. They think she might have access to something they want. Do you have any idea what that could be?"

"Lili, I am telling you, don't get involved. Run your fashion empire; have fun. Leave all the intrigue to the others."

"You are right!" She laughed sarcastically. "Perhaps I'll separate Ted from his wife and settle down with the chairman of the Church."

"Be careful—I don't like where this is going. I don't want to see you being used by the *Group*."

"Used?"

"You don't see? They are using you as bait to manipulate that poor idiot? They have plans for him. Be wise and keep your eyes wide open."

"Consider me forewarned."

"Now I must run," concluded Robert.

"But we haven't eaten yet."

"Sorry. Forget this meeting ever took place, but remember every single thing I've told you."

Lili remained at the restaurant and finished her meal. She watched Robert leave and felt a strange mix of emotions. Through the window, she saw him climb into his black limousine and disappear among the many other town cars and taxis on the crowded street.

She knew the other diners couldn't take their eyes off her, and for once, she wished they would leave her alone.

Suddenly remembering the precious vial in her purse, she rallied. *Nothing else really matters.*

It was a good decision to remain faithful to the Group, thought Lili. *They would not be easily defeated.* Even during that frightful war in the heavens, the rebels were not totally subjugated. All the leaders, or arch-rebels, as they are called, escaped. Well, most of them. Only the instigators had been imprisoned.

After a while, on the Sovereign's orders, they ceased to be ostracized or persecuted and were once again allowed to roam the galaxies. Lili had heard they had signed a treaty in which they agreed not to enlist any further mercenaries. Predictably, the treaty had not been honored, and now the threat of confrontation was once again real. The neutrals, like herself, had remained impartial and had never been pressed to take sides.

Her relationship with Arch-rebel Cirel had somehow changed everything. Cirel felt very strongly about the Luciel Manifesto, proclaiming *autonomy,* and fervently espoused it wherever he went. He was not an Edentian, but possessed their same brilliant vibration characteristics. At one time, he had even dazzled Lili.

Unfortunately, her relationship with him had cost her freedom. She was no longer allowed to move about the galaxy and had become subject to the quarantine that had been imposed on Urantia. She appealed to the *Foundation,* which had control of the vortex—the only channel for exit—but her pleas were always denied. She was treated as a rebel and became subject to their same rules and conditions. Their souls were imprisoned in mortal bodies that would deteriorate and ultimately die. At such time, her soul would leave Earth from her mortal form and begin the evolutionary trip back to her planet of citizenship. The *Group* had been more sympathetic to her situation and had helped her in whatever way they could. Thus, it was that she had become a permanent resident of the planet she no longer loved. She had made the best of it, however; she had become rich and powerful and had succeeded in her determination to remain eternally young and beautiful by any means necessary.

She hardly ever thought of the old life, of Edentia—the star planet that had revoked her citizenship—of her old feelings, of her creative powers, or even her loves. After a while on Earth, she had decided it wasn't so bad. There were many gratifications she would never have experienced. She had distanced herself from the Edentians, who had remained faithful to the Divine Plan. She was, nonetheless, touched by Robert's gesture. His warnings, unnecessary perhaps, let her know he had not forgotten that she, too, was an Edentian.

XI

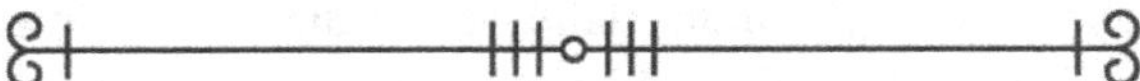

Los Angeles

Danielle dreamed of Orsef again. The vision vanished the moment she opened her eyes, but his words remained. "You must remember . . ."

His words shook her, even though she could not comprehend what he meant. Her time of relative peace under the cover of Danielle Peschard's body had expired. She now had to assemble the fragmented pieces of her immortal existence and conclude her assignment.

The complete report of Cirel's diabolical plans had to be transmitted to the life carriers, therefore, the Formation had to take place as planned.

Through the implant, Cirel had tried to control her and continuously attempted to access her memory. Danielle felt vulnerable, even when she slept. She could no longer transmit to Edentia or contact other Edentians stationed on the planet, and because of her, Kjell had been eliminated. Lili, her onetime companion, had been seduced by the *Group*, and Robert's loyalty to the *Foundation* was doubtful.

She was alone in the crucial responsibility for rescuing the Urantia 606 Project.

Yet there was something crucial that she had to remember!

Only Cam seemed cognizant of what was going on inside her and understood the episodes of her transient amnesia.

Things of major import had been wiped out from the memory banks of Daniela. As Danielle, she remembered everything about her physical life; well, at least since the car accident when she was nine. The Peschards had left a considerable amount of money to the Catholic Church and deemed Father Santis co-executor of their estate and tutor to their daughter. When he was assigned to the Vatican, he took Danielle with him to Europe. She went to boarding schools in England and, later, to finishing school in Switzerland.

The other executor of the estate had been Samuel Judd, a close family friend. Samuel Judd's son had been engaged to Deborah Drajanski, Kitzia's mother. This fact Danielle had never revealed to Kitzia. She was not to reveal it until the time was right for Kitzia to comprehend the omnipotent wisdom of the universe.

It was not quite seven o'clock when Danielle put on her jogging clothes and got ready for her morning walk with Cam. On her way down, she noticed Kit's bedroom door was open. Kit was in the shower and Danielle turned to go when her eye caught sight of the medal sitting on top of the dresser—the medal Chris Goodman had been given at the hospital as the only clue to the identity of the Scandinavian patient who had disappeared. Danielle took it and left the room quickly, wiping tears from her eyes.

Cam was already in the kitchen, waiting for Danielle. Maria had given up offering to fix him breakfast. He never ate and seemed to subsist on liquids. Although he never engaged in small talk, Cam was always courteous and helpful, and the staff liked him.

"Behind that face of indifference," Maria frequently told others, "there is a heart of gold."

Danielle signaled for him to meet her outside.

"The constant throbbing in my head, and the endless noise continues," Danielle said. Cam put his hands on top of hers and closed his eyes.

After a couple of minutes, he asked, "Is it better?" She nodded. "Danielle, tell me exactly what you are hearing."

"A roaring noise. I think they're voices, urging me to remember something I have obviously forgotten."

"It's a type of communication on the second air that you used to pick up and decode. But first, we must get your strength back. I think we can run faster and farther than yesterday."

Without saying anything else, Danielle placed the medal she had taken from Kitzia's room in Camiel's hand. After a few seconds, Cam returned it to Danielle.

Kitzia had been watching their exchange from her window and paid particular attention to his reaction to the medal. It was obvious the medal had special meaning for them. She watched as they began jogging toward the front gate. Kitzia sighed, not understanding. She had a busy day ahead, with last-minute details for the party.

Robert Powers stood in front of the large, arched French windows in Danielle's house, watching with interest the arrangements for the evening party. A couple of men were carrying a gold harp and placing it in a corner of the terrace. A white baby grand had already been positioned in the other corner. The staff was busy placing candles along the garden path, while the caterers carefully draped the circular tables with copious yards of silk brocade. Several members of the secret service were conducting their customary security check.

Robert spotted Camiel standing by the terrace stairs. The two men held each other's eyes for a brief moment. Kitzia walked into the room holding a small silver tray and two glasses of Perrier.

"She will be right down."

Robert took one of the glasses and pointed to the secret service agents. "Parker?"

"Yes. Isn't it exciting? I was surprised when the White House called this morning to say he'd be here. I realized Danielle knew him after the attempt on his life. Cardinal Santis has also been invited. Did you know Danielle was supposed to be in Rome?"

He did not seem surprised. "Who else is coming?"

"Jean-Christophe, some executives from the Met, Danielle's assistant, a scientist from Puerto Rico, and Tom, of course."

"Of course." He smiled. "And your friend, the writer."

"That's right—Chris Goodman. How did you know?"

"I know everything." He looked in the direction of the second floor. "Who is staying here?"

Kit let out a small laugh at the same quiz she had just gone through with the secret service. They heard Danielle's footsteps and turned around.

"Hello, Robert," said Danielle.

"Well, I'll leave the two of you," said Kit. "I've got to get back to the garden. Look, I left them alone for ten minutes, and they have already disrupted the schematic for the tables!"

They watched her leave the room before looking at each other. There was an awkward silence between them.

"I just wanted to make sure everything was OK," Robert said casually.

"If you are worried about the security—"

"Security is apparently being handled quite efficiently." He looked in the direction of Camiel. "Danielle, please tell me what happened the night of the accident."

"You were there; you already know."

"I am not sure you do, though. It is very important that you tell me where you were going."

"After you bravely rescued me from those thugs, I flew to California. Kjell met me, and we almost made it to the safe house. You forgot to mention that we were heading for a trap. We tried to get away, but—"

Robert's expression tightened. "I didn't know."

She put her hands on her temples, feeling the pain surge.

Robert blamed himself for what had happened. He should have anticipated the lengths the *Group* would go to neutralize her. He took a vial out of his pocket—it was half full—and handed it to her.

She held it in her hand, puzzled. She did not recognize the significance of its contents. He took it from her hand and emptied it into the glass of water. "Drink it, and drink it fast!" he ordered her.

Danielle did as she was told, and when she finished, he placed his hand on the spot behind her left ear where the tiny incision had been. She experienced a sudden release from the agonizing pressure in her head, and both of them closed their eyes for a few seconds. The silence was shattered by the sound of an explosion. A large glass vase containing an arrangement of roses had shattered, spilling water and sending shards of glass across the room. Robert and Danielle did not move, not until Kit and Maria, followed by the service members came rushing into the room. Cam watched attentively from his post outside.

"What happened?' Kit wanted to know.

Robert volunteered an explanation. "The vase shattered."

"It sounded like a bomb!" exclaimed Kit.

"It must have had a crack in it. The weight and pressure of the water must have made it explode," continued Robert.

The secret service team looked about the room as if to verify that explanation.

"Are you OK?" Kit's eyes were wide with amazement as she waved instructions to the workers to clean up the mess.

Robert and Danielle, unlike the others, seemed unaffected by the incident, and without saying anything else, walked out of the room.

"The pain will abate dramatically, and you will begin to remember. I hope that when you do, you won't be too harsh in your judgment of me."

She felt an inexplicable sadness. "Will I see you tonight?"

"Yes, you will see me tonight." He kissed her cheek. *For the last time*, he thought painfully.

It was only after he was inside his car that he added to his thoughts: *I love you, Daniela. I always have and always will.*

Danielle hurried back into the house and ran upstairs, trying to hold back her tears.

Chris Goodman drove his rented Jaguar up the road to the Peschard estate at a dizzying speed. When he pulled up to the massive iron gates, he was surprised to see so many men standing at the entrance. The two guards in uniform were obviously part of the estate's staff, as well as several men in dark suits wearing the ear pieces that identified them as secret police covered the entrance. Two of the agents approached him, one carrying an electronic notebook; the other, a list of guests.

"Christian Goodman," said the writer as he watched the man mark his name off the list.

"Identification, please."

Chris handed over his driver's license while the other man extended the electronic box he was holding. Chris placed his thumb on it and waited a few seconds before the man retrieved the box.

The man's face remained expressionless as he signaled Ramon, who was operating the gate, to open it.

Chris slowly drove to the front door. He passed limousines, uniformed drivers, and more secret service agents smoking and standing around. He left his car with the valet. Eddy, the young houseboy in a white jacket, greeted him at the door and pointed him in the direction of the living room.

The atmosphere was relaxed. He noticed the gigantic fresh flower arrangement in the foyer and remembered once seeing a similar one at the entrance of the Met. The crowd was relatively small, thirty guests at most, but the arrangements were quite elaborate. As much as he had hated parties in his parents' home when he was growing up, they now produced the sweetest of memories. Through the French windows he could see the piano, several violinists, and a harpist. Lavishly laid tables, laden with enticing foods, over which elaborate ice sculptures of Egyptian monuments held sway.

The reason for the presence of the secret service was immediately apparent when President Parker was the first figure he spotted. Not much had been said about the president since the attempt on his life in Rome. Parker was engaged in what appeared to be an amusing conversation with a cardinal in long robes and a crimson sash. Next, he noticed a man standing close to them, yet not with them. He seemed grave and kept a constant eye on the entire room. He was an unusual-looking man, Chris thought, hard-pressed to make out his nationality. No one ever failed to notice the unique combination of Cam's rich, dark skin and brilliant pale green eyes. Chris identified a couple of senators and a film director; across the room was the billionaire Robert Powers, whose larger-than-life stature made him stand out.

Chris recognized Danielle in the center of another group. He knew it was she; although this radiant woman had little in common with his mental picture of the frail, wounded woman his friend Jones had described. Danielle Peschard was more beautiful than he could have imagined. She was about five-foot-eight and looked much younger than her thirty-five years. In the last couple of weeks, he had learned an awful lot about her but had never imagined her to be so stunning. Chris could not take his eyes off Danielle—a fact that left him slightly light-headed. He was love-struck.

Danielle was a red-haired Aphrodite in a black jersey shift that draped off one shoulder. On her feet were mile-high satin sandals. Close around her slender, creamy neck she wore a heavy gold necklace with a Roman coin—the ancient artifact setting perfectly in the small indentation at the base of her throat. Her hair was parted in the middle and fell gracefully to her shoulders. She was the epitome of natural elegance. The man with her had to be the guest of honor, his mannerisms dictated by his nationality. It was also obvious the French archeologist did not feel at ease in his dark suit.

A waiter approached Chris with a tray of champagne. He picked up a glass and ambled casually about the room. He looked at Robert Powers again . . . definitely imposing. Another man—a latecomer, like himself—walked in. Chris turned around and introduced himself. The man extended his hand cordially.

"Thomas O'Neil. I was afraid I'd be unforgivably late, like in the past." He reached for a champagne glass from the tray of a passing waiter.

"You must be Ms. O'Neil's ex-husband," said Chris.

"Yes, we used to be married."

At that moment, they saw Kitzia gliding toward them in clouds of sky-blue chiffon.

"So glad both of you are here!" She kissed Tom first. I see you have met Chris Goodman."

"We just met," said Tom.

"Let me introduce you to Jean-Christophe, and you, Chris, have never met Danielle."

The three of them walked in the direction of Danielle's group. From the corner of his eye, Chris watched the president and the cardinal walk out of the room and enter an adjacent one. Chris assumed it was the library. Two men followed them and remained on guard outside the door.

Tom kissed Danielle and whispered something in her ear that made her smile. She then turned to Chris.

"This is Chris Goodman," said Kit. "I was telling you about him."

"Welcome, Mr. Goodman. May I introduce Dr. Jean-Christophe Girard. I believe we'll be hearing a lot about him."

"Nice to meet you. That was some discovery!" said Chris, extending his hand.

The Frenchman smiled proudly.

"Dr. Jean-Christophe Girard . . . Dr. Tom O'Neill." Kitzia's formality in introducing her ex-husband and her friend betrayed a hint of apprehension.

The two men shook hands, and Chris did not fail to notice Kitzia's sigh of relief. Later on, she'd tell him her fears. Tom had always expressed a disdain for homosexuals, and she had feared he might not be friendly toward Jean-Christophe. Noticing her suspicion proved unfounded, she was enchanted at their mutual cordiality. Furthermore, Tom became immediately interested in the bandage on Jean-Christophe's hand. The Frenchman explained—pointing to his ankle—that he had sprained both extremities when he fell on his last day on the dig. Tom seemed genuinely interested in the condition of the ankle, and Chris took the opportunity to turn to Danielle.

"You have a beautiful art collection," he said, hoping to engage her in a private conversation. "Is that Picasso on the stairway from the Maar collection?"

"It is. Would you like to see it?"

"I'd love to."

They started walking toward the foyer.

"I've read your books," said Danielle. "I admire your brutal honesty." He knew it was not meant to flatter his ego, but it did. "It is nice to see that you and Kitzia have settled your differences."

"As a reporter and a law enforcement officer, it was hard to believe in metaphysics. I have to deal in facts."

"And now?"

"Kitzia's insight proved me wrong. She has a gift I don't have."

"She had influences you did not have. She grew up in an atmosphere of extremes, with a dogmatic father and a highly intuitive mother."

They had reached the top of the stairway and stood in front of the Picasso abstract. Danielle stopped to check Chris's reaction. It pleased her to see he was intellectually keeping up with her. "You admired and singled out this painting because you have been schooled to choose the best."

Chris blushed. It was obvious Danielle knew he came from a privileged background, one he often downplayed. He liked the idea of having others think of him as a self-made man. Despite multiple threats of disinheritance, he had pursued what he liked. He had grown up surrounded by works of art and had been taught to be discriminating. Perhaps he had hated what wealth did to little boys—it separated them from their parents.

His father, a veritable workaholic, was obsessed with making money. The only words Chris remembered coming from him were those of advice regarding investments. His mother, despite her lavish gifts and display of affection, had little time for him. All her energy and enthusiasm were spent on her many charity and social functions. Chris's true family had been the household staff and the security guards at the gate of the exclusive complex where his house was located. He would ride his bike to the gate and spend long afternoons with the policemen who worked the gate during their off hours. He would listen to fantastic stories about the heroic officers and the various ruffians they encountered. To the dismay of his family, upon graduating from high school, he announced he wanted to be a police officer. For three years, he patrolled the streets and chased petty criminals, much to the embarrassment of his parents. Afterward, he went into the Army, then put himself through college and majored in journalism. He knew he could make the two things he loved work for him.

He remembered the smile of satisfaction on his mother's face on his graduation day, followed by her dumbstruck horror when he informed her of his intention to rejoin the police force. He came to understand that their continued disapproval gave him the opportunity to be free.

Knowing what he was thinking, Danielle added, "You chose the environment you came into because it gave you a good frame of reference from which to make your departure. From it, you took what you needed—education—and discarded what you abhorred, the pompousness and snobbery of political correctness. Had you been born into poverty, your first objective would have been to escape and run in the direction of education and affluence, which you would have, eventually, put aside to be free to search—a much longer journey, you see."

Chris laughed at her wit, knowing she was absolutely right, although he had never viewed the course of his life from that perspective. "My father wanted to go on living forever; he wanted to ensure I followed in his footsteps and became his image."

Chris was shocked he had uttered those words. He had never before admitted that his father had dangled his inheritance in an effort to subjugate him.

"Now," she continued, "your knowledge of art tells you it is the most expensive one in the collection. So you are impressed that I have the means and the taste to have acquired it. I assure you I picked it out for totally different reasons."

Once again, he thought Danielle's face to be the most beautiful face he had ever seen. "Please, tell me exactly what it was that drew you to the painting," he asked.

"The freedom of expression," answered Danielle. "The brushstroke in the outline of the woman and dog is an unbroken line that moves with the simplicity of a romantic melody. Not all of Picasso's work has this freshness and spontaneity. Some of his work betrays the madness of his genius.

"This was painted during one of his happiest moments. The thoughts and feelings of an artist are forever imprinted in the canvas. Picasso's thoughts at that moment are playful and full of mischief. He successfully executed the message as a reminder of the playfulness of existence.

"The truth that most eludes us all is that this art is simply a piece of cloth upon which dabs of paint have been distributed. An accumulation of molecules joined together for an infinitesimally brief moment in time, void of emotion or even color—a mere illusion. We are in front of an accumulation of gray matter. The sooner you realize that, the closer you will be to absolute freedom."

Chris wished he had something clever to say, but he did not. What she had said rang like madness in his heart. Yet somewhere within his soul, it was welcomed as an utterance of indisputable truth.

"I am glad you are here, Chris Goodman. I have wanted to meet you for a long, long time."

They walked downstairs in silence. Someone was signaling Danielle. "Please make yourself at home."

Chris felt an unfounded pang of jealousy. Though he knew it was childish, he didn't want to share Danielle with the rest of the guests and wished they could have continued their conversation for hours. But he barely knew her and had already monopolized her time.

Mingling with the guests, Chris discovered Angela had been Danielle's private nurse during the last six weeks, and John Larkin had known Danielle for over twenty years. His heart lightened when he realized he would soon learn more about Danielle's private life. All the while, he noticed that neither the president nor the cardinal had emerged from the library. In fact, a rolling cart was now being wheeled in that direction. It appeared they would not be joining the rest of the guests for dinner.

Angela did not feel like talking about Danielle's recovery. She casually shifted the conversation to more current and lighter affairs, and Chris focused more on John Larkin as his source of information. He learned John had met Danielle in Europe and had kept in touch with her over the years.

With no formal seating arrangements, the three of them shared a table with a young couple from New York. The woman introduced herself as Linda Teresi, Danielle's private assistant in New York. Her boyfriend, Ricardo, was in the fashion business and worked for Donna Karan.

Linda was more than happy to talk about Danielle. "She was absolutely wonderful, from the day I started working for her."

"The most extraordinary person I've ever met," added John Larkin.

"How did you say you first met her?" asked Chris, hoping that by having John repeat the story he might pick up something new about her.

"In Europe, right before I was admitted to Cornell. Danielle leased a yacht that summer. I didn't know such a world existed. You know, I was having such a hard time just floating my education. Then the grant that made it all possible came. I always suspected it was her behind it. Though, she won't talk about it. That is the greatest thing about her. Under no circumstances would she want to diminish my personal sense of accomplishment. But I know better."

Chris smiled. Much of what was being said touched him personally. He imagined for a second that the woman they were praising belonged to him. Chris cast a glance in Danielle's direction and immediately realized the absurdity of his thoughts. Danielle was engrossed in conversation with the billionaire Powers. For the first time in his life, he understood what jealousy meant. He could have sworn Powers guessed what he was thinking because he shot Chris a glance that made him shrivel.

"Even though I'm now well-established," John continued, "Danielle must guess the pay at Arecibo is not great, so she keeps me occupied on my off time with different projects."

"What kinds of projects?" Chris became very interested.

"The movement pattern of certain stars, random noise, the approach of RA, the cold interstellar body in the constellation of Orion, which we are mapping at Arecibo, anyway."

"You are working at SETI?"

"Yes."

"So, this is Danielle's hobby?"

"I suppose it has been. Recently, she has shown a keen interest in a particular area."

"What area is that?"

"I am afraid I am not at liberty to say. We have a confidentiality agreement." Chris had finally hit on something. Some of the strange documents Kit had been interested in had to be originating from Arecibo.

"You recently sent a star chart . . ."

John looked at him with renewed interest, although there was nothing secret about that particular document. "Yes, Danielle requests that I keep her informed on the position of some stars at certain given coordinates on specific days. I have always assumed she is compiling data that would coincide with her own archeological research."

Without wanting to disrupt the train of the conversation, Chris pulled a small piece of paper from his wallet. He had photocopied the symbols in the presumed angelic writing but had been unsuccessful in finding anyone who could decipher it. He unfolded the paper and handed it to John.

"Was that part of what you sent her?"

John looked at it and responded, "No."

Linda joined in. "May I?" She took the paper from John's hand. "I recognize the symbols. I don't know what they mean, though."

"Where have you seen them?"

"In Danielle's office. From time to time, things like that come in through the fax machine."

"From whom?"

"Some colleague who might want them deciphered. I'm really not sure."

Chris wanted to put the paper away. He had not meant for it to become part of a wider discussion and didn't wish for Danielle to find out he and Kit had gotten into her private correspondence. He reached to take it from Linda's hand. Angela looked at the symbols as the paper was being passed back.

"You should ask Ms. Peschard's physical therapist." She pointed to an athletic-looking young man chatting with a young girl. "I think I have seen those symbols scribbled on some of the notes he takes."

"OK. I will." He put the paper away.

John asked Angela to dance, and they headed for the terrace. Linda and Ricardo continued kidding and amusing themselves as young people do.

"Tell me, Linda," Chris broke in. "You seem happy working for Danielle."

"I am. She got Ricardo a job in the field he loves."

Ricardo added, "I was trained in fashion design, but all I could find in this very competitive city was a job repping a line. Linda talked to Danielle, and she got me to interview with Donna Karan. I am now a production assistant for DKNY—still not designing, but Danielle is sure it will happen. She says I must learn every trick of the trade."

"She is awesome," said Linda. "We miss her in New York. It's good to hear she is coming back soon."

"Really? When?" Chris suddenly felt like an outsider, which he was . . . well, until a few weeks ago.

"Very soon. In a week or so."

Chris had barely settled down in the beach house and liked it. He had imagined himself comfortably writing and conducting his investigation, which Kit had now put on the back burner, because of Danielle's recovery. He figured the matter of the man who had disappeared from the hospital would now be put to rest. Yet it was something the writer in him could not abandon. The whole affair around Dr. Peschard had stimulated his imagination. It was all too mysterious, too exciting. There was so much intrigue around those two beautiful women who rubbed elbows with the most powerful. He had found all the components for a great mystery. It was true he had promised Kit not to write anything about this, but he knew in time, he'd find an honorable way to renege on such a promise.

Chris would write about what he was about to experience. What he did not know was that it would not be a glamorous mystery that would bring him fame, but a much more profound book that would influence the way people thought for centuries to come.

"I hope you are having a good time," said Kit, taking Angela's seat.

"Let's dance." Chris led her toward the dance floor.

Neither of them missed the smile of approval on Danielle's face as they walked by.

"What did you think about Danielle?"

"She is beautiful, intelligent, witty, and everybody adores her," Chris answered.

"True. What I meant was, and this is probably hard for you to say since you didn't know her before, but does she seem OK to you?"

"More than OK. She seems perfect."

"Everyone is saying that, and yet—she still seems a little different . . . distant," Kit admitted.

"How?"

"Well, everything is fine if we are with other people. But she is avoiding spending time with me. I'm the one person in the world that would know if something is not totally back to normal."

"Give it time," Chris said.

"I suppose so."

"I was hoping to have a chance to speak to Jean-Christophe . . ."

"You'll get your chance," Kit replied. "People will start leaving and then there will be a more intimate group. Be sure to stay."

They watched Jean-Christophe return to the table where he had been sitting and pick up the conversation with Tom.

"It's seldom I see Tom enjoy himself like this," sighed Kit. "He has always worked so hard and taken life so seriously. I could never get him to relax. Look at him now; he is actually laughing. He must be mellowing with age. Life should have always been like this. I thought he might feel uncomfortable with Jean-Christophe, but I was wrong. Maybe I was wrong about a lot of other things. . . . Remember, do not leave." She walked back to her table.

By now, just about everybody had gotten up from the tables and had begun mingling again. The door to the library remained closed, which piqued Chris's curiosity. He noticed the door adjacent to the room where the men were meeting and guessed it might be a powder room. Perhaps he would go in and see if he could hear something of what was going on.

"Wow! That's Lili Keller!" exclaimed Linda behind him.

Chris turned around to see a very tall, slim woman enter on the arm of Senator Nielsen. The Republican senator had often been in the spotlight, and there was a constant swirl of controversy around him in Washington. He was a major opponent of gun control reform. Lili's face was well known too, frequently appearing in the media. Chris had, despite public opinion, never considered her beautiful. He had always found something extreme about her, whether her astonishing height or her immoderate slimness.

Chris watched with interest as Robert and Danielle walked up to greet them. The greeting was civil, but the stiffness in their demeanors bespoke their irritation with the arrival of these two. The four exchanged peremptory handshakes and spoke without smiling, and Lili effected a counterfeit, socially correct charm. Chris would have given anything to know what was being said. Danielle separated from the group and went in the direction of the library where the security guards still flanked the door. The senator engaged with the other Washington, DC politicos, and Lili and Robert moved aside, involved in a little tete-a-tete.

"Lili, I thought I made it clear that you were not to come," said Robert.

"We all have to do what we are asked to do," she whispered as she picked up a glass of champagne.

From another corner of the room, Jean-Christopher exclaimed, "That is a tall woman! She is pretty though," he added, calculating that she had to be as tall as he.

"It's Lili Keller," Kit said. "I don't know what she is doing here. She was certainly not on the list. Danielle has never liked her."

Lili had, as usual, made heads turn. Chris heard Linda's voice again from behind him. "She owns Montaigne Enterprises and Keller-DeWinter Fashion Group. That is exactly who Ricardo wants to work for. We have never been able to reach her." Linda withheld the fact that she had mentioned it to Danielle in the past, and it had been the one comment Danielle had always ignored.

"Well, this opportunity is as good as any. Come, I'll introduce you." Chris said.

"Do you know her?"

"No. I'll meet her now too." He signaled Linda and Ricardo to follow him.

Chris understood why Lili was intimidating and unapproachable. She wore an air of self-importance that could not be denied.

"*La Deesse de la Couture!* [The goddess of fashion!]" exclaimed Chris.

Lili turned at the sound of his voice and smiled. He had been right in assuming that exorbitant flattery was the path to engaging her.

"I'm Christian Goodman. I did not have the opportunity to meet you at the Bal de Tete in Paris last spring, which I've regretted ever since."

"You were there?"

"I was," he lied. "And I must say, you were the true fashion goddess of the evening. I would like you to meet my friends, Linda Teresi and Ricardo Duran. I felt it was imperative that you meet one of our newest talents in New York. Ricardo is currently working for Donna Karan. He is a gifted designer. I think you should see his work."

At first, Lili eyed the young couple with a hint of disdain, but something changed in her expression when she heard the names Jeff had mentioned previously. Chris witnessed the sudden change with intrigue. Her facial muscles relaxed, and her sapphire eyes lit up as she smiled.

"I suppose I should. Can't let the competition hoard all the talent." Then she turned to Ricardo. "Call my assistant Monday morning to set something up."

Ricardo could not contain his excitement. "I will—thank you. I know Jeff personally."

Lili had no time to reply. Danielle had just emerged from the library and stood in front of the guarded door. Lili took that as her cue, and without a word, moved toward the door to meet her. Senator Nielsen joined her in route. Danielle stared at them with an expression as cold as ice.

The door closed behind them, and Chris knew he had to find out what was going on in that room. He heard, without really listening, the profuse expressions of gratitude from the young couple for the introduction to Lili. He excused himself and headed for the powder room.

The walls that separated the library from the bathroom were thicker than Chris would have expected, and despite his effort to make out what was being said, he could only pick out random phrases such as *truce, others, inaccessible entrance . . .* Something was being negotiated. He left the powder room and rejoined the party. He continued to mingle, determined to speak to every guest, if only for a moment.

Chris had the opportunity to speak with Robert Powers, who, despite his commanding presence and earlier irritation, turned out to be surprisingly friendly. When the library door opened, Robert's head turned toward the door with an interest as keen as his. They watched the hostile couple stride out of the room. Lili wore a frozen smile, while the Senator's face was flushed with anger.

"I could swear they did not reach a congenial agreement," Chris kidded. Robert excused himself. He reached the library at the precise moment Danielle walked out. Chris watched them speak for a few minutes, after which Robert kissed her cheek and left. Danielle returned to the party, her charm restored, and cordially said her goodbyes to the guests who were taking their leave. Chris noticed that Jean-Christophe went into the library and shortly after, John Larkin was summoned as well. Kitzia, still by Tom's side, kissed the last of the guests goodbye.

What remained was the intimate group Kitzia had asked him to join. In the living room were Angela, the therapist, and the tall dark man who had reappeared in the company of another man—not a guest obviously, for he was wearing a casual white turtleneck.

Despite Kitzia's earlier request that he stay, he felt it appropriate to take his leave.

"Please stay," repeated Kitzia. "Danielle asked me to make sure you and Tom stay as part of a more intimate gathering."

Chris saw no reason to object; he thought there might still be a chance for a personal introduction to the president. The waiters were busy picking up empty glasses, and the musicians had stopped playing. Apparently, he and Tom would be asked into the library, so he was not surprised when Kit came up to him and took his arm. "Shall we?"

They walked behind Danielle, who was leading Tom into the room.

The president greeted them by name, and Danielle showed them where to sit. The spacious library had served as a sitting room for the two distinguished guests. The walls were covered with French Impressionist masterpieces, all displayed in masterfully carved wooden frames. There was an eclectic combination of French and modern furniture, along with two comfortable leather sofas and massive armchairs covered in a mushroom shade of suede.

The president took his seat behind a large pine desk, and the cardinal occupied an armchair to the side. John Larkin, intimidated perhaps by the presence of the two dignitaries, had placed himself on one of the smallest chairs by the French windows, while Jean-Christophe, somewhat stupefied, remained standing by the fireplace.

The waiters had taken the opportunity to serve coffee. Moving to their assigned seats, no one spoke while the cups were passed. Kitzia and Tom situated themselves on one of the sofas, and Chris and Danielle sat on the other. In the back of the room, against bookshelves containing antique leather-bound books, Camiel stood next to Zephon—in his white turtleneck—Angela, Lenny, and Joe. As the door closed behind the last of the waiters, Danielle spoke. "It was a hard decision to bring you into this. After much deliberation, it was President Parker who decided that we do."

"We have a situation," added the president, "that we can no longer ignore. Some of you have known Danielle for a long time and, without knowing it, have been under her protection. But times have become extremely dangerous for the *Foundation,* and I must step in at this time to reinforce security. But I cannot lie to you; there will be times when you will have to rely on your wits for survival. It is only fair that we instruct you on how to identify the threat, so that's why we are here tonight, to run down the list of precautions."

Too astonished to ask questions, all gave the president their full attention.

"It should no longer be a secret that Danielle's injury was no accident. It was a premeditated criminal assault, an intolerable act of cowardice, and an affront to our organization. I want to thank you all for your collaboration in saving and protecting her life." He said, directing his words to the group in the back. The eyes of the president and Danielle met and silently agreed she should continue with the details.

"I'm sorry, Kit, that I got you involved. After I was attacked, I gave you something that had to be protected at all costs. In his attempt to protect it, one of our agents lost his life. I had no choice but to place it in your hands for safekeeping. We will now take that back from you and lower the danger it brought you.

"This is the reason I have been avoiding you, but only as a means of taking the focus off of you. I was so afraid you would mention that you have the stone, and that knowledge in the wrong hands puts your life in danger. I wasn't sure to what extent I was being monitored. Alone, you did what I would have done, wisely and quietly enlist the help of those whom you trust." She looked at Tom and Chris. "In doing so, they have become involved as well, and from now on, will also need our protection. Tom, you have been extraordinary and the primary instrument for my recovery. And I know that even now, you remain in constant jeopardy, both physically and professionally, at the hospital."

Kitzia looked at him in dismay. He had not mentioned any further problems, past the original incidents when Danielle was at the hospital.

"What you discovered is true. Something was implanted in me that monitors and relays information. I am being helped to overcome it both mentally and physically, and eventually, we'll figure out what to do about it."

"Who are you?" Chris finally asked, voicing the question the others were afraid to ask.

She would have answered it had the president not intervened. "We are a secret organization devoted to maintaining peace on earth. Cardinal Santis is here as a representative for the head of the *Foundation*. Situations arise from time to time that we have to deal with to maintain order and balance on the planet. There is another organization—we call it the *Group*—whose ideology conflicts with ours. They feel they have as much of a right to be here as we do and want to direct the destiny of the world—according to their desires.

"For millennia, we have moved in parallel paths with our pursuits, assuming we would prove right. However, time is running out. That now places us in open conflict."

Chris noticed that Jean-Christophe, John, Tom and Kit were as speechless as he was, but Angela and the rest of the group behind them were not in the least bit surprised by anything said.

Startled and a little frightened, Chris voiced the first concerns that came to him. "Why would they come after Dr. Peschard? What could your opponents gain from injuring a private citizen, even if she is a member of your organization?"

"She is a highly placed member. They suspect she has information they need. We don't mean to sound elusive, but there are facts we are not free to discuss yet, mostly for your own good. The less you know the better."

"I don't understand," continued Chris. "I believed Dr. Peschard had been injured by a bolt of lightning."

"She was."

"You don't mean—"

"Yes, unfortunately her injury alerted us to the fact our enemies are attempting to manipulate the atmosphere."

"*C'est fou*!" exclaimed Jean-Christophe. "That is absurd!"

"There are atmospheric currents that originate somewhere deep inside the planet," continued the president. "They have gained control of at least one of them."

John Larkin, without speaking, began to understand. He realized this meeting's discussion had given substance to a lot of what Danielle had asked him to monitor.

The president then turned to Larkin. "You, Mr. Larkin, have done an outstanding job. You have provided us with information that is aiding us in locating their base of operations. What Danielle asked you in particular the night she was attacked is very important to us, and we wish you to know it's imperative that you continue your monitoring and investigation. There are likely to be other signals. We must locate the origin of those transmissions. The planetary blackout was intentional; it was a preliminary test. There will undoubtedly be others to follow."

The president then turned to Jean-Christophe. "Dr. Girard, Danielle related to me your experience in the tombs. To assuage your doubt, we can assure you that it was a real experience. The collapse took place and you fell. You located the Chamber of Sharah."

"But the others on my team saw nothing. They assured me the dig had not collapsed."

"It did. What they saw was an illusion fabricated to prevent others from going in. You came across the medians, who, thank goodness, are still with us. They saw you wearing the sign of Michael and knew they had to help you. You mentioned that they talked about the arrival of the others. That means the *Group,* with their new alien recruits, has also found the site and is already searching for what we are seeking in the tomb. It is imperative that we go back as soon as possible to retrieve it before they find it. We will be asking you to return and help us.

"The blackout and subsequent attacks on our members dictate that we implement intense safety measures. This house, for one, will become a 'safe house' where we can meet. The *Foundation's* scheduled meeting was canceled because Danielle was not present. Our main objective then became to find her and protect her. You all heard about the attempt on my life—one more indication they are getting desperate.

"The medals given to you serve three purposes: they identify you as members or friends of the *Foundation*, prove that you're under its protection, and alert us to your location."

The president next addressed Chris. "Mr. Goodman, will you take this?" He handed him a chain with a medal. Chris immediately recognized it as the medal he had acquired at the hospital, the one belonging to their lost agent. "Our agents will always identify you, and when activated . . ." Parker pushed a switch, and a bookcase behind him opened, displaying a large screen and a complex conglomeration of buttons. ". . . it can pinpoint your location anywhere on the globe."

On the screen was a three-dimensional map of the world, where tiny specks of light flickered like stars in the firmament. There was an inset map of North America and another of California, where the flickering lights became more widely scattered. When another button was pressed, the screen zoomed in on Danielle's house. A double beam of blue light surrounded the property.

"The double Code Blue!" exclaimed Kitzia.

Above the house, a dome of a lighter blue concealed the property.

"It is a shield composed of an element not known on Earth."

"What is it called?" John Larkin wanted to know.

"Veregonium." The president then remained silent for a few seconds, giving the others a chance to absorb all they had just heard.

"If at any time you feel threatened, you may come here," said Danielle. "Come to the gate, and as long as you are wearing the insignia, the gate will open when you say your name. The couple that arrived earlier, Senator Nielsen and Ms. Keller, came tonight as representatives of the *Group*. We have agreed on a temporary truce. However, the members of the *Group* have been known in the past to break their promises; therefore, their word holds little weight. It is better to be on constant alert."

She then turned to the group in the back. "Let me introduce you. . . . This is Camiel." The man with the pale green eyes bowed courteously. "He was sent to protect me while I was vulnerable." Her eyes moved to the man in the white turtleneck. "Zephon, as you have already guessed, is no vagrant. He has tenaciously guarded the gates of this place for some time and is capable of frightening not only the fainthearted. And Lenny and Joe, who work with Camiel, came as technicians to the hospital to ensure our safety."

"Messengers," said Parker. "Even though, at times, they have to act as guardians."

The cardinal, who had been listening quietly, finally spoke. "I have never before witnessed such cowardly and brutal attacks on our members. His Holiness believes this has dictated the need for a review and adjustment to our modus operandi." There was kindness yet a force in his voice, which Danielle had always admired. "We have dedicated our lives to the preservation of peace, but now that the core of our belief system is being threatened along with our existence, we have to act. We are first and always the Keepers of the Truth and vassals of our Creator. If war is being launched against Him once more, we must protect His Kingdom on all levels. If fight we must; we will fight!"

"Forgive me," interrupted Chris. "You are talking of things that are beyond human comprehension. Spiritual warfare? A group that is technologically advanced enough to manipulate the atmosphere, to make bodies disappear without a trace, and erase identities?" Chris could not forget the incident involving Mr. Ullman. "And you are capable of producing invisible domes and coexisting with angels—messengers? I want to know . . . I need to know what exactly is going on? I am, as you previously stated, already involved. Therefore, I think I have the right to have some of my personal questions answered, like . . ." He turned to Danielle. "You did not exactly answer my previous question, Danielle. Who are you?"

"Mr. Goodman," the president interrupted, "I have already stated that at this point, the less you know, the better."

"If I am already involved, with all due respect Mr. President, I'll decide what is best for me."

Danielle intervened. "You are right, and we had no right to bring you into this. I did not think it was a good idea, and perhaps it would be better if . . ."

"Now, wait a minute. I simply want to make the decision for myself." He was so intrigued, but didn't want to risk being dismissed.

"It is our duty to let you know what is happening, but only you can decide if you are with us and willing to help us. Circumstances brought you into this, but you can walk away and forget this meeting ever took place," concluded the president.

"I can't exactly forget what has happened here and what you have revealed."

"Yes, you can," said Danielle. "We have the means to make you forget."

"What exactly does that mean?"

"You can walk away, and tomorrow, when you wake up, you will remember nothing. You'll be eager to return home and continue with your novel."

"It is still our responsibility to look after your safety, and we will do anything within our means to protect you." The president seemed to be addressing Kit and

Tom as well. It was evident that John Larkin and Jean-Christophe, during their earlier meeting, had already pledged their allegiance to the cause of the *Foundation.*

"No need to ask me," said Kitzia. "You know I'll always stand by you, Danielle."

To Kit's surprise, Tom placed his hand over hers and said firmly. "So will I."

Chris watched them and picked up on Kit's emotion, realizing how much in love she still was with Tom. It took him a moment to answer. He had no reservations about what he was about to do; he was simply trolling for more information. Danielle looked him in the eyes. He knew then that he'd go to the depths of the earth if she asked him. What he did not know was that it was precisely what she would ask him to do one day, and that he would do it gladly.

"I'm in," he said finally. "But please indulge me. You told me a little bit about your *Foundation* but not about yourselves."

"Mr. Goodman, you will find out more about us and our cause than you might possibly want to know." The president's words seemed vague and distant.

Chris did not press further. Danielle had taken his hand and gently whispered, "Thank you."

XII

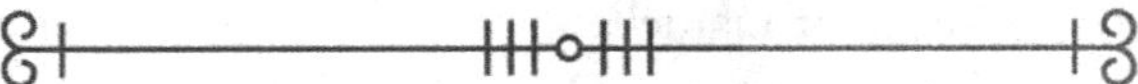

The seventy-ninth floor of the Keller Building in New York City was where the *Group* held its general meetings. The building's location on Park Avenue, with its high traffic and private elevators, made it accessible to all *Group* members. They could come and go without being recognized.

Lili knew of all scheduled meetings ahead of time and would make a point to drop by. The matters discussed, for the most part, had to do with political situations, and she tried to remain uninvolved. Recently, she had been asked to attend all meetings and become more active in the affairs of the *Group*. She feared that her attendance at the Peschard party marked a new entanglement with the *Group* that she was not sure she wanted.

She had been asked to accompany Senator Nielsen to Danielle's party to deliver a message because the *Group* had feared the senator, given his penchant for outbursts of temper, might not be a model of diplomacy. Lili was an Edentian—but one uninvolved in the current conflicts. Robert Powers would have been the *Group's* first choice. But they were aware Robert, despite his open neutrality, had uncertain allegiances, and Robert's close relationship with Danielle would be of tremendous importance later on.

Despite having known Danielle for eons, Lili had failed to recognize her in her present incarnation. Seeing her again face-to-face had been unsettling. There was a peace and reassurance in Danielle, which Lili had lost a long time ago.

This morning, Senator Nielsen and some of his colleagues from Washington sat at the center of the oval table in the conference room. The advertising executives, who worked strictly for the *Group* and at times collaborated with Keller Enterprises, sat to the side. Lili and Robert Powers positioned themselves at the other end. A large screen appeared as the doors to a huge bookcase slid open. One of the advertising assistants started the projection. The purpose for the meeting was a review of a taped presentation of one of Theodore Edwards's television broadcasts to his ardent congregation. Any other time, Lili would have excused herself, but now, the *Group* insisted on her presence. She was to become more involved in his career and more supportive of his ambition. The *Group* would maneuver his career and ensure his success. She was to manipulate his greed and his sexuality.

The advertising team was furiously taking notes in preparation for their critique—Ted's pose, tone of voice, and stance were carefully evaluated. Lili's mind kept wandering. The image of Danielle kept flashing before her eyes, teasing her into anger and irritability. Robert, as an Edentian, picked up on her thoughts. His look reprimanded her and jolted her back to the present.

"The suit is a shade too dark. Ted looks better in beige," she volunteered to show she was paying attention.

"The hair is thinning too much," said one of the image consultants.

"Let's get him a hairpiece, and for Pete's sake, get him to lose ten pounds," added Nielsen with annoyance.

"He still looks like a used car salesman, not God's emissary," said Robert.

Lili smiled, amused. She wished Ted could hear how they really saw him. She looked at the screen and unexpectedly felt a surge of pity for this man whom they had chosen as the "emissary." They would groom him, use him, and dispose of him in a second when he was no longer of use to them. *Poor, stupid Ted.* She sighed.

The camera zoomed in on Theodore, and the volume increased as he continued his rehearsed speech. "Christ said to his disciples: Go and become fishermen of souls! And I say unto you, we've got to catch the fish!"

"Hold it!" exclaimed someone, and the screen froze, leaving a cartoon image of the minister with puckered lips and his fist raised in the air. "That will make a good billboard—let's adjust the image. We haven't used the fish nonsense before, have we?"

"I don't believe so," another voice answered.

"Next!" It was Nielsen's voice. The projection fast-forwarded. "Let's work on the Thanksgiving sermon. That's going to be a big one! We've got forty-five channels across the nation." He turned to Robert. "Is it a go?"

Robert nodded. "Yes." Powers Occidental Broadcasting was to line up the markets for Theodore Edwards's TV appearance on Thanksgiving.

"The message has to be clear, gentle, and generic. Let's see what we have so far."

Theodore Edwards reappeared onscreen. He stood behind a table set for a traditional Thanksgiving meal with a horn of plenty and spilled fruit. In his basso voice, Theodore began his prayer. "This Thanksgiving will be a very special occasion. Sadly, skeptics and modernists, view this day as just another holiday. Let's remind—"

"Whoa . . . whoa . . . stop it!" exclaimed Nielsen. "He can't start attacking and passing judgment before dinner. We don't want anyone to turn off their TV."

"That kind of sugar-coated bigotry only goes well with his congregation, where the average IQ is at or below room temperature," added Robert humorously.

They all laughed.

"He needs further coaching on national appearances. Next!"

The clips that followed showed Theodore walking through Disney World alongside his wife and two children.

"The wife is too mousy," said Nielsen, "and the children have buck teeth."

"People relate to the commonness of their appearance."

"Can't do Disney World, anyway. Have you forgotten it was boycotted a few years ago by the Evangelicals?" added Lili humorously.

"Yeah, I remember something about it but refresh my memory."

"It had something to do with Disney allowing homosexuals to spend their honeymoons in the park. Mickey Mouse became an affront to Christianity," added Lili.

They laughed again.

"How did we end up with all this evangelical nonsense?" a Washington consultant wanted to know.

"It was the one up for grabs," Robert said sarcastically. "Open positions for the greedy and ruthless."

"I see," added Nielsen with annoyance. "Let's review the interview for the *New York Times*. We've got real problems with the direction. Hand me the actual article." The newspaper clipping was produced and handed to him. He read the headline: "Theodore Edwards, Chairman of the Church."

"I see what you mean," commented one of the associates.

The projection began. Theodore sat behind an enormous modern desk. His pose was that of a corporate executive. He began speaking to the interviewer. "We are a church, but we are also a corporation, responsible to our members. Members of our congregation like to know their money is well spent."

"The worship centers definitely show it," said the interviewer. "How much would you say this center cost?"

"About fifty million, and we have eighty-nine of them across the country so far," Ted said proudly.

The projection ended abruptly. Robert was the first to speak. "Well, it looks like we have inflated his ego to the maximum."

"Perfectly calculated," assured Nielsen. "What do you say, Lili?"

She raised her shoulders. "He feels God has called upon him to be a leader. He has tasted power, the worst of aphrodisiacs, and has also fallen in love with himself."

"Pride has taken root in his soul," murmured Robert.

Nielsen smiled approvingly. "Pride . . . hmm."

"Yes, pride," continued Lili, "the ruin of Agamemnon. Pride that made Luciel turn against his Creator and launch the worst rebellion in the history of the universe. Manipulate that pride, and you'll have what you want."

"Well said, Lili! And it is up to you to foment that feeling."

The door opened. Servers appeared, carrying trays of delicacies, and an armoire opened to reveal a fully stocked bar. The *Group* members relaxed and conversed casually among themselves.

The words Lili had uttered revived in Robert's long repressed, painful memories—the chaos that spread throughout the galaxies, and how it had affected his destiny and that of his associates. Although the Edentians had not been involved in the insurrection, they had been trapped in the aftermath.

Earth was not the paradise of the book of Genesis. It was a planet chosen arbitrarily among many as a location for the rehabilitation of fallen angels and other repentant dissident spirits. Here, the rebel spirits were to undergo a period of purification. The rebel soul was split into a thousand fragments. Its wisdom, accumulated during eons of celestial existence, was wiped out in a second. Each soul fragment was to evolve, re-learn, and ultimately attach to other purified fragments until the soul became whole again. Transformed to human form, the rebel soul would pass through hundreds of incarnations until it achieved its state of grace once again. The purification process had been given the name "Project Urantia 606."

The rehabilitation mission was more complicated than the Edentians would have imagined. Urantia's atmosphere, filled with self-doubt and fear, had been dubbed Earth—after the lowliest of its four ruling elements.

Kadmon (Adam) and Eva were chosen to head the Urantia 606 project and ruled the planet for five hundred years. Kjell, Robert, Lilith, and Daniela were also assigned to the rehabilitation project.

Then one unforeseen event took place.

Some Edentians involved in the project, fascinated by the oddities of the planet, began their first phase of experimentation. They projected themselves into several material forms and manipulated the atmospheric conditions. They tested power, excessive pleasure, the thrill of danger, and enjoyed them. Robert, indulged in certain mortal pleasures, coveted and fell in love with Daniela—Orsef's spouse. Only Kjell remained incorruptible.

Unlike the evolving spirits, the Edentians retained certain supernatural powers, but as their immersion in mortality progressed, their ability to morph into other forms ended. They captured a human form, held it, and protected it as best they could, for they knew it would be their last. They continued to live and move through innumerable centuries in those semi-mortal bodies.

Through the ages, Robert's obsession was to find Daniela, who had separated from the project during its early stages and vanished, perhaps because of his amorous advances.

He first spotted her in the temple of Ishtar, later as a young scribe of Ramses II, and much later as a highly placed member of the Solomonic elite in Judea. After each brief encounter, she managed to disappear.

Now, 35,000 years later, they were still here. Daniela's identity was discovered by Cirel, Lili's body, which had traveled through the ages but was now withering, and Robert's neutrality and freedom were about to expire.

His involvement with the *Group*, involuntary at first, had now become too deep for his own comfort. He had originally assumed that by staying close to them, he could provide Daniela with a certain amount of protection. But now that the *Group* had zeroed in on her, Robert wondered how much longer he could protect her.

Cirel was obsessed with capturing Daniela, finding the secret to modifying DNA, locating the key of Sharah and the set of crystals and microchip instrumental for communication between worlds to open and close vortexes and to access interstellar transports. He was convinced it had a safe-keeper and was being passed on from generation to generation. The most logical group was that of "the Chosen Ones."

"Those Jews! They think they can outsmart me!" Cirel would scream in rage. His loathing had led him to persecute generations for their faith throughout the ages. As the Führer, Cirel made up his mind to annihilate them all. He stripped them of their possessions, down to the gold fillings in their teeth. But the piece never turned up. He would have succeeded in full extermination of the Jews had it not been for a mandate from Edentia that he be stopped and brought back to be tried for cruelty. Cirel barely escaped, and when the body of Hitler was found, it was nothing more than the discarded mortal shell of the terrible arch-rebel.

Cirel went into deep hiding on Earth. From his secret lair, he continued to threaten his adversaries in the *Foundation* and run the network of the *Group*.

The approach of RA, the interplanetary transport that ferried the life carriers, refocused Cirel's attention on his obsession with finding the stone. And he tried to prevent communication between RA and the *Foundation*.

Astronomers had long viewed RA as either a mysterious celestial body that moved randomly among the galaxies or as a large meteorite headed toward the solar system. The speculation was that once it entered the solar system, it would fall into the orbit of Neptune and circle the planet as a permanent fixture, causing no further threat to Earth. So far, no scientist had the slightest suspicion that RA was a ship or that it was also an organic body similar to a small planet, which carried technology beyond the imagination of even the most visionary of mortals.

The ship and its crew monitored the evolving planets of the decimal order. When the life carriers determined a planet had reached the denomination of three, they deemed it ready to receive the gift of life. For Urantia, the carriers had projected a sodium chloride order for the basis of life. The protoplasm of the planet would forever function in a suitable salt-solution habitat. Therefore, the same salty solution that housed the most primitive living cells would continue to run in the veins of all living organisms, just as it did now in the bloodstream of humans. Several hundred thousand years later, at Stage 4, living organisms were endowed with the gift of intelligence, which the life carriers considered the most valuable gift the Creator would allow. In time, they would return to evaluate the progression of these gifts and how they were being used. Those periodic checks provided markers for leaps in evolution and the advancement of civilization. Since *mind* was the most precious thing in the universe, they closely monitored its progress. Every time the evolution of life on a planet reached a predetermined goal, it would be lifted to a higher level.

The planet of Urantia, offspring of the Nebula of Andronover, had remained on level 7 for over 5,000 years. And now, the life carriers were on their way to Urantia's solar system for its periodic evaluation. If pleased with the progress, they would lift the level of understanding to a new level, an age of enlightenment. They would pick up the signal from the Edentians that would be transmitted from Earth with the use of the key of Sharah. The signal produced by the *Formation* would advise that all was well and proceeding according to plan. At that point, the course of the ship would be set in the direction of Urantia. If they did not receive the signal from the *Formation*, they would bypass Earth.

Lili had been staring at him while he reminisced. "Do you miss it?" she asked, well knowing he would understand that she meant Edentia.

"Don't you?"

"You know we can never go back home. The most we could ever hope for would be to return as ascending mortals. Cirel promised he'd find a way of getting us out. He has spoken of a newly formed nebula in the southern-most part of Splandon. There is a planet in an early stage 4."

"I never took you for a rural pioneer, roughing it through primitive planetary stages."

She surrendered a small laugh. "No. It is not like that. With the right technology, we will accelerate the process and make it habitable. We'll make it an impregnable fortress, a safe place for our displaced allies in the universe. Together again, we'll have the strength to fight all the Seraphic ships."

"That is an ambitious plan! You will need a large number of mercenaries."

Lili smiled coquettishly. "That, my love, we have all figured out."

Robert tried to conceal his interest. He had gotten the first hint as to what the rebels were after. The nebula was not the actual place they were considering as a base. Although distant and somewhat inaccessible, it was too easily visible from Splandon.

Robert saw that the others in the room were ready to resume the meeting.

"Well, I believe . . ." Senator Nielsen continued, "our choice of, and investment in, Theodore Edwards will prove correct. The masses believe he is chosen by God. We've placed him in a conservative environment, mostly Republican middle- to upper-class, that will soon recruit Latinos. As we discussed previously, the uneducated masses will be better manipulated through their forthcoming conversion to Islam," Nielsen reminded them.

"How much revenue did each of the churches under his ministry bring in last year?"

"About one hundred million, give or take," the voice of a CPA answered.

"Excellent! Edwards will float his own conversions from now on. We need to give him extra exposure and expand his patriotic image. People need to imagine the possibility of him as a political leader."

"Not all people want to see their spiritual leader so involved in politics." said one of the publicists.

"We'll play on their phobias. We'll stage some terrorist attacks. Anyone can be manipulated through fear. One way or another, we are going to take the country! Protestants, Catholics, and eventually Black Muslims will be behind Theodore Edwards.

"We have officially begun Phase I. We will be going into Latin America earlier than scheduled. Theodore Edwards's ministries will start opening in small towns in Mexico, Guatemala, Costa Rica, and Brazil. "Despite the poverty of the rural areas we are targeting, we will get a phenomenal response. We will be dealing in volume. We will arrive with food, medical supplies, and Bibles—lots of Bibles. I really don't think it will be too hard to turn Latinos against the Catholic Church that has held them prisoner for centuries. Our coup de grace will be to convince them that the worship of saints is a deadly sin in fundamental Christianity. When released from the grip of their saint-centric, fear-mongering priests, they will be as docile as sheep.

"Once we have everyone familiar with the Scriptures, we can start matching world events with those foretold in the Bible. Theodore Edwards will not only be the political and spiritual leader of the mightiest nation in the world, but also God's emissary.

"We'll stage an attempt on his life followed by his miraculous resurrection. Sacred scrolls will be discovered somewhere, prophesying Theodore as the chosen prophet."

"And you are sure the world will accept the writings as *authentic*?" asked Robert.

"There is only one person qualified to refute them. That is your friend, Dr. Peschard with the Met, and you will make sure that doesn't happen."

"You are moving too fast. What is the rush? You could lose it all by acting in such haste," Robert warned.

Nielsen straightened up and swallowed. "Well, gentlemen, this concludes our meeting," he snapped. "Keep up the good work. We'll meet again next week."

His words were taken as a sign of dismissal, and, gathering their notepads, portfolios, laptops and charts, everyone left the room, except Nielsen, Robert, and Lili, who remained seated and immobile.

Nielsen turned to Robert. "Haste? You call this *haste*? I am trying to do things as smoothly and discreetly as I can, so as not to betray our true purpose. Have you not heard that we've run out of time? You, of all people, should be doing everything you can to cooperate with us and not question our decisions."

"I said I'd be with you!" answered Robert firmly. "And that I would place all my earthly possessions and influence at your disposal. But I am still entitled to an opinion. And that opinion is that I seriously question your competence in handling the enormous responsibility and magnitude of power entrusted to you by the *Group*. I am getting a taste of the sloppiness with which things are being run."

Nielsen flushed crimson, and his frosty arrogance gave way. "Sloppiness? There would have been no errors had you not stepped in and interfered!"

"Interference is called for when an order can't be carried out without smashing and crushing everything in one's path. That behavior is brutish!" Robert was steely.

Nielsen took these comments as a direct affront. His arm swung back and forth in a mad attempt to punch Robert in the face, but the blow never connected. His fist was halted five inches from the Edentian's face when the senator's fist smashed into an invisible, ice-cold barrier, harder than anything Nielsen had ever contacted. It smashed every bone in his hand. The pain shot up his arm and into his chest. Everything in the room began to roll around him. The last thing he heard before he hit the floor was Lili's voice calling for an ambulance.

XIII

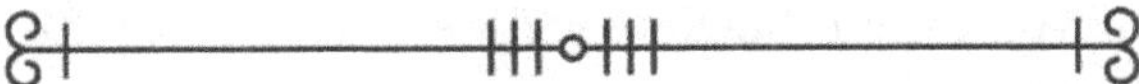

What a shame about Senator Nielsen's heart attack," Theodore whispered into the phone. "Yes, I'll review the videos and adhere to the format this time." Theodore was sitting on the edge of the bed, his back to Lili. She was tracing the outline of his ear with her fingernail while he spoke into his phone.

"What is it, darling?" she asked.

"The *Group*." He put the phone on the night table and turned to her. "They are becoming so demanding of my time."

"Poor darling! Every successful man's complaint . . . not enough time. And we waste precious time like this." Lili lowered the sheet.

"Lili, my beautiful Lili! You are the reward for all my hard work, as well as my temptation, the one I cannot resist."

"Amen."

He did not like her frequent sarcasm. It made him feel foolish, and he was no fool. Ted stood up and paced about the room.

She noticed his hurt look. "How can I be your weakness as well as your reward?"

"Life is full of contradictions," he said. "You believe in nothing but pleasure; that is why God put you on my path. I know that I can help you."

"Rehabilitate?"

"Absolutely! Jesus always said the conversion of a sinner had more merit than any other act."

"Oh, you are trying to help me!" She was having a hard time hiding her amusement but made an extraordinary effort as she continued. "I thought I was just absolutely irresistible."

"You are. You are my Mary Magdalene. I might still make out of you the biggest disciple. I believe God has handed me money, respect, and your love in exchange for doing his work."

"Apparently, God, in all His omnipotence, still needs help policing the world!"

He flinched when he heard a noise in the cabin's living room. He was always paranoid about being found out. "What is that?"

"My boys, Jeff and Ricardo. I asked them to bring us breakfast before they go fishing. They are staying at my other cabin."

"You have so many properties, Lili. So much wealth and so much loyalty from your employees. I could also ask the question. Why me? You could have any man in the world. Why choose one as complicated as I am . . . married, I mean?"

"Because it is you I want. I believe you were born for a greatness you haven't even imagined."

"Thanks," said Ted, beaming with satisfaction. "It's true. There are things I know I will accomplish that no one has ever accomplished before. I'll let you in on something. The *Group* feels the time is right to tie religion and politics together to unify the country, and they think I can do it. I'm going to be nominated for the presidency!"

"Oh!" Lili feigned surprise. "What better man than you to create a Theocracy?"

"I know." But his face showed concern.

"What is it?"

"Oh, nothing. Some of their immediate plans seem a little radical. But they know what they are doing. If, in the process of unification, we act a little harsh, then so be it."

"Harsh? In what way?"

"The *Group* thinks the first step in strengthening our position as a Christian nation is by fomenting discrimination toward other beliefs. A little fear has never hurt anyone. If that is what it takes to get the lambs back on track, we will do it."

"It worked in the Dark Ages and the Inquisition."

"These are dark ages too. What we are about to accomplish is truly great. We are starting National Youth Camps, athletics and all. We will start excluding Jewish boys from athletics, then social clubs and so on. They will feel the ostracism build and build—"

"The Jews?"

"Not only the Jews. We can't have a great nation if it is divided into segments of different religious belief. Catholics are already feeling the tyranny of the Church. We are going to take Latin America by storm. There will be an extensive building of worship centers, even in small villages that have been paying homage to the Vatican. Some of those people have never even seen the Bible!"

"Could that be because some of them can't read?"

"Not entirely. The Church wants to control and manipulate the masses. You know, once the Catholics become familiar with Scripture as we teach it, they'll toss all their saints and beliefs out the window and will stop supporting the Vatican."

"Well, of course! All that money can then go directly into your fund. You are so clever, Theodore."

Theodore looked at Lili, once again not knowing whether her flattery was sincere. Guessing he might be thinking precisely that, she feigned more interest.

"Later, you'll have to tell me more about you indoctrination—I mean, youth camps."

The little game of deceit Theodore played with others, and even with himself, made her weary. Lili got up and put her robe on. "Well, let's go out and see what they brought us for breakfast."

After Theodore took his departure, Lili decided to take the rest of the day off and went back to bed. There was so much she wanted to block out. She fell into a deep sleep and dreamed of Edentia and of a time when everything was full of promise.

Jeff used the key she had given him and was startled to find her in the living room. "I didn't see the car, so I thought you had left." He looked around. "Is your friend gone?"

"Associate," she corrected him. "Yes, it was a short meeting."

He pretended to believe her. "I just stopped by to see if the place was locked up. When would you like me to send the car for you?"

"Will you stay and drive me back?"

"Of course," he hesitated. "Let me tell Linda and Ricardo to go on."

He returned in a few minutes. There was something different about Lili. She seemed preoccupied. An unaccustomed feeling arose in him—a wish to protect her. The absurdity of the thought amused him. Lilith Keller DeWinter, vulnerable? That would be the day! He had better be prepared for whatever she had in mind.

"Some tea?" She began pouring before he had time to answer. To his surprise, she treated him like a visitor, not an employee. "I thought we might have a chance to spend a little time together, away from work."

"Great!" He hid his surprise. "I am glad the meeting with your associate was brief."

"You really don't like him, do you?"

"Does it matter whether I like him or not?"

"Perhaps not, but I'm still interested."

"I think the man is a clown."

Lili smiled as if in agreement.

"Your sense for smelling money never fails you. This man and his church are big business."

"You wouldn't buy into his dogma?" she asked.

"Me?" Jeff laughed heartily. "Never."

"You are smart, but the majority of educated people aren't."

"I agree. Education simply provides information. It does not guarantee the ability to process it properly."

She smiled with satisfaction. "Come on, let's go for a walk before it rains."

"It's a beautiful day!"

"It will rain."

Jeff set his cup down and followed her. *She is right,* he thought. The weather had been most peculiar. They walked up the road for a few minutes before the clouds darkened and began to whirl in an ominous circle. The sporadic shifts in precipitation were a frightening sign that unnatural forces were maneuvering meteorological circumstances. Even Lili feared what those currents could do when unleashed for purposes of destruction.

Like Danielle, she also suspected the end of life as they knew it was approaching. Lili had spent eons bemoaning her predicament. Condemned to live in an under-developed world, she was eager for the opportunity to escape. As the possibility of that time drew near, she felt a certain apprehension. To her surprise, she had developed an unexpected fondness for Earth, which had become her home.

"There is something I want to tell you."

Jeff was not sure where the conversation was going.

"I like your mind . . . it is far too keen to sacrifice to the Law. I am about to launch a new division in my fashion house. Ricardo will be the designer, and it will reshape the face of fashion around the world. I want you to help me run that enterprise. It will be successful beyond your wildest dreams. We will make hundreds of millions of dollars."

Jeff's astonishment made him stutter. "M-Me?"

"I trust you. I can't be watching my back every second. This will be my last venture. All other divisions will diffuse and integrate smoothly into the new one."

"I don't know what to say."

"There might be a few rough spots along the way, but ride with me, even when you might not fully understand the logic. It has all been carefully planned."

"Planned by whom?"

"The *Group,*" said Lili casually.

"The *Group*?"

"Yes. The *Group* is an international business consortium, a secret organization of successful entrepreneurs. We've been doing things together forever. You will meet them all, but you must never speak of them to anyone outside Keller-DeWinter. The *Group* has its own code of honor."

"I understand."

"We are the backstage choreographers, responsible for the efficient management of global business. We support each other. Therefore, our enterprises can never fail."

Jeff looked at her with keen interest. "I always suspected that much. So there really is a world business . . . " he didn't want to say *mafia* . . . "brotherhood?"

"And a very affluent one. Some may be a little apprehensive about my bringing you in because of your youth and inexperience, but they will learn to respect you."

"I will not let you down, Lili. I will always—"

She put her fingers to his lips to stop him. "I know you will, darling."

In his exuberance, Jeff felt a weight had been lifted from his heart. He remembered all the times when he had suspected that she kept him around to amuse herself.

"I know what you are thinking, but I had to be sure, sure that I could take a chance with you."

He took her hand and kissed it. "You won't regret it."

"I reiterate . . . this will be my last venture. After that, I might go away."

"Away where?"

"Far from all this." She gestured in a vague manner.

The thought that she might one day vanish from his life unexpectedly dismayed him, and the realization that he had feelings for her came as a shock to him.

Once again, reading his mind, she added cheerfully. "Don't be sad. I'm not going yet.

He laughed in relief and embarrassment.

"Would you be going home, wherever that may be?"

"No, I could never go back home."

"Why? Where is home and why not?"

She laughed. "Believe me. You wouldn't understand."

"You are the most intriguing person I've ever met. Such a high-profile woman, yet your background remains such a mystery. It is rumored that you are a Russian princess or a Danish countess. Even . . ."

"What?"

"Oh, nothing."

"Tell me. I'd like to know what people say."

"The craziest rumor is that you are a South American gold digger who marries wealthy men, strips them of their fortunes, and—"

"Kills them! I have heard that one."

"Were you running away from something?"

"Oddly enough, I was running toward something—love. Sooner or later, we are all victims of love, of at least one brutal episode of unrequited love."

"Who betrayed you?"

"It wasn't betrayal. I simply felt to be a better match for him and would have been a better ruler."

"He was a king?" asked Jeff in surprise. Jeff noticed for the first time that Lili seemed detached from the moment and immersed in the memory. He thought he detected pain in her words when she spoke.

"He chose another mate. I was devastated, and for the first time, unbalanced. I sought pleasure and amusement. To my surprise, I liked it, and that became my way of life."

Lili pulled a small sealed envelope from her pocket and handed it to him. Jeff recognized Lili's crest embossed on the golden seal, which she used on all personal correspondence.

"Don't ever misplace it. One day, you will understand its importance and will appreciate how I feel about you." Confused, Jeff put it away, and they returned to the house in silence.

XIV

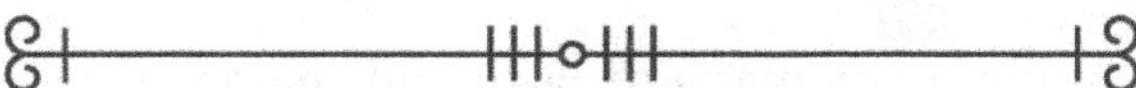

New York

"I understand . . ." There was a long pause before Danielle added calmly, "I know you did your best." She held the receiver gracefully. The phone seemed weightless in her hand. Danielle's movements were always refined, Linda thought, as she finished placing the incoming mail on a silver tray.

Linda knew the phone call was from Dr. Tom O'Neil, who was in Switzerland, and couldn't help wondering if something was wrong. Danielle had been back at work for a few weeks now. There was no more talk of the accident or what had happened at the penthouse. Yet Danielle seemed to be suffering from migraines.

"I understand. Please stop worrying about it," continued Danielle, speaking into the phone. "I'll try to get Jean-Christophe to meet you in Paris. It will be easier if he takes you to the institute himself." Another pause. "Destroy all blood samples. . . . Of course, you can trust him fully. Be careful, Tom."

Linda looked disconcerted. "Would you like me to tell you what is on the agenda?"

"Go ahead," responded Danielle mechanically.

Linda read as Danielle listened dispassionately.

"Here is a stack of invitations for charity functions. Please check the ones you are accepting, and list the amount of contribution, etcetera."

"Anything else?"

"The Vatican sent another list, including sixteen paintings. Eight of them are in private collections. We need to locate them and negotiate their purchase." Danielle took the list from Linda's hand and looked it over.

"OK."

"Is this a new phase of your work with the Museum?" inquired Linda.

"No. Until completed, I trust your confidentiality."

"Sure. I won't mention it. I work for you, not the museum."

"Do you have the destination for the first group of pieces? I'll call the art forwarding company," Linda offered.

"No. We will not be using them. Other arrangements are being worked out. In the meantime, try to locate the eight pieces in private collections. Go through Darren Bristow at Sotheby's."

Linda made a note on her pad." Oh, I forgot to tell you! Ricardo got the job at Keller-DeWinter Fashion Group."

"Oh?"

"He was offered a position as a designer and couldn't turn it down. I know you don't like Lili Keller, but he hasn't had to deal with her much. They've got him working on his own collection. Can you imagine? He is going to present his sketches to the board this week!"

Danielle watched the excitement in Linda's face, so she concealed her apprehension. "If Ricardo felt ready, you should have talked to me."

"Danielle, you do so much for us! It's just that sometimes he has to feel that he is doing it all on his own."

"I understand."

"You really don't mind that we are connected with someone you don't like?"

"It's not that I don't like Lili. I have always liked her. I just no longer understand her. I don't know what that whole organization is all about or what they are up to. It worries me sometimes. I would not want to see Ricardo get hurt in any way."

Linda could not see how designing clothes could hurt her boyfriend. Even if his position didn't work out in the long run, the experience at DeWinter would look great on his resume. Then she considered if Danielle might be referring to the open sexuality in the DeWinter ads.

Danielle smiled faintly. The open sexuality campaign was not what worried her. It was what was behind it. She was sure there was a full-blown scheme behind it.

"You said you used to like her?"

"I said that I have always liked her. I'm angry with her. She has chosen to run with the wrong crowd. One day, she will be trapped in their maneuvers. Anyway, has Mr. Goodman called?"

"Oh, yes. I was about to tell you. He got in this morning. He is staying at the Westbury. He called from his publisher's office—said he'd be free after lunch and asked where you would like to meet? Here?"

"No, not here. Tell him my place at 4:30."

Just then, the intercom buzzed, and the receptionist announced a flower delivery for Dr. Peschard. Linda stepped outside and came back carrying a tall glass vase with an elaborate arrangement of red roses. Danielle got up from her desk and helped Linda place the arrangement on a table.

"Speak of the devil . . ." Danielle said, smiling.

"He must be in love," added Linda.

"Nonsense. He is Kitzia's friend."

"But Kitzia only has eyes for her ex. She just got back from Frisco. That only means one thing . . ."

"Don't speculate so fast. Life has such intricate twists."

"Well, I am glad Dr. O'Neil is happy. Actually, everyone's lives seem to be going well. Even the weather has been lovely. Have you noticed, Danielle? After such a rash of extreme weather, everything is so calm and mild. Ricardo even commented on the decrease in crime. I think we must be going through one of those spells where the stars or the planets are in synch."

"We must be." It was precisely that calmness that made Danielle nervous.

The *Group* had backed off from their attacks. The weather was not being tampered with. Yes, these silent periods worried her. She couldn't help but wonder what was brewing in the minds of those twisted souls.

The elevator opened into the private foyer at Danielle's penthouse. Chris Goodman, who prided himself on having seen it all, could not help but gasp. The foyer was a circular room structured entirely of marble. Two Doric columns framed the main door. The doorknob was a huge carved hunk of 18-karat gold, which shined like a precious piece of jewelry. The barrel-vaulted ceiling displayed a splendid fresco in the unmistakable style of Tiepolo. Upon further examination, Chris felt certain it was an original Tiepolo, and then, not a fresco at all but an enormous canvas made to fit the concave shape of the foyer ceiling. The subject was an allegorical study of war and peace, showing the glorification of Venice. Centered in the marble floor were two concentric circles outlined in gold, the same as those on the medal he had been given, and which he now wore at all times. In its center was a circular glass tabletop, upon which an authentic ancient Greek vase held a huge flower arrangement at least five feet tall. He laughed to himself, thinking how insignificant the roses he had sent to Danielle were by comparison.

The door opened, and a butler dressed in a formal striped satin vest invited him in. The foyer had set the stage for the opulence of the penthouse, and he was not disappointed. The entry hall was flanked by enormous canvases by Robert Motherwell and opened into a spacious living room that was a contemporary re-interpretation of a neoclassical motif. Contemporary masterpieces stood next to ancient life-sized Greek marble statues, and glass pedestals held Hellenic busts.

Chris could have spent hours admiring the art, but Danielle appeared, wearing a black tailored suit and high-heeled pumps, with her hair pulled straight back into a chignon.

"Thank you for the beautiful flowers." She walked up to him and kissed him on both cheeks—in the French custom.

"This is a fabulous place!" He could not get over his amazement.

"Thank you. Let's sit down. What would you like to drink? How about a martini?"

"Sure," he replied, not sure how she knew that was his favorite drink.

The butler was already at the bar, shaking the vodka and ice. Mai Li, an Asian woman in a black uniform, came in carrying a tray of finger sandwiches and a pot of tea.

"You are not going to let me drink alone, are you?"

"I'm afraid so. I do enjoy my tea at this hour," Danielle said.

Chris looked around and then remembered what he had heard. The place had been ransacked and vandalized, although there were no visible signs.

Danielle observed him inspecting the surroundings and added lightly, "All material possessions are replaceable. I did hate to see the artwork damaged. But even those paintings have been satisfactorily restored."

They made themselves comfortable on armchairs facing each other next to the window. "Do tell me about your meeting, Chris. How is the book going?"

"All right, I suppose. I left part of the manuscript with my publisher this morning. That should appease him."

Danielle pretended not to hear the last comment. She was well aware of the pressure Chris was under and the tension caused by the postponement of his delivery date. In an effort to put him at ease, even though she knew already of his writing, she said, "Tell me about the book."

"It's a psychological thriller based on the true story of a young African American man who shot and killed a policeman while trying to evade arrest for a minor violation."

"You are a good writer, and the book will be a big success."

"Thank you. I should have finished it by now, but I have not been able to focus."

"I know, and I apologize. What we have asked you to do has been selfish on our part, but it was so important that we—"

"Hey." He did not let her finish. "I am more than glad to do it. I have come across certain things in the process that have made the hair on my neck stand up. It's actually because of what I've found out that I have had to reconsider whether it is important that I finish my book at this time."

"But you must. It will help re-evaluate and increase public awareness of the conditions that lead such youths to commit murder."

Chris knew she was right and that he had to find the means to juggle the two assignments. He opened the briefcase he had been carrying. As he took out a large folder, Danielle continued, "The *Foundation* has been impressed with your reports. They are most anxious to see what you are bringing today and would like me to inform you that they do not wish to cause you any further problems with your publisher. We'll be forever thankful for what you have done."

"What are you trying to say?" he wanted to know, before handing her the folder.

"Chris, we realize we are not only jeopardizing your career but may be placing you in physical danger. We do not wish to see anything happen to you."

"I can and will take care of myself. This is bigger than I imagined. Please tell me you will allow me to continue."

"Chris, you have done enough. If you really want to help me, then help protect Kitzia."

"I will do that too. But I will not quit. It is suddenly clear what I must do. Screw the novel! My place is here, doing whatever I can to help. Tell the *Foundation* that I am here to stay."

Danielle smiled. "I had to ask. However, under the circumstances, you may no longer refuse to be compensated for your services. The *Foundation* is very wealthy."

Chris waved his hand in dismissal, but at the same time, felt a sense of relief. The installments on his book had been delayed, and he was concerned about how he was going to make ends meet if he didn't concentrate on finishing the novel.

"Then it is set. We'll have our CPA contact you. Now tell me what you have found out."

"There is absolutely nothing on the disappearance of the body of Kjell Ulman."

"Even after the leads I gave you?"

"I'm sorry. The blood donor was a dead end—no records and nobody remembers him. The body was removed in secrecy from the hospital."

"It was not one of our people. So it had to be one of the *Group's,*" Danielle concluded.

"Yet he still died."

"I am having trouble believing that. In a situation of annihilation, Kjell would have left a clue to let us know what had happened. I would sense the vibration void. They might have him, and we won't stop until we find him."

"What exactly is a vibration void?"

"We Edentians are very sensitive to the vibrations around us and can detect a change in a vibration pattern. We would certainly notice the entrance or exit of one of us. An annihilation would leave a tiny void in that atmosphere of the planet. Unless . . ." Danielle thought of all the recent disturbances in the weather.

"I am totally overwhelmed by what is going on—your *Foundation*, beings from other galaxies who look just like us."

"I am human, of flesh and blood," said Danielle.

"Yes, that confuses me. When I touch you, I know you are a woman. Yet you admit to being from another galaxy."

"My spirit is. And, for that matter, so is yours. Most of the spirit essence inhabiting human bodies comes from far, far away . . . an unfathomable distance."

"That clearly explains the fervent desire of the human spirit to return to the stars."

"Yes, the ultimate desire of all beings is to return home."

"There is so much I want to know. I hope one day to be able to write about this—but I promised Kitzia that I would not write about you or what was happening around you, and I will keep my promise."

"Kitzia was only trying to protect me, just like I have reasons for keeping things from her."

"Are you telling me that you will not mind if I write about this one day?"

"I am telling you that the intrigue and unveiling of these current conspiracies will be of little interest to you one day. You will be much more fascinated with the truth. When that truth is revealed to you, yes, I would be very proud if it were you who recorded it for posterity. Your help and loyalty at this time of crisis will not be forgotten. If it is up to me, I will allow you to see 'The Manuscript.'"

"The Manuscript?" asked Chris.

"Yes. There is a manuscript. It is a record of the entire history of your planet. It will answer all your questions about why you are here."

"Understood. But I am also in agreement that Kitzia shouldn't be involved in pursuits that could harm her physically. She doesn't see it like that, though. I think she feels a little left out of what is going on."

"One day, you will understand, Chris, why her survival is essential."

"Now, about Robert Powers." Chris noticed Danielle's eyes widen with anticipation. He felt a touch of jealousy, which he tried to hide as he pulled the next sheet from his portfolio. "There is definitely a surge of activity in all his holdings, mergers, and acquisitions, as well as the dissolution of some of his companies. I'm no financial wizard, but I see a meticulously planned strategy here, leading to what, I'm not sure."

"World financial collapse?"

"More likely total financial control."

"He wouldn't do that. There has to be something else," added Danielle.

"He has certainly been busy and doing a lot of shopping. Back in the eighties, his banks financed a lot of small businesses. He made loans mostly to minority groups, the ones most banks would not touch. The only specification noted in their contracts was in the fine print. One day, these businesses would be sold back to Mr. Powers. Well, it looks like that day has come. As of last Friday, Robert Powers has been calling in his chips. He has taken over all the businesses he helped finance. They are as diversified as you can imagine: entertainment, fast-food chains, video games—all the small stuff you'd think wouldn't interest him. Big and small, they all have come under the umbrella of ARCH, which you can guess is a handsome part of the conglomerate of Powers Enterprises. I suspect it may be the largest of all privately held international businesses."

Chris pulled out a sheet that looked to be a financial statement and continued, "Annual Revenue of POWERS ENTERPRISES: approximately 100 billion US dollars. Primary Holdings: Powers Occidental Oil & Gas, Occidental Broadcasting and Occidental Futures. Secondary Holdings: Powers Advertising, high tech, graphic art, supermarkets, pharmaceuticals, soft drinks, retail stores, meat and fish packing, movies production and finance, skin care, perfumes, flower distribution . . .

"And now some of the beauty and skin care companies are merging with Keller Enterprises and DeWinter Fashion Group. Here is one of the odd questions. Why would an oil and gas magnate want to invest so heavily in the fashion industry?"

"Lili Keller, of course. They are up to something."

"Monopolize the economy?"

"No. They are trying to reach the masses. It confirms all my fears. How could they have persuaded him to betray us?"

He reached for the next documents but stopped when he saw Danielle close her eyes and reach for her temples. "Are you all right?"

She did not answer.

"What can I get you? Water? Medicine?" He moved closer and held her by the shoulders, afraid she might faint. Mai Li rushed in with a glass of water.

Danielle blinked, and because he was so near, he looked straight into her eyes. Chris was slammed with the most powerful emotion he had ever felt. Love in all its power gripped not only his soul, but his body. It was then, for the first time, he heard her voice inside his head. *This is not what I wish of you. I am banking on your inner strength and courage, relying on your wits to help me confront the adversary.* His passion dissolved in a heartbeat, and he was again himself, Danielle's friend and advocate.

He looked deeper into her eyes. The glorious rays of crystal green made him think of emeralds. In each, he detected a dark fleck at the outer edge of the iris.

Those tiny flecks made them unique to any other eyes in the world. He never suspected that those tiny holes were what gave Danielle the extraordinary distance and night vision she possessed.

The spell broke when Danielle turned to Mai Li and reached for the glass of water. Chris let go of her shoulders and moved away self-consciously. Danielle sipped her water, and the three remained silent. Danielle thanked Mai Li and passed her the glass in dismissal.

"You haven't totally recovered, have you?"

She shook her head. "Please do not mention any of this to Kitzia."

"I won't. But I thought Dr. O'Neil had removed the implant from your head."

"He did. It was a tiny neurotransmitter. Robert gave me something to neutralize the effects. That's why I know he didn't have anything to do with it. Tom attempted to remove it. Some of its chemical content spilled during removal. I am having a hard time convincing Tom that it was not his fault. I'll be OK."

"Would you like me to go? We could continue later."

"I'm OK, really. Let's see what else you have."

Chris fumbled for the right document. "Here is your worst fear: confirmation of connections between Powers's holdings and those of the *Group*." He handed her the sheet showing contributions to the Republican Party from the previously mentioned companies. Those made to Senator Nielsen's funds, particularly, were huge and only matched by those contributed by major weapons manufacturers, the tobacco industry, and various pharmaceutical companies. Nielsen, in turn, was financing guerrilla groups in South America and South Africa.

"I have not confirmed this a hundred percent, but I believe there is some type of menacing device being manufactured in these third world countries. I suspect it is some kind of instrument for torture. These sadistic enterprises are being financed through funds exhorted, or *extorted*, from the burgeoning congregations of the New Christian Church, headed by Dr. Theodore Edwards. Somebody has to be behind the proliferation of these churches. All signs point to the *Group*."

Danielle seemed upset. "President Parker has to read your report."

"Sure, I could send this to him immediately."

"No, no. You can't send it, and you can't just walk in to see him. You must take a tour. I'll arrange to have him meet you accidentally. You can pass him the report, by USB naturally, in the course of a casual handshake. I'll set it up for tomorrow afternoon. Be at the White House for the afternoon tour. President Parker or one of his trusted men will find you. I'd let you use my plane, but that would be a little conspicuous. We never know who is watching. I'd like to keep these papers if you have copies."

"I do."

"From now on, it will be better if you do not carry such information in your briefcase. Put it on USB. I'll give you a key to a PO Box. If you want to pass information to anyone else in our organization, just drop it in there, and I will make sure it is delivered."

"Very well," he said, "now, may I take you to dinner?"

"Not tonight. Tomorrow night will be fine . . . when you return from Washington. We still have a lot to discuss."

"There is a little bistro I like. It's called Les Artistes. Do you know it?"

"One of my favorites," said Danielle.

"Good. I'll call you when I get back."

"My car will be waiting for you at the airport. You will recognize Cam."

"Then, until tomorrow." He walked up to kiss her cheek, but once again, their eyes met. The surge of passion again struck him. He kissed her lightly on the lips. To his surprise, she allowed it.

XV

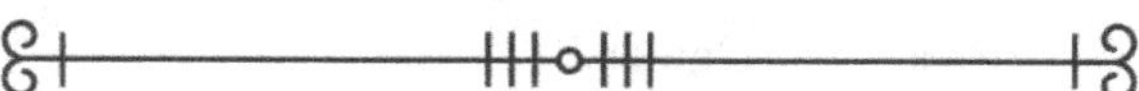

It was hard for Kitzia to get her routine back. Before Danielle's accident, Kitzia had taken a keen interest in one particular young patient and had been distressed upon hearing Denis had tried to take his life while she was away. The teenager had been committed to a sanitarium for his safety. Kit had gone to see him a few times at the facility and was shocked to see the blank expression on his face. That image remained with her, along with a sense of guilt.

The disturbed condition of two of her three new teenaged patients was oddly similar to that of Denis, her committed patient.. She wanted to consult Tom on the other two cases, thinking he might find a physiological correlation between them and was surprised to discover Tom had left for Europe unexpectedly, without even mentioning it to her. Recently, they had resumed regular communication, and there was a friendly intimacy that had not existed during their marriage. In Kit's mind, their relationship had taken a turn that she hoped just might lead to reconciliation.

Tom confided that he was under a lot of pressure at the hospital. A great number of his senior colleagues had turned against him. He was being unfairly criticized for things he had previously been lauded for and now had the constant sensation that his every move was being watched and second-guessed. He was convinced this surveillance had started shortly after he stepped in to take Danielle's case and studied her DNA.

When Kit suggested coming down to San Francisco for the weekend, he joyfully agreed.

It was the most wonderful weekend Kitzia had spent in years. They had taken casual strolls along Fisherman's Wharf, eaten Indian food overlooking the bay, and laughed like they did when they first met. Although they had not been physically intimate as she had hoped, she understood this to be Tom's way of respecting their friendship—no mixed signals. She had no doubt that they would one day get back together.

Kitzia checked her wristwatch. It was 10:30, and her patient was late. She checked the news. The first article announced the merger of Powers Broadcasting with ERIN Microchips. Robert Powers would now be a giant player in the manufacture of computer software. She spotted a photograph of Robert Powers and Lili Keller above another article announcing another merger in their various enterprises. It was the third one she had seen this week. They were not only becoming partners but also somewhat of an item. She was suddenly annoyed. She had always believed he loved Danielle. However, past his initial interest in coming to Danielle's assistance after the accident, he had distanced himself from her life. Danielle acted as if she had not noticed, and Kit decided not to pursue the subject. Her time with Danielle had also been limited by circumstance, which made Kit a little sad.

The intercom buzzed, and Michelle announced that her next patient had arrived.

After an hour, her patient left. Kitzia reached for her tape recorder and began speaking. "September 2. Devin Stevens, fifteen years old, depressed, showing early signs of psychosis. Seems to be experiencing an identity crisis. Devin spends hours on his cell phone, admits to staying up late listening to music by a group called Demonica that validates his feelings of entrapment in the present environment . . ."

It was almost lunchtime and such a pretty day that Kit took a walk and grabbed something to eat on the street. There was something wonderful about New York in the fall; Kit loved the crispness in the air and the new window displays. It was a perfect day to walk to the bookstore, so she headed for the one located a couple of blocks from her office.

The music department was crowded, and every salesperson was engaged. Kit had to walk up and down the aisles before she spotted the famous Demonica CDs. She had decided she had to listen and figure out the attraction kids feel for this kind of music. She picked up one CD and looked at the cover. On its cover was a road scattered with roses, leading to a rainbow. The roses became abstract spots as they receded into the horizon. Kitzia thought of pools of blood. She picked up another one. The cover showed tiny dots in the sky making up the configurations of certain star clusters. She felt the compulsion to pick up a third CD. Carrying the three Demonica CDs, she walked to the register. While she stood in line, she spotted a magazine featuring the Demonica rock group and reached for it.

"Hi, Kit!" The voice of a young woman reached her. She saw Linda, Danielle's secretary, working her way through the crowd. "I wasn't sure if it was you." She looked at the selections Kit was holding. "And didn't know you were into hard rock."

Kit laughed. "I guess I have to keep up with the times. I need to understand what this music is about. Are you familiar with it?"

"Not really. Ricardo listens to it."

"Really? I thought it was mostly music for the very young."

"The beat is a little depressing, if you ask me. But Ricardo likes it when he works late at night. Which now is *every* night."

Have you had lunch?"

Linda shook her head.

"Let me take you. We haven't had a chance to chat since Danielle's party."

"Super!"

Kitzia and Linda went to a bistro where Kit was always sure to get a table. While they were sitting comfortably at a table by the window, Linda opened the magazine she had just purchased and placed it in front of Kitzia.

"What do you think of that?"

Kit looked at the photograph of Lili and Robert. It was a picture she had not seen. The caption read "Merger of Fortunes: The Two Most Beautiful People."

"I don't know what to think. I am as confused as you."

Linda closed the magazine, moved it from Kit's plate, and stuffed it in her oversized handbag. "It's OK, I guess," said the young woman. "Danielle has a new admirer. Chris is younger."

"Chris Goodman?" Kit seemed a little taken aback.

"Of course, who else? He has been sending her flowers, and I know they are having dinner tonight. They make a nice couple, don't you think?"

Kit nodded in agreement. She remembered how angry she had been at this reporter. Who would ever think he would enter their lives and perhaps become important in her friend's life? She also wondered what Danielle had made of all the information Chris had come across regarding the disappearing corpse at the hospital. Perhaps it was not a romance at all, but more of an interest in what Chris was uncovering. Not wanting to gossip about her friend's personal life, Kit changed the subject. "So tell me about your boyfriend's job."

That afternoon, the weather changed. By the time Kit left the office, it was raining heavily. She was glad she lived only a few blocks away, and with her big black umbrella, she ventured into the street. It was hopeless trying to find a cab in Manhattan on rainy evenings. Once at home, she discarded her wet clothes and changed into a pair of sweatpants and a T-shirt. It was the perfect evening for staying home, so she turned the TV on and made herself a cup of tea.

She caught the last of a report on the Vatican. The pope had apparently become very ill. The next story was about Northern California, where slaughtered cows had once again been found. That marked the tenth incident of the vicious slaying of cattle during the last two years, with no leads or clues as to why this senseless slaughtering continued.

She didn't have time to dwell on the report, for the next news item was even more disturbing. A six-year-old boy had shot and killed his two sisters, ages five and three. Kit's heart sank. She was used to dealing with guns and violence, even in early teens, but had never heard of that kind of violence involving pre-school children.

Kit switched off the TV and inserted the first of the Demonica disks into the CD player as she opened her mail. The music was as she expected: loud, monotonous, and incoherent. She had to make a real effort to understand the lyrics. They spoke of anger, betrayal, and disillusionment. She thought of Danielle and Chris having an intimate dinner somewhere, a dinner in which she had not been included. Chris had forgotten their lunch plans and had not even bothered to leave her a message explaining he'd be away. Danielle used to include her in all her plans, and considering it had been she who had first brought Chris to help during Danielle's recovery, she felt a little hurt and left out. It would have taken Tom one minute to pick up the phone and let her know he was going to Europe. Had he perhaps gotten scared of their closeness? And she hadn't heard from Jean-Christophe in weeks. Suddenly, loneliness sat right down in Kit's lap.

The psychologist inside her jumped to the rescue. She recognized the negative thoughts that were encroaching and immediately put a stop to them. She really did not feel this way. She was not lonely. She was alone and not about to make a neologism of the word. The only thing she felt was exhaustion and a desire to rest. She curled up on the couch and was sound asleep before the second CD started playing.

Her dreams were disturbing. She found herself once again alone, back at the ranch where she had grown up. Her mother was dead and lay among the slaughtered cows. She saw Danielle, Tom, and Jean-Christophe pass by. They were laughing—laughing at her. Chris Goodman joined them and laughed too. His laughter was so loud, it could be heard all around her. "Kitzia, the psychic!" They all continued laughing as they ridiculed her talents. She felt so angry that she wanted to get out of there and disappear into the dark after killing them all!

She woke up in a jolt at the madness of the dream. What in the world was the matter with her? She then remembered the music. There was no doubt in her mind there was something bizarre in the music that produced those irrational feelings. It wasn't the lyrics, though. Something else in the beat produced a subliminal feeling of anger and despair that played on inner fears.

She went to her computer and searched in her files for any information she might have on her former young patients. She found enough similarities in the personal feelings of the youngsters to continue her search on the internet and found ample information relating music to feelings of aggression.

She would write to her congressman and present her suspicions. She also thought of Chris Goodman. He was very good at this sort of thing, and besides, he had all the connections at the police department and FBI. She held no ill feeling toward Chris. It was OK if he felt more attracted to Danielle.

She looked at the CD cover again. *Why would anyone want to embed subliminal messages of self-destruction into lyrics or music? The* Group! *Danielle had said the members were obsessed with creating havoc.* She looked at the CD cover for the name of the distributing company and realized it was a recent acquisition of Powers Enterprises.

Kit immediately placed calls to Danielle and Chris with urgent messages. Both returned the calls within the hour. Neither one mentioned their dinner date. Because of the urgency in Kit's voice, Chris and Danielle agreed to meet her early in the morning at Central Park for a morning jog.

What little Kit had told Chris over the phone about her suspicions was disturbing enough to spur Chris to follow through that very evening with some former acquaintances. Officer Jones, in California, had already provided him with evidence of similar suspicions. Now he just had to run a couple of things by the FBI for verification.

Danielle had wanted to keep Kit out of it all, at least as much as possible, but Chris realized it would not be possible to keep her in the dark. She was smart and was figuring out single-handedly what was going on around her. By morning, Chris had obtained what he needed. Yes, there was a sinister plot. That music contained a subliminal message recorded at a lower pitch. So low were the vibrations that the ear was not able to transmit them to the brain in its conscious state but picked them up clearly at a subconscious level. What Jones had uncovered was a type of secret graphic embedded in the artwork of the CD covers. At a certain angle, the faintly visible outline of a dragon could be made out. Jones was certain the particular graphic in question was subliminally presented to create some type of sub-cult. It led a person to the next object containing the graphic, and so on. Youths, like a group of zombies, were led from graphic to graphic. In the process, they became part of a group brainwashed into self-destruction.

Kitzia found both of her friends waiting for her at the agreed upon spot in Central Park. The three of them began a slow jog among the rest of Manhattan's early morning exercise fanatics. Kit candidly related her experience, including the dream. She expressed her concern for young people addicted to their cell phones, who were being manipulated in such a sinister manner. She was going to run EEGs on her young patients before and after listening to the music to make an intelligent assessment. She would then request a meeting with her congressman to present her findings, hoping for support that would lead to a congressional hearing. Kit was convinced the beat played on one's particular fears and turned them into full-blown phobias.

Danielle listened carefully and concurred that Kit gather all the evidence possible and present it to Congress, although she was not sure how helpful they would be. The *Foundation*, however, would act upon it. So the first report should be given to Danielle to pass on to the *Foundation*.

Chris then told her everything he knew and handed her a CD he had made with the information he had found and names of contacts—Officer Jones, in particular, who had found Danielle in California.

Kit was speechless. She put the small CD in her pocket. *So there is a conspiracy!* With her friends' support, she was about to start the biggest crusade of her career.

"Did you know Robert Powers bought the distribution company?" Kitzia asked.

"He is buying everything," responded Danielle. "But he is not behind this diabolical scheme."

Kit remained silent while she continued her jog. She had become preoccupied with Denis Bundrock, her suicidal patient who had been institutionalized. The new information might be of help; she had to check on him immediately. She would drive up to the facility that very afternoon.

Danielle looked at Chris and he understood this would be one more assignment he would have to follow to a conclusion. She also wondered if she was overloading him with responsibilities. Chris smiled back, letting her know it was OK. He would gladly do it.

His life was becoming surreal anyway, Chris thought with amusement. The previous day, he had flown to Washington, DC, as instructed, had taken a cab directly to the White House, and had joined the touring group. Halfway through the tour, a president's aide had come out to greet them. He had welcomed them all and had shaken hands with the tour guide and several of the other tourists. Chris had been the last one. Then the aide made eye contact with him, alerting him that he was the contact. Chris released the chip during the handshake and felt another one simultaneously placed in his palm.

Without any further incident, Chris returned to New York. As he came out of the airport, he spotted Camiel in his chauffeur's uniform, standing next to the black town car. Danielle was waiting inside. Chris handed her the button-sized chip, and she placed it inside her bag. The limo dropped him off at his hotel and picked him up again later in the evening.

During dinner, the conversation had been light, mostly about art and literature. She had confided in him that she was in the process of acquiring the largest and best art collection in the world. The *Foundation* had entrusted her with that mission, and the Vatican had requested her help in locating a number of religious pieces in American collections. She was limiting her purchases to the Renaissance masters and French impressionists and would be purchasing mostly from private collections and known art dealers.

For philanthropic reasons, she also wanted to acquire the work of abstract impressionists. She had compiled a list of possible acquisitions. Would he help her locate them and buy them on the spot?

"But I would not know where to begin!" he had gently protested.

"I know you can do it," Danielle had replied, handling him a list. "And if you come across any other paintings that you consider exceptional, will you buy them as well? I will place a several-million-dollar account at your disposal. Don't waste time bargaining. Time is more of the essence right now."

She then proceeded to instruct him on how the purchases were to be handled. He was to act as a representative of a newly formed corporation owned by Peschard Interests. He was to transfer a 10 percent fee of any transaction into his personal account as remuneration for his services. He was to keep acquisitions as confidential as possible. The handling, packing, and shipping of all art pieces to their ultimate destination would be handled by the people Danielle had designated and no other. Someone would show up after each purchase and wrap and take the piece for forwarding. Similar procedures would be used for any book recently published that Chris deemed worthy of "rescuing"—he was sure she had said *rescuing*, before correcting herself with "acquiring."

After dinner, they had driven for an hour to a warehouse in New Jersey, where several trucks with workers were loading and unloading wooden crates. He had been surprised to see so many people working at such late hours. It was almost midnight when they arrived. He found out that this warehouse would be the first destination for the shipments. They exited the first warehouse and entered an adjacent one through a back patio. The second one was as spacious as the first one and thousands of books were piled in six-foot-high stacks. A group of young workers was busy cataloguing the titles and placing the books inside thin metal boxes and then into large wooden crates. The workers smiled at Danielle, but no one spoke.

On the drive back, Danielle was vague as to the destination of the books, and he did not push. His mind kept going back to the calculation of the 10 percent fee. "But that might come to millions," he had pointed out.

"I know," she had replied simply.

The first thing Kitzia did when she arrived at the office the next morning was phone the youth rehabilitation center where Denis had been institutionalized. She advised the person who answered the phone that she had been Denis's former therapist and was requesting permission to have a session with him that afternoon. The woman replied that someone would be calling her back.

The call from the director of the institution came about an hour later to inform her that Denis Bundrock had committed suicide the previous evening.

XVI

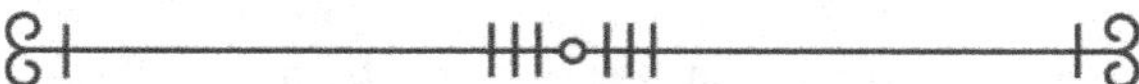

New York

Ricardo Duran had been waiting for this moment all his life.

To be a fashion designer was all he ever wanted. He had left Brazil, much against the advice of his family, who, as they had in the old days, still considered fashion design an effeminate profession. With the little savings his older brother had given him, he headed for the Fashion Institute of Technology in New York.

After the first semester at the institute, he received a merit scholarship, and used the money to continue his training. After graduating from FIT, he was only able to find employment repping a line. He had expected his impressive portfolio to open the doors of top designers to his talents, but after three years of struggle, the best he could get was a job as an assistant pattern maker at DKNY.

When his friend, Jeff, went to work for Keller DeWinter Enterprises, he promised Ricardo he'd do whatever he could to wangle an introduction to the fashion wing of the company. Jeff had actually talked to Lili about him from the beginning, touting his friend's talents whenever the opportunity arose, but Lili had shown no interest until recently. After the party at Danielle Peschard's house in California, where Ricardo had been introduced to her by Mr. Goodman, she showed an interest in him.

At Lili's instructions, Jeff had set up an appointment with a division manager at DeWinter Fashion Group, and Ricardo had been hired immediately and assigned to design a full presentation for Ms. Keller. And now here he was, with a series of full color drawings and made-up samples of his designs.

Ricardo was tingling with nervous apprehension. He had not seen Lili Keller since the party in California and had heard all kinds of rumors about her. Lili could be witty and charming or cold and cruel. He fervently prayed that today it would be the former.

Sweeney, the division manager, had informed him that Miss Keller wanted to come down to the workrooms, a very unusual thing for her to do, for she rarely descended from the executive suites. He and the division and production managers had been waiting for her for three endless hours. The atmosphere was charged with anxiety. The four pretty young models wearing Ricardo's samples wandered around restlessly, sipping Evian, unable to sit down for fear of wrinkling their fabrics. Other associates tried to keep busy grading and truing patterns. Ricardo continued to go over and over his sketches and, from time to time, would stop one of the models and adjust some minor detail on the hem or the collar of the garment.

They had not heard from Miss Keller's office, and Ricardo feared she might not show up at all when the intercom buzzed to life and the voice of the receptionist informed them Miss Keller was on her way down. Everyone straightened up and tried to look busy. The elevator door slid open, and the slim, tall figure of Lili Keller appeared, followed by Jeff Montgomery.

Lili nodded her head in greeting, dispensing with formalities. She was led to the seat that had been prepared for her. She whispered something to Jeff, who relayed the message to an assistant, who immediately produced a glass of water. Lili slipped a handful of green Chlorella pills into her mouth and drank the full glass of water.

Lili Keller was, indeed, the gorgeous, formidable woman Jeff had raved about; she exhibited that casual elegance one saw on the pages of *Town and Country*. The white silk pants and T-shirt fitted her perfectly. She was wearing sunglasses, which Ricardo found odd on an overcast day like this.

Lili signaled Bill Sweeney to proceed, and the division manager stepped forward to introduce Ricardo. Lili extended her hand without smiling and nonchalantly said, "I am anxious to see what you have come up with."

"Miss Keller, in compliance with your request, I have worked out sketches for an innovative line based—"

Lili waved her hand, indicating that he skip the speech and proceed with the presentation. Ricardo understood.

"My first group is reminiscent of Saint Laurent's '76 Ballet Russe collection. I have carried it several steps further, into an opulent terrain of luxury."

Lili took the set of illustrations Ricardo handed her and raised her eyes to look at the first model.

"Tanya is wearing an emerald green brocade vest trimmed with sable." The model moved gracefully around Lili. "Prussian blue silk blouse and a fuchsia triple-tiered silk faille skirt."

A second model, dressed head to toe in white, stood in front of Lili. Ricardo continued, "What could be more luxuriant than Russian ermine jackets over white woolen skirts embroidered in 24-karat gold?" He stopped for a minute to observe

Lili's reaction. She was absorbed in the outfits and, from time to time, cast a look back at the drawings.

He hoped she thought him talented. After a few minutes, she finally spoke. "These are magnificent, but they are not exactly what I have in mind."

Ricardo's heart sank.

"Let's see your next collection."

Ricardo shifted his sketches and handed Lili a new set of watercolor renderings.

"For this collection, I have chosen the New Classical Period of Bonaparte's Josephine." Two models walked out together, wearing dresses made up of layers of see-through muslin. "In the days of the French Empire, women dampened their dresses in order to produce the desired clinging effect."

Lili shook her head. Ricardo moved on to the next collection.

"Here we have a futuristic concept: very short A-line skirts, fitted jackets with multiple pockets, hidden closures and zippers. It's a minimalist approach, with—"

Lili looked at the model and made an unmistakable sign of dismissal.

Ricardo's confidence was sinking fast. He hesitated before presenting his last collection. Linda had warned him it was too weird, and he should withhold it. "My last collection is based on revisions I have made to *street people* looks and the ways they have morphed in the last few years."

He reticently exchanged the set of drawings Lili was holding, expecting her to reject the sketches out of hand, but to his surprise, she not only looked at them with interest but also seemed to be scrutinizing them in minute detail.

"Tell me your concept," said Lili casually.

"Because some young rappers relate to the street looks, I observed the homeless and have taken the oddest things I have seen around town and turned them into fashion statements. I created a whole line made out of rubbish. Except for some pieces made out of old, torn, faded denim, I used every other resource that might be found cast off in the streets: plastic, cardboard, rubber."

Lili smiled for the first time. "An entire collection inspired by trash!" She sat up straight. "I think we have our new look and our new designer!"

Everyone in the room, including Jeff, was stupefied. Lili could not fail to notice. "This will be our new direction. Ricardo just stated it; young people identify with the street looks. They prefer to look more like hobos than well-to-do kids. Calvin Klein did phenomenally with his ad campaigns showing boys and girls in permanent disarray—unshaven faces and matted dirty hair. That look of *Je m'enfoutism* made him millions."

No one could disagree.

"We are about to take that concept to the limits! Our advertising campaigns will be the strongest and most expansive we have ever undertaken. We'll fill the stores with clothes that give them the looks that play into their rebellion. These young people have lots of money to put into the marketplace, so let's give them what they want. A large percentage of the customer we'll be targeting is on drugs, let's face it. If they're not, they seem to want to look like it! Goodbye, blonde, athletic, suntanned young models. Hello, pale, big-eyed brunettes who are all about a different kind of fun. These kids don't jog; they stay up late, drink, and smoke too much. Get very young models. We want some natural beauty to show through the grunge.

"Line up everything to finalize the project. I'll need all design and production division managers, marketing, advertising, and PR directors working as many hours as it takes. I want full proposals and dates to launch this line. Jeff will coordinate and act as your liaison among divisions. Submit all proposals to him for approval."

She then turned to Ricardo. "I want a full line developed immediately. Sweeney will furnish you with whatever working staff you need. I want the line in the stores by mid-April," she said to her executive. "We can't rely on the spring market to test our line. We will have to launch it ourselves. We'll also be opening our own boutiques. We'll provide co-op advertising to major retailers and have plenty of media coverage. Understood? That only gives you eight months. Time is of the essence, so get moving. We meet at my office next Tuesday at 9:00 a.m., sharp. Good day."

She stood up, and without saying a word, Jeff followed her from the room. He was too stunned to speak. Everyone, like him, was sure Lili Keller had just lost her mind.

"I am telling you exactly what she said," Ricardo repeated to an incredulous Linda.

"But that line is so ugly. I mean, so crazy!"

"Crazy or not, that is what Lili liked, and I will give her the most incredible trashy line ever invented!" He picked up his fiancée and swung her around. "Honey, it will be a success! Be happy for me . . . for us."

"I am. Did you get a raise?"

"Raise, expense account, and . . . a staff. I can now have an assistant, a pattern maker, a sample maker, whatever I ask for. Wish you would consider coming to work for me—I mean, with me."

"I would. It's just that I really like working for Danielle."

"But Danielle is just an employer. Come with me, and we'd be working together for our future."

"I know, baby. Danielle is not just an employer. She is like a mentor. She's a friend."

"You'll change your mind when you see how cool this setup is. You could start looking for a new place; we can afford it now."

"That is—if the line is successful."

"It will be," Ricardo assured her. "Don't be pessimistic. I don't think Lili Keller would go out on a limb with a venture if it were risky. And by the way, I haven't told you about Jeff. He will be heading the entire division."

She kissed his neck. "How about going to the bedroom and showing me how very happy you are?"

"Boy, I hate to turn down a proposition like that, but I may have to take a rain check. I have to draft these patterns by tomorrow morning."

Linda pouted. "Don't stay up too late. I love you."

The Penthouse

Lili was becoming intolerable. Her nerves were so ragged, no one around her knew what to say or what to do. The smallest incident would send her into a rage. She was verbally abusive to all her employees, and during these rampages, nothing and no one was safe. It was better to just get out of her path. Even Jeff, despite his new position and attractive salary, had twice considered walking out on her. Then he would remember their walk at the cabin and the conversation they had shared and would make extra effort to try to fathom what was going on in her head.

Something was upsetting her. Lili was not eating and was subsisting on glassfuls of her hideous green potion. She had not removed her sunglasses, nor had she left the penthouse for days. The dark glasses were no longer capable of concealing the irritation around her eyes, and a thin red line was beginning to spread beyond their frames. Lili began smashing every mirror she encountered. Jeff tried to stop her. He ended up wrestling her to the ground and was surprised at the uncommon strength of this slender woman. The glasses fell off, and he could see the full extent of the redness around her eyes.

"It's just an allergy. Lili, you are acting irrational!"

"It will grow worse until it consumes me!"

"What are you talking about?"

"I am wasting away. Can't you see it?"

He pulled her head toward his chest and held her tight. "It is just a rash. There must be something that will alleviate it. I'll get it for you."

She began sobbing. "There is no more of it. You don't understand? You are stupid like the rest of them, like every earthling on this forsaken planet!"

"There you go again with your mad ravings about this insufferable planet. If I haven't left by now, it's because I will never leave you. Have you seen a doctor?" he asked.

"You are really pitiful! You think I would be this upset over something a doctor could fix?"

A little beep emitted from a laptop Lili kept near her. She swiftly got up from the floor and went to it. A message appeared on the screen, and she immediately entered a response. The fear and anger vanished from her face.

"OK. It is set. I am leaving at once for Switzerland," she informed him.

"What's in Switzerland?"

"My clinics. They have just informed me they have devised a special treatment."

"Would you like me to accompany you?"

"Robert Powers is going to an OPEC meeting and will give me a lift in his plane. Darling, please have my secretary call him and let him know I am on my way."

"I will. I wish you'd let me know what is going on."

She was busy jotting down instructions for different people in the company. "I'm having a very specialized rejuvenating procedure. It is done with a series of plasma injections. I will be out of pocket for a little over six weeks. In the meantime, I want you to take care of anything and everything that has to do with the new line. Sorry, I have been such a devil."

She then reached for and opened a crystal Lalique box, pulled out handfuls of one hundred-dollar bills, and spilled them casually over her desk. "I've been a monster to all my assistants. Please give them this." She pointed to the money. "It is amazing how this green stuff can pacify almost any situation."

Within the hour, the black limousine bearing the Keller DeWinter crest was waiting by the side door of the building. Jeff escorted her to the car, carrying a couple of leather travel bags, and kissed her goodbye. She continued to remind him to pay attention to each and every detail of the Trash Campaign.

He was not surprised at the change of mood of the penthouse assistants when Jeff asked them to help themselves to the money. It was as if nothing had happened. The money had greased the atmosphere, and empathy for Lili's ailment abounded.

Jeff turned his full attention to the campaign. He spent the next few days in the advertising offices and saw the campaign take shape. It did not seem as absurd anymore. Well, no more than any other campaign making the rounds of the fashion industry. He reviewed composites and approved the selection of the new models. It was obvious to all that he had become Miss Keller's right-hand man, and he was given their respect. The corporate executives agreed with all of his suggestions. For the first time in his life, Jeff had a taste of power. He liked it and promised himself he would not abuse it.

At Linda's request, he tried to spend more time with Ricardo under the pretext of following the campaign every step of the way. She had expressed concern over his obsession with work, his inability to sleep, and the fact that he was beginning to use too much "stuff" to get through the day. Jeff suspected she might be right. Ricardo, knowing that Jeff was trying to catch him in the act, became careful to conceal his addictions.

In the process of monitoring Ricardo, Jeff became aware that the use of drugs was widespread in the organization. He had managed to stay clean—not out of propriety, but simply because no drug had ever enticed him—and he had tried almost all of them at least once. Lili's preoccupation with youth kept her from ingesting any potentially harmful substance. He was surprised to learn that the most serious abusers were Lili's executives. Jeff at first considered documenting the drug use and bringing it to Lili's attention upon her return. To his surprise, he realized that she was aware of it and did not mind, as long as her employees remained productive. He would look for other ways to point out that drug use at work was not in the best interest of the company.

The first ads for *Vogue* were ready within two weeks of Lili's departure. The new look was integrated into advertising for a new fragrance that had been incorporated into DeWinter from one of Robert Powers's conglomerates. The new look in make-up was out as well. The new image was one of relaxed allure.

Jeff thought he understood Lili's desire to create a new look. Fashion trendsetters who snapped up new product lines created by Tony fashion houses, such as DeWinter, tended to lose their enthusiasm as the products reached mainstream stores. Once the trend became popular at the discount store level, it was time for the pacesetters to switch directions. Jeff wondered how long it would take this "trend" to run its course.

To serve as the face of the campaign, he had selected a sexy, dark young woman with unusually full and seductive lips, who, despite the messed-up hair and tattoos, still looked desirable. Jeff was delighted with the photographs and was sure Lili would be too.

It was amazing that business ran as smoothly as it did under the circumstances. As the days went by, his responsibilities and Lili's absence made him privy to many company documents and memos circulated among executives that he might not have otherwise seen, some of which pointed to somewhat questionable incidents. At first, he ignored them, justified that there were things that did not concern him—things that had happened before his time. But the lawyer inside him could not always be appeased, and his curiosity was aroused.

He came across governmental sanctions, environmental protests to ban the use of certain toxic products, and congressional investigations. The gravest offense had been the use of certain solutions in the manufacture of Keller's hair color. Chemicals in the dyes were believed to be carcinogens. The legal archives contained endless copies of lawsuits against Keller DeWinter Enterprises, most of which appeared to have been settled out of court. The organization seemed well aware of the toxicity of its products but never made the slightest effort to withdraw them from the market, choosing instead to compensate its victims with handsome settlements. Other offenders were creams, suntan lotions, make-up—there was no end to the products using the toxic ingredients.

Lili had left in such a hurry that she had neglected to lock her files as she usually did, so they were accessible when Jeff needed information. He tried to put the questionable procedures out of his mind. For a successful corporation of this magnitude to succeed, there had to be a certain degree of ruthlessness. He vowed that, in the future, if he had the power, he would attempt to elevate its social consciousness and erase the company's motto: "Keller DeWinter is in business to make a profit, not to win a popularity contest."

It was not until Jeff tried to locate Penelope Velez—a South American model who he had worked with when he first joined the company—that Pandora's box opened.

Penelope had resigned a couple of months after she had done a photo shoot with Jeff. He asked around, but there were only rumors and bits of gossip. Penelope had apparently gotten involved with Tracy Jackson, Lili's corporate lawyer, and feisty as she was, had pressed him to leave his wife and promote her career. Then she dropped out of sight.

Rumors about her disappearance swirled, and Jeff's initial interest turned into curiosity and finally, into obsession. Farhad, who worked in the mailroom, was the last person to have seen her. When Jeff asked Farhad, the Iranian denied knowing her.

There was no question in Jeff's mind that something terrible had happened to the girl. He went down to the law offices to see Tracy Jackson under the pretext of needing clarification about a contract technicality and casually asked Tracy, "Have you heard from Penelope Velez? She would be perfect for this campaign."

The portly attorney stiffened. "I think I remember the girl. Died in a car crash—terrible thing!"

"Oh, sorry to hear that. If we ever come across someone who looks like her, let's hire her."

"No problem." The attorney relaxed, seeing that Jeff's interest was merely professional.

One morning, Farhad caught Jeff in the hall, and having been informed of Jeff's new position, addressed him with a new aura of respect.

"One year after the fatal accident that had supposedly killed her, Penelope called me. She asked me to procure a certain file so she could nail them. I didn't do it. It was dangerous."

Farhad reached into his pocket for a crumpled envelope. It showed an address, and he slipped it into Jeff's hand, then hurried away toward the stairs.

After a morning meeting, Jeff instructed the staff to take over, explaining that he had some things to do outside the building. He ordered a car and headed for Queens. He needed a day off, and it was a good opportunity to follow through with his investigation—though he wasn't quite sure what he was looking for.

On the freeway, he saw the first billboard for the new Keller campaign. It was powerful. Although, admittedly, it appeared to be promoting drugs and not a new fragrance. A minor confusion registered in his thoughts, one that he mollified by the fact that the evening gala launching the new product had been an enormous success. "Damnation" perfume had been welcomed by the media and was already showing healthy profits at the retail level.

A few hundred feet down the road was another billboard featuring Theodore Edwards. The preacher's oversized image with his fist up in the air struck Jeff as somewhat comical. Behind him was a luminous cross with the fish symbol of Christianity in the center. Bold white letters made up the ad. "We've got to catch the Fish!" Passing drivers would probably identify with one group or the other—excessive conservatism or rebellious, indifferent abandon. The irony was that both worlds came under Lili Keller's jurisdiction, and she was somehow involved in the campaign of that lunatic.

He almost missed the Queens exit and so decided to concentrate on finding the address. If and when he found Penelope Velez, he hoped his fears could be put to rest. If he found a logical explanation, he would never again doubt or even question the things that went on in the company—especially those that did not concern him or had to do with his colleagues' extra-marital affairs.

If Penelope had fallen on bad times, he would help her. He remembered how he had once wanted to take her out. Those had been the times when his life was his and his destiny a wide-open field of choices. That had all been before Lili Keller.

He found the address, parked, and entered the tenement. The door of the dark apartment was ajar. Jeff stood there for a moment, observing the shadow of the woman sitting in front of a television. She remained immobile as if she did not care to acknowledge his presence.

"Penelope?" said Jeff, almost sure he was in the wrong place.

The woman turned around with a jolt and faced Jeff. "What do you want?"

He was not able to answer. He took a small, hesitant step toward her. With each next step, his heart ached more profoundly. He had not found the beautiful young girl he had once known but a skinny, worn-out woman, whose face had been dismally disfigured.

She recognized in his face the inevitable expression of horror. "This is why I never go out," she muttered.

"Penelope, what happened?"

She did not answer the question but asked one of her own. "How did you find me? Does anyone else know?"

"I asked around, and I was finally given your address."

"Ah, Farhad . . . poor guy . . . still trying to help."

"Penelope, please tell me what happened."

"Are you still with the company?"

Jeff nodded, not wanting to elaborate on his new position of authority.

"So what is it that you want?"

"To find out the truth."

"What concern is it of yours, anyway? Are you one of them now?"

"Penelope, if Jackson did this to you, I swear I'll kill him!"

"No, not him." Her voice softened upon seeing the impetuousness in Jeff. "Jackson . . . how is Tracy? I've often wondered as I sit here if the jerk ever loved me? He cried like a baby when he saw me. He gave me some money to go away and try to do something about this," she pointed to her face. "Then I never saw him again."

"I have to know the truth. I heard you were going public, that you threatened Jackson, that you had a car accident."

She moved closer to him and lifted the frizzy black hair that covered half of her face. "This was no car accident. Look closely at what acid does to human flesh!"

Jeff was horrified. Her right eye was gone and the severity of the burn scars was even more repulsive.

"Forget you ever saw me," she added.

"I can't. I have to know. I must know. Did Lili Keller have anything to do with it?"

"Tracy always said Lili did not ask many questions. She simply gave orders and expected results. How people got things done was no concern of hers."

"This can't be true. She is not a monster."

Penelope made a grimace, perhaps intended as a sarcastic smile. "I curse the moment I thought I was clever enough to scare them. Tracy told me things he should not have. With such information, I had the bright idea of demanding a magazine cover. Nobody puts demands on the company. They ignored me. I decided to play hardball and went to the media. After my meeting with a reporter, two punks assaulted me as I was getting into my convertible. One stabbed me; the other poured acid on my face.

"There was no link between what happened and the company. But I know. I know those men were hired by the *Group*. Tracy told me about the *Group* once—about how powerful they were. As you can guess, all the information and documents I handed the reporter vanished into thin air. No report or complaint was ever filed.

"If you really want to help, then stay away. Let them think I'm dead."

He did not notice the two bottles of sleeping pills on the small table next to the chair where she had been sitting. Yet if he had, he probably would have done nothing to stop her.

"I'll give you something, though." She reached under the sofa and took out a small spiral notebook and handed it to him. "My diary. This might help you understand . . . what the company is about."

"If they're in any way connected, I'll make them pay!"

"You don't get it, do you? You can't betray them. You can't even leave them!"

Jeff recalled his episode with Lili and Tracy when he was determined to go back to law school. No, he could not leave. They made him an offer so attractive that he could not refuse it. Had he rejected their terms, would they have done away with him? That was absurd, he thought. He was not dealing with the mafia. What could an assistant know that would be considered a security risk? The funny thing was that he had been too naïve to suspect or notice anything untoward. His eyes had been only on Lili. His concern had been only to do a good job and look good to Lili. Lili . . . always Lili.

The drive back to Manhattan was a torment. Penelope's ruined face had been imprinted on his soul. The thought that Lili could be involved in something so macabre was more than he could stand.

XVII

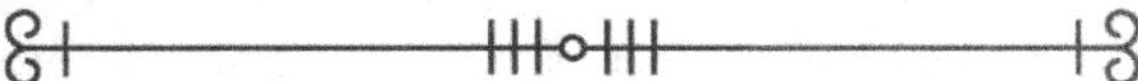

Penelope's Notebook

The first pages of the crumpled, faded notebook were incoherent. Jeff had to read them several times before he could make sense of the notes. They were made chronologically over six months. The sentences were short and childlike—like the cryptic reminders he jotted down for himself, with the intention of elaborating later.

He realized Penelope was not very intelligent and had always relied on her looks to get ahead. She had started seeing Tracy and, because of his initial gifts, had assumed this would be a lasting relationship. Jeff deduced from her notes that she had become possessive and irrational. Eavesdropping on his conversations and snooping on his classified documents. She didn't understand the nature of Tracy's job or his frequent trips to Switzerland. Somehow, in a moment of weakness, he confided to her he had been admitted into the *Group* or Brotherhood, which sounded like a satanic cult to her. He mentioned the beginning of "Phase I" and the wealth and power it would bring him.

Tracy moved her into a new apartment, and she became more demanding. In a fit of anger, she stole a vial labeled "IPS" along with classified documents from his briefcase and contacted the press. At that point, things fell apart. Jeff knew the outcome of her actions.

Jeff tried to sort out fiction from fact. The indications of wrongdoing in the company, he had already figured out, but association with a satanic brotherhood was beyond credulity. He had to remain impartial and not be blinded by sympathy for Penelope's tragedy.

The notes told the story of a foolish girl trying to take a shortcut to the top and of a love affair gone sour. Yet there were enough clues in the notes to alert him that Penelope had stumbled onto something big. Something that could definitely compromise Keller DeWinter's reputation if it were to get out. *It was decided she must be silenced. Thugs were hired to teach her a lesson. The hoodlums got carried away and did the unspeakable!*

The Brotherhood was obviously the *Group* that Lili had often referred to. The multi-million-dollar fashion group was a front for something even more lucrative. That was definitely a possibility. Keller DeWinter was in the import-export business. It received huge daily shipments from all over the world, including raw ingredients to process in its cosmetics and fragrance plants. It could be possible that shipments of illegal drugs were being smuggled along with the powders and flowers.

The IPS solution? He was familiar with the term. He had seen it often enough in documents having to do with the labs in Switzerland that performed Lili's rejuvenation research.

Something he had almost forgotten popped up in his mind—Phase I. Jeff recognized the phrase; it also appeared frequently in interoffice memorandums. That would be where he would start. His access to Lili's files would prove to be of tremendous help in clearing up this matter and fully understanding what this Phase I was all about.

His first few hours of research produced no startling discoveries. There were numerous references to the *Group*, but they were vague. It appeared that not all executives in the company were members. Lili had actually warned him once of the resistance the *Group* might pose with her bringing him in "because of his youth and inexperience," she had said. That meant she had considered making him a member one day.

Jeff really did not want to shatter the bubble of his success at Keller DeWinter. The campaign was doing phenomenally. His head, like a computer, kept constant track of the dollars in over-rides he was to get from the total sales. The clothing line was not out yet, but freestanding stores were being built on schedule and *WWD* magazine had already done its first feature story on the upcoming looks by DeWinter.

He decided to pursue a simpler approach. If Lili had asked him to check something on her computer, and she often did, he would have no problem accessing her files. He typed "Phase I."

The screen responded, giving him a choice of categories: Advertising, Apparel, Edwards, Fragrance, Health Products, Hair Products . . . more categories in alphabetical sequence.

Jeff opened the first two. He scrolled swiftly through the list. The only category out of context was the one named *Edwards*. He opened it.

It listed dates for reviews, promotional campaigns, and revision of formats, television, and so on. Jeff had never realized the company was footing the bill for so much of Theodore Edwards's promotion.

Jeff closed the file. He was getting nowhere, and there was only one person in the world that could shed light on what he wanted to know. Lili.

On Thursday morning, Jeff booked a first-class seat on a flight to Europe for that evening. First time to Europe! He reveled in the fact he was in a position to indulge his sudden impulsiveness and set about enjoying his trip. Sitting at the bar of the VIP room drinking a vodka tonic, he was trying to sort out his feelings. In a way, he wished he had never looked for Penelope. His discovery of her circumstances had opened up so many questions about his company, and the last thing he wanted was to cast doubt on his circumstances, especially Lili.

What would he say to her when he saw her in Switzerland? Would she be pleased or annoyed to have her treatment interrupted? Well, it was too late now. He was at the airport, on his way to Europe. The flight would go to Paris where he'd switch to Lufthansa and proceed to Switzerland. He even considered staying in Paris for the night to take a quick look at the city then head for Lucerne first thing in the morning.

A couple came in and sat next to him at the bar. The man, a Frenchman, promptly ordered champagne.

"Not for me," the pretty lady with him interrupted. "Mineral water."

The Frenchman put down his carryon bag and turned to her. "What are you going to do, Cherie?"

"What I usually do, Jean-Christophe, keep fighting," added the woman. "Sooner or later, someone will listen. I will not abandon this crusade. I will find out the truth."

Jeff had to turn to observe the woman who spoke with such assurance. He was pleased to find out he was not the only one searching for answers. The Frenchman's cell phone rang.

"*Oui,* Evans? I was wondering . . ." He turned to his companion. "Pardon, Kitzia." After a few seconds, he yelled, "What?" His champagne spilled. Kitzia tried to blot the spill with a paper napkin, and the barman immediately came to assist with a towel.

Jean-Christophe's voice grew louder. "I don't believe it! How can they revoke our permits? I am already at the airport!"

Everyone in the waiting room was now looking at him, so Jean-Christophe lowered his voice and moved away from the crowd. Kitzia remained at the bar and smiled at Jeff as a sign of apology. She opened the *Vogue* magazine she was carrying and flipped through the pages. She stopped and stared at the Demonica perfume ad. With a pen she pulled out of her handbag, she circled the bottle.

Observing her with interest, Jeff asked, "What do you think of it?"

Kitzia looked up. "What do I think of what?"

"The ad. You circled the item."

"It seems to be glorifying addiction."

Jeff introduced himself. "Jeff Montgomery, Keller DeWinter Fashion Group."

Kitzia shook his hand hesitantly. "I don't understand it," she said, pointing again at the magazine.

Jean-Christophe came back and interrupted, ignoring Jeff. "You won't believe this! They have revoked our permits just now, without warning and for no reason." The voice in the speaker announced their flight was about to begin boarding.

Kitzia made a gesture so the Frenchman would notice the young man. "This is Jeff Montgomery." She said his name slowly so Jean-Christophe would remember, "with Keller-DeWinter."

Jeff noticed that the Frenchman's manner changed, as if momentarily forgetting the bad news he had just received.

"He is responsible for these ads," she pointed at the magazine.

"Nice . . ." was all Jean-Christophe managed to say. He shook the young man's hand with interest.

"It was a pleasure," Jeff said to both, and picking up his belongings, he headed for the gate.

Kitzia waved and then kissed Jean-Christophe. "Be careful, you crazy Frenchman. I worry any time any of us separates these days."

When Jean-Christophe came aboard first class, he was pleased to see Jeff was sitting next to him. "Going to Paris on business or pleasure?"

"Going to Switzerland. I've never been to Paris, though. So I am seriously contemplating staying in Paris for the night."

"Absolutely! What is there to do in Switzerland after 7:00 p.m., anyway? Are you expected?"

"No. Actually, they don't even know I am coming."

"Champagne?" Jean-Christophe requested of the approaching flight attendant before she asked. The girl then turned to Jeff.

"The same."

"*Alors*, please allow me to show you the city. I'll take care of things. Put you in a charming hotel. Drive you around a little, take you to a great restaurant for dinner. I'll make it memorable."

"You are too kind. I would not want to inconvenience you."

"Not at all. I am suddenly free. My partner just canceled on me—problems with the Egyptian government."

"What do you do?" Jeff wanted to know.

"I am an archeologist, working in the Valley of the Kings."

"Oh, I do remember hearing about the discovery this summer. Were you part of the expedition?'

"Of course." The Frenchman did not want to elaborate. "And you said you work for Lili Keller . . ."

"Yes. Do you know her?"

"I know of her. What exactly do you do?"

Jeff realized he did not have a precise title. "At the moment, I am sort of a jack-of-all-trades. I'm heading a new campaign for the company. The fashion house is changing the direction of its look, and I am overseeing the transition."

"Interesting."

The flight attendant handed them their champagne flutes, and Jean-Christophe offered the toast: "To the *bon chance* of meeting! I want to hear all about your campaign."

Jeff explained that they were taking a more relaxed approach to fashion in an effort to keep up with the times and give the buyer something to identify with.

"Let's not kid ourselves," said Jean-Christophe, "fashion and style are gone. Beauty will go next. The process announces the beginning of the end of civilization. Do you agree?" He watched carefully for Jeff's reaction.

Jeff laughed. "We are not killing fashion. We are merely giving its pompousness a bit of a rest."

"I have watched carefully the trend you are pushing. Even in Europe you have made your statement. But why such an angry approach to fashion?"

"Angry?"

"Yes, angry. How else would you describe the last Keller collection? Taffeta gowns with combat boots, leather outfits with burned holes, bleached and torn denim—every piece in your collection put through undeserved torture."

"Terrorist chic!" said Jeff with amusement.

The Frenchman laughed. "I suppose we are getting more of it, yeah?"

"You are a tough critic."

"I am an archeologist. Show me a piece of clothing from any time in history, and I can tell you with fair accuracy what the society of the period was all about.

Clothing tells us not only everything about the individual but also reflects a society's morals and aspirations."

"So what will posterity see in our present civilization?"

"Corruption and decay."

Jeff let out a small laugh. "You are a pessimist."

"Not me. You asked what future civilizations will see and think of us."

"But if you, yourself, don't think so, why will others?"

"Because I'm one of the few who are fighting to let it be known that the world situation is not as hopeless as that. But I do suspect a conspiracy working hard at creating the illusion that it is."

The flight attendant was now standing in front of them, handing them menus. Jeff chose the filet. The archeologist started arguing in French with the attendant about the options offered. Jeff realized the archeologist was definitely the type who was never quite pleased with the state of things; he had also hit exactly on what Jeff had been seeing take shape in the company. Despite the beautiful models, the message was one of hopelessness and apathy.

Once Jean-Christophe stopped arguing with the flight attendant, the Frenchman turned to Jeff. "Do you like *gigot*, lamb?"

"Yeah, I did not see it on the menu."

"That is because they don't have it. So don't overeat. There is a great little restaurant in Paris where they have the best gigot in the world. We can have lunch or dinner.

"Anyway, I was saying that garments speak a clearer truth than typical advertising. For example, give me your idea of an Egyptian 4,000 years ago. What was he like, and what did he wear?"

"Gosh, the only one that comes to mind is tall, muscular, tanned, and bald. I'm seeing Yul Brynner in *The Ten Commandments*. Seriously, let me think . . . OK, the wall paintings. Egyptians were tall, thin, and wore those headpieces that matched the loincloths."

"Wrong. The wall paintings are the advertising I was talking about. Most people now believe that is how they looked—lean and tall. The truth is that most Egyptians were short and fat. Their diet consisted primarily of carbohydrates. Paleopathologists have demonstrated that the huge folds of excess skin on the mummies indicate the presence of severe obesity. The ancient Egyptians painted and carved idealized pictures of their people."

The attendant returned, and their conversation came to a halt. Dinner was served. Jeff noticed Jean-Christophe had taken a micro-recorder from his leather bag and began speaking into it in French.

Jeff reviewed in his mind what they had just discussed. He wondered why he had not defended Keller DeWinter with more zeal. But he could not deny that the Frenchman was right. The astuteness of his observations had astounded him.

It was a fact that in the last few seasons, the company had been pushing that unsettling look. Grunge turned to the aggressive, then to implied addiction, and now what they were launching was the ultimate look of sloth. The Trash Collection, as it was now referred to in the company, was out to destroy fashion as it had existed through the ages.

This was not really what Jeff had pictured his life to be. He had always hoped to become a successful lawyer, but beyond financial success, he had envisioned his life as having some purpose. He had pictured himself on some worthy ecological crusade or fighting for some principle worth preserving. Instead, he now headed a campaign of destruction, and spent his free time looking for justification for unethical corporate maneuvers.

Jean-Christophe, while pretending to be totally immersed in his dictation, continued to observe Jeff carefully. Jeff ate slowly and pretended to be absorbed in the movie. His thoughts had returned to Lili. His longing for her again made him ache. That was something he had to control. He was glad the Frenchman had convinced him to stay in Paris. He needed to distance himself from his feelings and his doubts and become integrated into the rest of the world again.

It was a little past two in the afternoon when they arrived in Paris. The Frenchman informed him that he had secured accommodations for him at the Plaza Athenee and invited him to share his cab. He told Jeff he'd be calling for him at 7:00 p.m., which gave him time to have a light lunch, take a shower, and relax.

At 7:00 sharp, Jeff was at the door of the hotel, and with the same punctuality, Jean-Christophe's red Ferrari roared up and screeched to a stop. Jean-Christophe drove around the city and treated him to a quick tour of such points of interest as the Trocadero, the Champs Elysees, and the Eiffel Tower. Paris was everything Jeff had imagined—and more. There was a sense of magic about the city, a *joie de vivre* as Jean–Christophe put it, that Jeff knew was the antithesis of the image his company was determined to establish. It was almost ten o'clock when they stopped at a popular bar. With mutual agreement that the gigot dinner would have to wait for another occasion, they ordered a bottle of champagne and a board of charcuterie. The archeologist told Jeff amusing anecdotes about his profession that put the American in a jovial and relaxed mood. They drank a second bottle, after which Jean-Christophe suggested they take a stroll.

They exited the restaurant and ambled down Avenue Montaigne. Jeff wondered if Jean-Christophe had chosen this particular street by design, aware that it was the famous avenue occupied by extravagant boutiques where top French designers displayed their creations. He was ready for another witty put-down of the DeWinter look. Instead, the Frenchman said, "I'm glad life gave us this opportunity to meet. You are a good guy; I think I can trust you. We are on opposite sides of the fence, but we are not enemies. I believe you neither know how deep you're in, nor how muddy the water has gotten."

Jeff stared at him blankly, an icy feeling creeping up the back of his neck.

"You are with the *Group,* but you're not in it," said the Frenchman.

"What do you know about the *Group*?"

"Apparently, a little more than you do." He took out a card and handed it to Jeff. "I want you to know that you can call on me if you are ever in a jam you can't get out of. You seem naïve but not stupid. I think you will start noticing that things within your company are not as they seem. When it's time to bail out, we can help you."

Jeff's immediate thought was that the Frenchman might be with the law, the CIA, or whatever.

"Who *are* you?"

"An archeologist, as I told you. But I am also with the *Foundation*."

"The *Foundation*?"

"You have never heard of the *Foundation*? . . . Hmm. You are with a company affiliated with the *Group* and have never heard of the *Foundation*. Brother, you are in the dark!"

"Will you explain to me what is going on?"

"You have affiliated yourself with very dangerous company," added Jean-Christophe. "Not really understanding your position, I have perhaps put you in danger by being seen with you. They may think you are selling out. When they question you about me—and they undoubtedly will—tell them the truth. Say I made a point of meeting you so I could extract information from you, which you refused to give."

"But I don't have any information."

"You certainly do. You probably don't even know it."

The two men had just rounded the block when a car coming toward the intersection made a straight dash for them. Jeff saw it first and yelped, "Watch out!" The Frenchman reacted forcefully, pushing Jeff out of the way, causing the black Citroen to crash into a post. Three men jumped out and were upon Jean-Christophe in a flash. Jeff tried to punch one of the guys in an effort to help his companion. The man responded with a blow that sent Jeff crashing into the wall of a jewelry store. Before Jeff could get up, two other figures dressed in black leather seemed to fall out of nowhere and onto the scene. The first one, a dark man with light, curly cropped hair moved with the swiftness of an acrobat and the force of a wrestler. He was a good match for the first attacker. Then the second newcomer did a somersault in the air, landing on one leg and using their left heel to smash the jaw of the second attacker. During one of the lightning turns and ninja kicks, the cap fell off the new defender, exposing a ponytail of flaming red hair. Jeff noticed Jean-Christophe was having a hard time fighting off the third attacker and rushed to help, throwing himself once again over the man's back. The battle continued for a few more minutes.

The dark-clad man and the red-haired woman overcame the men they were fighting, and before long, they rendered them unconscious and bleeding on the pavement. Then the pair turned toward Jeff and the Frenchman, still duking it out with the final assailant. The dark man shot a blast of light from what looked like a laser gun, and the attacker fell to the ground, releasing Jean-Christophe. The explosion produced an intense vibration, which caused Jeff to fall backward. Despite the confusion, Jeff noticed the Frenchman was bleeding, but the two defenders were helping him to his feet.

The woman went and kneeled next to Jeff. "Are you all right?"

Jeff nodded. He was too stupefied to think straight. He had never seen the swiftness and agility these two possessed. It was then Jeff noticed how beautiful the woman was.

She picked up the wallet he had dropped in the fight and handed it back to him. "We must get out of here before the police arrive and find the bodies. Can you make it back to your hotel? We must tend to Jean-Christophe."

Jeff got up. "I'm OK. My hotel is just around the corner."

He watched the dark man and the red-haired woman pick up Jean-Christophe and disappear into the darkness of the street.

Jeff crossed the boulevard as he heard the faint sounds of an approaching police car.

XVIII

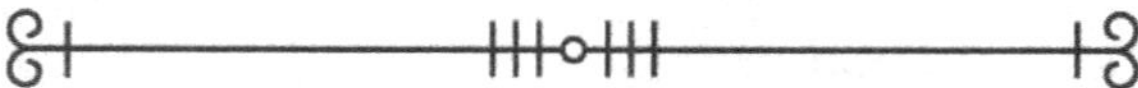

Lucerne

A man in a white uniform holding a sign with Jeff's name met him at the airport. He had not told anyone in the company that he was coming to Switzerland, and a sense of apprehension came over him. The sudden realization that, no matter where he went, the company had tabs on him bothered him immensely. Nonetheless, Jeff smiled cordially at the man and thanked him for his thoughtfulness.

The driver took his carry-on bag and escorted Jeff to the car—a white limousine displaying the well-known gold crest of the DeWinter-Montaigne Clinic. When they arrived at the clinic, a woman in a white suit greeted him, introducing herself as Heidi Schiller.

"Monsieur Montgomery, we expected you last night. Miss Keller feared something might have happened to you."

"Oh, really? Is Miss Keller available?"

"She is expecting you. Please, follow me." She started toward a spiral stairway facing the main entrance of the chateau while someone carrying his bag walked in the direction of the elevator.

Despite extensive renovations, the chateau retained an Old World look, unlike everything Lili owned in New York, where the ultra-modern style ruled. They entered a salon. Above a massive carved limestone mantlepiece hung an oil painting of a beautiful, raven-haired woman dressed in black, and wearing an obviously rare and perfect ruby pendant. Lili.

He walked toward it, and Heidi commented, "*Baroness DeWinter* by Van Dyck."

"I thought it was . . ."

"Everyone does. It is an amazing likeness."

The door opened, and Lili entered, dressed in a white caftan and turban. Jeff stared at the translucency in her skin—which looked almost unreal—and her eyes shone with the radiance of sapphires. Jeff noticed that, in their uncommon brilliance, Lili's blue eyes carried the same intensity as those of the green-eyed, red-haired woman in Paris.

He breathed a sigh of relief when he saw the welcoming smile on Lili's sensuous lips.

"You finally made it!"

Jeff started to kiss her on the cheek, but Lili searched for his lips. The door behind them closed. Alone with her, Jeff kissed her passionately. Her body felt light and youthful, and he became immediately aroused. He no longer thought of intrigues and conspiracies. He lowered her to the floor. Nothing mattered at this moment but to have her.

They both lay exhausted on the Aubusson rug for a long moment without speaking. When Lili's breathing returned to normal, she sat up and slipped the caftan back over her head. She walked to a mirror and re-wrapped the silk turban around her head. "So what do you think?" asked Lili with an air of pride. It was her looks she was referring to, not her performance.

"Sensational."

"I am very pleased. I think we have perfected the technique," said Lili casually.

"Definitely."

"You haven't told me what kept you from coming straight to me."

"Madness. I gave in to a sudden whim to see Paris and paid for it handsomely."

"Oh? How so?"

Lili had now straightened up, and her tone changed to what Jeff called her professional mask—cool and detached. She looked at him, anticipating a full and accurate report. The Frenchman's words came back to him. *When they ask you about me, and they undoubtedly will, tell them the truth.*

He related the story as dispassionately as he could. He expressed ignorance as to why the archeologist wanted to befriend him or why they were attacked on the street.

"You should have waited a couple of days and come in on the company plane that is arriving tonight. Ricardo is coming, along with some of my key people from both Keller and DeWinter."

"Ricardo? He didn't mention anything to me."

"It was a last-minute thing. Some of the *Group* members would like to meet him. Besides, I've been told he has serious sinus infections and has been taking too much medication. His doctor suggested surgery. So I thought, why not bring him here? I have access to excellent surgeons. It's a rather simple operation, and

Ricardo will recover in a couple of days. Then we can all return to New York together." She headed for her desk. "If you want to freshen up, Heidi will show you to your room. Then we'll have a light lunch. I must go back to sleep for the rest of the afternoon. It is part of my treatment."

"You are still receiving the IPS shots?" he asked matter-of-factly.

"No. I'm glad the plasma shots are finished. The lamb plasma is very strong."

Jeff noticed she emphasized the word *lamb*.

"Perhaps you should take a nap as well. That way, you can be rested and fresh for tonight. You will meet a lot of interesting people."

"Let's go to lunch," he said.

She took his arm, but before they reached the door, she cast a mocking glance at the mirror.

The two men standing behind the two-way mirror had watched it all. Cirel always enjoyed watching Lili perform, and she obliged at every opportunity. Robert Powers was not amused.

"I would think the act of seeing your beloved copulate would be a little painful. She gives herself so freely to men . . ."

"Lili never gives herself," Cirel corrected him. "Lili takes. She was made for pleasure. So she is indiscriminate about her choices. That is the one flaw in her character."

Robert remained silent.

"You cannot admit that such a beautiful Edentian can be defective," Cirel laughed maliciously. "The boy will last for a while, then we will get rid of him. I don't like him poking his nose where he shouldn't."

"What if she were more taken with him than you imagine?"

"Absurd notion!"

"She wants to bring him in."

"Fine. As long as he continues to do a good job for us, he'll be OK. We need everyone working for us at a time like this. Now, let's get back to reviewing our mergers and acquisitions."

The tables under white umbrellas emblazoned with the gold crest were scattered far apart on the lawn that overlooked the artificial lake. A waiter in a white jacket and gloves escorted Lili and Jeff to the most remote of all the tables, near an enormous elm tree. The tables were elegantly set, and chilled white wine awaited them in a silver cooler. Lili motioned the waiter to begin pouring.

Jeff was served a healthy poached salmon with dill, fresh asparagus, and a terrine of broccoli. Lili, in turn, was served a clear broth and strips of something that looked like iridescent green rubber.

"What is that?" asked Jeff, incredulous.

"I don't think it has a name. It's the heart of a plant that grows in the bottom of the ocean."

"OK." He turned to his infinitely more appetizing food.

"Why don't you ask me now?" said Lili. "What were you searching for . . . on my computer?"

His heart stopped. She had known all along that he would try to break into her computer. He had to think fast.

"I had to get some files. I hope you feel I managed OK without you."

"I couldn't be more pleased with your performance. The campaign is doing extremely well. What was it precisely that you needed to know?"

Jeff took a drink. *I better come up with something believable.* "I wanted to bring a model I know into the campaign. I thought she had the right look. A can of worms opened and sent me on a wild goose chase. It just left me wondering what really happened to her. Who is lying?"

"The girl, of course." She reached for the laptop that had been placed on the chair next to hers, placed it on the table, and logged in. She continued nonchalantly, "We have to deal with our share of accusations and lawsuits, but treason within our company is a rare thing, and we don't condone it. The girl was an opportunist. She tried to manipulate us through blackmail and bizarre threats of scandal. Oh, here it is. . . . Poor Tracy, he really fell for the girl. It was the only time I have seen him lose his judgment. She stole confidential information and tried to sell it to our competitors. She tried to embarrass the company by selling some crazy story to the media. The *Group* has no tolerance for that kind of behavior."

"She must have come across something pretty damaging to make her confident that she could get away with it."

"Jeff, for heaven's sake!" she snapped. "It really does not matter. We are always trying to improve our products, spending billions trying to make them as safe as possible, but we'll never stop every attempt to sue us."

"I still would like to know what she found that gave her enough confidence to come after a company as powerful as Keller DeWinter."

"You are living in Wonderland!" She logged into something else and turned the computer toward him.

"Here. Take a look. If you are looking for harmful stuff, you don't have to turn to products that we manufacture. We do not create the poison. Just look at the world you inhabit. It, and everything in it, is already contaminated. Look at our confidential reports from the US Congress and various labs. We are living on a contaminated planet—a dying planet—and there is nothing anyone can do about it. The air you breathe, the water you drink are all contaminated. The food you eat has been poisoned."

Jeff scanned through page after page of government documents outlining the depletion of minerals in the soil and highlighting the presence of toxic substances. The Environmental Protection Agency pointed out a priority list of 129 dangerous pollutants in the water, including PCBs and chloroform.

"Now, part of our responsibility in the *Group* is to take the veil off and show the truth as it really is. I believe you will now understand the goal behind our present campaign at Keller DeWinter.

"Go through our private files," said Lili. "Look under 'Contamination.' After you do, I never again want you to doubt or question the motives of the company.

"Now, if you will excuse me, I must return to my treatment. I will see you at dinner tonight."

He stood up when she did and watched her leave, annoyed with himself for having upset her. But he doubted that what was nagging at his heart would ever be put to rest. The euphoria of what he had accomplished in the company had evaporated. He took a swig from his wineglass and entered the word *Contamination* into the computer.

He discovered that, indeed, the dyes in the hair colors contained the same toxicity found in artists' oil-based pigments and were most likely responsible for millions of cases of brain cancer. Cosmetics used highly toxic powders and the Keller deodorant contained such a high level of aluminum that several documents linked it to Alzheimer's disease. Jeff felt sick. Was Keller DeWinter just a typical twenty-first-century corporation, acting under norms dictated by the times? It was all about money. There was no more social consciousness. And here he was, at the crossroads. He could live a successful and prosperous life, ignore the truth, and be loyal to the company. Or not.

At that moment, he saw Heidi Schiller approaching. He closed the laptop and got up to join the flirtatious fräulein.

She walked him through the reception rooms, the sunrooms, and the spa. She showed him the operating rooms and the floor where the rejuvenating procedures were conducted. Jeff was allowed to peek through the glass window into a room where several women lay in a state of suspended animation. Heidi explained the procedure and the function of the boxes and wires connected to the patients.

"Temperature and metabolism are kept at a minimum during the hibernation periods. Patients receive heavy doses of antioxidant vitamins: A, C, E, K, and chelation treatments," Heidi informed him. Jeff focused his eyes on the IV bags and identified the one marked distinctly as IPS. It appeared to be the main and constant fluid going to the body. He questioned Heidi no further.

She punched in the combination on the electronic pad next to the door of his room, and the door popped open.

"You should take a nap," she advised him, handing him a tiny yellow pill. "It's a mild sedative to relax you."

Jeff had the distinct impression that she was not going to leave until he took it. He had no choice but to put it in his mouth and pretend to swallow it with a gulp of water. Heidi smiled approvingly and promised to ring him in plenty of time to get ready for dinner.

As soon as the door closed behind the assertive German woman, Jeff took the pill out of his mouth and threw it away. He waited a few minutes. Just as he suspected, his door was locked. He was glad he was an observant man and had picked up the combination when Heidi punched it in. Just three numbers. 009. Jeff stepped outside. Total silence filled the building. He walked down the corridor to the first intersection and peered carefully around the corner. He saw Heidi sitting at a desk at the end of the hallway. She would certainly see him if he tried to cross. He then noticed the door across the corridor marked "Supplies."

To his delight, the 009 opened it, too, and he slipped in. The linen closet led to a large room full of unmarked boxes, then to a narrow passageway and into another room with several tables and computers. No one was in the room, so he assumed the operators were on a break. One of the images on a computer screen stopped him sharp. He identified the room being surveyed as the IPS Lab. The words *71 degrees* flashed on the screen, the IPS temperature. Stacked on racks were cylindrical containers connected by wires to vertical metal posts on both sides. Jeff's curiosity made him click the zoom tool. He enlarged the image and distinguished the outline of the object within the jar—the unmistakable shadow of a human embryo.

He clicked back, unable to process the shock. *Are they breeding infants? Cloning them? What is going on?* He suddenly understood what the letters IPS stood for: infant plasma solution. The idea that the clinic was using infant blood plasma as the primary rejuvenation ingredient was too staggering to process.

Jeff walked out of the room and took the elevator down to the second floor. No one was around, and he headed in the direction of the chateau. He navigated the back rooms of the facility, past kitchen pantries and storage rooms. The sound of voices made him pause as he became aware of activity in the chateau.

Jeff opened a door, crossed a terrace, and reentered the building through an open French door that led to a library. Bookcases lined every wall except one, where a large mirror hung. He walked toward it, wondering if his face reflected the shock he had experienced, when he noticed his reflection change. It became clear this was a two-way mirror looking into the salon where he had made love to Lili. He wondered if anyone had watched them.

His shock turned to indignation. He needed to get out of the chateau without being spotted. But as he started back to his room, the sound of distant laughter drew him down a hall toward what he suspected was a party or meeting. On a wall was an oval Florentine mirror. Not to be deceived again, he confirmed it was a two-way. There were about a dozen men and women of diverse nationalities. A man whose back was to him spoke in German. There were smiles and occasional bursts of laughter among the listeners. *Is this the* Group*?* he wondered.

A slender, dark man wore an Arabic headpiece, another an Indian turban, and a woman dripping with diamonds held a white cat—with a diamond-studded collar—in her lap. On her side, a large man smoking a cigar listened to what was being said. Jeff spotted Robert Powers. He appeared to be the only one bored by the discussion. Powers stared at the floor, as if impatient for the speech to end. Then someone spoke in English about the importance of moving through Phase I and into Phase II. Robert Powers looked up and replied that the components were all in place and awaiting the catalyst to begin the transition. OPEC would soon be announcing that oil and gas resources were almost depleted, that the situation dictated the world turn its full attention to the use of nuclear power as its main source of energy—through the use of uranium and its by-product, plutonium.

The man with the cigar spoke. "We all know the planet will annihilate itself before one tenth of the supply of uranium, now dormant in the USSR, is extracted."

Robert Powers responded in English, "Possibly . . . since the *Group* has violated all laws governing the sale and transportation of *Yellow Cake.*" *Refined uranium,* Jeff guessed. Suddenly, Robert Powers looked in Jeff's direction. Jeff knew Powers could see him through the mirror, knew he was there. There was nothing Jeff could do now but await the inevitable.

To his surprise, Robert turned away and continued speaking. The conversation continued, languages alternating among the members, who seemed unaware of any change, as if a universal language were being spoken. Jeff tried hard to piece together what was being said about Phase I. He understood the US would soon be following the influence of *someone.* He thought he heard the name Theodore Edwards and shook his head in disbelief. He scanned the room for Lili and was pleased not to find her there. He harbored one last thread of hope that perhaps she was not a key element in this scheme of madness. But then, the vision of the IPS lab returned to him.

"So what about the European situation? How are we going to deal with my problem?" The woman with the cat spoke in an accented English that Jeff could not identify. She raised her hand to her head to adjust her wig, and her skin, a portion of her face moved with it. Jeff was startled; he suspected she might not be human.

Not until someone else spoke in English did Jeff understand they were now talking about food additives. From his recent computer search, he recognized the terms—BHC, chlordane, DDT, heptachlor, HCB, and lindane—as carcinogens.

"But the European market has banned the sale of US-grown beef treated with hormones. They have detected the deleterious effects of antibiotics and sulfa medicines added to animal feed."

"We'll find a way around it. Soon enough, all European beef will also be full of long-term carcinogens."

Jeff recalled that mutagens were chemicals that damaged cellular reproductive material. Once again, Jeff had to wonder what benefit these individuals would reap from poisoning the food of the world.

"If there are any cattle left on the planet after your ongoing worldwide slaughter!" Robert Powers seemed to violently oppose any further tampering with foods and insisted everything would be ruined by such uncontrolled greediness. There were loud protests. Robert's voice became stern, almost threatening. "None of you is going to push me into doing something that is absurdly stupid. Don't forget that most of our enterprises have merged. Any in-depth investigation into our activities will result in a twenty-five percent decline in the value of stock in our major enterprises. As of this moment, I am going on record with my opposition."

The threat of loss of revenue served to make some of the members rethink the proposition. A man in the assembly changed the subject. He inquired what was to be done about the "zeroing in on the zone."

The man with his back to Jeff, who by now Jeff had identified as someone of importance within the *Group*, responded in German. His voice became agitated as he directed everyone's attention to something on a table. Three-dimensional images appeared. Jeff was reminded of the futuristic scene in *Star Wars*, where Princess Leia's hologram pleads Obi Wan Kenobi. He recognized the image of Jean-Christophe. The German's frantic body language made Jeff wild to know what was being said. The projection switched to an image of the woman with the red ponytail. Without hearing their words, his instinct told him the *Group* wanted those people killed. In unison, everyone in the room barked out an affirmative vote and raised a hand in the Nazi salute. Everyone except Robert Powers.

Robert Powers purposefully looked in the direction of the mirror. There was no doubt in Jeff's mind that Robert would not betray him. Maybe the meeting was about to break up, and this was Jeff's cue to move on. He quickly retraced his steps without any difficulty.

When he approached the monitoring room, he noticed three people were back at their desks. Jeff picked up a box from a stack, and placing it on his shoulders, walked past the room and into the linen closet.

He reached his room without further incident. Ten minutes later, there was a knock at his door, which was no longer locked. "Me . . . Sophie," said the busty blonde. Her English was limited, and she made use of her hands to communicate. "Miss Keller says you get massage."

"OK."

She handed him a robe and signaled for him to change. Jeff took the robe and headed for the bathroom while she set up.

From his balcony, Jeff watched two limousines emit the arrivals from New York. Tracy Jackson stepped out of the first car in the company of what looked like two other corporate lawyers. From the second car came Ricardo, his assistant, Fonda, Lenny, the fashion show choreographer, and two models from the current campaign. It was not until cocktails were served on the terrace by the pool that evening that Jeff was able to speak to Ricardo. Even then, he realized there was no way he would be able to talk any sense into him. Ricardo was drinking vodkas as if they were water and seemed to be high on something else. The young designer's eyes were glossy, and all he uttered was, "This place is so cool!"

Jeff was stupefied.

This was not the Ricardo he knew. Ricardo, creative designer . . . the intellectual who would spend hours discussing the meaning of life. Jeff had always been a captive listener, fascinated by his friend's knowledge of the Kabbalah and his lifetime interest in Hermetics.

"I thought you were having surgery in the morning," said Jeff, "so I don't think it's such a good idea to drink."

"Will you chill?" responded Ricardo angrily. "You sound like my mother—or worse, like Linda."

"She is worried about you and not without reason."

"Will you get off my back? Everyone is freakin' telling me what to do!"

"Ricardo, this doesn't sound like you!"

Jeff walked away. It was useless talking to him in his present condition. It was painful to see his best friend slip away into this dangerous netherworld of addiction. As soon as they got back to New York, he would speak to Linda. They had to get Ricardo into rehab.

Lili, wearing a diaphanous sheath of moss-green gauze, came to find Jeff leaning against the balustrade, immersed in thought.

"Tonight you are supposed to have fun." She took his arm and returned him to the crowd. She introduced him to a successful-looking gentleman from Spain, then to a defense minister from Saudi Arabia. Over drinks, Jeff observed the very weird bejeweled woman with the cat and learned she was in the food import and export business.

Jeff met Robert Powers for the first time. Lili praised Jeff's achievements with the new campaign. As they shook hands, Robert looked Jeff directly in the eye with an unmistakable look of complicity. Jeff was struck by his gray eyes . . . they shared the same brilliance he had seen in those of the red-haired woman, a luminosity that, now and then, shone from Lili's blue eyes. It was a clarity and shine that, in his experience, was peculiar to these three people.

Jeff liked Robert but made a cautious mental note to remember his affiliation with the *Group*.

"You know, love," Lili said to Robert, "I think that as soon as Jeff can separate himself from the fashion campaign, he should move to one of our new mergers, the digital campaign." She turned to Jeff. "The industry is about to change. The entire world will now be hooked to Powers Digital." She laughed. "But now, no more business. This is a party night. Jeff, I hope you enjoy yourself."

Someone signaled from the upper terrace, and Lili and Robert moved on. Jeff wandered among the crowd. He could not put his finger exactly on what it was, but a number of the guests' faces reminded him of human masks.

"Sorry I snapped," Ricardo said to him, still holding a vodka in his hand. "I've been under so much freaking pressure! And I can't get rid of this horrible headache. I've taken everything I can think of."

"Perhaps you should partake less and not more."

"I will, after they open my freaking breathing passages."

"Are you happy, Ricardo?"

"What do you mean? I'm miserable—the sinuses, the headaches . . . the pressure . . ."

"That's exactly what I mean. I don't think things were supposed to turn out this way. We were always like brothers. Now we are drifting apart. I see you slipping away, and I can't let that happen."

Ricardo sobered up momentarily. "If this is what success is all about, perhaps we have to reconsider."

"You are wasting away, and I find myself sandwiched between people who are trying to kill each other." Jeff gave Ricardo a short version of what had occurred in Paris, as well as what he had uncovered about Penelope.

"Oh man, that's heavy! What are we gonna do?"

"I don't know. We have to watch each other's backs. I will figure a way out. The timing has to be right." The two young men clasped hands.

"I didn't want to tell you . . . if you only knew what I've found out," added Ricardo. "Some of the people around us are not who they appear to be. And I mean physically—we have entered Geburah's Den."

"Geburah?"

"Yes, the fifth emanation of the *Otz Chiim*, the tree of life. He is Geburah, the destroyer. This entire setup operates under its influence. It is force unbalanced, but force, nevertheless."

Jeff thought he understood. The *Group* amassed force and power through destruction. "I should have guessed that you, of all people, would pick up on it. You have known all along?"

"I didn't want to shatter your dream, but the world is about to be destroyed," said Ricardo.

They both laughed.

"You see. It's still us, covering each other's rear ends."

"Ricardo, you are hooked on the stuff, aren't you?"

"I'm afraid I am but working on stopping it."

"Hang in there. I'll pull you through."

"I do get irrational. I must warn you . . . I blab, get violent sometimes."

"I know."

"It will be easier after the surgery."

"Would it not be better to wait and have it done in New York—later?"

"Will you lighten up? It is just a sinus operation. Don't be so freaking paranoid!"

Jeff witnessed the moment of lucidity in his friend begin to slip away.

The crowd was now separating into two groups. Some of the guests were being ushered into the upper terrace for supper. The rest, those associated with Keller DeWinter, including the ones Jeff had previously considered wearing weird human masks, were heading down the terrace stairs and crossing the garden into what appeared to be the entrance to an underground wine cellar. There was joy and anticipation on the faces of those guests who had previously tasted the sumptuous hospitality of Keller DeWinter. Ricardo and Jeff joined the queue and resigned themselves to enjoying yet another extravagance of the organization that had enveloped them, the one that held them, unwittingly, in its thrall.

Jeff tossed and turned in bed, able to sleep only fitfully. Images of last night's orgy writhed and twisted in half-awake dreams until he could hardly distinguish nightmare from reality. Nymphs and satyrs danced to exotic and erotic tunes around a crystal sphere, free-flowing fountain bubbling with a mixture of champagne, ecstasy, and who knows what other psychedelic drugs. Like everyone else, Jeff had drunk from it and had become deliriously intoxicated. Several nude young men and women, some of whom he recognized from the penthouse, offered themselves to the guests in exchange for gold coins. Jeff remembered rose petals falling from the ceiling, silver trays bearing rare and delectable edibles, and spirits of all descriptions. Beautiful acrobats twirled on golden ropes above their heads, and singers regaled them with music. It was an orgy for the senses that would challenge anything he had ever read about in ancient Rome. It was the drugs, he was sure, that had made him think the weird-looking individuals wearing human masks were aliens.

He had a vague recollection of Lili reclining on a divan with several adoring lovers at her feet, teasing him with a wicked smile and malicious eyes. He was certain that, at some point, Ricardo had been among them. Jeff had felt not only jealousy but also fear that Ricardo might betray his confidence. By the time Jeff decided to leave, Lili's smile—a mixture of triumph and derision—indicated she had extracted from Ricardo what she needed to know.

XIX

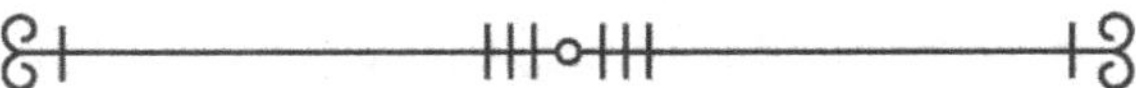

Paris

Legs crossed in lotus position, deep in meditation, Danielle sat on the French limestone floor of her Paris apartment's atrium. Still unable to transmit to Edentia, she was beginning to grasp segments of the horror unfolding in the universe. The Edentian council had closed the vortex and activated all seraphic posts surrounding Urantia. Danielle understood they were on the verge of celestial warfare.

The Luciel Rebellion was in full swing throughout the universe, despite the fact that Luciel had been imprisoned for nearly 1,500 Earth-years and that the trial of Gabriel versus Luciel was well on its way. Luciel would be charged with celestial treason and universal insurrection. The outcome of the trial would not be favorable and pointed to inevitable annihilation.

To pass such judgment on a brilliant Son of Light like Luciel had never been done in this universe. All rebel forces would join the legions of the Dragon and march on the legions of the Creator. They would create chaos and seize any opportunity to control the vortices. Chaos on a decimal planet like Earth could manifest in financial and political unrest, natural disasters, war, or pestilence—whatever it took to bring the planet down.

She thought of Robert's involvement, and her heart filled with pain. Everything pointed to the possibility that he had lost the last thread of connection with the Source.

Her meditation was interrupted by the sound of an approaching car. She opened her eyes and, as she got to her feet, the door to the guestroom opened. Tom had finished checking on Jean-Christophe's wound and changing the dressing. The car that would take Tom to the airport would be pulling in any minute now. The doctor stood under the doorframe, giving the Frenchman last-minute instructions about the medication he was to take, when he saw Danielle approaching.

"I think he will be fine in a day or two—at least able to walk," said Tom.

"Bah!" puffed Jean-Christophe in dismissal. "I'm OK. I think I can go with Danielle and the others now."

"It was a nasty cut," said Tom. "I'd take it easy."

"I've had worse things happen to me in the digs."

"Call us if you have any problems." Danielle said, pointing to the medal. Danielle and Tom embraced, and the doctor waved to Jean-Christophe. The driver picked up the suitcases and headed downstairs, followed by Dr. O'Neil. It was a chilly morning, promising snow. Cam and Danielle stood by the window, watching Tom get in the car. Cam left the room, and Danielle turned around to find Jean-Christophe out of bed, positioning himself on the living room sofa. "I'm telling you I can help."

"Absolutely not!"

The Frenchman shook his head. "I still can't believe it. You really are from another galaxy!"

"Well, yes, but so is your essence. The sojourn of your soul is on this planet."

"That still makes you an extra-terrestrial, doesn't it?"

"If you want to look at it that way."

"Do you still consider Yahweh "the Source?"

"Not Yahweh," she corrected him again. "Taoism has the closest definition to the truth. It says, 'If you can call *Him* by name, then *He* is not the *Eternal One*."

"Have you ever seen *Him*?"

Danielle laughed in delight. "No. Not the way you mean it. We are more aware of His presence in Edentia. We, therefore, live in a state of bliss. It is different here. We are trying to liberate humanity from the illusion that it is separated from the Source."

"Couldn't you just open the firmament and broadcast the truth to every corner of the world?"

"We must work without disturbing the perimeters of the realm. Only under very strenuous circumstances can we employ supernatural powers."

"The other night . . ."

"Yes. It was poor judgment on our part, but we had no choice. We must have looked quite bizarre to the young man."

"For sure. Jeff must think the champagne caused the hallucinations."

"I am worried about him . . ."

"So am I," said Jean-Christophe. "He is definitely not one of them."

"We have to be careful and discriminatory in our offense. Did you give him your card?"

"*Oui.*"

"Good. If he ever calls, the card will activate our tracking devices."

"Perhaps I should have told him more."

"No. He would not have believed you, anyway."

"I have a question that has been bugging me. You Edentians call yourselves immortals, yet if as you say, all the human spirit is immortal, then how is your kind different from ours?"

"It has to do with the levels of enlightenment. Your world exists as a new type of evolutionary planet. The souls incarnating into your matter have many lessons to learn and evolutions to accomplish before moving on. If you only knew how many times your planet has been on the verge of falling into the hands of the adversary!"

"The Creator, you have explained, is the direct Son of the Source."

"One of the begotten sons of the Eternal One. He is the Creator of all and everything in our universe. We call him Michael. Because of his incarnation in the flesh here on Earth, you know him as Jesus."

"So all this insurrection we are trying to prevent is against Him?"

"Yes. the Ancient of Days and Supreme Divine Courts of Nebadon have passed a final and irrevocable decree. Anyone charged with sin—that is, rebellion against the Creator Son, Michael—shall be found guilty by the Divine Council and will be annihilated. The Cirel *Group* is cataloged as a rebel group and will be brought to trial, sooner or later.

"The approach of RA, the organic interplanetary ship, is pressing matters. The ship is scheduled to pass through this galaxy, and it will await our laser signal before it heads in this direction."

"I can see why the *Group* will do all they can to prevent the *Formation* from taking place," Jean-Christophe said.

"Yes. They need more time to complete their nefarious plan."

"How long have you been a recorder?"

"Since the beginning of Earth's recorded time. I have submitted recommendations for its acceleration or advised restrain. Now, even my survival is at stake."

"Wait a minute, I thought you were immortal." Jean-Christophe flinched.

"Just as there is a secret to creation, there is also a secret to spiritual annihilation. We fear the arch-rebels might obtain that secret, which makes even us, the immortals, afraid."

"Has the enemy amassed such vast power?"

"Yes. Since this is not the only galaxy on the brink of war, we are trying to be self-sufficient. We'll attempt to contain the insurrection at the planetary level without further divine intervention," Danielle explained.

"What I am trying to locate in the tombs is very important to you. Why?"

"Our present lines of communication have been compromised. In the remote past, we used a giant crystal set into a gold base as a transmitter. The crystal was a potent firestone. But when circumstances caused us to fear that it could be misused by our enemies, it was separated into fragments and dispersed among several Edentians for safe keeping—so that no enemy could find it in one place and use it against us. This is one of those pieces."

Danielle showed him the small stone she had entrusted to Kit. "Several crystals similar to this fit precisely into the grooves of the metal piece that originally held the whole stone. The gold base is what you must find. It is said to be buried in the sarcophagus of one of the pharaoh's daughters."

"Clever," said Jean-Christophe, "as civilization made its transition from female to male dominance, a less prominent female tomb ensured that it would lie undisturbed for thousands of years."

"But now that you told me what the medians said, I am convinced the *Group* suspects where it is buried. We have to retrieve it before they do, or they will destroy it. Only with the transmitter, the stones—including the main crystal—and the right time and location, will we be able to create the *Formation*."

"How can those tiny crystals produce enough power to send such a transmission?"

"The crystals act in the same manner as masers—powerful lasers that amplify light waves. It is a form of electromagnetic energy, a method we have used successfully when stranded on primitive planets. On this planet, there is a monolith from Edentia that works in conjunction with the transmitter and the crystals. Together, they will produce the necessary power to send a signal."

"Monolith?"

"It is a sophisticated type of asbestos, non-conductive stones that pick up the radiation from stars, much like we now use X-rays from the sun and convert them to mutable energy. The rays ascend and descend at such speeds, they are invisible to the human eye. The *Foundation* needs . . ."

She could not complete the sentence. Alarm registered in her face. "They are in trouble," she stared at her watch.

"Who?"

"John, Angela . . . perhaps Chris. They are at the airport. I have to help them."

Before he could ask anything else, she had run out of the room and, within seconds, had put on her boots, a black leather jacket, and was running out the door in the direction of the garage. Jean-Christophe felt helpless but realized he could hardly move, and when he did, his wound hurt terribly.

During the drive to the airport, Camiel gave Danielle a full report. He informed her that her friends were at Charles De Gaulle. Chris had arrived safely from New York, but John and Angela, who arrived on a flight from Atlanta thirty minutes later, had been detained.

"A group of terrorists has blocked the passage leading from the plane and taken hostage some of the arriving passengers."

Danielle detected a troubling vibration while she continued to receive the report from Cam.

"Angela picked up my telepathic advice to exit the plane quickly and head for the main gate but could not avoid the armed terrorists. John and Angela have been pushed back into the waiting room."

"Is it a random hostage assault or are the terrorists targeting John and Angela?" Danielle wanted to know.

After a couple of minutes, Cam continued, "The majority of the hostages have been set free, except for a group of twelve, mostly Americans, who are to remain captive until the terrorists' demands are met. John and Angela are among the twelve."

Danielle was at De Gaulle in no time and managed to get through the crowd and approach the gate, despite the tight security that now blanketed the airport. The French police had arrived and had the terrorists pinned down from all directions.

Danielle, unseen, slipped through the chaos and climbed to a vantage point where she might be able to see and be seen by Angela and John. In the crowd, she could see Chris trying to move closer, waving his press credentials to the police to no avail. Then she saw Cam, positioned on a corner ledge opposite hers.

The twelve were now being pushed at gunpoint back in the direction of the tunnel and toward the airplane. The terrorists had apparently requested fuel and were about to re-board.

"The flight crew has not emerged," Cam let Danielle know telepathically. "We have to act fast."

Danielle understood. She fixed her gaze in the direction of her friends. Angela looked up and saw Danielle and then Cam. She squeezed John's arm to let him know they were there.

"They want us to start walking toward the exit," Angela whispered to John. "Then, when they signal, run toward the flight information screens on the left."

"We'll be shot!" he whispered back in alarm.

"They're telling us to do it."

"We can't."

"We have to." She took a couple of steps in that direction. Not meaning to, he followed. The screams of one of the terrorists, while pointing his gun at them, made them freeze. He was instructing them in broken English to step back and rejoin the group. They didn't move. He repeated his threat. Angela looked up. Danielle held her gaze for a moment and then moved her lips, instructing them to run.

Angela grabbed John's sleeve and without hesitation yelled, "Run!" He didn't understand what made him follow.

As they were rushing toward the screens, they heard the sound of gunshots behind them, followed by a loud explosion. Smoke and a blinding light followed them, but they arrived safely at the screens and hid behind them. Someone screamed that a bomb had gone off. After an exchange of gunfire, the paramedics were now moving in, trying to see in the midst of all the smoke. Two of the four terrorists had been shot, and the other two were now being taken into custody. Hysterical screams could be heard throughout the terminal.

The Edentians, without further ado, quietly headed for the exit. As they passed the first trash can, Cam opened his fists and discarded the handful of spent bullets that he had magnetically attracted when the terrorist discharged his weapon in their direction.

Away from the crowd, Danielle and Camiel waited by an emergency exit. Shaken by the experience, Angela, John, and Chris joined them, and the five silently walked to the car.

XX

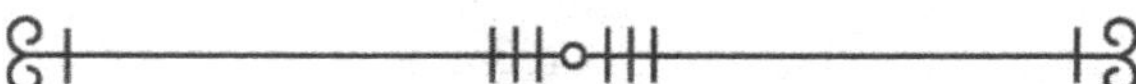

Paris

Jean-Christophe had followed the airport incident on television, the taking of the hostages and the explosion of a homemade bomb, followed by the capture of the two terrorists. Incidents of terrorism had recently escalated in Paris. The European press compared the current instability in Paris to the violent atmosphere reported in many American cities.

In a televised interview, the Reverend Theodore Edwards of the New Era Christian Alliance denounced the violent incident at De Gaulle airport as an act of Satan and urged all Christians of the world to send money to finance the war against Satan.

Listening to Edwards, Jean-Christophe's concern turned to amusement. When he heard the car stop, he was glad to see everyone arrive safely. It was agreed that everyone should stay in Danielle's apartment. Cam went into the library and posted himself on watch by the tall French windows.

Chris walked about the rooms in a state of amazement at the nineteenth-century Renaissance revival-inspired apartment. To the left of the salon, he noticed the library displayed eighteenth- and nineteenth-century literature. He returned from the salon but did not sit down. He continued to wander, examining the Bouguereau paintings. Simone, the French *domestique*, was busy setting the table in a small but formal dining room that opened into the atrium.

It did not take long for Danielle to make everyone feel at home and put aside the frightening events at the airport. During dinner, the French archeologist entertained them with amusing accounts of his digs around the world. Some of the funny anecdotes included joint adventures with Danielle. Chris felt a touch of envy. John and Jean-Christophe had known Danielle for years and included her as part of their past.

"Danielle is an anomaly," cracked Jean-Christophe, "starting with her Jewish and Catholic upbringing, her Hellenistic studies . . ."

Chris's Jewish heritage suddenly assumed a basic connection with her.

"She reveres all the deities," continued the Frenchman, "The Holy Trinity, Yahweh, Allah, as well as all the gods of pagan antiquity. She showed me how to extricate myself from every sticky situation in the Middle East. Now, I take the Star of David, crosses, and amulets, and just to be safe, I end every dialogue with the Arabic *Inshallah*, but this particular time . . ."

Chris continued listening with fascination. He could see Danielle in khakis, digging among the ruins and holding ranging rods to measure stylobates. Her claim to be of a different order of beings became irrelevant. Chris saw her only as a woman, with all the qualities that made her his ideal partner.

Jean-Christophe continued with his anecdotes. Danielle's laughter ceased momentarily, and she looked at Chris, interrupting and derailing his thoughts, which in her perception, were going in the wrong direction.

You need to understand, Christian. It is not all about possession and pleasure.

But I don't want to possess you. Danielle, I just want to love you. He was not even aware that they were communicating telepathically.

Chris, I need all of your energy channeled in the right way. Please help me do what I must do.

I will do anything you ask or need but don't ask me not to love you because I can't promise that. I will love you till the day I die.

She smiled hopelessly. *No, he would never understand her dilemma.*

Lucerne

It was a brisk morning. Jeff, emotionally numb, walked aimlessly by the lake. He raised glassy eyes toward the chateau. Everything that had taken place since he arrived in Europe seemed surreal, like a bad dream he wished he could erase. Anguish had crawled deep into his soul, and Jeff felt weighed down with sadness and guilt.

He had awakened the morning after the orgy with a terrible headache. Despite the nausea, he had jumped out of bed, remembering that Ricardo was scheduled for surgery. "Oh, no!" Surely Ricardo would not be crazy enough to go under the knife in his condition.

He jumped into his sweats and ran to the clinic, where he was informed the surgery had already been performed.

"Everything is fine," a nurse told him. "Ricardo is in the recovery room. In about an hour, he will be moved to a private room."

Jeff went down to the terrace and grabbed some breakfast. It was quiet, and the atmosphere was sober.

Still annoyed by his friend's betrayal, Jeff wondered why Ricardo would tell Lili about his experience in Paris? Lili would never fully trust him again. Ricardo's mind was more muddled than he had anticipated. But it was he who had brought Ricardo in, and he would be the one to take him out.

On his way to see Ricardo, Jeff found out from Heidi Schiller that Ms. Keller, along with the majority of the guests, had left right after the party for an unknown destination.

"One of the Keller planes remained behind," she informed him, "to take you back to New York. Ricardo will be able to travel within a day or two. In the meantime, why don't you take advantage of the spa's superb facilities?"

By the time he finished breakfast, Ricardo had been installed in a spacious room overlooking the lake. Jeff found him sitting up in bed, fully wake, nose bandaged, with mild bruising around the eyes. He was busily unfolding a small silver foil pack.

"I don't believe you!" Jeff exclaimed as his friend touched the tip of his middle finger to his tongue.

Ricardo blushed, refolding the pack.

"Give me that!"

Ricardo obeyed with the docility of a mischievous child caught in the act and sadly watched Jeff stick the pack in his pocket.

"Actually, I was saying goodbye to the stuff . . . forever."

"I'm sure you were."

"You'll see. You will be so proud of me!"

"Proud? Can you tell me why you told Lili about the incident in Paris?"

"I don't know. She somehow gets into my head."

"So it's Lili's fault that you are so messed up?"

"In a way. But no more drugs. I can do it." There was a moment of silence.

"OK. As long as you realize you have a problem, we'll work things out."

Jeff's mind spun. What had to be done, he had to do alone. He had to find a way to outsmart Lili and the others. "Get some rest now." His voice had softened.

"Will you hand me my phone from the leather bag on that chair? I think I'll text Linda."

"Good idea." Jeff searched the bag to make sure it didn't contain any drugs. "I will check on you later."

"Thanks . . . for not giving up on me."

Jeff went to the gymnasium, lifted some weights, and then had a refreshing swim in the indoor pool. On his second lap, he sensed someone standing near the edge of the pool. Without interrupting his strokes, he glanced up and recognized the figure of Heidi Schiller. When he reached the edge of the pool, he looked directly at her. She stood immobile, staring at him with a solemn expression in her pale blue eyes. Jeff felt a chill run through his body.

It was then he knew Ricardo was dead.

~

"Ricardo suffered a cardiac arrest resulting from complications after surgery," the attending physician informed Jeff. "Post-operative traces of cocaine were found on his tongue and throat. Your friend should have known that it was lethal to add drugs to the potent, lingering effects of anesthesia." Jeff stared at the man in silence. "We were unable to resuscitate him," added the physician.

Jeff then inquired about the surgery. "It went very well. It was performed by a highly competent surgeon, Doctor Eric Hansen."

"May I speak to Dr. Hansen?"

"Unfortunately, Dr. Hansen left for Geneva shortly after the surgery, once certain that the patient was stable."

Something didn't seem right; he still had the packet he had taken from Ricardo. He asked no more questions, only to be allowed to see his friend's body before it was taken to the morgue.

The nurse pulled back the sheet. Jeff held back his tears as he gazed at the peaceful face of Ricardo. He reached around his neck with an uncontrollable urge to hug him in a final goodbye and noticed a tiny cut behind his ear. He thought of asking what it could be but didn't. *What would it matter now?*

Jeff walked silently along the edge of the lake, his grief palpable and his hands in his pockets, clutching the tiny foil and his phone. He needed to summon all his courage to call Linda in New York to ask what she would have him do with Ricardo's body.

Jeff could not forgive himself. *I should have stayed with him.* He felt guilty and desperately alone. Then he remembered the Frenchman and reached for his wallet.

Yes, he still had Jean-Christophe's card.

~

Paris

"This was, after all, an experiment." Danielle spoke to her friends as they sat around a table on the terrace of the Paris apartment. "Because *you* represent that which is noble and beautiful in the human spirit, what is strong and good in the human mind. Each of you represents what is worth preserving in the human race. This is why I have chosen you to help me bring about this cosmic event.

"A few months from now, an interplanetary vessel known as RA will cross the intersection of Splandon and Mirria. Aboard the ship are life carriers—entrusted with the highest mission in the universe—to import life to the chosen planets and continue monitoring their progress. I have been delegated to signal them from Earth through a planetary *formation* that must be in place at that time, but our network of communication is compromised, and some of our members have disappeared. I need your help to send the signal. The window of opportunity to send it is only a few minutes."

"How exactly is this *Formation* supposed to happen?" asked Jean-Christophe.

"The *Formation* is accomplished by at least three Edentians, *Foundation* members and two members of the violet race."

"The violet race?" Chris asked.

"Yes, the offspring of the Edentians—the star seeds. One of the mandates for the realm is to preserve some individuals of the pure race who have residual traits of the Edentians, who could perform as magisterial parents to a new race if needed.

"I am relying on John to monitor the heavens and keep a strict account of every unusual energy formation that could be disruptive to our purposes. He has been tracking the energy patterns the *Group* is using, how they are accumulating power, and if they are receiving support from other alien races."

She turned to John, and he cleared his throat. "They have used what we call the high points of the planet to send signals and intercept the *Foundation's* messages. The four high points are bulges on the planet." He took a pencil and began drawing on a piece of paper. He drew a circle and inside it, a triangle with a point in the center. He then connected it with broken lines to the center of the angles in the triangle. "These four high spots roughly form a tetrahedron."

All of them stared at the drawing while John continued, "These spots are the same distance from one another. I have located the general areas but now have to fine-tune my calculations to pinpoint where the *Group* is hiding and the location of their transmitter.

"Their transmitter is getting power from a yet undetermined underground location. Unique energy currents flow under several geological layers of the planet. Danielle helped me map their position and enlightened me as to their nature."

"Advanced civilizations in the past," added Danielle, "manipulated these currents and brought about destruction."

"It seems the *Group* has almost total control of one of the currents. I discovered the signal had originated on Earth, somewhere deep beneath the crust."

"They are perfecting something they are about to launch," said Danielle. "It could be a world event of catastrophic proportions—a distraction while they throw this planet into the insurrection. I must inform the carriers that not the entire population of the planet knows of, or is in agreement with, the rebellion. Otherwise, the carriers perceiving the red aura of Urantia might label the planet 'hopelessly irreparable' and add it to the list marked for extinction. According to the prevailing mandate, the souls rebelling against the Creator will be annihilated."

"What would become of those who had nothing to do with the insurrection? Would they be destroyed indiscriminately?" Angela ventured to ask.

"No. Converted to spirit energy, they would be relocated to another training ground similar to this one. However, everything they have gained here will be lost to them."

She turned once again to John and took his hand. "I know you have been under a lot of pressure and scrutiny."

"I don't really know what will happen when I get back . . ." said John.

"President Parker has already arranged your transfer to Argos, the top secret military installation in Colorado. There, you will have access to extraordinary technology that will enable you to continue your work. We need to know the pattern being used to amass energy in manipulation of the Edenic currents."

Turning to Jean-Christophe Danielle continued, "There is a monolith that holds the primary element for either combining or destroying those forces. The *Group* is aware of its existence. We must get to it first. I believe part of it is hidden in the tombs of the pharaoh's daughters. It is the crucial element for securing our *Formation*."

"Tell us about the origin of the conflict between the *Group* and the *Foundation*."

"The *Group* and the *Foundation* have existed in parallel since time immemorial. Each has a different belief as to how the local universe should be governed. In the past, while aware of our differences, we coexisted on the planet and did not interfere with each other's views. The *Foundation* has been tolerant of the *Group's* dysfunction, thinking it was a passing phase in its members' evolution. But now their difference in philosophy has turned from disloyalty to open treason.

"A number of the repenting souls working out their karma have once again rebelled. Cirel has convinced them their leader, Luciel, currently on trial in the celestial courts, will be rescued and will lead the rebel army through the galaxies. What they lack in power, they are making up for in numbers. They are targeting the young people, confusing their minds, illegally taking souls, and forcing them to join rebel ranks.

"Angela has been sent to aid me in recognizing the trend. She is an epidemiologist working with the *Foundation*. She has been observing hospitals, their patients, and, in particular, the medical profession to determine just how deep the infiltration of the *Group* has gone, and to identify the effects of the *Group's* nefarious experiments."

John was the first to look at the Angela with a look of surprise

"The implant I had in my head is but one of many she has seen."

"In your case, it was used to prevent you from any further communication with Edentia."

"What do you think is their immediate plan?" asked Chris.

"I suspect the addictions they are causing will lower the body's resistance to a potent drug that will be administered globally. It could be a powerful form of heroin, introduced into the food we eat, the things we drink, and the medications and products we consume."

"Well, of course," Chris added. "That is why the *Group* is acquiring all kinds of businesses. They will have a hand in everything we consume, plus they control the subliminal messages constantly encouraging us to use the drugs. A new method of enslavement."

"It is getting increasingly difficult to stay ahead of them," said Danielle. "Not having someone on the inside, we have to rely on our hunches."

Jean-Christophe's phone rang. The Frenchman, who had been listening attentively, made a signal for Danielle to stop as he recognized the caller's ID name. "*Oui . . . oui*," he stood up and moved away from the others.

When Jean-Christophe closed his phone, he looked at Danielle. "We now have someone on the inside. Jeff Montgomery."

XXI

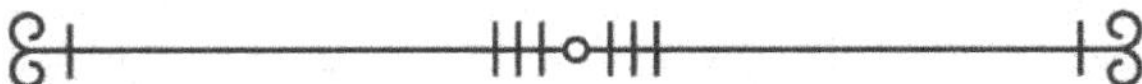

Paris

"Danielle, you have to remember where the other components are!" pressed Cam.

The two walked in silence along the Seine, past the *bouquinistes,* their telepathic conversation undetected by passers-by.

"The transmitter has to be assembled in the next twelve weeks. So far, we only have one vital stone. The *Group* should be moving into the second phase soon. Kitzia has discovered they are encoding the image of the Dragon and the sound of the roar into music, into the pop culture, subliminally hypnotizing youth into aligning with the *Group's* forces of evil."

"Do you think the *Group* suspects my earthly associates?" Danielle asked.

"Hard to tell."

"Cam, do you think I am terrible for involving them?"

"Not at all. They wanted to take part in saving their world. The *Foundation* hopes to be fully operative again in a fortnight. The web of communication will be re-established."

"What damage have we accrued so far?" asked Danielle.

"Nothing that cannot be repaired, except for the disappearance of Kjell. We don't have much hope of finding him again"

"And Robert . . . have we lost him, as well?"

Cam did not respond.

Danielle lowered her head and stared at the ground. "Kjell was my friend, quite often my guardian. We went through so many lifetimes together. I don't know what to think about Robert. What could they have offered him that would make him jeopardize his eternal welfare?"

"Are you sure he has abandoned us?"

"For him to take the stand he has taken, to ally his resources and spirit with the adversary, shows an irrevocable allegiance to the rebellion." After a few seconds of silence, she said, "Cam, tell me about the rebellion. You must be more up-to-date than me with what is going on. Is your planetary station involved in active defense?"

"No. Dresia is a training ground. We are not warriors; we are mostly messengers—guardian messengers. We are sent to protect in time of crisis. I was sent to protect you during an instance of vulnerability."

"And I am truly thankful." She smiled. "I became so involved in earthly matters that I became careless.

"The *Group* had long been plotting their assault. It could have been anyone in your place. Knowing the vortices were closing and the quarantine would be tighter, they were counting on one major transmission to the Council from a recorder. They didn't know it would be you. Kjell rushed to your aid."

"He was trying to deflect the lightning that struck me, wasn't he?"

"Yes. I was immediately dispatched with orders from Edentia, and the *Foundation* here mobilized its newest recruits. Angela has proven to be a real asset. She identified the presence of Cirel at work in this realm. We regret not having been fast enough to prevent his intervention."

"I am so sorry for Kjell."

"The Great Orsef, himself, wanted to come down."

Danielle's heart skipped a beat at the mention of the name, but she struggled to appear unaffected.

"The Great Orsef is kind. Do you know him?"

"No, only of him, of his greatness and particular interest in this mission. There is talk that someone dear to him is involved in this rehabilitation mission." Camiel suddenly smiled in delight. "Well, of course . . . I should have known." He bowed his head in acknowledgment. "It is a great honor to have been assigned to your guardianship."

During the week they had been in Paris, Chris noticed an extraordinary thing. There were times when Camiel and Danielle would exchange glances, not saying a word, yet Chris was sure an exchange of communication had taken place. He observed them closely, trying to tune in, and to his surprise, their nonverbal conversations began to pop into his consciousness with the same clarity as if they were being spoken. *I can understand them*! He picked up their discussions regarding common denominators in random world events and detected patterns form scenarios that could cause the collapse of an entire civilization.

Jean-Christophe's injury was healing, but characteristically, he was impatient. He told Chris about the assault on the evening he was with Jeff Montgomery and how Danielle had fought off the attackers. Danielle dismissed his story as an exaggeration. Chris gathered from a conversation between Danielle and Camiel that fighting was not something she was proud of. She would resort to it only when there was no other way. It was like the principle of Aikido; Edentians were supposed to set an example in the art of reconciliation and try not to break the connection with the universe through aggressive force.

Jean-Christophe started going daily to the Louvre, where he spent hours searching through large rooms of antiquities that had not been cataloged and prepared for display. Danielle gave him lists of pieces to look for in hopes of finding the missing stones.

Angela spent her days at the Institute LaSalle, where Dr. O'Neil had been weeks before, working in the labs, assisting in the investigation of newly discovered viruses. She was also tracking every move of Cirel, posing as Dr. Eric Hansen of Switzerland. The last piece of information Jeff Montgomery had passed on to Jean-Christophe presented the possibility that the *Group's* labs in Switzerland were experimenting with human infant cloning.

John Larkin was the only one of their group that did not remain in Paris. He left to meet with the *Foundation* members and from there to his new position at Argos.

On a late afternoon during their second week in Paris, the five gathered in Danielle's library to share their findings and discuss Danielle's conclusions in preparation for departing the city. Camiel, as usual, posted himself by the window.

On a screen, Danielle projected the image of an ancient rod with a gold circular headpiece. "The image shown is the famous rod, the pen, or key of Sharah, by which signals were sent to outer space." They all stared at the head of the rod, the circular plate made of gold, centered with two overlapping triangles that formed the Star of David. Christian, Jean-Christophe, and Angela gave their full attention to Danielle's instructions. Each one of them had an assignment and a deadline that must be met.

"We must think of ourselves as warriors," Danielle said. "The fight in our physical realm will soon begin. Use your watches to communicate and have your medals with you at all times. May the Power of Michael be with you."

Assignments in hand, Danielle sent the archeologist and the physicist on to their assigned journeys.

Jean-Christophe was to return to Egypt with Camiel and break a certain seal. Danielle would soon join them to enter the tombs and meet with the beings they called the medians.

Angela was to continue her research with other microbiologists to find an antidote for the virus that would be unleashed by the *Group*, intended to cause a world pandemic. Danielle asked Chris to remain with her in Europe a little longer.

When Chris found himself alone with Danielle, he asked, "If the power of the *Foundation* is linked with that of the universe, shouldn't it be omnipotent? Being on God's side, why should it feel threatened?"

Danielle smiled. "We all proceed from the Creator, but not all that He created will survive. Don't forget that when He gives free will, each soul shapes its own destiny. Out of respect for that gift of free will, which He has granted you, He cannot and will not interfere. He can put all his resources at our disposal to put us back on track, but He does not selectively withdraw the principle of free will.

"Think of this lifetime as a temporary school, with different levels of learning. You are here to remember *love* and everything else that you have forgotten. Love will reunite you with the Source."

Chris pressed forward. "We accept that we are here to do God's will, and at the same time, we are reminded that we do possess free will. Which one is it?"

"I don't think there is a contradiction," Danielle answered. "Free will has been granted, and that is God's will. He wants you to remember the path back to Him. And again, because of His gift of free will, He may not have a final word in the hearts of men. The learning process of the spirit is beset by certain inevitabilities."

"Then are you saying that a soul will set up its own parameters of experience?"

"Precisely. Consider:

> *If man is to relearn the meaning of Faith, how is he to trust that infallible Divine Voice within him, but by vacillating constantly in the predicament of trusting that which he cannot see?*
> *And Loyalty . . . how is he to develop that virtue, unless he personally experiences betrayal?*
> *Hope cannot be achieved unless he is surrounded by insecurity.*
> *How will he remember what Happiness truly is unless he is afflicted with misfortune?*
> *Truth can only be discerned when you inhabit a world where error is ever present and falsehood always possible . . . (The Urantia Book)*

"When you meet a man in less than desirable circumstances, do not judge or pity him. You must view him with respect and remember that his challenges are tougher than yours."

"Is everyone to experience the same things sooner or later?"

"No. You are here to remember what you have forgotten."

"Wow. Can you at least tell me how and why this happened to us?"

"It happened during the rebellion. Some spirits decided to separate from the Source and become autonomous. Even some members sent to monitor or assist in the rehabilitation project became corrupted and ceased to honor the Source, thus the origin of the *Group*. Since they can never go home, bitterness and resentment flow among the whole fallen population, and the rebellion continues. There have been many attempts to rescue them. The Creator himself descended . . ."

"Well, of course, so the Scripture says . . ." murmured Christian. "God sent his only begotten son to redeem man."

"Michael, Creator of this universe, came down Himself to remind the earthly inhabitants that they are children of the Universal Father and to show them how to get back home . . . not too many listened."

"So Earth's population is imprisoned in a self-imposed limbic lock?"

Danielle nodded. She knew she had said too much. But Chris pressed on.

"Danielle, what is reality?"

"God is real, and you are real. Everything else in what you call reality may or may not be. That is the challenge of life, the puzzle that you must decipher."

XXII

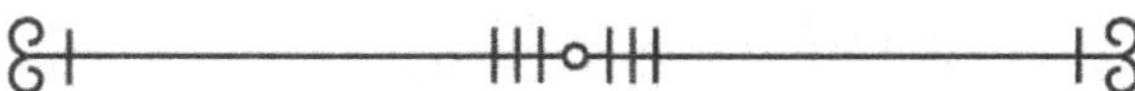

The French Countryside

The call came two days after Jean-Christophe and Angela departed.

Danielle and Christian would be going to meet with the *Foundation*. They quickly packed overnight bags and left Paris in Danielle's convertible.

Despite his love of adventure, Chris was happy to put his intrigue aside. It was a beautiful Saturday morning—cool and sunny. Danielle's hair blew in the wind, strands of copper and gold tossed into the bright sunlight, then falling naturally back in place. She wore dark sunglasses and Christian smiled, thinking she looked like a movie star.

She had insisted on driving, and he did not protest.

Leaning back in the passenger seat, Chris took the opportunity to observe this beautiful woman before he asked. "The other day, when you and Camiel were communicating wordlessly between yourselves. You said something about finding a 'rememberer'."

"We did." She looked at him, admiring his perceptiveness.

"What is a rememberer?"

"Someone who preserves memories of lifetimes."

"You speak of our lifetimes as swift passages."

"Well, they do go by in a blink."

"And then?"

"Then you momentarily return to your essence, the real you. Freed from the limitations of the five senses, you get to see the evolution of your soul without fear."

"So, fear is the great enemy?"

"When you conquer fear, you move toward love—the only other emotion that matters."

"Tell me about you in this lifetime. How and why you chose your life as it is."

"I came into this plane of existence via a close call. I had to escape into the physical realm to get away from my nefarious pursuers. The situation presented itself at a critical time and was favorable. Yvonne and Jean-Luc Peschard were a couple with a nine-year-old daughter. The three of them were vacationing in Provence. The car accident happened on a narrow curve on the road to Tourette-sur-Loup; they were all killed instantly. I watched their souls depart and respectfully requested permission of the Edentian Council to re-inhabit the little girl's body. So far as the rest of the world knew, Arlette Danielle Peschard, daughter of Yvonne and Jean-Luc Peschard—French ambassador to the United Nations—survived the accident. As the only surviving heir, Danielle inherited the Peschard fortune."

"What is your real name in Edentia?'

"Daniela."

"How coincidental! So, who cared for you as a child?"

"Father, or rather, Cardinal Santis, whom you met at my house in California and who is at the Vatican now, became my guardian. When I was twelve, the *Foundation* contacted me. After a series of verification procedures, they acknowledged my identity as an Edentian and put me back in touch with Edentia.

"It is a funny thing that happens while you are in the flesh; occasionally, you forget who you really are—it even happened to me."

The Jaguar made a sharp turn and headed for a quaint provincial inn off the main road. "Auberge Saint Michel" was painted on the sign above the front door. Danielle parked the car between two apple trees and jumped out, stretching her arms.

"How about cassoulet for lunch? "

"Sounds delicious!" said Chris, not sure what cassoulet was.

When they went into the rustic farmhouse-turned-restaurant, a petite, gray-haired woman emerged from the kitchen and greeted them with a smile.

"*Madame,* what a surprise! It has been so long!" the woman exclaimed upon seeing Danielle. "*Entrez, entrez.* You and your friend are most welcome."

Danielle put her arms around the woman. "Oh, it's good to see you, Martine." When she turned around, Chris thought he detected tears in Danielle's eyes.

"This is my friend, Christian Goodman."

The woman held Chris's hand between hers for several seconds and smiled at him warmly.

"Your usual corner table?" she asked.

"Yes. I was just praising your cassoulet, Martine."

"*Merci*, madame, but today, I have delicious paupiettes and falette as well."

"Veal rolls and incredible stuffed breast of veal," Danielle explained to Chris.

"Sounds perfect . . . and a bottle of good wine, a Bordeaux, perhaps."

"I will go down to the cellar myself and get the very best bottle we have."

When Martine walked away, they found themselves alone. It was not quite lunchtime, and they were the only customers.

"I love this place!" Danielle sighed.

Chris looked around. "So, this is one of your favorite places?"

"I don't mean this restaurant alone; I mean all of it . . . the whole world."

"I love it, too, now that you came into my life."

She smiled and let the implication slide by. "The sun, the sky, the meadows . . . how can you look at it and not be in a constant state of amazement?"

Chris loved to listen to her voice.

A server returned with a bottle of Chateau Margaux, compliments of Martine, and uncorked it for Chris to taste. It was pure velvet.

"Superb!" He signaled the waiter to pour.

A tray of *crudites* and a loaf of freshly baked bread were placed on the table.

"You are really very lucky," continued Danielle. "You get to experience almost all of it." She held the goblet and stared at its contents. "Do you know that angels envy you? They do. They will never get to know what this wine tastes like, have no idea of the meaning of hunger, cold, or anxiety. When I was twelve, I used to hear a recurring voice from within asking me what a 'lemon' was. It took me a while to realize the question was coming from my angel protectors. I recorded for them in detail, in the eternal collective consciousness, and explained what a lemon was—the taste, the color, the texture, and the smell. There is a universe encompassed in one lemon. At that point, I had returned to my job as a recorder and remembered that as you experience life, they get to experience it with you."

"I would have thought angels had all the answers. We see them as highly evolved beings."

"They are perfect and almost incapable of error. But your growth process fascinates them. Along with the inevitable discomforts, life gives you thrilling experiences, like falling in love. Angels love, of course, because love is the essence of their nature. But the act of falling in love . . . never."

"You mean the act of surrendering who and what you are for the mere chance of being near the loved one?" He looked at her rich, auburn hair, parted in the middle, curving so gently, and casually tucked behind her ears. He observed the sparkle in her luminous green eyes when she spoke. Her voice was brimming with vitality, without a trace of weariness in its tone.

"I love you, Danielle."

She looked at him like she had that afternoon at her penthouse. Chris knew there was a place in her heart that was his.

"Christian, the things that you expect to accompany those words are not possible."

"What things do you think I expect?"

"The normal things that people in love expect: marriage, children, growing old together . . ."

"And why not? Why can't we be together?"

"I have worked very hard at remaining detached from romance. I accept that those aspects of love are things that are not available to me as part of my mortal experience."

"What? Do you feel that falling in love is too trivial for Edentians, or so foolish as to detract you from your work? Danielle, I need you. Let me be with you. I'll help you however I am capable. But know, for what it is worth, that you are not emotionally alone; I love you as much as a human is capable of loving."

"I know, and that concerns me deeply."

"Concern is all you are capable of feeling?"

Danielle sipped her wine, trying to formulate what she needed to say in a way that he would understand and not be hurt by it.

"Chris, I am not like you."

"I know, I know. You keep reminding me that you are superior."

"Not superior . . . different. I have different goals, things I must accomplish."

"To me you are a woman—a woman with a mission—but foremost a woman. I see you breathe, eat, drink, and enjoy life. How can you convince me that you don't have needs, that you don't experience loneliness?"

Agitated, Chris accidentally tipped his wineglass over, breaking it and spilling the wine. He felt clumsy and embarrassed as a drop of blood slid down the side of his hand. Danielle reached across with her napkin, but he had already blotted the cut with his own.

"It's nothing," said Chris.

The waiter came over to sweep up the broken glass, blotting the spill with a towel.

"May I?" Danielle stretched out her hand, still holding her napkin.

Chris let his hand slide onto hers while she applied pressure to the cut. He raised his eyes to meet hers, and their eyes remained locked for a few seconds. The emotion he felt when she looked into his eyes prevented his noticing a tiny glass vial Danielle had concealed under the napkin, and into which she was slipping a drop of his blood.

"I think the bleeding has stopped," said Danielle.

Martine had appeared to say, "I'll bring a Band-Aid, *tout suite*." She took the soiled napkin and vial Danielle had concealed.

"I am sorry," said Chris. "I act like such a fool sometimes. Please forget everything I said."

"Chris, if things were different . . . if the *Foundation* were not in a crisis . . . if I were to choose a companion to live this lifetime with, it would certainly be someone like you."

He felt a surge of encouragement. "Thanks. If there is something I have learned from you, it is to be hopeful."

Martine returned with the Band-Aid and handed Danielle an envelope. It bore the two concentric circles of the *Foundation's* insignia. Danielle read the message without betraying any emotion. When she put it down, Chris noticed that it was written in the same archaic script as the document Kitzia had once shown him. He had not thought about it since then, but seeing this type of writing as a standard mode of communication among Edentians, he was reminded of what she had just said. They were, indeed, different.

"What is it?" he inquired.

"They are not ready for us yet. It looks as if we have the day to ourselves."

"It pays to be hopeful."

Danielle laughed, and the tension of the previous few moments vanished. A plate of stuffed veal surrounded by braised artichokes and puffed potato squares was placed on the table, along with a clay pot containing the cassoulet. It was a romantic setting and Chris decided to let chance take its course. He was not going to say anything else that would make Danielle put up her guard.

"Everything OK, *madame, monsieur*?" Martine's words were bathed with kindness. "Anything else I can bring you? We are preparing for you a special dessert, Kirsch souffle."

"What else could we ask for, madame? You have prepared a sumptuous meal!" Chris complimented sincerely.

"Martine, please sit with us for a moment," said Danielle. "It has been a long time. Tell me how you are doing. Your children?"

"Everybody is fine. We found more slaughtered cattle just recently."

"Martine . . ." Danielle's tone was sympathetic.

"Guy is at the Institute in Paris. He likes what he is doing. He tells me, 'Mama, you have to be careful with the food. Some of it is living poison.' What am I to do? Food is my livelihood." She laughed. "I will stop using peanuts and avoid chlorpyrifos, diazinon, dicloran, HCB, malathion, etcetera. But continue using raisins and live with the carbaryl, DDT, dimethoate, endosulfan, and so on."

Christian's senses became highly alert. This was no peasant woman, despite her demeanor. Danielle listened acutely to the information the French woman was passing on to her. He paid close attention and not ask questions, hoping to decipher it for himself.

"The world situation is becoming more tense," said Danielle. "Even the countryside is unsafe now. The threat of contamination has reached every corner of the world."

"I hear Paris is becoming very dangerous."

Chris had the distinct impression that Martine was referring to the incident at the airport. He watched Danielle as the two women continued their double-speak.

"Yes. Terrorists and explosives are turning up everywhere. People think their governments can no longer protect them."

"Everyone is taking up arms, even here in the provinces," sighed the woman. "They say that the arms manufacturers will become the real warlords, and even President Parker in the United States will not be able to stop them."

"Oh, yes, Martine. He will stop them."

"Our news tells us the wave of religious fanaticism in America has begun to spread throughout Europe. Korans, Bibles, and guns . . . what chaos that will be!"

Danielle took the woman's hand. "We won't let it happen, Martine."

The woman seemed reassured. "Do you stay in touch with your mentor in Rome?"

Danielle's face showed concern as she answered. "Yes. I do."

"Give the cardinal our regards. We all pray for His Holiness's health." Danielle nodded. The French woman rose before saying, "Enjoy your food. I will see you before you go."

"Thank you, Martine."

When Martine walked away, Chris had to ask Danielle. "Is she with the *Foundation?*"

"Yes. How would you like to go to Rome?"

"Rome? I thought we were going to a castle in . . . why Rome?"

"And I thought you were trying to decipher the double-speak, Christian. Well, did you?"

He laughed and said, "I should remember that you are always one step ahead of me. No, I did not. She was giving you information—"

"Disturbing information. The reason the *Foundation* is unable to meet with us just now is because Cardinal Santis suspects His Holiness is being poisoned. The *Group* has reached someone very close to His Holiness. We have to act fast. I will be advised of the arrangements as soon as they are set. There is nothing else we can do today. Perhaps we should rest. We may have some sleepless nights when we get to the Vatican. So today is your day, Christian."

During the rest of the meal, they talked about his life: the touchy relationship he had with his parents and the shocking discovery, when he was fifteen, that he had been adopted. Mrs. Goodman had spoken of his natural mother only once. She had told him that the dossier the agency had sent said the young woman had been orphaned at an early age and had spent time in a detention camp in Cyprus after World War II. She had been sent to America to be adopted. Her parents had probably died in Auschwitz or Dachau. The girl had gotten pregnant when she was very young. The best thing for an unstable, young, unwed Jewish mother was to contact an adoption agency, which is how Chris came to be adopted by a successful Jewish doctor and his Protestant wife. The term *emotionally unstable* was scary enough and made him incapable of sustaining a relationship with a woman, of making a commitment. Marriage frightened him.

Danielle listened compassionately, and he felt that for the first time in his life, he had shared his true self.

They spent the rest of the afternoon exploring the roads and villages of Provence. At dusk, they took a suite in a charming little hotel and decided to freshen up, order room service, and retire early. Stimulated and exhausted by one of the most wonderful days of his life, Chris fell into bed.

That night, Chris's dreams were of Danielle. But a surprising shift had taken place. When she had embraced him, the embrace did not lead to the passionate love-making he had envisioned. Instead, as she stroked his hair and held him close, he experienced a comforting sense of reconciliation between his spirit and his wounded heart.

About 3:00 a.m., there was a knock on the door. Danielle, who had come into Chris's room during the night, got up from the chair from which she had tenderly, and with some regret, watched him sleep, and walked over to him. Touching him gently on the shoulder, she whispered, "It's time to go."

When he awoke, Chris realized he had been weeping in his sleep. The damp pillowcases had absorbed all traces of a past that would trouble him no more. He got up and dressed quickly, gathered his belongings, and joined Danielle, who was wearing an androgynous, black leather jacket and pants and already had her overnight bag slung over her shoulder.

They quietly walked out of the room and followed the man who had knocked on their door through the back door of the hotel. The man whispered something to Danielle as they crossed an orchard and walked over a hill, emerging on the other side of the main road. Hidden behind a tree, a dark van awaited them. The man, who had not been introduced to Chris, continued to speak earnestly to Danielle in tones so low Chris, couldn't hear what he was saying.

When the man finished, he turned to Chris and, patting him on the back, said, "Take care of her, Herr Goodman. The others are already waiting in the plane. Remain quiet during the flight so your voices cannot be picked up by tracking devices. Once you get to the Vatican, you are safe. Security will be sufficient for your protection."

Chris nodded. They arrived at a small airport in Lyon. The engine of the Learjet was already running and ready for departure. Danielle and Chris walked swiftly up the stairs and onto the plane. Inside the cabin sat Angela, between two men. They embraced in greeting, and as instructed, did not utter a word until they arrived in Rome.

The mood at the Vatican was somber. Cardinal Santis explained that the pope's health had been deteriorating for reasons no one could explain. With no logical explanation, Santis suspected that small amounts of an undetectable poison were being introduced into his meals.

Santis had personally taken charge of His medications, keeping them in his possession and administering them himself; he had even implemented the ancient practice of sampling food. Before it was served to His Holiness, he tasted every dish. So far, he had discovered nothing irregular.

The Holy Father, as head of the *Foundation*, was the *Group's* obvious first target. By neutralizing his activities, they could disrupt the operation of the *Foundation.* No doubt a traitor was among those closest to the pope, someone set on keeping him incapacitated.

Recently, His Holiness, in one of his better moments, had reiterated to Santis the importance of the upcoming *Formation* and the crucial need to assemble the components of the key of Sharah.

Danielle had to uncover how His Holiness was being poisoned. The first order of business was to set up her team. Angela joined the group of physicians in direct contact with His Holiness and tending to his needs. The two men who had flown with them from Lyon were electronics technicians who were to check the *Foundation's* secret transmission equipment to see if it had been tampered with. Chris set about interviewing clergy and other Vatican personnel to detect any subversive attitudes or behaviors.

The moment Danielle began to walk around the Vatican grounds, she was struck by a powerful energy that could only have been emitted by one of the ancient stones. One of them was hidden in the Vatican. She placed a call to Jean-Christophe.

After three days of investigation, the team came up empty-handed.

"The food is being handled carefully," Angela informed them after days of painstaking supervision. "I haven't come across any irregularity in the medical protocols, and the doctors are clean. Yet the last lab reports show a residue of something in his blood. Something obvious is escaping us."

"Let's look again at his daily routine," said Chris.

Angela pulled a small notebook from her pocket.

> *Breakfast 7:30 am: tea, slice of bread. The tea gets sampled daily, and the bread is baked in-house. Everything is in order there.*
> *Mid-morning: orange juice at 11:00 am—sampled also.*
> *Lunch: clear broth, portion of chicken breast, small serving of rice—no spices or additives.*
> *Mid-afternoon: a piece of fruit from his own tree.*

"He cuts it himself. So there is no—"

"That's it!" exclaimed Chris. "We have checked everything but the tree."

Danielle understood immediately. Poison has been rubbed onto the fruit. "You are right! It's got to be the apples."

The three of them made haste to the patio. Using towels to protect their hands, they randomly picked apples that looked ripe. Angela placed them in a bag and headed for the lab.

Four days had gone by since Danielle's arrival at the Vatican, and today was the first opportunity Cardinal Santis had to visit with her at length. Awaiting the results from the lab, they sat in his study having tea.

"How many years has it been since we've had time together?" asked the cardinal as he poured her a cup of green tea.

"Too many."

"It is good to see you, Danielle." He finished pouring his own cup and sat on an upholstered chair next to hers. "I've tried to keep up with your life, your career . . . all your achievements. Always so proud of you! Last April, during the *Foundation* meeting, upon finding out that you were one of the missing agents, I became terribly scared. My little Danielle in danger! Next, I find out that Danielle Peschard is a highly trusted member of the *Foundation.* Furthermore, that she is an Edentian—one of the founders of our organization. I felt such gratitude for having been given the opportunity to care for you as a child, to mentor you as a young lady . . . and now look at you! I should have always known that such radiance was not in the province of humankind."

Danielle listened to him with the devotion a mortal woman has for a loving father.

He continued, "His Holiness said to me the other day that in his efforts to conceal your identity, he had chosen not to tell me. But now that the adversary knows, there is not much point in concealing it. On the contrary, we all should be on alert to protect you."

"And you have, you always have, my dearest Santis. Your prayers have always been the strongest shield for my protection."

"Protection? Hmm . . . I think now it is you who must protect us."

"With my life, if necessary."

"These are treacherous times. To think that we have someone who is trying to murder His Holiness! It feels like we have regressed to the Dark Ages."

"The *Group* wants to break down our position. But now, they must know we have regrouped."

"What good is it to continue trying to harm the pontiff?" the cardinal wondered.

Danielle sipped her tea slowly. "There is something else that is at stake here. Please tell me . . . what is His Holiness doing that is threatening enough to jeopardize his life?"

Cardinal Santis thought for a moment. "Well, we were not to talk about it, but I see no harm in telling you now. He is about to change the position of the Church—in more than one way. He has revised many of the points that have sat at a standstill for centuries, and he plans to revive rituals that have been put aside."

"I see. That could prove threatening to those who have manipulated the teachings of the Church to control the masses."

"Precisely," said Santis. "We know the *Group* has been manipulating the minds of the masses in numerous ways and has succeeded in turning many away from the Church. Its campaign to plant and expose priests as pedophiles has been most damaging. We fear most the movement of Theodore Edwards in America. He is a wolf in sheep's clothing. His message is sugar-coated, but he is fomenting bigotry, violence, and deceit. He will deceive a great number of people. When our message gets twisted, His Holiness feels it's time to disclose truths that, for various reasons, have been hidden from the people."

Santis got up and walked to his bookcases. "Our libraries at the Vatican are rich with authentic translations of the Scripture. Perhaps the time has come to share them with the world."

"Where would you start?"

"With the nature of the Church itself. Reinstating our position as keepers of the legacy and rememberers of what Christ taught us. The prevailing belief that Christ said to Peter, 'Upon you I will build my church' was, as you know, not entirely accurate. We possess no proof that Christ ever wished to start a new religion or cult and no record that he ever wanted to mingle religion with politics.

We know his purpose in coming here was to remind us of what this experience in the flesh was about and how to get back home."

"'With *love,'* he said. His message was so simple, it was misunderstood," added Danielle.

"You see, we have proof here that the early Christians adopted his teachings and went about spreading his doctrine while remaining true to their faith. The early 'Christians' were—and remained—Jews. The switch to Christianity was not a selective choice. It did not result from a Christian congregation in Antioch as is being preached in America by Edwards. Christians were forced to separate from the Jewish faith due to persecutions . . . by being singled out as a rebellious sect of the Jews. So much blood has been shed in vain. Salvation was offered to all, not just his followers." Santis returned to his seat before continuing, "I forget that, of course, you know all that. It is I who should be asking you questions. Like, this leap of consciousness that His Holiness mentioned. What does it consist of, and how will it be achieved?"

"Basically, it is an expansion of the five-sensory perception. It will start with the acceptance that we are more than what our senses perceive—that non-physical realities exist parallel to ours. It is about the realignment of the ego with the soul and the empowerment of the spirit. It will be a new way of looking at and understanding the hierarchy of the universe and accessing information from our non-physical guides."

There was a knock on the door. Santis was sorry to have the conversation interrupted, but he knew the anxiously anticipated report was back.

Christian came in holding a manila envelope. Danielle reached for it, looking straight into his eyes. She knew by his look the report was not conclusive. She read the first paragraph of the document and then flipped quickly through the pages. She handed them to the cardinal and waited until he had time to examine them before speaking.

"We were wrong; the fruit is clean. Yet the blood reports continue to show the presence of a toxin. Please bring Angela in," Danielle said to Chris.

Angela came in, bowing her head respectfully to the cardinal, and Danielle addressed her. "How is his condition?"

"Deteriorating. His symptoms resemble those of multiple sclerosis or lupus; his brain function is weakening. His Holiness is definitely suffering from fibromyalgia. His speech is becoming slurred, and there is evidence of memory loss and vision loss."

Danielle remembered her own condition. "You are absolutely sure no device has been implanted?"

"Positive."

"Then what has been given to him is still being administered on a daily basis." She addressed Santis, "When can we go back to his quarters?"

"Now would be a good time. He has been taken down to the chapel."

The four of them rushed down the hall in the direction of the pontiff's rooms. Father Lucci was busy clearing the cups and saucers from afternoon tea and replacing the fresh flowers. The last thing he put on the tray as he got ready to leave was a can of diet cola from the nightstand. Danielle and Chris simultaneously looked at the can.

Danielle reached for it, "May I?"

The priest handed it to her before walking out of the room. Danielle looked questioningly at Santis.

"Yes, His Holiness drinks diet cola because of his intolerance to sugar and because it settles his stomach. Actually, it is his only indulgence. He keeps a supply right over there," he said, pointing to the small refrigerator in the corner of the sitting room. "Since he opens the cans himself, we have never considered sampling them. You don't think . . ."

Danielle did not answer. She put the can down and reached for the cell phone inside her pocket. They waited anxiously as she dialed the White House. "Danielle Peschard for President Parker." After a couple of minutes, the president came on the line.

"Hello, David. We are at the Vatican, still trying to solve the puzzle. Can you do me a favor? Will you e-mail me the information Congress has on artificial sweeteners used in diet drinks? Yes, you can send it directly to Cardinal Santis's office. Thank you." She closed her phone. "The report will come in a few minutes," she told them.

"Then let's get back to my office," said Santis.

Jean-Christophe deduced from the pace of his friends walking down the corridor that perhaps this was not the best moment to inform Danielle of his findings. He continued on down the marble stairway.

Danielle spotted the fresco of the *Angel Musician* by Melozzo Da Fore in Santis's study. "Nice replica," she said as she entered the room.

"I think so. We had the original here till last Friday. It is already packed and ready to go, per your instructions."

Chris looked at them. Everyone seemed to be part of the art-hoarding conspiracy. He guessed there was still a lot Danielle had not told him. The computer beeped. The documents had just been e-mailed. Cardinal Santis proceeded to print them. As the pages began to pop out of the machine, Danielle gathered them.

"World Environmental Conference: Dangers of artificial sweeteners marketed as Aspartame, NutraSweet, Equal, Spoonful, etc. and the new potent product called *Draoxtil* . . ."

Danielle read on. The risks of chemical sweetener poisoning commingled with the many toxins and poisons posing as food in the increasingly contaminated world food supply. Millions of people were ingesting the poisons. There was a global epidemic of multiple sclerosis and systemic lupus, and not until recently had Congress figured out the link to artificial sweeteners.

But what is different in this case that's killing the pontiff? Danielle wondered.

Then the crucial page . . .

> *Draoxtil changes the brain chemistry and causes severe seizures. This drug changes the dopamine level in the brain. When the sweetener exceeds 86 degrees F, the wood alcohol in Draoxtil converts to formaldehyde and then to formic acid, which in turn causes metabolic acidosis. (Formic acid is the poison found in the sting of scorpions). Methanol toxicity mimics multiple sclerosis and lupus.*
>
> *In the last few months, when neurosurgeons excised a variety of brain tumors, they have detected in the tumors high levels of Draoxtil. (Phenylalanine, a component of Draoxtil, breaks down into DXP, a brain tumor agent.)*
>
> *The recommendation to ban the sweetener from the market was killed by powerful drug and chemical lobbyists. The use of the sweetener was approved by the FDA as a dietary supplement and endorsed by a bill proposed and lobbied by Senator Nielsen.*

Danielle knew then, with certainty, how the poisoning was being carried out. She handed the documents to Cardinal Santis before she spoke.

"The pope's diet drinks were put through a process of repeated exposure to extreme heat, then refrigerated. Through this process, the chemical properties in the sweetener were changed to formic acid before the drinks were delivered to Vatican City. This slow form of poisoning is nearly impossible to detect. Look for yourselves."

Danielle asked Chris to hold the cola drink in his hand with his arm outstretched.

"Hold your arm steady," said Danielle while she applied pressure to his arm. The arm gave under the pressure and lowered. The others looked at the demonstration, not understanding. "It is an ancient oriental method of detecting allergens, toxins, and substances that will, in general, weaken your system. A clash of energies is produced and the irritant usually wins." She exchanged the cola can in Chris's hand for an apple that she took from a nearby fruit bowl. She repeated the process. This time, she was unable to lower his arm, despite the force she applied.

"The toxin is in the drink. We have no way of knowing the amount he has consumed. It will take a few weeks for the body to divest itself of the poison. His system should be replenished with antioxidants," Danielle advised.

"Angela, will you make sure no more artificial sweetener, in any form, is included in his diet?"

"Chris, find out where this particular shipment of diet cola came from. We still have to find our traitor. Now, if you will excuse me, I must find Jean-Christophe. I believe he has also made a discovery."

"You won't believe it!" exclaimed Jean-Christophe when Danielle finally located him deep in one of the most remote storerooms in the basement of the right wing.

"Did you find it?" her voice was full of anticipation.

He put his hands on her shoulders and guided her through rows of broken sculpture parts, most of them not yet cataloged. "*Voila*!" he pointed to an unpolished marble Roman head, broken at the neck and badly damaged. "All the markings match. There is your head of Aphrodite! Now you won't have to continue digging under the scorching sun of Knidos, fighting off scorpions."

Danielle ran her hand over the rough and cracked surface of the face.

"Fourth century BC, for sure," he continued. "No one could guess it belongs on the body of the goddess you found years ago, making complete the most famous ancient statue of Aphrodite. How did you know it was here?" the Frenchman wanted to know.

"Just a hunch."

"The head was never finished."

"It was. The rough stone is a coverup. Hand me your tools." She began chipping at the rock around the head. A piece of the stone broke off easily.

"Ha! Not marble at all," the Frenchman was amused. "Even then, there were faux stone finishes." He took the tools from Danielle and continued chipping away the material. She helped break off the pieces. Her watch made a faint sound.

She raised it closer to her lips. "Take the stairway down, turn left, and go to the second door. It is open. We are at the very back."

In a few moments, Christian had made his way to where they were.

"What have we here?" he inquired.

"The head of the oldest known statue of Aphrodite. It's the missing head of the statue Danielle discovered in Turkey."

"That will endear you to your chairman of Greek and Roman art at the Met."

"I'm no longer with the museum. I thought it would be better if I resigned, knowing I wouldn't be able to spend much time working for them, anyway."

"Oh," said Chris. The Frenchman did not register surprise, indicating he already knew. "Well, so who gets the complete piece—the Met or the Vatican?"

"The last thing we want right now is to draw attention to this piece. We need to finish removing the cover without anyone knowing what we are doing or what we've found."

"Cardinal Santis asked me to find you," said Chris. "His Holiness wishes to speak to you. The cardinal has informed him of our findings and your assurance that he will get better. He insists on seeing you right away."

"I'll continue working on the head," said Jean-Christophe. "Chris could help me."

"No. I think it's better if you come out with me. It will look as if you found nothing. Besides, you need to get back to New York for the ceremony. It is not every day that an archeologist receives the silver plaque for the most outstanding contribution to the study of Egyptian history. And you well deserve it. My plane will fly you back. Chris, if you could continue chipping at the rock . . . I should be back within the hour."

"I'll be glad to." He took the chisel and hammer from the Frenchman. "Just make sure they don't arrest me for desecrating Vatican relics."

"Nobody knows you are here. Lock the door, just in case."

Danielle and Jean-Christophe walked away. Chris heard their voices become fainter as Danielle gave him instructions to deliver something to Tom and check on Kitzia.

A look of peace, or *beatific radiance*, as Santis called it, appeared on Danielle's face when she emerged from the chambers of the pontiff. The cardinal hoped she would share what they had discussed, but he dared not ask.

"His Holiness expressed his desire to go ahead with the conference as planned," Danielle said to Cardinal Santis. "You should therefore implement the arrangements."

"I will as soon as he regains his strength."

"Don't postpone the date. It is very important to him. Just as important as it is for me to keep my rendezvous with the *Foundation*, he told me. Therefore, I will be leaving shortly—as soon as I can make the arrangements for transportation of the last works of art. His Holiness has expressed complete trust in Mr. Goodman, although he has never been initiated into the *Foundation*. Mr. Goodman will assist me with the preparations."

Cardinal Santis bowed his head in agreement. He would never know what had transpired between the pontiff and his protégé. Cardinal Santis thought of mentioning the distinguished visitor that had come for the earlier meeting—the one that had been interrupted because of her absence. Then it occurred to him that perhaps that was what His Holiness had wished to relate to her in private. Santis was sure it had to do with her, but he would not broach the subject unless she mentioned it first. She did not.

As Danielle approached the room where she had left Chris, she felt a sense of apprehension. A draft of cold air was seeping eerily from under the door. Without waiting to check if the door was locked, she kicked it open. The room was much colder than it had been earlier, and there was a haze that gave the room a sense of unreality.

She called out Chris's name as she ran to the spot where she had left him. She thought she heard him answer, but his voice had the distant sound of an echo. She saw the head of the goddess almost completely free from its rock encasing. A hole in one of the eye sockets indicated the stone had been extracted and that Chris's life was in danger.

She called out his name again and again. "Danielle . . ." echoed back from a distance. The voice was agitated and continued to call out, "Over here, Danielle." She swiftly turned in the direction of the voice. A blinding light struck the ground by her side, then a deafening wind jetted past her. She saw Chris for a second. He was struggling with what appeared to be an assailant. Then they vanished. The blinding light struck again; it blasted from the ceiling, zigzagging down the wall, as if creating a momentary crack into another world.

Danielle understood that a portal had opened. The fissure was a cosmic crack, most likely caused by the *Group's* manipulation of an Edentian current. She had to jump through the opening immediately. Christian had been sucked through it. If the door closed behind him, she would lose him forever.

Reaching for the chain around her neck, she held the medal with the two concentric circles, and whispered, "May Michael protect me." Then she jumped in.

XXIII

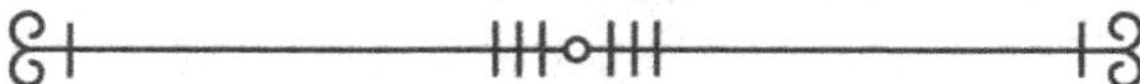

New York

It had been weeks since Kitzia had heard from Danielle, and that worried her. It was not like Danielle to take long trips to Europe and not call her at least once a week. Following Ricardo's funeral, Kit had to fill in for Danielle and console Linda.

Jean-Christophe had not returned, either. From the newspaper, she had learned he was set to receive a prize for his archeological discovery in Egypt earlier in the year. The event was to be a formal affair at the Promenade at Lincoln Center that week.

She felt a disconnect from everyone she cared about. Tom was, as usual, terribly busy at the hospital and had once again distanced himself from her. When she last visited him in San Francisco, he had remarked that she looked a little pale and insisted on checking her blood for anemia. She agreed to the test just to please him. He hadn't called with her the results.

Piled high on her desk were reports from the various agencies she was working with; they confirmed each and every one of her suspicions regarding the mind-conditioning of young people. A large percentage of people, now under the influence of Ted Edwards, overlooked the fact that children were being exploited by big business. There was a national brainwashing campaign going on. The most she could do at the moment was concentrate her efforts on saving her existing patients.

Kitzia looked at her watch. She had forty-five minutes to get to the youth rehabilitation center where her next patients were waiting. The call to Tom would only take a couple of minutes, so she dialed his number.

Bent over his microscope, taking copious notes, Tom picked up the phone.

"Tom, I just wanted to make sure the blood test was OK."

Tom slipped his glasses to the top of his head, rubbed the bridge of his nose, and replied, "Sorry, I've been swamped. Oh, your test was fine—just perfect." He smiled to himself with amusement as he pushed aside the file he had been reviewing. The file was marked "Kitzia O'Neil—abnormalities and differences." He closed the file as if to prevent his psychic ex-wife from sensing that she was the subject of his current study. As he closed it and put it aside, the new file, not yet begun, came into view. It was marked "Christian Goodman—preliminary blood study."

"Well, that is good to hear," said Kit. "You know, I have also been terribly busy with the congressional hearings. How are things at the hospital?"

"OK, right now. I am expecting to get a confirmation on the grant. We are on the verge of so many great things, but the money is crucial. I cannot continue to foot the bill for these studies."

"Tom, I know it will come in. You are a great physician, and they know it."

"Something strange is still going on. . . . Oh well, I don't want to burden you further with administrative intrigues. It looks like I'll be coming to New York this week. I am not sure when, though. I'll let you know."

Kitzia's heart skipped a beat. "That's great. Maybe we could grab lunch or dinner."

"Certainly."

She felt exuberant and once again ready to take on the world. She grabbed her files and left the office in the direction of the Bronx.

Tom returned to his work. He had just received the blood sample belonging to Christian Goodman and began cataloguing it in the same manner he had done for Kit's. Danielle had asked him to verify the variances, so he proceeded to enter the DNA information. He had already prepared charts, outlining the normal human cell configuration of forty-six chromosomes in pairs, including the one set of sex hormones, and had placed boxes to the right to enter the differences. He examined the genetic code with the four types of molecular bases, the adenine paring with thymine and the guanine with cytosine.

He gasped in disbelief at the extra step in the double helix. Christian Goodman possessed the same genetic variance as Kitzia O'Neil.

Washington, DC

"It is important to remember that all beings have a sense of connection with the Source." Danielle had once told President Parker this, and he tried to remember it before he made any decision that would affect others. He had in his hands proof of the horrors that were being initiated for humankind, and he wondered if those plans went so far as to include the annihilation of the species.

Throughout his presidential term, he had been working closely with the *Foundation.* Besides the usual national crises that made headlines, there were always the others, the more sinister ones, which were kept from the public to avoid panic.

The *Group* had grown alarmingly powerful. Not one area of life had they left unsullied. The president had faith in the power of the *Foundation,* of course, but at times, it seemed to be outmatched by the *Group's* enlistment of drug lords, ruffians, and unscrupulous businessmen, while the *Foundation* recruited from the honorable and erudite.

At the moment, one of the priorities was an attempt by the *Group* to influence everyone privy to digital technology. President Parker paid especial attention to the report—submitted by Dr. Kitzia O'Neil—outlining the present use of subliminal messages. The *Foundation* assured him they would be ready with measures to thwart the *Group's* plans, and the public would never know how close they had come to enslavement.

It was crucial for the *Formation* take place as scheduled, and he did not fully understand the *Foundation's* insistence that a single player like Danielle Peschard would carry out the arrangements. Yes, he knew that she was an Edentian and possessed supernatural abilities, but still, she was bound to a human body and restricted by many of its limitations. The proof was that she had been seriously injured. Yet the *Foundation* continued to insist that she work alone. Everyone was to offer assistance but limited protection. In her hands was the most important of missions. She had to gather the components necessary to activate the key of Sharah, find and make connections with those who were to effect the *Formation.*

"Mr. President." The voice of William Kramer, his advisor, made Parker realize his mind had wondered off. "Anything else on the digital?"

"No. That about covers it. Let's move on. Do you have the next figures?"

"Yes." He placed a chart of the globe, with several areas highlighted in various colors, in front of the president.

"My heavens!" murmured Parker, reading the figure at the top of the chart that showed the present world population. "It took over two million years to reach one billion, and now it is 8,012,700,000. The sustainable population of Earth is only eight billion!"

He read the numbers typed on the highlighted areas representing the most populated countries. "China, India, US, Indonesia . . ." The president remained silent for a moment.

Enough had been said about the pollution of the water, but right now, he was facing the possibility of a world crisis resulting from water shortages. The *Foundation* had information that one act of global terrorism the *Group* might launch was the contamination of most of the world's water supply. The *Foundation* had advised the government to be prepared for such an event.

Kramer spoke again, "So the most strategic places to have water miraculously appear would be where the red dots are."

The president did not miss the derision in Kramer's voice while he continued to study the chart carefully.

"Mr. President, you don't really believe that would happen—that the water supply could be contaminated?"

"I have to be prepared for anything and everything."

"Millions of people would die."

"Precisely, and it would certainly bring many nations to their knees," said the president.

"And this *Foundation* of yours, how would it come up with such vast amounts of fresh drinking water, short of performing miracles?"

"I have to believe it will," answered Parker emphatically.

"But how?"

President Parker looked at Kramer. They had worked together for almost a decade now. Parker trusted him. Yet recently, the word *trust* needed to be redefined. The president had spent sleepless nights wondering which of his colleagues were really with him. For months now, he had been carefully weeding out his staff. The attempt on his life in Rome had convinced him there were traitors among his elite circle. The plot to murder him had been conceived on the inside, and he had no doubt they would try again.

"I sincerely have no earthly idea," Parker affirmed. "But there will be water if the need arises. Let's move on. What do you have on Theodore Edwards?"

Kramer removed the global chart and exchanged it for a folder. "As far as I can tell, he is definitely going for it. He will run against you, David."

"I suspected that much."

"He is coming on strong. He is emerging at a time when people have become disillusioned with politicians and are turning to faith. People may turn to a religious leader."

"The country is divided," added Parker. "The polls have made it clear. So what you're telling me is that Edward's nomination is imminent?" Parker laughed ironically. "Twenty years ago, it would have been inconceivable to imagine a religious lunatic attempting to run the country."

"But the time has been made ready for such madness."

"You are right, Kramer; it is no longer a laughing matter. It happened in Iran and could also happen right here."

"I seriously don't think it will go that far. It will mostly be embarrassing that you might have to protect your position against that wacko."

"One way or the other, he will do more damage than you can imagine. One of Edwards's more basic principles is to undermine women's higher evolution. This pro-life attempt to block women's right to their own body is part of a series of attempts to re-enslave them.

"It's a funny thing about civilizations. Did you know they invariably run a cycle of birth, growth, and death, encompassing anywhere from 200 to 2,000 years?" He grabbed his pen and began drawing a diagram.

> *Bondage to spiritual strength. Spiritual strength to courage. Courage to freedom. Freedom to abundance. Abundance to greed. Greed to fear. Fear to apathy . . . and apathy back to bondage.*

"Kramer, where would you say we are now?"

He did not give Kramer time to answer. The watch on his wrist emitted a faint erratic vibration—too quiet to be noticed by his advisor. The president reached for his cell phone and said while turning to Kramer, "Will you excuse me?"

"Certainly." Kramer rose and headed for the door.

Once alone in the hall, Kramer took out his cell phone and punched a single number, direct to the *Group*. He placed the tiny phone inconspicuously in his hand and whispered into it as he continued walking. "Looks like he's been tipped about the water. No, they don't know the digital phase has already begun." After a pause, he concluded, "Understood." He shut the phone and smiled at the Secret Service agent walking in his direction.

The morning in late November was chilly. While hoping to hear from Tom on the weekend, Kitzia decided to pay Jean-Christophe a surprise visit. Jean-Christophe, probably exhausted from the previous evening's award dinner, would probably sleep late.

Wrapped in a cashmere coat, Kit walked down Third Avenue toward his building and picked up a bunch of flowers from a vendor. She made a stop at a coffee shop and ordered a couple of lattes and croissants to go. It had been a long time since she had dropped in like this, unannounced and bringing breakfast. They would chat for hours and catch up with their lives. Kit knew where he put the key but decided to knock. After all, she could not assume he would be alone.

After a couple of vigorous knocks, she heard the Frenchman's voice.

"One moment . . . Who is it at this freaking hour?"

Kit let out an amused giggle instead of answering. Still adjusting the tie on his terry-cloth robe, Jean-Christophe opened the door.

"Kit!" He exclaimed in utter amazement. "I don't know what to say."

"How about thank you?" She handed him the flowers and slipped past him into the kitchen.

He seemed shocked and she understood. "So you are not alone. OK. I'll leave your breakfast and go. Call me later. I want to hear all about last night." She moved in to hug him. Jean-Christophe, still holding the flowers, remained immobile. She wrapped her arms around him. The bedroom door opened, and Kit let go of Jean-Christophe. She saw a man in a similar white terry-cloth robe emerge.

At that moment, everything in her world collapsed; her dreams and hope for happiness vanished.

The man was Tom.

XXIV

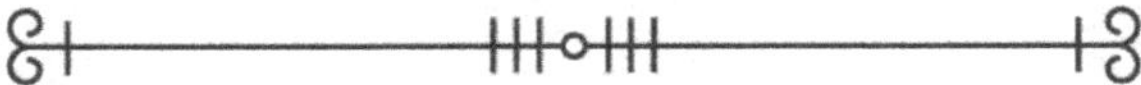

Rome

When Christian Goodman opened his eyes, Danielle was kneeling next to him. It took him a few minutes to assemble his thoughts and remember what had happened. His last lucid memory was of chiseling away the stone from the head of Aphrodite, when a stone set into the eye socket loosened. A gigantic shadow materialized from the darkness and fell upon him, striking him with a force that knocked him off his feet.

Chris realized he was more stunned than disabled. Aware that the stone had been wrenched from his grasp, he turned to throw himself on his attacker. As they wrestled on the ground, Chris gained some advantage over his adversary, whose priestly robes were clumsy garments for combat. He almost had the stone when a sudden blast of cold air hit him and powerful vibrations shook the room.

The wall split open, shattering the darkness, and both men were sucked through the chasm. Chris let go of the man as they tumbled through spiral layers of a helix-like tunnel. Behind him, Danielle tumbled through space, traveling through the rings at a more accelerated speed. Frantically, they reached for each other, but when Chris felt his head hit something hard, everything went black.

"We went through a cosmic crack," answered Danielle.

"A cosmic what?" Christian tried to get up, but the pain and buzzing noise inside his head made him fall back. "What is that noise? It feels like it's inside my head."

"It is. Be still. Your senses are still adjusting."

He obeyed. There was something different about Danielle—a translucency that was out of the ordinary. She did not seem solid.

Danielle looked around, assessing the situation. They were in a small room with white walls, surrounded by objects from another era.

"He is gone," announced Danielle, moving about the room.

Then Christian remembered the attacker. "He has the stone!"

"I know. We have to find him."

"He was a priest."

"No," corrected Danielle, "he was only dressed like a priest." She went back to his side. "Tell me something about him that will help me identify him—anything."

"There was madness in his eyes. His hands were large, and he wore a ring."

That caught Danielle's attention. "What did the ring look like?"

Her face was close now, looking at him intensely. Once again, Christian was disturbed by her appearance. The radiant green had dissolved into rings of diverse colors, much like a rainbow.

"Christian, what did the ring look like?"

"It was like a snake coiled around his middle finger."

"Catilina!" she exclaimed.

He noticed they were in what looked like a kitchen vestibule. Two youths, possibly slaves, came in carrying a basket of fruit and a large decanter of water. The youths did not seem aware of their presence—neither did the plump woman who followed them out of the room. Christian was surprised she did not see them. He immediately noticed the smell—an unmistakable burning odor and the foul stench of sewage coming in through an open window.

Chris stood up and dusted off his clothes. "Where are we?"

"Same place we were before but back several centuries." Danielle now looked solid, but her appearance had changed. Her hair was pulled back, and she was wearing long woolen robes and fur-covered boots. He could not hide his amazement.

"How did you do that?" asked Chris

"You wouldn't understand."

She put a cape on his back. "We need to get out of here, and it's cold outside."

He followed her through the atrium in the direction of the stables. When they arrived, she burst out laughing. He laughed also, not quite knowing why.

"Christian, look at yourself!"

Until then, he hadn't realized that he had become as amorphous as Danielle had been earlier. "What is it?" he asked alarmed.

Still amused, she added "You have to will yourself into this reality. . . . Much better," he heard Danielle say. At that point, he realized that at least his physical being had become solid. "I'll get you the right clothes," she said.

They headed into the street. It was late afternoon, and the sun was setting. There was a loud roaring noise in the street and a clacking of vehicle axels.

"*La Roma Antica*," she replied, pointing in the direction of a marketplace.

He followed, concealing his attire under the wool cloak. The crowded streets stank of burning brick and dying vegetation. Danielle explained that this was the busiest time of the day. Men and women were closing shops, stalls, and places of business and heading home. Chris was too fascinated to ask many questions.

At the market, Danielle skillfully bargained and procured an entire set of clothes for him. "Nobleman's clothes," she explained. He could not move about the city in a peasant's attire. To his surprise, she also produced sesterces from her pocket to pay for the purchases. Danielle appeared to be fluent in the language, and no one looked askance at them. Danielle and Christian resembled a normal, affluent couple from the outskirts of the city. After obtaining the name of an inn where they could spend the night, they strode in that direction.

Danielle's calmness disconcerted him. "I thought we were in urgent pursuit of the man who took the stone," he said.

"We'll find him," she answered. "Now I know that this particular world still has an open cosmic portal, and I will be able to seal it."

"What year is it?" asked Chris.

"I'm not sure, but I would say we are in the last century before the Common Era."

"If I were to choose a time and spot to be trapped with you for all eternity, I think Ancient Rome would be it."

"Don't be too sure," Danielle advised. "Even though the aggression and coldness of your century has probably prepared you well for existence in this one."

Danielle asked a passerby if the building they were approaching was the inn of Ovintus. The man pointed to a side door through which they could enter. Danielle entered and made the lodging arrangements—a spacious room almost devoid of furniture but for a wrought iron double bed, barely wider than a twin-sized bed, with rough linens and a small coal stove placed near the bed. This chamber, they had been told, was the most luxurious room in the inn, reserved for wealthy merchants. Better lodgings could be arranged at the villa of one of the well-to-do residents for a much higher fee. Danielle requested that a suitable residence be found for them, for she did not know how long they would be staying.

Shortly thereafter, two slaves came in and set up a table in the alcove—a wooden board over two wooden blocks and two large pillows. Neither Chris nor Danielle complained. The arrangements seemed quite cozy under the circumstances. Another slave brought in a tray with hot meat pies, figs, sweet cakes in shapes of fawns and snakes, a jug of wine, and a pair of hand-blown glasses.

The slave girl poured the wine then joined the other servants as they retired, walking backward out of the room.

Chris and Danielle sat on the pillows and took a sip of the wine.

"Strong!" exclaimed Chris with irony. "Not a Margaux . . . hmm . . ."

Danielle laughed and drank the wine, not minding the taste that much. "It's not too bad."

He pulled his pillow closer to hers. "Tell me fair maiden, how are we going to find the man with the ring?"

"We must find our way to the Brotherhood. The ring represents an arcane fraternity of powerful men. We now know the ring is the key to open the doors between worlds."

He was studying the fabric of her chiton as he lightly massaged her shoulder. "Who is this Catalina that you mentioned?" he whispered.

"I'm referring to Lucius Sergius Catilina, one of the most corrupt men of this era. He destroys everything that crosses his path. It's no surprise that he would be a key member of the Brotherhood here."

"He was the man that attacked me?"

"I doubt it. You did not mention his good looks. It was probably one of his emissaries. Catilina is remarkably beautiful and physically imposing. No one would miss that."

"I guess in my fight for survival, I forgot to notice his physical attributes." The wine was making him feel lightheaded. "So let me get this straight. This is not my reality, correct? And I am not bound by the physical laws of my world. Therefore, I can be an avenger, a fearless warrior?"

"No, no!" she stopped him. "You must be more careful than ever. I can handle the duplicity of this reality's crisscross, but I don't think you can. To put it bluntly, if you are killed in this reality, you will certainly die in the other."

"Well, that definitely puts a pall on my sense of adventure." He continued rubbing her shoulders. "Then romance is all that can flourish in this one."

"I think you are getting drunk," she said with amusement.

"What this wine lacks in quality, it makes up in potency."

Danielle moved away and looked at him. "Tell me something, Chris. What do you think of Kitzia?"

"Kit?" He straightened up. "What does she have to do with this moment?"

"I am curious."

"She is fine. Ethical, intelligent . . . dedicated to whatever cause she chooses. She is all right."

"Do you find her attractive?"

"Yes, she is. A little nutty, I thought, when I first met her. Can we forget about her for now?"

"I just wondered."

"Oh, that's what this is all about? You don't think that . . . Oh, no, I have no personal interest in her, if that is what's worrying you. It is you I love."

"So you say, but I wanted to hear from your lips how you feel about her. She is everything you say and more."

"OK. I believe you. Now, can we toast to our first night in this romantic place?"

Danielle lifted her glass and clinked it with his. She kept the tone light for the rest of the night and let Chris indulge in his fantasy of romance.

Chris became groggy after his fourth glass of wine, and Danielle helped him to the bed. After covering him with a blanket, she quietly slipped out of the room. Wrapped in her woolen cloak, she left the inn and disappeared into the night.

The chattering of the people on the street below could be heard from the room, but it was the smell of freshly baked bread that awoke Christian. The weather warmed up, and the sun came out, promising even milder temperatures.

He smiled at Danielle. "Good morning. So what's our plan of action?"

"We need to make contact with the *Foundation* and tell them we are here and why. I have already sent a note this morning seeking help. They will come to us shortly. They will also welcome information regarding the opening. We will find the stone and return home. The *Foundation* might also be preparing for the *Formation*. That is, if they want to be acknowledged by RA."

"You said the *Formation* occurs every so many thousand years. How can you count if things are occurring simultaneously?"

"Don't even try to figure it out because you won't. Simply understand there are worlds or realities that share the same space and that a soul can live an existence split into diverse layers of those realities. Do not be surprised when you encounter all the similarities they have in common.

"Ancient Rome and modern America are perfect examples of those parallel realities. The errors of Rome are well documented in your history books, and you are to learn from them. Just like President Parker has a strong devotion to the Bill of Rights, someone here is also upholding those values and trying to save the nation through a bill of rights similar to yours."

Chris noticed that Danielle was referring to the other world as *his* and not *theirs*. "You feel less a part of that reality now?" he asked.

"That world, like I said before, is a training ground for most and a place of work for me. My world is Edentia."

Suddenly, it was clear to Christian that, besides recovering the stone, they were here for another reason. Danielle had brought him to this place to discover and clarify his true life's mission—to record from his new and unique perspective the comparative histories of Rome and the America of his reality.

"You will write about this in a manner that the people of your time can understand and reference the similarities," she told him. "All the concepts of freedom are alive here but threatened in the same way they are in the US. Likewise, the corruption of politicians is spreading fast and reverence for life is being lost. The *Pax Romana* is surprisingly like the United Nations in America, and both are losing ground. Socrates once said, 'Those nations that ignore history are doomed to repeat the same mistakes.'"

"I understand what I must do. If only I could understand the language!"

"It is the message being transmitted that matters. Tune in to that energy, and you will understand. The essence of what you learn here will be imprinted on your soul forever."

I will employ my every capacity to prevent history from repeating itself. I can expose those who are trying to destroy America and plunge it into darkness, just like what happened to Rome before its decline into the long night of the Dark Ages.

Danielle handed him a small scroll.

"What is this?" he asked.

"I went out this morning and got one. It is called the *Acta Diurna,* and it's comparable to your *New York Times.*"

"There is a daily newspaper?" he asked incredulously.

"Actually, there are three competing journals."

Chris looked at the publication, with columns signed by different editorialists. He was surprised to discover satirical political cartoons. "So what do we have that they don't, a stock market?"

"Have a look at the last entry. You'll see their stock market and commodities report."

Chris continued to study the ancient journal. There was a knock at the door, and Danielle went to answer it. She returned with another papyrus scroll and seemed excited. "We are moving to a residence on the Palatine, and we have a contact. He will meet us after today's session of the Senate."

"The Senate? Has Brutus murdered Caesar?"

"Funny that you should ask. You might be in for a treat and have occasion to meet Julius Caesar as a young man, while he is still a member of the Populares. We are to be house guests at the home of one of his friends."

Chris was surprised at the number of temples in the city. Just about every other building was dedicated to one deity or another. Every temple portico swarmed with congregants. It looked as if half of the working day was spent in worship.

There was also turmoil in the streets, which Danielle explained was because much of the populace was unhappy with the government. What they encountered in the streets was equivalent to the demonstrations in the US. A phrase echoed wherever they went: "Must end the advancement of despotism!" Not being totally up-to-date on his history, Chris asked for an explanation of what was going on.

"One consul has replaced another," Danielle told him, "only to bring the country further into debt. Carbo has replaced Cinna, who was murdered in Thessaly, and in turn, Sulla replaced Carbo. The recent wars have depleted the Treasury."

Sheets and sheets of political commentary were posted on every wall. Danielle and Chris stopped at the temple of Leda to read the posts.

Maritime shares were at an all-time low due to the recent sinking of several merchant vessels. The quarrel with Egypt was impeding the shipping of grain. Propaganda cried out for citizens to invest heavily in the manufacturing of instruments of war and military supplies.

"Ah . . . the proliferation of arms dealers!" said Chris. "Not much different from our time."

They ducked away to avoid the melee when dissident groups set violently upon one another, yelling obscenities and support for opposing political figures. The screaming turned physical and escalated to sword fights and stabbings, and within minutes, the portico was running scarlet with blood, which flowed in more abundance when soldiers came to quash the riot.

Danielle and Chris separated from the crowd, leaving behind the bloodstained steps and the echoes of voices proclaiming the return of "the age of tyranny."

"Say what you're thinking," said Danielle, when they found themselves alone again.

"It is all so shocking."

"You want to know why I don't help, become involved . . ."

She caught him off-guard, but then he remembered. "You told me before; you cannot interfere."

"That's right. Do remember that."

The home of Jarred ben Joseph was on the foot of the Palatine Hill. It was by far the most beautiful villa in the area. Jarred ben Joseph was an affable man in his fifties, a highly respected Jewish merchant most admired for his investment skills. He dressed expensively but conservatively, unlike his countrymen, who tried to outdo one another with the lavishness of their togas. Although Jarred ben Joseph befriended all, his loyalties were well established and his word was his bond. When

Danielle introduced Christian to Jarred, the man repeated the name *Christian* softly to himself, with the solemnity of receiving an omen. The host did not ask many questions of the travelers, as if instructed to respect their privacy.

On the main terrace, they came upon an empty altar. Jarred explained that it was the altar to the unknown God.

"In our religion," he said, "we believe God will send us a Messiah. We await him eagerly. For not until then will our sorrows end."

Danielle and Chris exchanged a glance, both knowing there was no response either could make.

By now, Chris was able to understand conversations in both Latin and Greek, though he could not speak them in kind.

Jarred continued, "I am very interested in hearing your noble thoughts on the subject. I wish to know about the prophecies that foreigners may have heard. Egyptian acquaintances tell me that the Pharaoh Aton predicted Horus will descend from Heaven and become a man. He will reconcile all nations under God.

"The Hindus believe man can only be rescued from his state of sin and corruption, as it is stated in the Gita, when some god takes the human form and leads man to grace.

"Our Torah foretells that the Messiah will be born of the Jews, that he will establish his kingdom on Earth, and that his empire shall spread across the earth. However, according to our Prophet Isaiah, few will know him. Alas, how could that be?"

He pointed to the luxurious silk couches by the crystalline windows of Alexandrian glass that overlooked his Roman pool and bade them to sit. He continued, "Lady Daniela, I have been told that you possess the gift of prophecy. Will you lighten my heart and tell me that the Messiah will be born to my people?"

"Yes, Jarred ben Joseph. Your prophecies will come to pass."

"Ah," he sighed with relief. "You are the awaited sign. Anyone backed so firmly by the *Foundation*, be blessed! I am honored to have you and your companion under my humble roof." He motioned to the servants to begin serving refreshments.

"I suspect our stay will be short," replied Danielle.

"I understand the place of States United, where you come from, is a long way from Rome."

"A very long way."

"I am an old man, almost fifty-three. It is good to know the *Foundation* has expanded farther than the Roman Empire."

"In the place where we come from, fifty-three is not old," said Danielle.

Jarred laughed. "You are kind, beautiful lady, and wise for your young age. The *Foundation,* despite its insistence upon secrecy, has begun to acquire a reputation for recruiting intellectuals. It is rumored that its existence dates back to the time of the pharaohs in Egypt. It was a privilege to be asked to join the organization. There are some members who will not disclose their identities but whose presence is feared and respected in Rome."

"Jarred, can you tell us something?" inquired Danielle. "Do you know of anyone who wears a ring in the shape of a snake?"

The man thought for a moment. "No. I don't believe so. But Julius would certainly know; he tries to keep up with everything. As a matter of fact, he had already heard, somehow, that you were in the city and should be paying us a visit today. He is a brilliant man, extremely diplomatic, who hides his disappointments well. You see, he was refused admittance to the *Foundation*. I am sure it was because of his association with Sergius Catilina."

"Is he talking about Julius Caesar?" whispered Chris to Danielle.

"Who else?" She then turned to Jarred. "If Julius maintains a friendship with Catilina, then he is undoubtedly a member of your opposing group."

"The Brotherhood, the Prince's *Group* you mean?"

"Yes."

"I heard rumors about the organization. A group of individuals proposing the theory that once Earth was ruled by a planetary prince who served Luciel and was deposed of by God Almighty." Ben Joseph waved his hand in dismissal. "It is just a dying fable. Such a group, if it does exist, has absolutely no power. Julius would not consider that affiliation of use to him."

"Don't be too sure, my dear Jarred." After a pause, she said, "Jarred, do you have a wife?"

"Yes." His eyes lit up. "Here she comes . . ."

They turned toward the steps and watched the young woman, no older than twenty-six, with long black hair, uncovered, unlike other Jewish women of her time.

"My wife Rebecca." Jarred Ben Joseph announced proudly.

When the young woman smiled and bowed her head, Chris knew without reservation that she was Angela, or an aspect of Angela, as Danielle put it. Chris looked again at Jarred and now saw clearly what Danielle had not missed. Jarred ben Joseph was none other than John Larkin.

A sense of well-being came over Chris with the realization that the bond between people who loved each other was eternal. The evolutionary journey was not a lonely one; one undertook it, quite often, in the company of eternal loved ones.

At that moment, the house overseer announced the arrival of Gaius Julius Caesar. Jarred ben Joseph excused himself and walked to the portico to meet with him. Rebecca left the room to attend to some domestic duty.

Danielle and Chris remained silent but smiled at each other, amused.

Gaius Julius Caesar entered the room dressed in what was considered splendid attire. Yet Chris could hardly hide his disappointment upon seeing the legendary Caesar. Julius was small in stature, of medium build, slightly muscular, but altogether unimposing. His hair was sandy blond, and his pale eyes a nondescript color; but his manner was gracious and his look, engaging. He kissed Danielle's hand and embraced Chris with the enthusiasm of encountering an old friend. It was easy to see what made him likable. He seemed to have a way with people. He possessed that unusual trait, very favorable to politicians, of making everyone feel particularly special. Julius inquired about their journey. Danielle was vague, but Julius took no offense.

"It's a real pleasure to meet foreigners like you, representatives of the Pax Romana, no doubt. I understand you come from an island beyond Britannia. I have never heard nor known of such a place called the States United."

"We were once under Britannia's rule, but no longer," volunteered Danielle.

"Interesting . . . very interesting," commented Julius, eyeing the couple keenly. "The Pax Romana has a noble purpose, but I feel that it is one that has not been effective."

Jarred ben Joseph interrupted, "Julius has glorious dreams for Rome if he does decide to pursue a political career."

"I believe all nations should come together under one rule, one God, undivided, where there would be justice for all," added Julius.

"An empire?" asked Danielle sarcastically.

Gaius Julius laughed with his usual charm. "No, a democracy! An exemplary democracy—one the entire world could look up to for uncompromising protection. A Rome that would guarantee peace." He began pacing about the room. "I love the people, the common man. It is he, and his hard work, that makes our nation great. Don't you agree, my good Ben Joseph?"

Jarred felt cornered. "Well, if someone is able to bring the people together, it has to be you. Who else has been able to defy Sulla and yet remain in his good graces?"

Julius smiled and drank the wine that had been served. "And may I ask what brings you to our city?" Julius interrupted.

"We wish to make contact with the Brotherhood," answered Danielle.

"The *Foundation*?"

"The other one. The one whose members wear the ring with the coiled snake," said Danielle, pointing to her middle finger.

Julius appeared quizzical, but the smile never left his face. "I am afraid I can't help you. No, I have never seen such a ring or heard of the Brotherhood. I will be glad to inquire, though."

Like Danielle, Chris could tell he was lying. It was precisely the mention of the Brotherhood that made the future dictator cut his visit short.

"My beautiful lady and distinguished guest, I must take leave of you. If there is anything I can assist you with while in Rome, I'd be most happy to be of service."

Chris and Danielle bowed their heads in acknowledgment, and Julius threw his cape over one shoulder, preparing for departure.

"I'll walk you out, my friend," offered Jarred.

Danielle and Christian followed the two men with their eyes, not missing the arrogant bearing particular to Julius.

"Devious but charming," commented Danielle. "I suppose there is a grain of honor in his design—the unification of the people under one government. Unfortunately, his craving for personal aggrandizement overshadows his purpose."

"And Brutus says he is ambitious . . . and Brutus is an honorable man . . ."

When Jarred returned, Danielle informed him they had to leave to meet their contact at the senate building. Jarred offered to accompany them or send an escort along. Thanking him cordially, Danielle insisted that Chris would be escort enough, and they would enjoy walking through the city. So they took their exit, despite Jarred ben Joseph's insistence that the city was dangerous and not what it used to be.

XXV

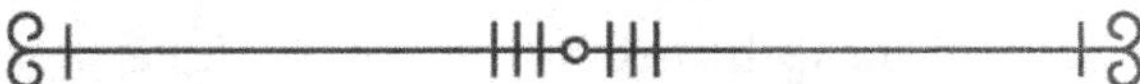

Rome

Marcus Tullius Cicero, who had been recently appointed Curule Aedile, would be addressing the Senate. Danielle and Christian walked to the forum and mingled with the senators and distinguished public officials descending from private litters. Christian was splendidly arrayed, his toga was gracefully draped and made him look like a true patrician, and Danielle's radiant beauty commanded unquestioned respect. They walked undisturbed into the chamber and took up places at the back of the room.

Silence fell when Cicero entered the hall; only distant cries from the street hailing the famous lawyer echoed in the chamber. From where he was standing, Chris could catch only glimpses of the tall, slender man in his white tunic, golden girdle, and armlet. His two clients followed and took seats next to the podium.

Cicero's voice was clear and eloquent as he solemnly read the charges that included contempt for authority and society. "I must remind the court of the philosophic principles of jurisprudence—principles that are now ignored by magistrates bent of voiding the rights of Roman citizens. Republics die," said Cicero, "when the people do not insist that the law be honored, the constitution observed, and justice served."

A young boy tapped Danielle on the shoulder and handed her a note bearing Cicero's crest. Danielle signaled Chris to follow her, and they exited the Senate chamber and walked to the spot where the orator's litter awaited them. As they came down the steps, they spied a tall, slim woman getting out of an extravagantly opulent litter. They stared in disbelief. The woman was Lili Keller.

"It's all beginning to make sense," said Danielle. "The *Group* has been using the cosmic portal to move in and out of our century. I wonder if she saw us."

Chris, disappointed to miss the rest of the discourse in the chamber, nodded. "Probably."

"Can you ride?" asked Danielle when they were in the litter.

"Not well, but I think I can manage."

"Good. Cicero's litter will only take us so far. He has arranged to have horses and an escort waiting to take us to our destination."

"He is your contact here?"

"Yes, one of the most incredible men of his time."

When the litter reached its destination, they were provided riding clothes. Shortly, a man galloped up with their two horses on leads and urged them to mount quickly and follow him.

The three rode rapidly in the direction of the hills, creating great clouds of dust. After a few kilometers, they heard the sound of hooves behind them. Chris turned to see four hooded horsemen in pursuit and coming up fast. Danielle signaled him to ride faster, but the pursuing riders were swift, and, in no time, caught up with them. They rode, two on each side of the group, for another kilometer. Danielle and the escort moved closer to the pursuers, opening the way for Chris to pass and pick up speed. Chris did his best. He knew he was ahead when he could hear the ring of the hooves of Danielle's horse behind him. But the hooded horsemen managed to overtake them again and tried to cut them off when they reached a narrow passage on the road.

The escort, who had been instructed to protect the couple at all costs, turned around, pulling his sword. Danielle looked back. The escort had engaged one of the pursuers in combat, and she had no choice but to go back. She yelled for Chris to keep going, but he ignored her and turned around. Chris was blinded by the dust but galloped through. Then a second gust hit like a strong wind. Danielle circled her hand in the air as she rushed to the aid of their escort. The cloud of dust changed into a lavender mist that enclosed Christian within three concentric circles.

Danielle produced a small sword and charged the attackers. Chris realized he had no weapon but felt he had to do something. He rode straight into the fight; he could at least distract their horses. No one seemed to take notice of him. He did not realize that Danielle had made him invisible.

One of the attackers threw his hood back and produced a short, thin pike, then threw it at the escort, spearing him in the neck. The horse reared, throwing the escort to the ground. In fright, Chris's horse reared also, and suddenly, Chris was on the ground. He realized this was the same man who had attacked him at the Vatican. He was wearing the snake ring. As their wounded escort lay dying, the other two horsemen headed straight for Danielle. She had reined her horse in and allowed herself to be maneuvered into the trap the four horsemen had formed around her.

Chris was at some distance from them, so he ripped the weapon from the dead escort and charged on foot to Danielle's side. The four men had swords drawn and were closing in on the Edentian. Before Chris could reach them, a man jumped from a tree onto the back of one of the horsemen, knocking him to the ground, disabling him instantly. Another horseman came in his direction, leaving two men to fight Danielle.

The man who had come to their aid was a seasoned warrior—swift beyond anything Chris had ever seen. He unseated his second opponent within seconds and was wrestling him on the ground.

Surprisingly, Danielle had also dismounted and was taking on her two attackers on foot. Christian joined in the fray. When Chris threw himself at the man with the ring, he realized something odd. The attacker, though momentarily stunned, failed to react. Again, Chris swung his sword at the man but missed. The man continued to focus his attack on Danielle. Chris was amazed that his efforts were having no real effect.

Danielle had disarmed and disabled one of her attackers, but the one with the serpent ring went after her aggressively. She evaded him by doing an aerial turn several feet above the ground and landing behind him. The fight continued for several more minutes in fierce hand-to-hand combat. Here and there, brilliant sparks of light flashed from each one of them as they clashed in physical contact.

The mysterious man, who had appeared out of nowhere, had now put both of his combatants down and turned to help Danielle. With all three of his allies on the ground, the serpent-ringed fourth realized he was outnumbered. In retreat, he made a gravity-defying leap and mounted his horse. His departure was swift, and when he was out of sight, Danielle rushed to embrace the rescuer.

"My dearest, you are here!" Tears ran down her cheeks.

"I am," answered the man, still holding Danielle tight. "But we must get away." He turned to Chris. "Can you still ride, Christian?"

"Yes." He felt embarrassed that he had not been of more help. *And who is this man who calls me by my name?*

They mounted their horses and headed again into the hills. The Nordic-looking guide took them through sheep meadows and groves of olive trees. Finally, they entered a neglected vineyard and dismounted next to a well.

"We can enter through here," said the man with the pale hair, and he jumped into the mouth of the well.

Danielle followed, signaling Chris to do the same. The well was shallow and dry. Inside, there was an opening the size of a small door. The three of them entered and walked a few feet down a narrow passage before it opened into a wider tunnel with a metal door, which led to a spacious square chamber with a minimalist, modern Roman style. It was built mostly of limestone. The clean architectural lines reminded Chris of the apartment of the vanished Kjell Ullman.

With a questioning look, Chris turned to face the man who had rescued them.

"I am Kjell Ullman. You have been tracking me for a long time."

The two men shook hands as Chris looked at him intently. He recalled the picture of Kjell and Danielle when she was much younger and was amazed to see Kjell had not aged since. He also possessed the same strength, gentleness, and physical beauty as Danielle. Before Danielle could speak, Chris understood that Kjell was also an Edentian.

"What is this place?" he asked.

"One of the *Foundation's* safe houses."

"How did you get away?' asked Danielle of her friend.

"Supposedly, you died at the hospital," added Chris before Kjell could answer.

"And I almost did before a friend came to my rescue."

"Who? I don't understand," said Danielle. "The *Foundation* does not know of your whereabouts, at least not back home."

"It is a complicated story, one I cannot yet fully disclose. Some of the members of the *Foundation* do know that I am here. It is better if the majority thinks I have perished."

"Such a horrible thought!" shuddered Danielle.

"Well, the *Group* disabled us for a while. We underestimated them and their resources . . . how they managed to keep a portal open despite our strict quarantine."

"Right under our very noses. Who would ever suspect them to have a door at the Vatican?"

"Here, they have been able to test their weapons without interference, making it all appear as disasters from nature. "Now tell me, how did you two end up here?" Kjell wanted to know.

Danielle recounted the happenings from the time she had been in the hospital, what they were doing at the Vatican, the uncovering of the statue of Aphrodite, and the theft of the stone.

Kjell listened carefully, connecting pieces of the puzzle.

"We also saw Lilith."

"Lili . . .Lilith," repeated Kjell with amusement. "Was she with Catilina?"

"Perhaps. We couldn't tell," said Danielle. "Logically, Catilina would be her favorite recruit."

"I think this time, a number of them have entered. I suspect they are readying this space for habitation—once they ruin the other one."

"Here, take this . . ." He took off a chain from around his neck and removed an oval stone. Then, while turning to Christian, said, "I believe you are wearing my medallion."

Christian removed it and handed it to Kjell. The Edentian inserted the stone in the center of the concentric circles and returned it to Christian.

"I believe it will be safe with you. I will retrieve from Catilina or Lilith the stone that was taken from you."

"The one in the Valley of the Kings must also be retrieved soon," added Danielle.

"Your friend, Jean-Christophe, must leave for Egypt immediately. It won't take the *Group* much longer to locate it. They are planning to reenter the tombs from here. They have already been there a couple of times."

"Well, of course, the medians told Jean-Christophe about it," Danielle explained. "The *Group* no doubt expects Gaius Julius to take them."

"No wonder Julius felt uncomfortable discussing the *Group*. Is he with them?"

"Probably not, but being paid well for his services."

"Did you meet Cicero?" Kjell wanted to know.

"No. Wish we had," said Chris. "What eloquence!"

"Cicero has a soft spot for Julius. They grew up together, but I think he would tell us if Julius forms deep alliances with the *Group*."

Kjell turned to Christian. "You see, this original U-606 mission was overseen by a member of the Council of Sages and headed by six Edentians. They were Adam and Eva, Daniela, Trebor—whom you know as Robert Powers. Trebor and Lili, after completing their initial assignment, separated from the mission and chose to remain on Earth. Their refusal to become part of the *Foundation* forced them to relinquish their stones, which were placed in a secret location for safekeeping."

"It is now our job to find the pieces and reassemble the disk. We have two stones so far," said Danielle.

"I'll get Catilina's, which belongs to Adam. Eva's stone has to be the one in Egypt."

"I think I might locate Robert's in Mexico."

"We need to locate the sixth one, and we have not a clue where to start looking."

Kjell once again addressed Christian, "Did you have trouble getting into this dimension?"

"When I was struggling with the man in the Vatican, a huge crack in the room sprang open and pulled us in."

"And I followed," finished Danielle.

"Hmm . . . that's what I suspected. They brought you here. It is a trap! They want you in here, Danielle."

"But I would just interfere with their plans."

"Quite the contrary. Their real plans are outside. They had no qualms about eliminating me. If they wanted you dead, they would have killed you back in California."

"I suspected as much. I was practically in Cirel's hands."

"If he let you live, Danielle, it is because he was restrained. They need you. They had to incapacitate you, but you must remain functional to serve their purpose."

Kjell and Danielle looked at each other, then he said, "There is only one other reason why they need you so desperately. Tell me now, Danielle, am I correct? Do you have . . ."

"Yes, Kjell. I do have it."

"I thought so!"

"What are you talking about?" Chris broke in. "What do you have that they want so badly?"

"It's something I was given for safekeeping."

"Another stone?"

Danielle laughed. "No. A secret—something that can aid in changing the destiny of man."

"What?"

"The formula for DNA modification."

"We are all participants in this experiment called Urantia 606, or life on planet Earth; and, of course, we want to succeed."

Danielle took Chris's hand. "We are here to aid you, and our mission is to free you from the fetters the rebels have placed on humanity."

"What fetters?"

"The fetters, or limitations, that imprison you in this fabricated reality—the one you now accept as real and controls your mind."

"And this starship of yours . . . is it real or fabricated?"

"Real," answered Kjell. "The life carriers are aware of the human predicament and check on its progress periodically. Most of you are undergoing a purification process."

"The rebels established a station on Earth, and a group of them settled here and became known as the *Luciel Group*. For a while, they tried to keep up communication with other rebel bases in the galaxy that were supporting the Luciel cause.

"The Celestial Courts of Edentia agreed that this communication only fostered unrest and confusion and decided to put a stop to it. Seraphic forces were dispatched to Earth to seal and protect the vortex, the only 'door' for accessing other worlds or realities, and from then on, only members allied with Edentia were allowed in or out. This is how the *Foundation* came to be established. Its charge was to recruit humans of the highest order and concentrate on maintaining peace and balance on Earth, mainly by keeping an eye on the activities of the *Group*.

"The *Group* members living on Earth, now cut off from their superiors, continued to follow the instructions previously given to them, the purpose of which was to make the plan for salvation fail, recruit despondent souls, and set them against the Creator."

"Didn't those leaders have any accountability?"

"The Creator gave the order to leave them alone, thinking that, in time, they would see the error of their ways and repent. A few did while others, stripped of their privileges, became more and more embittered and dedicated their energies to Arch-rebel Luciel."

"Tell me about Luciel or Lucifer. I gather he is not the horned and hooved creature with a tail, portrayed in stories?" Chris asked.

Kjell and Danielle laughed. "Far from it," said Kjell. "He is a beautiful being whose radiance is blinding. He was one of the most magnificent Sons of Light—a favorite of our Creator Michael."

"Like a brother?"

"More like a son," answered Kjell. "That is why the betrayal was so painful. When he began to exhibit hateful ways, like a loving father, Christ Michael allowed him to go free, always hoping for his return and repentance. But Luciel began to create havoc throughout the galaxies, which continued to escalate. A council of the Most High approached Michael and asked to be allowed to deal with the situation. Michael sorrowfully agreed, and Luciel was arrested and imprisoned and a trial scheduled. Thus began the trial of Gabriel versus Lucifer in the celestial courts.

"The trial has now been going on for some time, and deliberation for a verdict will soon begin in Enza. We have information that all the rebel stations will join in a massive attack and attempt to liberate their leader," Kjell finished.

"We are to keep order as much as is possible," said Danielle. "But this time, the attacks on us are unprecedented. Because we have taken human form, our bodies, like yours, are vulnerable."

"Chris, we could stay here and talk about this for days. But why don't you take a look at our documents in the library? A lot of your questions will be answered."

Christian followed Kjell down another corridor and into a well-lit room. It had no oil lamps or torches, and it was impossible to see where the light came from, but he did not question Kjell further.

"Unfortunately, you cannot take any of these records back with you. They belong to this time. You might find in here the answers you are looking for. Danielle and I must meet with the elders. We will be back for you. Make yourself at home. You are safe here."

After the Edentians left, Chris paced around the room, not knowing where to start. The room was lined on two walls with wide shelves containing leather-bound books, the pages still retaining the charm of handmade paper—extremely thin and semi-transparent. The other two walls contained a stack of wooden boxes that held a vast number of carefully rolled scrolls. He understood that the scrolls had been methodically placed, each containing commentaries on particular epochs of civilization.

Wondering what time of the day it was, he looked at his wrist, where up to a couple of days ago his Cartier watch had been. He was sure he had not taken the watch off, and it occurred to him that perhaps the time warp had disintegrated it. He turned to the first shelf and stared at the books. He had no trouble recognizing the symbols. He was overjoyed that he understood.

To his surprise, he thought of Kitzia. She was very much like him. Two mortals that handled experiences much in the same manner. Two beings who continually searched for truth and were driven by the desire to do the right thing, not particularly to serve the ego, but for that inner need to know they had done the very best they could.

Chris grabbed the first volumes, setting them on top of a mahogany table. He sat on a chair—the only other piece of furniture in the room—and arranged the books in the order he would examine them:

The Primary Nebular Stages of Urantia and Crustal Stabilization
Planetary Beginning of Life: Continental Drift
Reign of the Planetary Prince (The Urantia Book)

Suddenly, he caught sight of a volume that interested him more than any other. It was marked *The History of Atlantide*. "Atlantis!" he whispered excitedly as he walked to the shelf. That was where he would start.

One side of his brain told him he was looking at documents written in Latin, Greek, and Aramaic; the other side of his brain encouraged him to proceed and read them as if they had already been translated into English. As he opened the book and began reading, Kitzia came back to his mind. He wondered if she had any idea that they had, for all practical purposes, vanished from her world?

XXVI

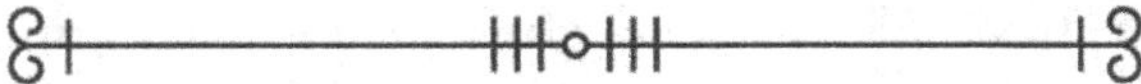

Kitzia pondered the paradigm shift taking place all around her, compounded by feelings of loss that came with acceptance that Tom had slipped away from her. On her desk, a photo of Deborah, her mother stared back in disbelief. The irony was that her professional success, of which her mother was so proud, had kept Kitzia from seeing her parents more than once or twice a year. She was stung by regret. Her father's health had deteriorated—the Wilsons had moved out of their ranch and bought a house in a suburb of Dallas.

They had been stunned when Kit and Tom separated, and Kit felt as if she had somehow failed them. Danielle must have always known what Kit failed to see. But now that Tom was gone, the struggle was finally over.

Kitzia looked at her calendar and began shifting her commitments. She rang for Michelle. The perky Black girl came in and placed Kit's incoming mail on the desk.

Kitzia stared at her assistant's outfit—a faded Army-green jacket and a skirt with torn fringe. "What in the world are you wearing?"

"I gather you don't like it? It's the newest look, trendy and awfully comfortable. Everyone is wearing it. Haven't you seen the new Keller boutiques? There is one around the corner . . ."

Kitzia shook her head. "Michelle, I need to go away for a couple of days to see my mother."

"OK."

"No word from Danielle?"

"No."

The phone rang. Michelle picked it up and handed it to Kit. "It's your mother."

"Oh, Mom, I was just about to call. . . . Oh . . . I'll leave immediately." She turned and addressed Michelle, "Book me on the first flight to Dallas. My father had a heart attack."

Plano, Texas

"You could have told me," Kit said to her mother reproachfully.

Deborah was silent. She cast a sad glance at the casket sitting by the graveside, and the two undertakers waiting for the last of the cars to depart before they lowered it into the ground. The two women climbed into the limousine, which led the procession of cars back to Deborah's house in the suburbs. The sprays were lovely, and the funeral for her husband had been simple and tasteful, she thought.

Inside the limo, Deborah removed her sunglasses and, looking at her daughter, finally answered the question. "Yes, perhaps I should have told you. But how would that have changed anything?"

Kit thought that perhaps she was being a little tough at a time like this, but she pressed on. "It is a little too much to take in one gulp. My father dies, and at the same time, I find out he was not actually my father. What a month for eye-openers!"

"How did you figure it out?" Deborah inquired curiously.

"At the hospital, when I looked at his records. Our blood types were not a match."

"I am sorry you had to find out this way."

"Who was my father?"

"I will tell you all about it but not now."

"I don't see why not. Dad is gone. Did he even know?"

"No." Deborah's voice displayed no remorse. "He loved you."

"And I loved him. Who was my father?" Kit insisted.

Deborah bit her lip as she pushed strands of blonde hair behind her ear. In her early sixties, she was still an attractive woman. The time had come to open the past, and Deborah saw no point in delaying it.

"His name was Martin Judd. He was killed in a car crash weeks before the wedding." An expression of wistfulness and nostalgia came into her eyes, a look Kit had never seen. Deborah related the story—the shock of her pregnancy and the determination to keep her child. "I met Gene, he fell in love with me, and . . ."

Deborah lowered her eyes, and Kit reached for her hand. "I know you did your best, and you chose the next best man in the world," whispered Kit. "I just wish you had told me earlier. It would have made everything much easier to understand, like why Dad and I were so different. I think I would have tried harder, worked on our relationship longer. I had so much to thank him for."

"I suppose it was that kind of feeling I wanted to spare you, the need to make up for something that was not your fault. You brought Gene incredible happiness, and that is all that matters."

"So I gather that I am a hundred percent Jewish?"

"Yes."

"That explains why I've always hated to pay retail for anything," she quipped.

Deborah smiled for the first time in a long while.

Their car pulled into the driveway, and several cars behind them parked on the street. *More people extending condolences,* Kit thought with resignation.

"You didn't tell Tom about the funeral," said Deborah suddenly. "Didn't you think he would want to be with you at a time like this?"

"Mom, please. I don't want to discuss Tom right now."

Deborah ignored her protest. "I thought he should know, so I called him . . . and see . . ." she pointed to a man in a dark suit coming toward the car. "There he is!"

Tom opened the car door and helped Kit out. She let herself be guided and pulled into his arms.

"I am so sorry about your dad," he whispered in her ear.

Kit ached to tell him what she had just learned but remained silent, savoring the comfort of his arms. It was at that moment the anger subsided. She saw Tom as the brilliant doctor, an exceptional human being, whom she loved and admired, and not as the husband and lover she always wanted to possess.

Not understanding why, in his arms she experienced a sense that her healing had truly begun. She knew she would be all right. He held her tightly, hoping to convey what he had never been able to verbalize—and his sorrow that she had to find out in such a brutal way. That the nature of his inclination did not in any way diminish the affection and admiration he felt for her.

Tom kept his arm around her as he escorted her into the house. His feelings toward the small, beautiful woman were those of awe. He felt enormous respect for the way she had handled the discovery of his homosexuality.

He also thought about what he had recently found out.

He wished he could share with her what he had discovered in the lab about her blood, but he had made a promise to Danielle not to disclose any of his findings, and needless to say, he was still having trouble processing the results in his own mind. He consoled himself with the knowledge she was no ordinary woman, that there was something unique in her that elevated her above the average mortal. An extraordinary variance in her DNA.

When Danielle was in the hospital after her accident, he had been astounded to discover that she had a complete set of additional chromosomes, compared to those of normal human beings and different from anything he had ever seen, as well as inexplicable configurations in her brain.

Tom's thoughts wandered to Christian Goodman, who he had also found to possess the extra variance. If they ever came together, Christian Goodman and Kitzia would likely produce offspring that would share most, if not all of Danielle's superior traits.

That had to be Danielle's plan all along, and Tom could not help but wonder how long it had taken the Edentian to find the perfect mate for her friend.

XXVII

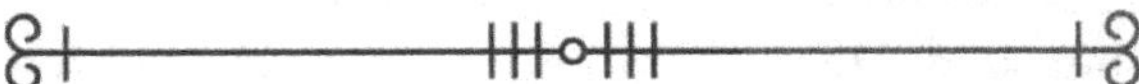

Surviving accounts of the island of Atlantide

Christian flipped excitedly through the papers, reading with anticipation. It covered material as recorded in "The Manuscript," furnished by the rememberers, to whom such accounts were entrusted:

> *Atlantis the third and last Garden of Eden recreated the grandeur from the universal memory of Edentia . . .*

Chris scanned preliminary notes that had been entered by *Foundation* members over time and Plato's introduction to the narrative. He opened other scrolls and read on, alternating among volumes. Finally, a clearer image of events began taking shape in his head.

> *Because of a deviation from the celestial plan in the Garden of Eden, Project U-606 had been classified in default, and its inhabitants were forced to relocate. Atlantis was the final resting place of the Edenic caravan. The Edentians monitoring U-606 accompanied the exiles to their new island . . .*

Chris was electrified. He continued flipping the pages.

> *Atlantis was the original seat of the Aryan race, as well as the Semitic. . . . The settlers sought to recreate the magnificence of the first Garden of Eden. The Edentians constructed magnificent structures out of gold. The rumor spread throughout the galaxy—gold was abundant in Urantia.*

Visitors, sympathizers to the rebellion, began to arrive. They reminded the souls in evolution of their right to autonomy, and the progress many had achieved began to reverse itself. . .

He was so captivated by what he was reading that he failed to smell the combination of smoke and sulfur filling the room. When he did, he rushed out to the living area. The entire room was engulfed in flames, the thick smoke making it hard for him to see, let alone breathe. He rushed to the door. He pushed with all this strength, but to his horror, the door that looked like wood was actually metal and was shut solid. He tried twice more, throwing all his weight against it, disregarding the burns on his shoulders. When he began to choke, Christian ran back toward the reading room and scanned the walls, looking for another way out. The library was now on fire; he saw the scrolls burning, and some books on the shelves disintegrated before his eyes. He could hardly breathe as smoke and darkness choked him.

He fell to his knees, grabbing the chain around his neck and clasping the medal in his hands. As he drifted into unconsciousness, he felt himself being lifted by strong arms.

He opened his eyes a couple of times and saw that he was outside, away from the flames, but no matter how hard he tried, he could not wake up. He felt the jolting of hooves hitting the ground beneath him. No, he could not be riding a horse. He was not even awake.

The Countryside

"He is not there," Danielle said to Kjell, her voice filled with anxiety.

"Then he got out before the fire."

"I have to go back and find him."

"Danielle, this will only take a little longer. We have almost sealed the portal."

It was sunset and the light of the receding sun bathed the top foliage of the trees with a veil of fading lavender. Danielle and Kjell were standing between two large umbrella pines, and Kjell moved his hand in the air with the agility of a painter saturating a canvas with paint. The two trees were slowly converging and overlapping to become one. Danielle was bent over, working horizontally, while Kjell closed the gap vertically.

She suddenly stopped and said, "I'm going back.

"Wait," said Kjell as he received a mental vision. "I've got him. He is riding toward us."

Within minutes, the horse carrying Chris appeared around a hill. Still coughing, Chris had regained consciousness and rode, letting himself be guided by the horse. When he reached them, they helped him dismount. It was apparent that Chris had suffered from smoke inhalation and seemed delirious. Danielle made him lie down. Chris was trying to tell them about the fire, but they gently bade him to rest, answering that they already knew.

"It is all gone! All the writings, everything!"

"It's OK," she whispered. "You must go through the opening. We are going to seal it behind you."

"And you?"

"We'll finish closing the portal, and when we are done, we'll slip through at another point. Tell Jean-Christophe that I will meet him in Egypt in a fortnight . . . and Kit, that I am sorry for her loss." She reflected for a moment. "About His Holiness, this is the way he chose to help us fight. Most important, not a world about Kjell to anyone. Now, hurry! Walk between those trees in a straight line toward that rosebush and do not look back."

Chris did as he was told. As he walked between the trees, Kjell's hand movements continued to bring the trees together until the gap between them closed, and one tree overlapped the other, creating one thick umbrella pine.

When Christian arrived at the rosebush, he looked back. Danielle and Kjell had vanished. The sun was setting, and the Vatican gardens were deserted. He was wearing the clothes he had been wearing in the storeroom, and the Cartier was back on his wrist.

He was not sure how long he had been gone. To his surprise, the watch indicated that only a few hours had passed.

Angela was the first person he encountered.

"I was looking for you. Is Danielle with you?"

"No. His Holiness?"

"Resting peacefully. He needs to have all his strength for tomorrow. He insists on having the conference as scheduled. Despite the opposition, he will pass all the changes that are so overdue. That is actually what I wanted to talk to you about. His Holiness handed me a draft of what he is covering for the press release, and he wants you, and only you, to see it and write it."

"Well, of course. I will be honored."

"Then come with me. Cardinal Santis has the notes in his safe. Oh, by the way . . ." Angela reached inside her pocket and handed Chris a white card. "He asked me to give you this, a pass, a papal mandate that will give you access to the Vatican archives. It is issued by the Board of Vatican Libraries and should give you access to anything you might want to see. His Holiness thinks you might be interested in looking at some of the surviving documents related to Atlantis."

The two Edentians watched Christian cross safely through the portal.

It was important to close the opening before dark, when it would be harder to weave the layers of reality together. The shadows of dusk descended upon them. But something was wrong. Daniela and Kjell noticed it simultaneously. The sun was setting on the wrong side.

After a second of confusion, Daniela turned around and walked about ten feet before she ran into a solid but invisible barrier. She ran her hands across the impregnable surface. Kjell had run back to the vanishing point of the realities they had just woven together, trying desperately to pry them open, but to no avail.

"We are trapped!" yelled Daniela in horror.

Someone had sealed the remaining space behind them, catching them between realities, in a prison of undefined time and space. Night shadows continued to fall, turning the space behind them into utter darkness.

Facing the barrier, they could still see the last rays of light on the Roman countryside, and the faint outline of four figures, among them the despicable Cirel. Kjell thought he recognized the figure of the evil patrician Lucius Catilina. There was also the unmistakable shadow of their onetime friend, Lilith.

"Lili!" pleaded Daniela, resting her hand and face against the glass-like barrier. "I know you are there. I know you can hear me . . ."

But it was Cirel's despotic voice that answered, "Both of you escaped me once. Now, enjoy your sleep." Then, turning to the hooded figure, he added, "Comrade, take one last look at beautiful Daniela." The man wearing the hood did not move. After a short pause, Cirel addressed Lili. "Are you coming, dear?"

"Not yet. Go on. I'll catch up with you."

"As you wish. Shall we, Lucius . . . Trebor?"

The sound of horses' hooves indicated that they had departed.

"Trebor?!" Daniela screamed in agony. *No. Robert cannot be part of this!*

"Why do you insist on being so boringly naïve?" asked Lili. "What made you think that Robert's fascination with you would be eternal? Sooner or later, he had to come to grips with the truth, realize who would win, and side with us. You are finished, and so is your *Foundation* and your cause."

"Lili, why are you doing this?" pleaded Daniela.

"Are you not listening? We have a chance. You don't." Lili moved closer to the barrier so Daniela could see her. "Too bad you will miss all the action. Trebor feels you are safe in there," she laughed. "Oh, you will be taken out sometime when we are done. Maybe by then, you will be more willing to support us. Besides, your role as a human is coming to an end, as you have already figured out."

Kjell approached the glass. "Lili, I never thought you very clever. Now you have totally justified my suspicion."

Lili laughed, amused. "Me, not clever? Actually, look at the predicament you are in."

"You're simply being allowed to play out your treacherous role . . . sinking yourself deeper and deeper in the quagmire," said Kjell.

"Well," sighed Lili, "we are close to the conclusion. We won't have much longer to wait."

"Lili, you are delusional," said Daniela. "There is no detachment from the Source. As a neutral, you might now be charged with divergence, but as a rebel, given the mandates of the Most High, you will be charged with treason and annihilated!"

"I see no seraphic troops coming to rescue you," answered Lili. They are so busy preparing for the war that they have forgotten about you, even your beloved Orsef. The way I see it is RA reaches the intersection and, with no signal, it continues on. We assume control of the currents and establish our base. We position the monolith and open communication with our allies. It will then be quite easy to launch an attack from here on the legions of Salvington.

"I'll leave the real fighting to those who enjoy it and move myself to my next adventure—with your help of course. I have no intention of moving about the galaxies as a gas form. I want a body. You realize now that part of keeping you alive is my doing. I know Eva gave you the secret, and that you will share it with me.

"Daniela, you and I are the same. We were best friends once. We wanted the same things. We've had the same setbacks. We wanted brilliance, power . . . love."

"No, Lili, we are not the same. I never sought power, and you have never wanted love."

The smile vanished from Lili's lips. "I don't understand why you insist on our loyalty to a Creator who abandoned us. We were left down here to rot, along with this decaying creation of his. He should have foreseen the perils and made provisions. He should have sent us help when we needed it. Instead, we had to survive by our wits. You and I have carried the heaviest burden."

"Lili, there is something very wrong with your thinking. Your vision of reality is twisted."

"The Manifesto of Lucifer clearly expressed our sentiment. Why should all the universes be ruled under one God? One that we are not even sure exists. No one has ever seen him!"

Daniela continued listening in disbelief. "You have seen Christ Michael in our universe. One needs not seek further."

"How do you know for sure that He is indeed the Creator Son? That the whole scheme is not a myth invented by the Celestials to ensure them rule of the universes?" Lili demanded.

"We know it in our hearts. That's where love comes in."

"On the contrary, I believe the Lucifer Manifesto states it well. The day has arrived when we will put an end to the absolute reign of the Ancient of Days, those 'Foreign Potentates,' who, under the name of a universal Father, continue to interfere with the affairs of the local systems and universes." Lili's voice softened as she continued, "We simply want autonomy, Daniela."

"Listen to the contradictions coming from your mouth," urged Danielle. "You seek autonomy, and yet you rob individuals of their right to choose. I have seen the zombies you are creating and the accumulation of thwarted spiritual energy thrown into the collective consciousness. Where is the freedom in autonomy?"

Daniela's worlds angered Lili, especially because of the images they produced inside her mind—lost images of times gone by . . . of Edentia, of Orsef, the Magnificent Orsef. Lili reproached herself for thinking of Edentia. Those were distant memories, painful images of love unrequited. *Love—such a disruptive feeling!* She had sworn never again to be carried away by emotion, and she had succeeded, so far . . . or had she? Jeff's face suddenly appeared in her mind. She snapped back to the present for fear Daniela should guess her thoughts. "So I guess we won't be seeing each other for a while."

"Poor beautiful Lili!" added Kjell. "You feel so unloved when it is not so. With understanding comes the realization that love is more than ego or sexual gratification. I love you now, even during this most stubborn period of opposition to the truth."

"We have all loved you," added Daniela. "It was because of that feeling that . . ." Danielle could not complete formulating the lost memory. The veil of night had by now almost completely fallen upon the imprisoned Edentians.

"Lili, I can't believe you have forgotten your link to Daniela," was the last thing Kjell said.

Daniela's voice pierced the darkness. "I swore I wouldn't leave you and Robert here to an uncertain fate. Now I see that the two of you are no longer Neutrals. You have whole-heartedly embraced the rebellion and have pledged your allegiance to the Manifesto. I can no longer help you!"

Rome

Christian worked on the press release for the pontiff. The draft needed no editing. The pope's insistence on his editing the document was a way of making sure Chris understood what was being proposed. The pope was about to shake the ground the Church had stood on for 2,000 years. No representative of Christ had ever before taken such a firm stand in the reformation of the doctrines of the Catholic Church. Chris viewed the forthcoming conference with an inevitable sense of apprehension.

There was bound to be worldwide outrage. His views would revolutionize the way of thinking about God and religion. He was cutting through the gridlock of bureaucracy and dissipating the barriers between Judaism, Christianity, and, he hoped, Islam. His Holiness also displayed an unwavering respect for the Eastern religions and the ancient noble principles of the Tao.

The days of ruling through fear were to come to an end.

When Chris finished and satisfied with his notations, he returned the transcript to Cardinal Santis, keeping a copy for himself. He then retreated to the library containing the Atlantean documents and installed himself comfortably in the room.

He came across wonderful documents—antediluvian records—and was surprised to find out that he had retained the ability to decipher them. Among the most valuable documents he came across was a set of loose pages carefully protected between acrylic sheets. They were burned around the edges.

Besides saving him, someone had rescued the Atlantean documents he'd been studying, and knew Chris would come across those papers two thousand years later. Christian was immeasurably moved.

One of the pages, written in the Andonic language, was a surviving page from an ancient Edenic journal belonging to Eva, Adam's wife. Her recommendations and notes advised of the existence of a chromosome bank. Their mission on Urantia/Earth accomplished, they prepared for their departure.

> *They did not rest long in the oblivion of the unconscious sleep of the mortals of the realm. On the third day after Adam's death, the second following his reverent burial, the orders of Lanaforge, sustained by the acting Most High of Edentia and concurred by the Union Days on Salvington, acting for Michael, were placed in Gabriel's hands, directing the special roll call of the distinguished survivors of the Adamic default on Urantia. And in accordance with this mandate of special resurrection, number twenty-six of the Urantia series, Adam and Eve were re-personalized and reassembled in the resurrection halls of the mansion worlds of Satania, together with 1,316 of their associates in the experience of the first garden. (The Urantia Book)*

It was almost 5:00 a.m. when Chris decided to stop. He was overcome with the significance of what he had read. When he exited the library, he noticed a great commotion; guards were posted at the foot of the marble stairway.

Obviously, something dramatic had taken place. After ten minutes of searching for a familiar face, he saw Angela emerge from the crowd, still in her white uniform. She headed in his direction.

"It's over! His Holiness passed away in his sleep."

"They killed him, after all!" exclaimed Chris.

"I think so too. But how? We were so careful about everything."

"What was the cause of death?"

"Heart failure," said Angela.

Danielle's words about His Holiness came back to Chris, "This is the way he chose to help us." Chris pulled out his copy of the pope's press release. The closing words were a personal message to him. Had he been more aware at the time, he would have recognized the words couched as a farewell. His Holiness knew he was about to abandon the physical plane but never the war. In spirit, He would become one of their most powerful allies.

Angela and Chris headed for a tiny chapel away from where the clergy was congregating. Chris prayed for guidance. Within a few seconds, he knew what he had to do.

He had to speak to Cardinal Santis and reveal the whereabouts of Danielle. He had a foreboding feeling that Danielle and Kjell were in some sort of predicament and that only the *Foundation* could help.

XXVIII

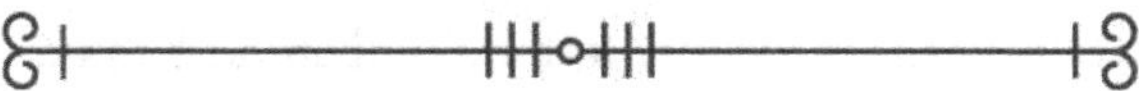

Air Force One lifted off from Fiumicino airport and soared over the Mediterranean with the usual escort of military planes following at a distance. President Parker, more preoccupied than usual, did his best to appear jovial and energetic as he conducted an informal meeting with the select staff accompanying him.

After drinks were served, Kramer, one of his personal advisors observed everyone attentively—every move, every word—a habit he had perfected during his White House service. All seemed perfectly normal, except for President Parker's insistence in having the new tall, thin secret service agent accompany them on this trip. Camiel stood at the entrance of the presidential cabin, watching, listening, and not blinking an eye. Kramer did not like him—those pale, penetrating green eyes. Nor did he understand why the president wanted him around. *It really doesn't matter, though. Not anymore.*

"What a relief to leave Rome without incident, Mr. President!" said Russell, a military advisor and one of Parker's close associates and confidants.

"It was risky. All in all, you should not have gone, David!" added Mark Ferguson, national economic advisor and Parker's most trusted man in Washington.

"I am glad I went to the funeral," answered Parker. "His Holiness was a friend."

"You're right. Your absence might have been misconstrued as an act of cowardice, with everything going on in the Middle East right now," said Kramer.

"Perez Levi's presence was a big surprise," remarked Parker, "especially to all the Arab leaders who thought they had him immobilized."

From his post, Camiel watched the men. They sat in two groups facing each other. "Indeed, since nobody expected Levi to be there," said Ferguson, "he was safe. While you, on the other hand, David, were in constant danger. I won't relax until we are safely on the ground. Such tight security surrounding the pope . . . and he still died."

"You don't believe the allegations that he was murdered!" Kramer exclaimed.

The president shrugged his shoulders. *Foundation* members attending the funeral had advised him how it had so cleverly been accomplished: a deadly agent had been mixed into the starch in his sheets, and the poison had entered his body through a small razor cut on the pontiff's cheek.

The *Foundation* accepted the pontiff's exit from the material world. There was no need to further upset the Catholic world by announcing their pope had been murdered.

"We were especially careful in handling the arrangements for this trip," offered B. J. Strauss, head of security, who was standing behind Kramer. "We can never disregard threats made on the president's life."

"Seriously, David," continued Ferguson, "this time we have very reliable sources advising us of a plot to assassinate you."

Parker smiled. "Well, as you can see, I'm safe."

Jean McCord, White House press secretary, came into the cabin, followed by Christian Goodman. She signaled the secret service agent that it was OK to let him through. Cam and Chris exchanged a surreptitious glance. The president signaled for Chris to come and sit down. "Mr. Goodman, here," said the president, pointing to Christian, "is writing a very important book. So when you get back to Washington, Russell, give him your full cooperation and security clearance so he can access all historical files he may need."

Russell nodded in agreement.

"Now, gentlemen, there are some points I'd like to cover before we land, and we don't have much time," continued the president. "We will not refuel in Ireland; we'll go Lisbon. There, I want you, Russell . . ." He turned to the press secretary. "Jean, Bennett, along with your secret service teams, to get off and take the plane that will be waiting to take you back to Washington, DC. Mr. Goodman will be going with you, as well."

Everyone protested, especially Bennett and the secret service agents, who knew it was highly irregular to leave the president with such a small contingent for his protection.

"It will be all right. I am keeping Ferguson, Strauss and his team, Camiel, and, of course, Kramer and his group. Once we leave Lisbon, we are adding more air escort."

"Mr. President, you cannot ask us to do that!" they protested in unison.

"I am not asking you. I am giving you an order. Kramer and I can handle the situation." Parker winked at Kramer who, after taking a deep breath, answered, "Certainly, Mr. President."

"Don't look so dismayed," continued Parker, seeing the expressions on Ferguson and Russell. "The most important thing right now is not to allow a breach in our security."

"I will be making a stopover in Bermuda for an important, top-secret meeting, which explains why I chose these men to accompany me. The rest of you are needed in Washington, and I have to let you get back to your posts. In a few minutes, you will be handed your advance team reports and a list of priorities to deal with on your return. Let me enumerate some of the points not listed on the report. We don't have too much time, so I'll cover these points quickly.

"Jean, I want you to put a stop to this epidemic of book burning. Get with Vice President McCann to get Congress involved. Russell, we need to get tough with Theodore Edwards and the incitement he is causing among his converts. Prepare for any violence that his so-called religious militia might cause in Washington during his religious conference. The threat of biological warfare is our top priority. The *Group* is fully backing our enemies."

The President took a report from a folder and read, "Listed possibilities are smallpox, SARS, and Ebola. The first and most logical to be unleashed would be smallpox. Now, what do we have on the vaccine situation?"

"We are on it," said Bennett, "but our supply is almost depleted. Our labs are working hard to increase the supply."

"When will our next batch be ready for distribution?"

"Three years."

"Hmm . . . that does present a problem," said Parker. "How many nations in the Middle East have the virus in liquid form?"

"Almost all of them," replied Russell.

"Any recent outbreaks?"

Kramer looked at his notes. "Iraq, Afghanistan, North and South Yemen . . ."

"Our reports indicate the virus is being manufactured by the metric ton in Russia." Parker turned to Ferguson. "Get in touch with Dr. Thomas O'Neil in San Francisco. He is working on a solution to weaken the virus. We have to be prepared for massive quarantines. In the event that I'm not here, you, Russell, have to support the vice president on his decision to destroy the labs in Russia."

Alarmed, Russell asked, "What do you mean in the event that you—"

"It was a figure of speech. I just want all angles covered. We must work nonstop at blocking the dispersal of biological agents."

"That's going to be a tough one!" added Bennett. "Whether it's smallpox or SARS, they are no doubt planning on non-explosive methods of dispersion. I never thought I'd say this, but it was better to be under the threat of nuclear attack! We at least knew how to prepare."

President Parker turned to Christian. "Mr. Goodman, writer of thrillers, give us possible scenarios of how these agents might be dispersed."

Chris thought for a moment. "The agents would have to be smuggled into the country, unless they are already being manufactured in the US."

"Unlikely. We would have been informed," said Parker.

"They could be smuggled in ordinary ways—for instance, on aircraft," said Bennett. "The virus can be freeze-dried, carried safely, then easily reconstituted."

"A central ventilation system in an airport," said Chris, "a mall, or just about any public place could infect thousands of people, who would, in turn, disperse the virus nationally in a period of hours."

"Yes, we have thought of precisely that," added Bennett.

"Anyone could utilize spray cans on buses, trains, and subways to spread SARS," added Chris.

The president and his advisors, including Bennett, exchanged looks of concern, then returned their eyes to Chris as he continued. "Of course, the first and most obvious thing would be to contaminate the food supply."

"OK, gentlemen," said the president. "There you have it! Get ready for it."

The captain's voice came over the intercom and announced they would be landing in Lisbon in fifteen minutes.

The president got up and, excusing himself, invited Chris into his private office, closing the door behind them. He asked Chris to sit. On the bulkhead behind the president's Air Force One desk were multiple television screens. Parker entered something into a computer, and on the screens appeared various views of the Vatican gardens.

"Now, Christian, where exactly did you last see Danielle?"

Chris scanned the screens until he found the large umbrella pine and pointed it out to Parker.

"Are you sure?"

"Absolutely certain."

Parker sent a copy to John Larkin at Argos.

"Mr. President, I wish you would let me go with you. I know I can be of service."

"No, Christian. I need you on the outside right now. We may be sending for you sooner than you think. Now, be seated and buckle up; we are about to land."

A jet was waiting on the Lisbon runway, its engines running and prepared for departure. Russell, McCord, and a group of twelve men, including presidential aides and secret service agents, descended from Air Force One, followed by Christian Goodman. The men changed planes as swiftly as possible, and no luggage was transferred—the less tampering with Air Force One, the better, the president had instructed. Chris decided to contact John Larkin as soon as he got on the plane to see if John knew what was preventing Danielle's return.

On Air Force One, President Parker asked Ferguson to join him in his office.

Kramer watched the departing men run across the strip in the direction of the jet. *The detour to Portugal doesn't make much difference,* he thought. His instructions were to activate the signal immediately after refueling. He was glad the president and Ferguson were inside the private office, busy and out of the way. Kramer sat down, opened his laptop, and entered a code.

Strauss had been told to distract the flight crew and had invited them into the cabin for a quick stretch. Outside the flight deck, they would not hear the faint beep indicating the new program had been installed.

The remaining passengers had again taken their seats in the main cabin. The president and Ferguson remained in the office.

Air Force One took to the air without incident, and Lisbon became a haze of twinkling lights in the dusk. Kramer knew the chip, newly installed in the navigation system, would activate within the hour. He didn't know exactly what was to take place, but Senator Neilson had waved his hand dismissively and told him not to bother himself with the minutiae, that some technology the *Group* had designed would emit an infrared light that would confuse the pilots and navigator, and a cloud of fog would make them lose the horizon. It would occur around the area of the Azores. When it happened, Kramer and his men would be all right, Nielsen reassured him, as long as they followed their explicit instructions.

Parker and Ferguson were still in the office when the plane encountered turbulence, and the seat belt signs came on. The plane was losing altitude.

A sudden storm was adding to the confusion. Air Force One was entering a vast cloud bank, and the pilots could detect no horizon. They had lost contact with their escort planes.

The first pilot's voice came on the loudspeaker to announce that the flight was in trouble, that the aircraft computers were non-responsive; all communications had shut down. Air Force One was losing altitude quickly. The president's escape module would be activated, and he was to board it immediately.

Camiel headed for the cockpit. The pilot's voice came on again, frantically announcing that the flight could not be saved, and Air Force One would plunge into the water within minutes.

Kramer rushed ahead of the secret service agent. His instructions were explicit: he was to prevent the president from boarding the module.

The pilot instructed all passengers to put on life jackets, head to the back of the plane, and grab a parachute from the cargo hold. The rear-loading ramp would open when the airplane reached 1,200 feet. They should jump when ready.

Two flight attendants rushed the men down the passageway to a stairway that led to the cargo hold. When the ramp opened, those with parachutes began to jump.

Strauss was already at the president's side, helping Parker and Ferguson into the module. Kramer rushed up behind him to take over. He yelled to Strauss to head for the exit ramp, which he did without hesitation. Kramer finished buckling the president in, but, instead of activating the ejection buttons, he pulled out his revolver and shot both Parker and Ferguson in their chests.

Kramer rushed out of the cabin and ran toward the ramp. He noticed that a number of the president's aides had remained firmly buckled to their seats—pillows on their laps and heads bent forward over their knees—prepared for the impact.

"Fools!" muttered Kramer as he ran past them. That would save him the trouble of shooting them.

"Nine hundred feet and descending," announced the voice on the loudspeaker.

At the open cargo door, an attendant was hurriedly trying to help Strauss put on his parachute. They were standing between Kramer and the open door. Kramer took his own parachute by the straps and swung it forcefully at the two, causing them to lose their balance. They fell awkwardly through the opening. Shock registered on their faces, and their arms and legs flailed uselessly as they disappeared into the void.

Kramer expertly secured his own parachute and approached the jump ramp. The whole procedure had been nerve-wrecking, but Nielsen and the *Group* had assured him he would survive—just keep calm and follow the instructions. One of the *Group's* planes was following Air Force One closely and would alert their ships near the Azores, where the men would jump.

With that thought to reassure himself, Kramer jumped into the darkness. Kramer—an experienced chutist—confidently counted off the seconds before pulling the ripcord. He pulled, and waited to hear the rush of the fabric releasing and filling with air, and then to feel the yank on the harness that stops the free fall. Nothing happened. He tried again. Nothing.

When his parachute did not open, he realized his had not been the only one; neither had those of his men opened. Countless thoughts flashed through his mind as he plummeted toward the dark ocean. Kramer had done what the *Group* had asked—what was required to cause the presidential plane to crash. He had been loyal to the *Group* to the last breath, and they had tricked him! There was no wealth or position of power awaiting him, as Nielsen had promised. He had been used and disposed of, as had everyone else on his team.

A sardonic laugh burst from his throat. At least he had done his job. Momentarily, Air Force One would plunge into the ocean.

News of the disappearance of Air force One dominated every television screen around the world, overshadowing the death of the pontiff. And yet, no one suspected how closely related the incidents were.

Air Force One had vanished. It had disappeared in the vicinity of the Azores. The plane had taken off from Lisbon, and no malfunctions had been reported during the flight. Then it had disappeared from the radar. Two of the escort planes had seen it lose altitude and enter the cloud bank but had not seen it dive into the water. Air Force One had never transmitted a distress signal.

Senator Nielsen fabricated the report that one of the escort planes had seen Air Force One plunge into the ocean. Acting on that single report, Navy and Air Force rescue teams roamed the waters in the vicinity of the Azores.

No evidence of the wreckage could be found. After twenty-four hours, only three badly mangled bodies had been fished out of the waters. Because the bodies had been partially devoured by sharks, it was impossible to make immediate identification. Through dental records, it was finally determined that two of the bodies were the remains of J. B. Strauss, head of White House Security, and William Kramer, the personal advisor to the president.

Pressure built at the White House. Without concrete answers, Jean McCord could not make a public statement. Had AFO been shot down by enemy missiles? There was no sign of impact. Had it been hijacked by terrorists? There was no ransom request.

The only logical explanation was that it had crashed and sunk into the ocean. But why hadn't there been a distress signal? The search for the wreckage continued. When Russell and Bennett opened the instructions packages, they found specific directives on how to proceed during "the period of confusion."

"It's as if he knew this was going to happen," Russell said to Bennett.

"He probably knew something was up but didn't know who would be the Judas."

"Why didn't he confide in us? We could have saved him. Why didn't he trust us?"

"He did trust us. That's why he made us get off."

"I still hope that somehow Air force One managed to . . ."

"Managed to what? Russell asked. "There is nowhere it could have gone! We must face the facts. AFO is gone and so is our president and a handful of good men. The world has suffered a great loss."

The only thing President Parker did not foresee was the weakness in the character of his vice president, Clayton McCann, in the face of these circumstances. The president had always trusted McCann, for he knew him to be a man of good judgment, a man, Parker felt confident, who would not sell out to the *Group*.

Indeed, Clayton McCann could not be bought or bribed, but shortly after the disappearance of Air Force One, he became conscious of the weight the *Group* carried around the world, and the unexpected happened. He was suddenly afraid.

Fear gave way to hesitation and, ultimately, to poor decision-making. During the days following the disappearance of the president, McCann chose to keep a low profile. He made himself unavailable to both the minister of Defense and the CIA director.

The first critical call McCann was forced to answer came from Perez Levi in Israel, three days after the supposed crash. The violence on the left bank had escalated. There was an unprecedented rash of suicide bombers, and barefooted, ragged Palestinians were suddenly armed with modern, sophisticated weaponry. Palestinian youths opened fire on military and civilians alike. The Israeli Army retaliated and, as in the past, Palestinian casualties were in far greater numbers than those of the Israelis. It was inevitable there would be severe retribution once the neighboring Arab nations came together.

McCann had no choice but to offer Perez Levi full military support. After an emergency meeting with military advisors and a confrontational session of Congress, McCann dispatched the first of a series of nuclear missiles to be positioned in defense of Israel. Recognizing the possibility that chemical weapons might be used, hazmat suits and gas masks were once again made ready for distribution.

"The house of Isaac and the house of Ishmael, in eternal conflict, now make way for a final confrontation," preached Theodore Edwards. "A certain prelude to the end of days!" The preacher's tone was somber as he appeared in a brief teleconference broadcast worldwide.

Both Russell and Bennett were disappointed and infuriated by the unreliable behavior exhibited by McCann. They met with the CIA director and planned their strategy for determining which Russian labs were manipulating deadly viruses to wipe them out.

Christian felt numbed by the rapid course of events. He could hardly believe that President Parker, their most powerful ally, was gone. Neither did he fully understand what all this had to do with Danielle. In vain, Chris tried to contact John Larkin. Dr. Larkin did not return his messages.

Later, when John finally called back, Chris was taking a shower. John's message was apologetically brief and simply said he would try later. So Chris decided not to leave his apartment again until he called.

Cardinal Santis was incommunicado, as well, while the conclave—the ceremony around the election of a new pope—was in session.

Chris called Linda, Danielle's secretary, who was not at all alarmed by her boss's absence. But she did hint at having been in contact with Danielle, which of course, made him crazy with curiosity. But Linda had nothing more to say. He decided to break down and see Kit; he asked her to dinner.

New York

The morning John Larkin finally called Christian back, things fell into place. He was puzzled at John's clipped, impersonal tone, and annoyed at Chris's continued attempts to reach him. They spoke briefly, and Chris didn't have a chance to ask many questions. Chris realized there had been a nervousness in the timbre of John's voice. It was not until he hung up that Chris identified it as fear.

Despite John's unresponsiveness, Chris pressed on. After all, John was the only person he could reach who could shed light on what had happened to Danielle. He told John he was aware of the message the president had sent him from Air Force One before the crash. John reluctantly agreed to meet him in two days, perhaps not wishing to speak further about his communication with the president. Chris made arrangements for his trip to Colorado, then dialed Danielle's office. He caught Linda on her way out, and she agreed to meet him at the loading dock.

He found her speaking with a young man, whom Linda introduced as Jeff Montgomery. The young man shook Chris's hand then departed hastily.

"Now, who did you say that was?" inquired Chris.

"Jeff Montgomery, an old friend of mine. He was Ricardo's best friend. I think he is the only person in the world who knows how sad I still feel." She wiped a tear from the corner of her eye with her knuckle. "He is a Keller vice president. I think his job has taken him well beyond his expectations, but the funny thing is that I don't think he is happy."

"Well, that's the baggage that usually comes with money," said Chris, remembering his affluent and lonely childhood. He took another look at Jeff as he climbed into his car. Chris remembered the name. Jean-Christophe had received a call from him while they were together in Paris and had announced they now had someone on the inside. The young man seemed aloof, but Chris knew the shaky territory that informants walked.

The wind was blowing, and wisps of black hair were playing over the face of the young woman. She pointed to the harbor. "Well, there it goes!"

Chris looked at the freighter sailing at a distance.

"The last of our shipments."

"The paintings and the books? Where are you shipping them?"

"To a safe place. One more phase that we're shutting down."

"You are shutting what down?" It seemed to him as if Linda was speaking in riddles.

"Just following Danielle's instructions."

"That's what you said on the phone. Danielle is still communicating with you?"

"Well, of course!"

"You know where she is?"

"Not exactly. She emails me daily with instructions. I'm shutting down her residences, finalizing projects, closing accounts, etcetera."

Chris knew right then that something was not right. Linda did not seem herself, and he doubted the validity of her communications.

"Linda, I don't believe those messages are from Danielle."

"What an odd thing to say! Who would they be from?"

"I don't know. Would you let me see one of them?" he asked.

"I guess. Come by the office early one morning. That's when I open the emails. After I read them, I'm supposed to delete them."

"I will do that. By the way, I am having dinner with Kitzia tonight. Why don't you join us? I'm sure Kit would like to have news of Danielle."

"Oh, I do keep her up-to-date," said Linda in her matter-of-fact tone, and Chris understood Kit's complacency. "Thanks for the invite, but I can't. I'm having dinner with Jeff. You see, now that Danielle's interests are shutting down, I'm probably going to be out of a job. I'm trying to talk Jeff into hiring me. I don't understand his reluctance." After a short pause, she continued, "Jeff has insight, you know. Nobody thought this trash look would catch on and look, everyone is starting to wear it." She pointed at her own ragged denim, faded leather, and ribbed rubber jacket.

"I see . . . looks like the entire country has gone on a fashion strike."

When Chris got back to his apartment, he switched on the television. He had to surf past several infomercials touting the urgency of joining the Reverend Theodore Edwards's fight against Satan. The catch phrase at the moment was "Get on the bus and join the combat force." When Chris finally got to the news about AFO, he was disturbed to learn there was no longer hope of finding any survivors. The unanimous conclusion was that the plane had plunged deep into the ocean, and the search teams had turned their energies into recovering the black box.

The global atmosphere was tense. There was unrest and rioting in several US cities. Once again, the government was facing severe criticism for its aggressiveness in dealing with Edwards's youth conditioning compounds. Many young boys had committed suicide rather than surrender. Chris remembered that Powers Broadcasting had taken charge of editing most news reports.

The phone rang. It was John Larkin.

The scientist's voice was trembling noticeably. "Can you come to Colorado tonight? There is a flight that leaves New York at 7:30 p.m. I could meet you at one of the airport's coffee shops around 10:30."

That would barely give Christian time to get to the airport. But, picking up on the urgency in John Larkin's voice, Chris agreed. He threw a few things in his overnight bag and walked out of his apartment ten minutes after receiving the call.

From the moment Parker disappeared, much of the country had spiraled down on a course of self-destruction. Kitzia was shocked by the TV reports, especially the raids of the youth camps.

In retrospect, she couldn't help wondering if her reports had indirectly been a catalyst for the suicides.

Crime had increased tenfold. The sounds of police and ambulance sirens intruded nonstop into the once quiet atmosphere of Kitzia's apartment. Most of her patients had canceled. For the first time since she had moved to New York, Kitzia dug out the gun Tom had given her years ago for self-protection. These would be lonely holidays if Danielle did not get back! It was almost Christmas, and holiday spirit was the lowest she had ever experienced. Stores were not busy with the usual indulgent shoppers, and those who did go out clutched their handbags close, and kept watch of their surroundings. Kitzia was seriously considering closing her office and spending a few weeks in California with her mother. Her usual Christmas dinner group would probably not get together this year. *Would Jean-Christophe be coming to California this year to spend Christmas with Tom?*

XXIX

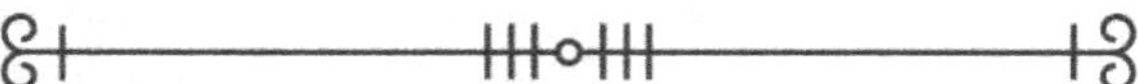

Denver, Colorado

The plane arrived on time and Christian rushed to the appointed meeting place—the smallest and darkest bar in the terminal. He spotted John Larkin sitting at a corner table, reading a magazine. Larkin saw Christian come in but made no attempt to get up from the table and barely looked up until Chris sat down.

"I'm glad you made it on time," said John, returning his eyes to the magazine. "I was afraid I might have to leave before you got here. I can only stay a couple of minutes."

Chris set his bag down. "I sure didn't come up all this way just for a couple of minutes," said Chris, unable to hide his annoyance.

John looked up past Christian and glanced furtively around the bar and out into the concourse. "I'm sorry; I just have a few minutes tonight. I'll meet you tomorrow morning too."

"John, what is going on? Why didn't you just let me fly in tomorrow?"

"I thought we might have the opportunity to speak tonight, but we don't. Anyway, we're wasting time. Let me have your index finger," John said, taking out a small black box and pulling a wire from it.

"What?" Chris said as he extended his hand to the scientist and allowed him to connect the clip to his finger. The gadget looked like a pulse monitor, and it further added to his agitation.

"Please be still," urged John.

Within seconds, a series of numbers appeared on the tiny screen, and John jotted down some notes on a small notepad he had pulled from his coat pocket.

"Would you mind telling me what the heck that is?" asked Chris.

"It measures your molecular density and your atomic vibration," said John before mumbling to himself. "That explains how your sub-atomic particles can travel backward."

"Good! Now that you have satisfied your scientific curiosity, would you mind answering my questions? Like, where is Danielle?"

"She is trapped in the cosmic warp. Because of the high velocity at which we are traveling, it's hard to pinpoint the exact spot where the convergence of time and space fuse into the molecular wall. We are trying to detect a weak point in the sub-molecular structure where we can split it or create a portal."

"Come on John, speak English!"

"I really have to go," said John, getting up from his chair. "Please meet me there tomorrow morning." He handed Chris a piece of paper with directions and a hand-drawn map. "Let's meet at 7:00 a.m. The place is about two hours from here, a little longer if it snows tonight."

Chris took the paper, but before he had time to protest, John walked away. He sat motionless, bemused by the eeriness of the meeting. He watched John disappear down the corridor and mingle with the flow of late arrivals heading for the escalators. A man cut through the crowd and Chris saw that he was following the scientist. Only then, did he grasp the reason for John's apprehension.

Chris rented a car and, following John's directions, drove through a light snowfall, down interstate 70 to the lodge that same night. John was being followed, and his news of Danielle's entrapment was frightening. Danielle and Kjell were stuck between two worlds. Now he understood the president's questions about his exit into the Vatican gardens. The *Foundation* was trying to figure out how to rescue her.

The *Foundation*! sighed Chris. It remained elusive.

He felt certain Kit had not yet been called into service, for she seemed oblivious to the course of events. He recalled that someone had been assigned to watch over her. *Was it Camiel? But Camiel had been on Air Force One. Had his assignment been switched to protection of the president? If so, he had utterly failed!*

The thought struck him as he pulled into the parking lot of the lodge . . . *what if he hadn't failed*? It occurred to him that John had been the only person he had encountered lately that had not made any reference to the tragedy of Air Force One. Perhaps John knew if the plane had landed at another destination, somehow avoiding both the radar and the escorts. Nothing should surprise him after the things he had witnessed during the past year, thought Chris.

Now energized and encouraged, he looked forward to meeting John in the morning and hoped for an explanation of these very puzzling recent events.

9:00 a.m.

Already two hours had gone by, and Chris still sat in the lobby of the hotel reading the papers, trying to be wait patiently. John was not answering his cell phone. He inquired at the desk one more time to see if he had any messages, and for the seventh time, the clerk politely stated that no one had called for him. Even though it was Saturday morning, and most likely their offices would be closed, he decided to have one more cup of coffee and call Argos. As expected, the operator told him John's office was closed. Chris realized he had no other means of reaching him—no address. There was no recourse but to continue waiting and hope that nothing had happened to him.

6:00 p.m.

The sun was beginning to set when Chris walked back into the coffee shop. The room was now filling up with skiers coming in from the slopes. He reclaimed the stool he had occupied off and on since morning. The bartender smiled and set down his drink, then turned up the volume on the TV for a special report.

Everyone's attention turned to the screen as a CNN anchor announced that the search for the missing plane had been called off, and according to the rules of succession, the swearing in ceremony of Clayton McCann as President of the United States would take place. A statement from the White House would be forthcoming within the hour.

There was stunned silence. The next report sent seismic shockwaves, not only through the coffee shop, but throughout the globe. Meeting in emergency session, OPEC had decreed that global rationing be put into effect immediately because of the depletion of the oil and gas reserves. The world would now have to turn to nuclear power as its chief source of energy.

Voices were raised in panic and disbelief; glasses shattered as angry patrons slammed them on the bar or to the floor.

No one understood the implications of the bulletin better than Chris. He grabbed his cell phone and booked his flight. He knew he had to get out of Colorado before the airlines began canceling flights. As he left the coffee bar, he heard way too many voices expressing that Theodore Edwards should be president since the world was entering a time of tribulation.

Chris knew this was the beginning of chaos. *Why hadn't John shown up? Another link to the Foundation gone . . .*

New York

The next day, back in New York, Chris located Kitzia late in the afternoon at Danielle's penthouse and headed there immediately.

Standing where he had once stood, admiring the Tiepolo that covered the rotunda, he now stood watching the workers dismantle the huge canvas. He would have questioned the workmen, but at that moment, the door opened, and he saw Kitzia. He walked up to her and took her in his arms. Chris was surprised at how right it felt to hold her. But when the hug had gone on a bit too long, he whispered in her ear, "What is going on?"

She released him. "I really don't know. Linda said Danielle had told her to do it. I just came to make sure it was done properly."

They walked into the penthouse. Chris saw the vacant walls and empty pedestals.

"All the art is gone," announced Kit. "Danielle started taking it down before she left."

Kit took Chris's hands and stared at him with genuine concern. "What are we going to do about John? I am dumb-founded!"

At the mention of John's name, Christian's eyes widened and upon seeing his expression, Kit released him and pointed him to a seat in the living room.

"You obviously have not heard! It is all over the news. John has been accused of espionage and seems to have fled. Supposedly, he was selling secret information. Apparently, disks containing secret military information disappeared from Argos."

They reached a couch. "Something to drink?" she asked.

Chris shook his head, not wanting her to interrupt her story.

"Anyway, there is a manhunt going on . . ." She shook her head. "It sounds so unlike him! I have advised the staff everywhere to look out for him.

"I think this is what Danielle was referring to," continued Kit. "I questioned her about the double Code Blue security after her accident. She said that when the infrared beams were in evidence, the places had been rendered impregnable. She added that I would know when the second button should be activated."

Chris did not believe any more than Kit did that John was a spy, and he sincerely hoped that John had gotten away.

"If the place is safe, why remove the art?" Chris finally spoke.

"I don't understand. But Linda insists those are Danielle's wishes, and it must be done immediately."

"Do you think Linda could have misunderstood?"

"I don't think so. Linda is trustworthy and very meticulous."

"But Linda told me the last of the art shipments were off."

"You spoke with her lately?" Kit wanted to know.

"Yes, I saw her at the docks a couple of days ago."

"Don't you think she is acting a little strange?"

"Strange in what way?" asked Chris.

"Oh, I don't know. I can't make sense of anything. Danielle has been gone for weeks now; I'm very worried. The only thing that sustains me is that she is in constant touch with Linda. You'd think she'd give me a quick call just to let me know that she is OK, no matter how busy she is."

"Kit, I was not quite truthful with you the other day on the phone."

"What do you mean?"

"I saw Danielle in Europe. In fact, we were in Rome . . . at the Vatican. We separated there, and I have not seen her since."

"I spoke with Cardinal Santis shortly after the pope's funeral, and he did not mention seeing you or Danielle."

Chris took a deep breath. "I think I am beginning to understand. Danielle has been trying to protect you. She foresaw things like what happened to the pontiff, the president, and now John Larkin."

"It is happening!" gasped Kit. "She once warned me that the *Foundation* and the *Group* might come to open conflict. But she also said she'd be here and ready . . ."

"Kit, I don't really understand her reasons, but she made us promise—Jean-Christophe, John, Angela, Tom, and me—to protect you at all costs. She said that your safety was the most important facet of any operation that we undertook."

"My safety?" Kit looked confused.

"Yes. I also promised to keep from you what was going on, but I think now it would be to your benefit to know a little more. First, though, New York is going to be one of the most dangerous cities to be in, and we should get out of here while we can. I would strongly suggest that you avoid any public transportation, like the subway."

"Oh, actually, I did use it today. And now that you mention it, something struck me as peculiar." Chris's heart began racing. "There was a crew of men in white suits diligently cleaning the turnstiles, using some kind of disinfectant." As she raised her hands, he noticed the inside of her palms had red blotches. "I told you that cleaning stuff was powerful!" said Kit.

Chris took her hands by the wrists and stared at them in dismay.

"What is it?" she noticed his astonishment.

He didn't answer. Slowly, he let her hands down and walked to the window. Kit got up and followed him, waiting for him to speak.

"Are you feeling OK now?" he asked when he finally turned back to face her.

"I'm fine."

"Good! Is there a computer I can use? I need to retrieve some info."

"Yes. In the study—second door to your right. What are you thinking?"

"Give me a few minutes. And do us a favor: book us a seat on whatever airline you can get. We should leave New York as soon as possible."

"Actually, I was already planning on leaving. I just have to wait for someone."

"Who?"

"Jean-Christophe has adopted the young brother of his friend Mustafa and is sending him to the US. Tom is going to enroll the boy in a prep school in San Francisco."

"When does the boy get here?'

"The day after tomorrow," she answered.

Chris pulled out a credit card and handed it to Kit. "Here, book us all out of New York the day after tomorrow. We'll leave with the boy."

"She put the card in her pocket and focused again on her hands. "Tell me, what is it that worries you about my hands?" she asked while wiping them with a Kleenex.

"Kit, I believe the *Foundation* is fighting back. Don't rub the spot. I'm sure it's a very potent solution, an antidote to the poison that was released on the subway. It is brilliant!" he exclaimed. "Everyone that goes through the gate has to touch the bar. It was, in fact, the contact with that solution that saved your life!"

Kitzia had become pale. Without further explanation, Chris headed in the direction of the study. She turned her attention to the window, gazing out. She could see something going on in the streets. She distinguished the distant outline of crowds blocking traffic.

From up here, people look so small, almost insignificant, she thought. Kit wondered if this was how they appeared to the Edentians who watched them. She was convinced the entire race was being monitored. She, herself, now lived with the constant awareness of being watched, and such realization gave her a fuller understanding of her position in the scheme of things. Quite often, she experienced the awareness of her smallness and was filled with a sense of wonder, knowing the human race was not alone. There were guardians and monitors and direct connections to the great beings—just as she had been connected to Danielle for most of her life. If the time and the situation had been different, she probably would never have known. *Nonetheless, it is reassuring*, she thought, *to know "they" are living among us.*

She picked up the phone. Fifteen minutes later, Chris returned.

"Did you find what you wanted?" asked Kit.

"Unfortunately, yes. I was right. Things are going to get bad. We had better get out of the way. Were you able to get us tickets?"

"Yes," answered Kit, still looking at her hands. "Many flights have been canceled. The tickets were $12,000 each."

"Start packing. We must be out of here, at least for the holidays."

"I'm taking Mai Li with us. Her son works at the LA house. We will all be at the airport to pick up Ali, then catch our flight."

Twilight was beginning to fall cross the Hudson River. The pale shades of lavender from the receding sun were replaced by the shimmering lights from the buildings as lights switched on.

"Will you stay and have a bite to eat with me?" asked Kit. "I so dread being alone nowadays."

"I'll be glad to. Then, when the workmen leave, I'll take you home."

"OK. I'll even surprise you with a talent you didn't suspect. Actually, I'm a good cook."

By now, the entire city had lit up and had virtually erased the people below, the only indication of their presence being the clamor from the street they could hear through the open windows to the terrace. Chris and Kit moved into the state-of-the-art kitchen, where Chris discovered that Kit's gourmet abilities consisted mostly of delegating tasks. Mai Li began taking orders as to what and how to chop the ingredients for her famous pasta. Kit opened a bottle of Gloria-St. Julian and decided, at least for tonight, to put aside the anxiety nagging at her heart. They finished the first glass before sitting down to eat at a small round table in the room just off the kitchen.

They had not quite finished when the blackout struck. The penthouse, the building, and the entire city sank into silence and darkness for three unbearable minutes.

The blackout was universal. Electricity, satellite telecommunications, and radio frequencies were interrupted. Mai Li produced a flashlight but could not get it to work. The workmen in the foyer, holding matches, tried to pry the private elevator door open to rescue a screaming woman trapped inside.

Following the dim glow of the matches, Chris walked in the direction of the foyer. Kit followed, holding his sleeve.

The electricity was restored as quickly as it shut down, and brought with it light, music, and heat. But traffic noise from the street escalated to a disturbing level. When the elevator opened, Linda jumped out in hysterics.

Kit ran to her. "Are you all right?"

Linda took a deep breath to control her shaking. "I thought I'd die. There was no air in there. I could have suffocated! We really need to speak to the building super!"

"It was a blackout," answered Kit.

"Oh! Another one?" Linda was calming down.

"Come on, let us fix you a drink." Chris took her by the arm.

"Make it a double of the strongest thing you've got."

One of the workers came in to announce they had finished rolling the canvas, and it was ready for shipment. Kit offered the man a beer, and asked Armand, the butler, to get some bottles for the rest of the crew. The superintendent accepted the bottles, saying he would take them along since his crew had decided to walk down the stairway.

"Don't be silly," interrupted Kit. "I'll activate the generator right now, just in case the blackout should repeat. The private elevator will not be affected."

The man thanked her, but he and the crew still opted for the stairway.

Mai Li turned on the TV. The blackout was already being analyzed by the media. Brief though it was, the incident sent waves of panic throughout the world. The notion that the entire world could be paralyzed and communications cut off without warning was mind-shattering. What would happen if incidents of world immobilization became longer? What would happen to factories, hospitals, national security systems, and air traffic control?

Theodore Edwards appeared on the screen all too quickly with words that sounded too much like a speech pre-planned for the event. Chris and Kit exchanged a knowing glance as they listened to the preacher rave on about an impending doomsday and quoting from the book of Revelation.

Linda was the first to dismiss the preacher. "That's all we need—another prophet!" Then turning to Kitzia, "Are you staying here?"

"No. I was just about to go home. Chris is going to walk me. Can we take you home?"

"No, thanks. I need to be here for a little while. Have to finish some things for Danielle. You two run along."

They looked at each other and then back to her.

"Are you sure?" Kit insisted.

"Positive," Linda assured them. "Just have to get some invoices from the office. A friend of mine is picking me up in a few minutes. So go on. I'll be fine."

"OK," said Kit. "I wouldn't want you to be alone in the streets with the way things are." Kit was not sure what it was that bothered her. She walked back into the living room and picked up her coat. Chris helped her put it on, and she said no more. Kit gave last-minute instructions to Mai Li and left with Chris.

Linda watched the couple disappear into the elevator before returning to Mai Li in the kitchen, putting away the last of the dishes.

"I won't be long, Mai, but you can go ahead and leave as well. I'll lock up."

Linda walked through the splendidly furnished living room, now devoid of art, with a sense of excitement she had never experienced.

She had never, for a second, contemplated the notion that life would give her the opportunity to be part of this lifestyle. She could be very rich. Now, it all seemed possible and within her reach.

Danielle may not understand my motives, Linda murmured to herself. *But then, how could she? Danielle has always had it all.*

She pulled out her cell phone, punched in a number and whispered into the phone. "Now, what is it exactly that you want me to find?" She listened attentively to the voice at the other end. "OK . . . got it! I'll come out through the back door of the building. Just give me a few minutes."

Robert Powers closed his phone and instructed the driver of the black town car to move from the parking place to the back door of the building.

XXX

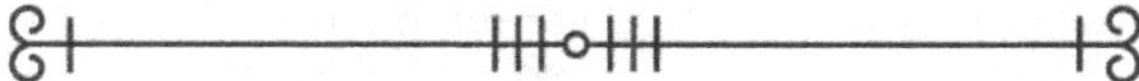

Christian and Kitzia got their affairs in order within thirty-six hours of the blackout. TV and the internet continued spreading messages of doom and gloom, with constant predictions of further blackouts. Economic tension was heightened all over the world. An economic depression seemed imminent as a number of venerable establishments went out of business.

The morning they were to leave New York, an article was posted online, ridiculing Dr. Kitzia O'Neil and her unfounded allegations of subliminal satanic messages presenting in pop lyrics. Fortunately, Kitzia didn't see it. Kit and Mai Li awaited Chris in the lobby with eleven suitcases of "bare essentials," as Kit explained. On the way to the airport, they encountered mobs protesting the gas rationing, with signs and banners promoting Ted Edwards for president and warning of the end of the world.

Their limousine took some flak before it even reached the 59th Street Bridge, where it came under attack by a group of skinheads. Both the limo and the van carrying their luggage were surrounded by the motley group screaming insults and threats.

Chris urged them to remain calm, but when the crowd began to pound fists and bricks on the car, Mai Li sobbed. Kit pulled out her handgun and handed it to Chris. A couple of the thugs close to the window saw the weapon and pounded harder, shouting, "Get the bit—! Get them all!"

We are going to be killed! Chris, Kit, and Mai Li thought simultaneously.

The vehicles unexpectedly emitted a light, and the assailants were startled into silence. Among them stood a man dressed in black trousers and a turtleneck. His steely gaze stopped the thugs in their tracks, and they slinked away. A tunnel of violet light formed around the two vehicles and opened the way ahead. When the driver saw the space open up in front of them, he jammed his foot on the accelerator, and sped, unencumbered, through the crowd. The van followed. Chris and

Kit snapped around to look through the back window. They saw the imposing figure of Zephon.

The violet light faded from view but protected them all the way to the terminal, and nothing else slowed their progress as they made their way to the gate to meet the flight from London and pick up the boy. Ali was a handsome lad of thirteen with bright black eyes, who spoke little English but communicated with a warm handshake and a smile. After retrieving his baggage, they headed to their gate and boarded the plane for California.

Without opening her eyes, Linda reached across the bed and fumbled about the expensive sheets. Finding the space next to her empty, she opened her eyes. Across the room, Robert Powers, wearing a silk paisley robe, sat at his large, burled maple desk working on a laptop computer.

The young woman observed him in silence. He was magnificent! Never did she ever imagine that she could feel this way about an older man. He was old enough to be her father, she realized, but so handsome, so imposing! Being with Robert Powers was like nothing she had ever experienced.

Her euphoria had vanquished her feelings of guilt and disloyalty toward Danielle.

Robert looked up. "Go back to sleep," he whispered. His voice sounded more like a father's than a lover's.

"It's three in the morning. Don't you ever sleep?"

"I don't have much more to do," he answered, without taking his eyes from the computer.

She rubbed her eyes and got out of bed. After slowly tiptoeing over the silk Nain rug, she stood behind him, looking at the incomprehensible chart he was mapping. Robert kept at his task, absorbed in what he was doing. She wrapped her arms around his neck, kissed his ear, and gently whispered, "Come back to bed."

Without looking up, Robert removed her arms, releasing her grasp, and continued working. Linda was pained by his rejection. "What is so important that can't wait until morning?" she asked, trying not to show her hurt.

"More than you could ever understand," answered Robert, matter-of-factly.

"Why do you treat me like a moron?" She felt the anger begin to rise.

"Go back to sleep."

"No," she said. "I don't want to go back to sleep. I want to have a conversation with you."

Robert, aware of the young woman's pain, tried not to show annoyance. "Linda, you could not possibly understand the importance of what I'm doing.

I am in the midst of a crisis that could be of disastrous proportions. I have been asking you to leave New York; it's not a safe place to be right now. I have a plane at your disposal, ready to take you to my ski lodge in Colorado, or anywhere you might want to go."

Linda tried to calm down. She thought of his generosity and was still amazed that he had allowed her into his world.

"No, I really want to stay here," she said sweetly. "If you'd only take the time to explain what you are doing, I'm sure I could assist you. Just think, you'd have a twenty-four-hour assistant!" She smiled, raising her eyebrows flirtatiously.

He was not amused.

"It's Danielle, isn't it?"

He returned to his computer without answering.

"I don't know what happened between the two of you," Linda blurted out, "but it's quite obvious that you still carry a torch for her. If you love her so much, why are you betraying her?"

Robert was silent but shot her a piercing look. His eyes were so intense, they sometimes frightened her. Yet, at that moment, she knew that she had found his Achilles heel. He pushed the laptop aside and, placing his elbows on the desk, propped his chin on his hands. "How do you propose that I am betraying her?"

"Why would you have me steal information from her penthouse?"

"Because she is away, and it is essential that I conclude the work we were doing together."

Linda was not convinced. "You know, Robert, I am beginning to suspect that she is not OK, as you keep telling me. Something has happened to her. I know your lunatic friend was talking about her, even though he never mentioned her by name. What have you done to her? Is she alive?"

"Of course, she is alive!"

"I know none of those emails were from her. You were sending them, weren't you? You wanted to make everything seem normal so that no one would suspect anything. What have you done to her?" Her voice rose in agitation.

Robert got up from his desk and went to her.

He took Linda by the shoulders and shook her gently. "Listen to me. Danielle is all right, and you have to forget everything you saw or heard. It had nothing to do with us." He used *us*, knowing nothing else would placate her.

She wrapped her arms around him and began sobbing. "Robert, I love you so much. I know you did not make any promises, but we are so good together. Don't toss me aside. Please, let me be with you. I'll do anything you ask."

"Sit down," he said, his voice soft as he sat her on the bed and took a seat next to her. "And listen carefully. I would never hurt Danielle. Yes, I have loved her, but nothing is to be between us. Just like nothing really can be between you and me now. You are so young and so lovely! You have your entire life ahead of you. It was wrong of me to allow you to think that something lasting could possibly develop between us. True, I needed you to get those codes for me and saw no other way of doing it. Danielle is not here, and this was a matter that could not wait. With the crises arising daily, I needed to map out some strategies, and millions of lives depend on what I am doing."

Linda was having a hard time controlling her emotions and allowing reality to set in.

"Furthermore, I will take care of you. I will afford you the opportunity to do whatever you want with your life in a financially comfortable manner. You just told me last night that you wanted to raise horses one day. I'll buy you a ranch and the most beautiful of Arabian stallions. But my first concern for you right now is to get you out of the city, away from forthcoming catastrophic situations." He continued, "What we had is lovely, sweet girl, but it will come to its conclusion, and we must go our different ways."

"I should have been prepared for this," she said with a deep sob. "For one moment, Linda Teresi stopped existing, and I became someone else. It was such a nice feeling to be wanted by someone like you and not have to worry about bills!"

"And you won't have to again."

"You really mean it . . . about the horses and all?" she asked incredulously.

"I really mean it," he said, stroking the hair away from her face. "But promise me you will start packing and won't do anything to draw the attention of my business associates. They are paranoid about business confidentiality."

"Who is that guy Cirel who came by the other day? Something about him is frightening."

"Very perceptive of you. He is ruthless. Don't cross his path."

"Why do you do business with him?"

"I have no choice at the moment. I hope our association will be brief. Now, will you try to sleep? I must go back to what I was doing and try to make some sense out of it. Something is not fitting. You are sure you took every code you found?"

She nodded.

"OK. Then the key is in here somewhere. I'll find it."

Linda went back to bed and closed her eyes. She was sorry she had confronted him and made him say what he had, what she had dreaded from the beginning—the painful and inevitable goodbye.

She played back his words in her mind. He had said their relationship was coming to an end. He had not said it was over. She would not put pressure on him again. She would simply go with the flow, be docile, she decided. He would learn to love her and everything would work out. *It has to work out because I will die without him!*

Lilith's Penthouse

Recently, Jeff had noticed with dread a constant glint of mischief in Lili's sapphire eyes. He watched her hang up the phone with satisfaction, after which she clapped her hands jovially.

"Have you put another competitor out of business?" inquired Jeff indifferently.

"Better than that. The whole Joel Harvis chain of stores is closing. That leaves us the undisputed fashion leaders in the southwest. Everything is going so well for us!"

"Why such greediness? If you succeed in killing fashion, what will happen to your cosmetics line?"

"It will continue to flourish, my darling. Every woman will buy my products in an effort to look natural."

"I should have guessed! Your preacher friend is the catalyst, right? Has he been condemning the use of make-up as an act of vanity?"

"Perhaps, but nobody wants to look made-up anymore. The sales margins from internet shopping are phenomenal! We are getting the population right where we want it—in front of a computer. The streets are dangerous, with all those terrorists and militia groups going wild! That's why I like to have you close to me, my darling Jeff. I feel more secure."

Jeff could not contain his laughter. "Lili, why are we supporting both the militia and the terrorists?"

"We have a group of mercenaries attempting to keep balance during these tumultuous times. A lot of nutcases have created their own fanatical factions. With the weakness of the present administration, we cannot curb this national discontent."

"Clayton McCann is doing what he can under the circumstances, tolerating the daily theatrical rantings of the self-anointed messiah Edwards!"

"But it's not enough. Stability will only be brought back by force," Lili argued.

"Here at Keller DeWinter, we seem to be the only ones unaffected by recent events. But how long can that last?"

"Jeff, will you stop worrying? Things have a way of working out."

He looked down, unable to face her continuous deceit. "We are behind every single thing that is going on, aren't we?" he asked.

Lili picked up her purse and briefcase. The sound of a helicopter could now be heard, announcing its landing on the roof. She evaded Jeff's question, and he understood.

"But the hail storms, how will they be accomplished?" he asked with feigned interest. Lili smiled. "It is brilliant! I'll explain it all to you when I get back." She threw him a kiss and moved toward the door.

After watching the helicopter take off, Jeff looked away from the huge window of his penthouse office and buried his face in his hands, trying to block out the reality of what his life had become. He now existed in a surreal world, where his main concern was appearing unaffected by what he saw. But the façade was wearing him down. Lili's constant vigil was making it difficult for him to pass information to Robert Powers, who always found a way to pass it to the *Foundation.* Lili was an astute woman. So far, he had been able to get by her. But sooner or later, she would figure it out.

Robert's position had been difficult to define. Jeff realized that Powers World Enterprises had been placed at the disposal of the *Group,* its worldwide net of communications utilized to broadcast its messages, and his international oil trading position was manipulating the course of the economy. In spite of Robert's powerful position, his enigmatic behavior belied his complete allegiance to the *Group.* In turn, many members of the *Group* withheld certain plans from him until ready for implementation.

Robert didn't appear to care whether he was involved in the details of every operation. But Jeff knew better. Whatever his reasons, Jeff knew the two of them were in similar circumstances, which had necessitated a bond between them. On occasion, there were silent exchanges of complicity.

At Lili's suggestion, Robert had recruited Jeff to collaborate in his new digital campaign, which had provided them with some unexpected, private moments. One day, Jeff took a gamble and made a couple of casual, witty comments about an operation, as if he assumed Robert to be involved. Robert seemed amused but disinterested. After that, when at Lili's invitation Jeff attended a few of the *Group's* meetings, a comment would be made to the effect that the "cursed *Foundation*" had counteracted the offensive. Jeff knew with certainty who had issued the warning. In this manner, the bond between the two men was established.

Nonetheless, Jeff decided to watch his step, and now he had one more thing to worry about: Linda. The infatuation Linda Teresi had for Robert Powers was absurd, not to mention dangerous. Jeff had tried to reason with her, but she would not listen. Overnight, Linda, whom he had always known to be well grounded, had become a little bit crazy. She couldn't sleep or eat. Hers was one of the worst cases of obsession he had ever seen. It was not a love affair; Jeff was sure Linda barely knew Robert. They had gone out a few times, but where did she get the notion he would marry her? How had this whole thing come about? Suddenly, a piece plopped into the puzzle! Linda was Danielle Peschard's assistant—that had to be Robert's one and only interest in her, and Linda had latched on to a handsome, wealthy man, trying to write her own beneficial scenario.

Now, she called Jeff a dozen times a day from some ski resort in Colorado, where Robert had sent her so she would leave him alone, asking him if he knew where Robert was. She was becoming hysterical, living beside the phone, awaiting Robert's calls. When the call never came, she called Jeff.

Jeff had watched as Lili's secretary had passed phone messages to Robert, all of which he dismissed with indifference. They were assuredly from Linda.

What he had to tell Linda seemed cruel, but in the larger scope of things, it was for her own good, Jeff rationalized. The next time she called, he would tell her that Robert had gone off with Lili Keller, as he did almost every day.

What Jeff told Linda about Robert burned like acid in her heart, but it had the opposite effect from what Jeff had anticipated. Jealousy and rage served only to make her all the more determined.

She was back in town. Linda planned to tell Robert that because he had not returned her calls, she had become worried about him and flown back. At home, her apartment looked grim in comparison to Robert's luxurious place. She had all too quickly grown accustomed to the different world of affluence—one that she was not about to relinquish without a fight. Deep down, she recognized she was no match for Lili Keller; but no matter what, she would fight with all the tools she could muster.

The whole thing was making her sick, she realized. She scrutinized her reflection in the bathroom mirror. Her skin was sallow, and dark circles had erupted underneath her eyes—brought on by a lack of sleep and poor nutrition, which she failed to acknowledge. *Pregnant! I must be pregnant! That's why I am feeling so nauseated!* Triumphantly, and without any verification, she decided to tell Robert.

I know we were only together a couple of times, but there was love; we had love from the beginning. The age difference absolutely doesn't matter to me.

Another thought crept into her head. *What if I am not preg—impossible! I've got to be. Why else would I feel sick?*

What Jeff had told her about seeing Robert and Lili leaving work together, she quickly dismissed. *Jeff has to be mistaken! It is all business, strictly business. He probably hasn't gotten my messages. Those receptionists are such morons!*

She rushed to her closet, and instead of the Keller trash look, she dug out a gray flannel suit, heels, and a black leather bag. As she was transferring her wallet and other personal items from a vinyl handbag studded with bullets, she came across a small, thin, metal card etched with symbols. It was one of several that she had taken from Danielle's penthouse.

Oh no! This is what Robert has been looking for. How could I be so careless? He said the entire sequence was invalid without this code! She reprimanded herself harshly, not feeling so pregnant anymore. *He'll want to see me right away!*

The wind blew gently, but the air felt colder than usual. Jeff strolled around Central Park's Columbus Circle monument, alternating his glance between the paper he was holding and the pigeons pecking about for food.

He couldn't remember how long it had been since he had begun trying to decipher it. But he might be finally be making some headway.

He looked closely again at the paper Lili had given him at the cabin, with its incomprehensible combination of characters within a circle.

JXIIM4911
000000
L______ L____
206976

He was deeply focused on the second line of circles or zeros, and did not hear the man come up behind him until he spoke.

"You seem perplexed by the digits," said Robert Powers in his resonant voice.

Startled out of his concentration, Jeff turned around, folding the paper and placing it in his pocket.

Robert cordially shook Jeff's hand. "I thought that might be you, so I took the opportunity to talk to you about a dear acquaintance of mine, whom you know well."

Knowing what was to follow, Jeff tried to evade the situation. "Hey, I'd really rather stay out of it, if you don't mind."

"But I do," Robert said firmly, "because you are the only one that Linda might listen to. You see, you must get her away."

"From you?" Jeff asked mockingly.

"From the city. I just found out she has returned. I thought I had her in a safe place, at least until the storm passes."

Jeff grasped that Robert was not making metaphors for an emotional relationship. "There is going to be bad weather, I assume?"

"Yes, very bad."

"Hail storms?" Jeff remembered overhearing that term during one of Lili's conversations with a member of the *Group*.

"Hail storms and more." The Edentian paused for a moment. "I am very sorry about it all—about what Linda imagined it could be. It was unforgivable of me to assume she would not be hurt. Will you talk to her?"

Jeff nodded. Robert looked at his watch and said, "Well, I must run along. I am already late for a meeting. I don't suppose you'll be attending this one?"

"Oh, no. This one, I understand, is top level only. Actually, I'm on my way to another meeting."

"May I give you a lift?"

"No, thanks. I am staying here for a few more minutes."

Robert smiled. "Take care." He cast a glance at the nearby statue of a reclining man. "Interesting monument. What a shame to deface it! His left hand has lost its digits."

Jeff watched Robert walk toward his town car, where the chauffeur stood holding the open door. *Robert Powers is definitely a strange character,* Jeff thought. Who in the world referred to fingers as digits? Jeff looked back at the statue of the man with the laurel wreath and the missing fingers.

Digits . . . fingers . . .

"Bingo!" He pulled out the piece of paper, and his mind tossed back Robert's words of greeting. "You seem perplexed by your digits," he had said, referring to the zeroes that Jeff was studying on the piece of paper.

The zeroes had a double meaning. Fingers . . . numbers . . . absence of digits! The last circle on the row stood as the sign for a male.

The male with the missing digit! Jeff jubilantly raised his fist into the air.

It all started to make sense now, and Jeff had been right about his first calculation. JXIIM4911 stood for a date. J, the tenth letter of the alphabet, meant October, XII . . . 12, M . . . one thousand, 4 . . . four hundred, 9 . . . ninety, 11 = 2 . . . two. Thus October 12, 1492, the day of the discovery of America, or *Columbus day*, inside a circle.

The marks on the paper were leading him to a location. The search for the clues started right there, at Columbus Circle; the male with no digits would point the way. That was what the arrow represented.

He rushed to the statue and climbed onto the base. Yes, carved on the knee of the statue and protected by the broken hand, a set of numbers was inscribed on the marble. He jumped down and wrote the numbers on his paper. They were not hard to decipher. The set of digits belonged to an address on the Upper East Side of Manhattan.

Cirel stepped out of the elevator at the seventy-ninth floor of the Keller building, followed by three bodyguards. He recognized the young woman in the gray suit at the reception desk and took a step in her direction. Linda turned around immediately because the receptionist had shifted her eyes and stood up to acknowledge the dignitary who had just arrived.

"Hi, there," said Cirel, not remembering the young woman's name.

Linda recognized him as the visitor at Robert's place. He was the one who had referred to Danielle's doom. But Linda did not dwell on that, figuring that Cirel might help her get to Robert.

"Hello!" She walked toward him, offering her hand and best smile.

"What is such a lovely girl doing in a boring place like this?"

"I just need to see Robert Powers for a second. I'm told he is in a meeting, but if I could just speak to him . . ."

Cirel realized how clever the girl had to be to make her way that far into the building. Security was extremely tight lately. Her short skirt, charming smile, and quick wit had allowed her to move successfully through the series of reception rooms. Cirel eyed her curiously without interrupting his smile.

"I am afraid that is impossible at the moment. Because of our foreign dignitaries, a strict security clearance is in effect. I can give him a message if you wish, and I promise to have him call you the first chance he gets."

"Oh, that would be wonderful! And I do have something to give him." She opened her purse and took out the envelope, moistened the flap of the envelope with her tongue, and sealed it. "Please tell him it's from Linda . . . and that I'm so sorry I overlooked this."

Cirel took the envelope from her as his smile widened with satisfaction when he saw the object through the envelope. "Why don't you wait a minute? I'll see what I can do."

Cirel disappeared through the double doors, followed by one of his men. The other two stood guarding the door, ignoring her presence.

In a few minutes, the man returned holding a card and handed it to Linda. It was Robert's business card, and on the back was a handwritten message.

Thanks. Meet me at the Met, Morisot exhibit 12:00 p.m.

Linda's face glowed when she read the card. She immediately headed for the elevator, not noticing that Cirel had given a signal to one of his men to follow her.

The smile on the face of the arch-rebel vanished.

XXXI

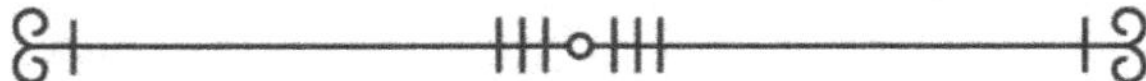

New York

By now, Lili had resigned herself to turning her business headquarters over to the *Group*. Therefore, many of its meetings were held at the Keller building. This had been Cirel's longest visit to the "outer world" from his secret hiding place. When Cirel came into the boardroom, everyone took a seat. Robert, as usual, sat next to Lili. On his way to the podium, Cirel paused next to Robert's chair and stared at him briefly. Lili observed the telepathic exchange between the two men.

"I have advised your latest consort to run along. You may seek her later," Cirel had derisively implied.

Robert was glad he had spoken to Jeff that morning. He hoped he had communicated the urgency of getting Linda out of harm's way. It was unfortunate that Cirel had run into her because the arch-rebel had most certainly accessed her memory banks. Robert's decision to ignore Linda's messages, which he thought to be the most effective method of deterring her advances, was no longer working. The resourceful girl had managed to track him down to the Keller building. She didn't realize how dangerous it was to come under Cirel's attention.

What had Cirel discovered while plundering Linda's mind? Did Cirel suspect now that he had been working to put the puzzle together for the benefit of the Group, *with plans to destroy it in the end?*

Cirel's malevolent voice boomed across the room. "It is a great pleasure to announce the conclusion of Phase I. We have a small group here today, colleagues who have worked together to accomplish our goal. Our most sincere thanks to Kim-Sui in the Asian chapter, Mohammed Riezk, as well as our visitors who have responded to our call from far-away galactic realms. Friends and comrades," Cirel continued pompously, “we chose the Western Hemisphere as our point of departure, because the US remains the undisputed leader of the world. Whatever cultural attitudes and way of life it conceives, other nations are sure to follow.

“Our Phase I consisted of a period of preparation in mind-conditioning. The end result of our labors will be eminently apparent at the completion of Phase II. The global program consists of three stages: conditioning, preparation, and implementation. Phase I in the US has been entirely successful. Mental properties, in general, are being altered by the use of food additives that have weakened the degree of communication between neurons in the brain. Subliminal messages encoded in music and computer imaging have been phenomenal. We are ‘rewiring’ the brain to our specifications.”

The audience found Cirel engaging, even laughing at times. Robert remained silent, and he was gratified to notice that Lili only grudgingly showed any sign of amusement.

“We have placed plenty of addicting agents in the marketplace—from heroin to cocaine and prescription drugs to candy.” More laughter.

“Every individual has found his or her form of addiction. I want to thank Robert Powers for the use of his telecommunications and digital networks he’s placed at our disposal. I hereby announce that Phase II has begun!” he bellowed, shaking a fist in the air.

The sound of cheering and clapping filled the boardroom.

“We’ll be watching the population at large, like lab mice, destroy one another, and we will monitor the process from afar. When we are left with the fittest and most cunning, we will modify and clone them in large numbers to be our intergalactic warriors.”

There were gasps of amazement.

“As we watch this take place,” continued Cirel, “we will continue to perfect our interstellar communicator. We want every able person in front of a phone or computer screen. The programs we have installed will periodically emit a beam through the screen that enters through the pupil of the eye, giving us free access to the brain. This will capture the individual’s intellectual energy and join it to the force we have created that will propel our signal into outer space. Through Powers Digital, we will have the largest and most powerful computer communicator in the galaxy.” This time, the members were too astounded to clap. Robert wondered if they were finally getting a glimpse of the madness of the arch-rebel, who had apparently forgotten the fate of the Tower of Babel.

“Once out of our system,” Robert interrupted, “the *Foundation’s* allies will intercept our signals, and, not having the complete exit code sequences at this time, we simply—”

Cirel flashed a triumphant smile, "Oh, but we do have them," he said, extracting the envelope that Linda had handed him. "I congratulate you on your choice of efficient team members." He continued his speech, grinning and gloating all the while. "We'll be capable of preventing communication contact with RA."

Cirel raved on, outlining the dire consequences of the ongoing oil shortage. The Arab nations, China, and Russia would enact an embargo. Next, he praised those who had expedited the epidemic of mad cow disease in Europe, which dictated that all its meat be imported from the US, where an even more lethal agent had been introduced into the herds. And finally, the *Group's* financial wizard announced the program for enslavement of the population through credit card debt. The list went on and on . . .

At the first opportunity, Robert texted Jeff. So as not to arouse suspicion, he sent the text in view of everyone.

Will you come to my office and bring with you the project we discussed this morning? Don't let it out of your sight. I'll be there shortly. Robert knew that, for the time being, his Park Avenue building was safe.

Linda was rushing up the steps of the museum when her cell phone rang. She was annoyed to see Jeff's number on caller ID rather than Robert's, but she answered it anyway. "What? . . . Who said what? . . . Jeff, I can barely hear you. . . . I am already at the Met. Let's talk later. " She turned off the phone, threw it in her purse, and proceeded on to her rendezvous point.

Jeff tried repeatedly to get Linda back on the line, but there was no answer. He had a hunch something was not right. There was something Robert had insinuated but could not say openly. Jeff left his office and hurried to the Metropolitan.

He was across the street from the museum's front entrance when it happened. A ricochet of explosions ripped a path through the museum, decimating gallery after gallery, and in a matter of minutes, the facade, along with thousands of the world's most precious works of art, went up in smoke.

Police cars arrived almost immediately. Jeff was pushed back by officers trying to cordon off the area. Media trucks and helicopters flocked to the museum and jockeyed for space around the devastation. Screams of agony pierced the air in chorus with the sirens of emergency vehicles. Bomb squads arrived to secure the area and determine whether there were bombs yet to go off.

In a state of shock, Jeff broke away from the crowd and ran back to the Keller building. He knew the reign of terror had begun.

The loss of precious, irreplaceable paintings and objects of art from the Metropolitan Museum of Art was an unexpected blow to the American people. The tragedy of the loss had not set in when a second deplorable act destroyed the Library of Congress in Capitol Hill.

In the days following the two big blasts, several landmarks and museums suffered similar fates. In New York alone, the Guggenheim, the Public Library, the Frick Collection, and the Whitney experienced similar acts of vandalism. From Manhattan, the mindless destruction by these terrorists spread to other major cities.

Art and literature were to be the first of the muses to exit the stage.

"But she was my friend!" Jeff's voice mumbled painfully, his hands covering his face, and tears running between his fingers. "Linda was like family to me."

Lili moved closer to him on the sofa and took him in her arms. "I am sorry; I know exactly what it is to lose a friend."

She thought of Danielle, trapped in the cold and darkness.

"Lili, stop it!" Jeff blurted out. "Did you know about this?"

"No!" She paused, then said, "Jeff, I need to know why you were you heading for the museum?"

"To speak to Linda. Why do you want to protect me? We all seem to be going down, one way or another." He saw her concern, and added, "I worry about you, as well."

"I know, darling. We'll survive these treacherous times. I'm gradually withdrawing from the *Group*. We created and marketed the look they wanted; they can now take over the production. My fashion empire is ruined. Edwards considers wearing anything beautiful an act of vanity and a sin against God."

"I'm glad you are beginning to see him for what he really is."

Lili laughed. "I had no choice in the past but to humor him. Now, the idiot thinks he is above me." He and Nielsen are conniving to take over the country, manipulate the Constitution, and take over the presidency by rigging the election process. Edwards, the new Messiah, will run the country."

"Lili, you are inside the *Group*; you'll know how to disconnect us."

"The best thing for us right now is to give a good show of esprit de corps and wait for the right moment. I know you have deciphered the coordinates on the paper I gave you. You will know when to go there."

"Why?"

"You will know why and when," she repeated.

As often happened, her warmth faded and her business persona appeared. "Robert will be out of the country, so you are to take over a task that the *Group* wants to pursue immediately. We have been given the job of locating this man. Use our digital resources; I want you to get right on it."

She took a folder from the cocktail table and handed it to him.

"John Larkin . . . the spy who fled from Argos?" asked Jeff with surprise.

"Yes, the person responsible for selling military secrets."

"Why do they *really* want him?"

"It's a matter of finding him before he can find them," she surmised.

"If he is not really a traitor, he must be with the *Foundation*," offered Jeff.

"The *Foundation*. What do you know about it?"

"Just that it is an organization opposing your ideology."

"Have you met any members?"

"I wouldn't know how to recognize them."

"Good. Keep it that way. John Larkin is a member of the *Foundation,* but we are certain he has not reached them. We have set up measures to intercept him if he does, but as far as I know, he hasn't tried. He is communicating with the *Foundation* using our technology, but we have been unable to find him. When we do, it will appease Cirel and get him off our backs. He is becoming a raving maniac!"

"Sounds like you have marked him off your dance card."

She smiled. "I thought him brilliant once. Now I realize he is simply obsessed with destruction. The time it took to assemble the body of knowledge, the fine examples of human achievement that he blasted off the earth with such impunity. I never thought I'd care, but I do."

"Yet, you still want to help," whispered Jeff, having just verified the horror of his suspicions.

"I have no choice, but I'll find a way out."

"And Robert?"

"Robert? Might be in the same predicament. Let's find this elusive scientist, and perhaps Cirel will bring his bombings to a halt, at least temporarily. By the time we intercept a signal, John has already moved. So far, Powers's digital technology has been so efficient that it is working against us."

"Your new gold microchip is unbelievably powerful."

"Yes. Larkin is also hacking into communications going both to and from the *Group's* headquarters, where Cirel is perfecting the manipulation of the currents."

"I've heard you speak of the currents."

"They are underground currents that could control the way the earth behaves. Cirel wants to control the world."

"You're not kidding," said Jeff. "This man is insane."

"Don't ever let him know you think that," said Lili. "He can read thoughts and is very sensitive about how he is perceived. Cirel knows the universe is all about the mind, and the mere thought that his share of it is deranged is more than he can handle."

She moved closer to him. "Now, darling, will you get this job done? Will you find this John Larkin?"

Jeff looked into her eyes and swam into the depths of the sapphire pools. He understood his position. Jeff had finally been asked to prove himself. He had to be the one who delivered Larkin to them. *Have they figured out that I am the leak within the organization? I have to buy time.*

Looking at her, Jeff nodded sadly. "I'll see what I can do."

She smiled and left him to his task.

XXXII

Atlanta

There was unusual bustle in the fourth-level biosafety laboratory at the Centers for Disease Control and Prevention. New teams of epidemiologists, microbiologists, and physicians had been working nonstop, trying to identify the new strains of viruses popping up throughout the United States. Wearing the regulatory hazmat suits, the place resembled a crowded space station.

The *Foundation* had practically set up headquarters at the Atlanta CDC, bringing in experts from the Army biosafety labs in Maryland, as well as some of its own microbiologists and neurologists from around the world. The situation was tense. These doctors were not only trying to control outbreaks, but they were also trying to prevent new ones from happening.

The CDC had always worked alone and felt confident they could handle any emergency that might arise in the US. However, within the first forty-eight hours of the newcomers' arrival, they realized they were dealing with situations never before encountered. Parasites were contaminating the water supplies in different cities, and infectious bacteria had showed up in food. The *Foundation* set up powerful microscopes and additional equipment throughout the lab and immediately got to work.

The center was successful in preventing the spread of smallpox and neutralizing the effects of dispersed chemical agents. But now, they were facing a more critical situation. They were dealing with antibiotic-resistant organisms, which they called "killer bacteria." If they lost this battle, the world would be thrown back to the pre-antibiotic era, where millions died every year.

Dr. Thomas O'Neil had been brought in from San Francisco as a consulting neurologist. Wearing doubled rubber gloves and unaccustomed to the constriction of the hazmat suit, Tom looked into his microscope. Angela, a microbiologist, had come along as his assistant.

Dr. Osborn, director of the CDC, invited Tom to have a look through his scope.

"Unbelievable!" exclaimed Tom, doing a double-take at the budding viral particles on the glass. "This bacterium has mutated into a brand-new strain in just twenty-two minutes! The freakin' microbes have perfected evolution."

"Indeed," exclaimed Dr. Osborn. "I never thought I'd live to see the emergence of such sophisticated pathogens! What if these particular ones mutate and go airborne, like SARS or influenza?"

"We'll have the worst pandemic in world history."

"That's precisely why the currents must remain immobilized," Angela whispered to Tom.

"This microbe is a particularly interesting one," continued Dr. Osborn, producing a slide to show the couple. The virus itself had been locked up and removed from the lab. "Unlike those that die when the host expires, this one seems to thrive on decay. It is clear how entire civilizations disappear after certain epidemics."

"This could wipe out the entire human race," Tom added.

"That may be a little far-fetched," responded the director. "It is hard to visualize complete necrosis. Dr. O'Neil, you seem to be uncomfortable in your hazmat suit. Shall we take a break?" Right then, one of the messengers signaled. "It looks like your representative has arrived."

Tom set the slide down and began disconnecting himself from the red hose that entered the suit from the back. He signaled to Angela, and she followed his lead. The three of them headed for the door marked "Exit."

Once outside the room, they entered the decontamination chamber and were showered with a disinfecting mist. They removed their protective helmets. Angela shook her head, releasing thick strands of brown hair, then gathered them up again with a rubber band. They were helped out of their suits and escorted down a long, stark white hall with doors on both sides. When the door to the last room opened, they were informed that someone from the *Foundation* would be with them shortly.

"Good news, I hope," said Tom, hoping to ease Angela's mind. "I hope they have located John."

"I received an email today. He sounds exhausted. I am very worried about him," sighed Angela.

"He is a clever fellow. He knows how to take care of himself."

"But he is totally cut off. How is he getting by?"

Tom took her hand. "I am sure this visit has something to do with it."

At that moment, the representative from the *Foundation* came in and sat behind a black granite desk. Tom was surprised to see that she was a diminutive woman with a sparkle in her blue eyes, her gray hair pulled back severely into a chignon. "Martine DuChamp, I am pleased to meet you. I understand you have been working non-stop and must be hungry," she said.

The doctors dismissed her concern with a smile but were gratified to see the tray of canapés and drinks that had been set up on the console behind them.

"Go ahead, they are quite good, I assure you—my own recipes. You see, I used to be in the restaurant business," Martine said with a faint French accent.

Dr. Osborn helped himself, but Angela was too worried to eat.

"I'll have a scotch, instead, if you don't mind," said Tom.

"Please help yourself," Martine smiled, pointing him to the bar. "In the name of the *Foundation,* I want to thank you for the invaluable work you are doing. Tom, we appreciate your willingness to take time from your practice on such short notice.

"We have evaluated what you have submitted and have thus concluded: Dr. Osborn, the bacteria you are studying was apparently released as a trial run for dispersal of other viruses yet to come. It displays the mutation of a microbe kept dormant on this planet for millennia—frozen or embedded in stone. As we continue to stop the dispersal of bacteria and viruses, the *Group* will continue to unleash new ones, most likely into the water system. Therefore, we have established facilities for desalinization in several areas. Water will be not only become scarce but also unsafe to drink."

Martine read true alarm in the faces of the scientists. "Yes, we know that with the scarcity of water, famine will hit next, and when it does, we will have these ready . . ." The woman produced a can of thin, round wafers. "Consuming one of these daily will keep you alive." She offered them the can. Dr. Osborn took one and looked at it suspiciously before putting it in his mouth.

"Go ahead," Martine urged Tom and Angela. "They are not bad. They contain all the nutrients and vitamins you need to survive. Actually, I suggest that, for safety's sake, you begin to supplant your regular diet with them as soon as you return to private life. While we can make every effort to protect you physically, this is the only way we can control what you eat. It is very likely that the *Group* will try to have you poisoned."

By now, they were all munching on the wafers and found them tasty.

"We don't know when these senseless bombings will stop, but there is no doubt that fallout of their chemical residue will at some point come down in precipitation."

"Angela's reports are accurate. Miniature chips have been implanted in the brains of many randomly chosen individuals, creating a kind of network. The procedure works on the principle of Morphic resonance. When the chip in the mind of one individual is modified, the same chips in others are modified simultaneously. Of course, having an actual chip to work with has been invaluable to us," Martine informed them. "We were fortunate to retrieve the chip in Ricardo Duran's brain and examine it thoroughly. It is very clever, very evil."

Martine noticed the tension building in Angela's face and turned to her. "About John Larkin . . ."

Angela looked at her beseechingly.

"We'll have to bring him in shortly. We have not done so because we had to be cautious."

"Cautious?" Angela could no longer hide her apprehension.

"Yes. Mr. Larkin diverted from our instructions, creating a possible breach of security, perhaps to avoid interception by the opposition, but we have no way of knowing his motivations. We even wonder whether he has somehow been subject to an implant."

Angela shook her head. "That's not possible!"

"Let's hope so, dear. The *Foundation* was forced to back off and cease communications with him."

"He is out there all alone. I must go to him," Angela said, panic in her voice.

"No, we don't deem that advisable, Angela." Martine's voice was firm. "The *Foundation* will bring him in before the *Group* finds him. John has mapped the configuration of the Edenic currents. As we all know, the *Group* has been manipulating one of the currents for over a year now. But if John should be compelled to show them how to unleash others, the *Group* will have new and frightening power. The members will use the currents not only to bring about atmospheric catastrophes, but will also use them to mask reality. If a peaceful atmosphere on Earth is seen from RA, with no signal to stop, RA will bypass Earth and continue its voyage.

"But back to John . . . He has figured out the exact time and place to produce conditions necessary to rescue Danielle. The problem is none of us can go in, not the mortal members of the *Foundation*, nor the messengers. We all lack the correct atomic density to penetrate the cosmic shield. Her rescue is our top priority at the moment, and we need John's input for this dangerous undertaking. The spirit of the late pope is still with us, and he is urging us to get to Danielle now."

"Dr. Osborn," added Martine. "I will be taking Angela with me. We'll depart immediately." She turned to Angela. "Dear, I know this is too much to ask, but please cease all communication with John."

"But . . ." Angela's heart sank. Yet she knew she had to obey.

"Tom, I'll have another plane here in a couple of hours to fly you back to San Francisco. We need for you to finish the research on the DNA strands of the couple under investigation. Please be very careful."

"I'll be fine," said Tom.

"We know they are onto you, and we don't know how they will strike. Beep us if you're in trouble, and we'll be there."

Tom nodded, never imagining he would find himself in need of such help.

Texas

The line outside of McDonald's on Congress St. in Austin, Texas, became longer with each passing day. Not many restaurants were open these days, and a hamburger had become a luxury for which people didn't seem to mind the wait.

A vagrant with a scruffy beard and a backpack pulled out his change. He barely had enough for the meal, and this would be his last. It would have to be the soup kitchens of the New Evangelical Churches. He had avoided going there because he'd heard one had to go through some kind of indoctrination service before getting a meal, and he certainly had not been up to that.

The man behind him tried to engage him in conversation, but the vagrant, feigning drunkenness, ignored him. "I heard they are hiring laborers," said the man, handing him a crumpled pamphlet. "Here, in case you are interested."

The vagrant took it, put it in his pocket, and turned around without replying. He did not want to be noticed and, so far, by standing silently within the crowds, he had avoided attention. But John Larkin was reaching the end of his resources. He had managed to get to Texas on his way to Mexico, not quite sure how he was going to cross the border. One thought kept him going: move to avoid capture. His only communication of late had been with Angela, but she had stopped receiving his emails. They had all been returned "undeliverable." Like the rest of them, she had cut him off without explanation.

The small laptop he carried in his backpack was all he had taken with him. With his resources exhausted, he would have to trade it in somewhere to survive. His ragged clothes, beard, and dirty, matted hair gave him a degree of invisibility, but he remained cautious and made every effort to avoid confrontation.

His face peered out from flyers posted everywhere. Fortunately, no one had recognized him yet.

None of it made any sense to him anymore. He was being hunted like a criminal. The *Foundation* had directed him out of Colorado, asked him to check certain installations, verify security, and track the path of the currents. He had randomly encountered messengers that picked up his reports and handed him cash with further instructions. Then suddenly, everything stopped, and he was cut off.

He was sure it had to do with the last report he had sent. Yes, while in New Mexico, he suspected he was being watched and changed his method of communication. He thought the *Foundation* would understand, but apparently it had not.

John reached the door of the restaurant and went in. *Only ten more people ahead of me,* he thought. *How long has it been since I've eaten? Thirty-six hours? It seems like forever.* What sustained him was knowing that Danielle's predicament was far worse.

The *Foundation* had asked him to reconfigure the exact spot and timeframe for the rescue until he had no doubt. They would need to shift and overlap currents with exact precision to create the gap through which she could escape. They had to get her out before the next minuscule polar shift, when she would be crushed.

He had given the *Foundation* all the particulars, except for the last of his calculations, perhaps the most vital part of the operation—the one to get through the shield and get her out. Mortal entities were too dense; messengers had no density at all and could not slow down their vibration long enough to enter. This was a job for someone whose molecular density and vibration were variable.

Christian Goodman was such a man, but only John knew that. Chris was desperate to help Danielle but did not have a clue that he might be the only one able to do it.

Christian Goodman was what the *Foundation* called a star seed," a true descendant of the Violet Race—the offspring of the Edentians. John knew of the research Dr. Thomas O'Neil had been conducting and the findings. Chris Goodman carried the extra molecule in his DNA, which was absent in most humans.

When John reached the counter, he ordered a hamburger and fries. He desperately wanted coffee, but after re-counting his money, he realized he did not have enough and ordered water instead. The counter girl took his coins and handed him the coffee, anyway.

A scream in the back of the restaurant made him turn and move away from the counter before his order was ready. Someone had fainted. Several people gathered around the woman, while others pulled back. Such scenes were common, and John had seen people collapsing everywhere.

"She's sick," yelled a man kneeling next to her. "We need an ambulance!"

"An ambulance?" repeated another man sarcastically. "Ambulances ain't gonna come just like that anymore. First, they make sure you can pay. Does she have a credit card? They have to run the debit before they dispatch . . ."

"Oh, she'll die before an ambulance comes," another woman volunteered, observing the bloody nose. "She could be contagious!"

"She is not very sick," said the man kneeling next to her, wiping her nose with a handkerchief. "Can we just have some water?"

John Larkin moved closer to observe. He forgot his need to be inconspicuous and pushed his way through the crowd. He set his backpack down and pulled out a mask, covering his face before he touched the woman's forehead. She was burning up.

"How long has she been ill?" he asked the man, her husband.

"A few days. She started complaining of nausea this morning. I thought going out might help her. She didn't feel hot till now." The man tried to lift her head while another man tried to help.

John stared at the woman's face, the red eyes and the bloody nose.

"Don't touch her!" John warned, his voice belying his appearance and causing most of the onlookers to back off. "Ebola! Highly contagious," he barked, remembering what Angela had told him.

With a sudden retch, the woman died right before their eyes. The husband, ignoring John's warning, sobbed and hugged the lifeless body.

John moved back and headed for the door. There was nothing else he could do. He noticed a man staring at him from a nearby table. *Was I identified?* He knew the *Group* had informants everywhere. Someone tapped him on the shoulder. A young man in a McDonald's uniform handed him a paper bag. "You forgot your food."

John took it, thanking him with a nod, and cut through the line, walking away from the restaurant as fast as he could, continuing his pace until he felt he had not been followed. John could hardly believe this was America. Chaos and disorder in the streets, every other shop closed and boarded up, piles of garbage and broken glass, gangs of hoodlums roaming everywhere.

He had to find a quiet spot where he could eat and use his computer unseen. He had to take the risk of letting the *Foundation* know there was now an outbreak of Ebola. He spotted an alley and headed that way. Tossing his paper cup in a garbage bin, he reached into the bag for the hamburger. Instead, he found a box of wafers and something heavy at the bottom of the bag. He sat on the ground and emptied the contents with great care. After removing the curious box of wafers, he found a velvet pouch. In the pouch were a handful of gold coins, a roll of one hundred-dollar bills, and a car key. With incredulity, he counted the bills. Ten thousand dollars! He suddenly recalled the pamphlet that had been given him by the man at the restaurant and opened it to find a California driver's license taped to it, bearing the name Dale Sanders with a picture *of himself.*

John sighed in relief. They had not forgotten him! He removed the driver's license. Under it was a paper with three typed lines directing him where to find the car and Danielle's familiar address in Los Angeles where he was to go. He picked up the wafers. That was what he was supposed to eat, and now he knew where to go.

XXXIII

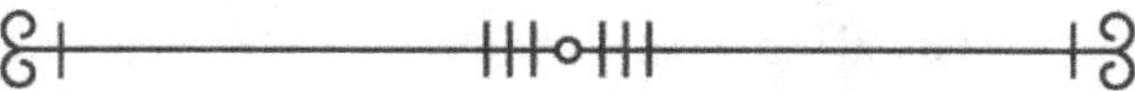

When Chris heard Kitzia's footsteps, he looked up with delight. He had been working all morning in her California library. She headed for his desk, tiptoeing through piles of books and files scattered on the floor.

"Sorry for the mess," he said. "Got used to having my assistant, Ali."

"We are going to miss him."

"I wonder how he'll adjust to living with Tom . . . and Jean-Christophe."

"He'll be fine," added Kit. "You forget his brother was Jean-Christophe's friend."

"You're right."

"This came for you." Kit handed him an envelope.

He opened it, and Kit noticed the change of expression in his face. "What is it?"

"I think it's from John Larkin."

Kit looked at the card with two vague circles and no signature. "You're right. He is letting us know he is OK."

"When I last saw him, he spoke of a cosmic portal. All I know is that he is the only one capable of helping Danielle. I wish I understood more. All I have learned is that our existence is composed of multiple layers, the integration of which constitutes our reality."

"You've had a glimpse into eternity," said Kit with a degree of satisfaction. "Danielle chose well when she decided it should be you that would explain to the world. Perhaps I could ask Mai Li to fix us a tray and bring it here so we can continue working."

"I was hoping you would say that." He kissed her forehead.

Nowadays, Chris's slightest touch made her blush.

During the days that followed, Chris and Kit continued to go through hundreds of documents and computer files as they waited to hear from John. The weather was once again deteriorating; rain poured non-stop, inundating and destroying crops and creating new mud slides. Then suddenly, it began to hail and sleet. It was the coldest weather recorded in California over the last two hundred years.

As usual, Californians coped as best as they could. An unexpected blow came with the contamination of large water delivery systems throughout the state with the appearance of a microbe that made a great percentage of the water undrinkable. Some towns that had already been contending with frequent blackouts, now had to face a shortage of water. Fortunately, the misfortune coincided with the opening of the first desalinization plant on the west coast, but the shortage still created fear and havoc throughout the state.

The Peschard estate, with its own water well and purification system, was not affected. Kit and Chris immediately put thousands of gallons of water at the disposal of nearby residents. But word spread, and people from as far away as Reseda came to stand in line all night, plastic bottle in hand, to get a ration of drinking water. In addition, many were given a supply of wafers. One day, among those standing in line, John Larkin showed up.

"Let him in immediately," said Kit, speaking through the intercom.

Ramon opened the gate and allowed him through, wondering who this scruffy man might be. Once inside, John could hardly wait to discard his filthy clothes. He tossed his parka, hat, and gloves on a bench. Kit and Chris ran out to meet him before he reached the main door. John explained how his connection with the *Foundation* had changed after the disappearance of Air Force One.

"I have no information on the whereabouts or fate of the presidential plane, but I suspect it is not the one the public imagines. The president texted me before the plane's disappearance. The *Foundation* believes Danielle was imprisoned in the warp between two molecular walls. Physicists working for the *Group* had successfully created a way of suspending molecular movement and freezing time in that exact spot."

Neither Christian nor Kit could comprehend what he meant, but they understood that Danielle was suspended in time, that she could not remain there indefinitely. John found it prudent to withhold the fact that it would be Chris who would enter the warp to rescue Danielle. He would leave that news for the *Foundation*.

"Do you know where Tom has been?" Kit asked.

"Working in one of the eight biosafety laboratories. Three of them are supported by the *Foundation*."

"John, what is happening?"

"We are at war," stated John. "Don't let the fact that we don't see the forces in direct combat fool you. The *Group* and the *Foundation* are in a deadly battle. The *Foundation* has temporarily gone underground. We are to enter one of the secret facilities somewhere between Santa Barbara and Montecito at the ruins of an abandoned pagoda. I have the location and exact time to enter."

"That's where Danielle was hit by lightning," exclaimed Kit. "She was trying to reach the *Foundation's* safe house!"

"I was warned that we might encounter difficulties. But nothing is to stop us from reaching the inside of the building. This will be dangerous . . . extremely dangerous."

"What isn't these days? I'm going."

"I just don't know what we'll encounter," was all John could say.

Chris turned to Kit. "What if I promise to call you as soon as we reach Danielle?" Chris stared into her eyes, and she knew she would have to give in. "We know that while you are inside this house, you are safe. If you could just remain inside for the next few days, you would put everyone's mind at ease."

Kit reluctantly agreed.

Surprised at the strength of the fear that struck her at the possibility of losing him, she casually asked him to stay with her that night.

The morning was crisp and bright and the drive uneventful. They allowed her to accompany them only to where they would park the car. Despite their protests, she had insisted on bringing along a couple of guns.

The abandoned pagoda was easily seen, perched on the crest of a hill. Chris drove up the small dirt road that led to the ruined structure and parked the Range Rover as close as he could, though it was still about 300 yards away. He hugged Kit, urging her to stay in the car. They had barely said goodbye when a cloud materialized above them. The cloud began to spin, growing larger and larger. The sound of thunder bellowed the announcement of a storm. John urged Chris to hurry, and with a quick thumbs up to Kit, they dashed up the hill to an uncertain fate.

Kit watched apprehensively as lightning flashed, but there was no sign of rain. A bolt slammed into the ground, but as Chris and John hit their stride, a circle of light formed around them, and their pace slowed. Shadows emerged from the trees on either side and began to morph into human form, opposing phalanxes challenging each other, zigging and zagging to dodge the arrows of lightning they flung at each other . . . then retaliating with bigger and ever more dazzling bolts.

Chris and John froze in the middle of the circle. The dark figures were in mortal combat, and the circle of light around Chris and John blocked their path. But Chris recognized Zephon in the melee and quickly signaled John to jump out of the circle. They hurtled forward and raced toward the building. Just as they reached the pagoda, a tree was hit, caught on fire, and fell in front of them, igniting trees and bushes to either side. The fire quickly spread. They stopped short and glanced back at the fight to see Zephon's signal for them to run through the fire. They did not hesitate.

"Jeez . . . it was just an illusion," Chris cried.

They raced inside the building.

The lightning stopped, the shadows vanished, and the dark cloud was sucked into the firmament.

Kit had watched in horror. She thought she had seen lightning strike her friends when the tree fell. She jumped out of the vehicle and ran toward the pagoda. Expecting the worst, she ran inside in a panic, but the building was empty. There was no sign of Chris or John.

The structure was no more than a concrete shell to hold the red pagoda top. It looked as if it had been neglected for years. She ran her fingers over the concrete but found nothing to suggest a door of any kind. Thoroughly puzzled, she left the building and walked back to the car.

A car passed her on the road. It was a rental with its requisite logos. *A tourist,* she thought, observing the young man driving slowly and speaking into a cell phone.

"Quite a light show!" said Jeff on the phone, watching Kit drive away. "But Larkin still made it to the door."

"Was anyone else with him?" asked Lili back in New York.

"Another man." Jeff did not mention seeing Kitzia. "What do you want me to do?"

"Nothing. You found him. That's all you were asked to do. We can't help it if he got away. Go on to Colorado. I'll join you there."

XXXIV

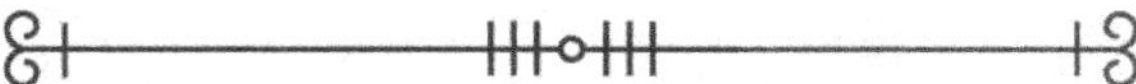

The door above John and Chris closed. They were taken aback by the presence of the splendid figure of Zephon. Only his face visible, a silvery suit covered his entire form. The messenger smiled and ushered them forward. The wall facing them dematerialized and gave way to a corridor. They passed through a gate, where a sleek, silver train with the promise of lightning-like speed awaited them. The men took seats opposite one another. Two other silver clad messengers boarded the train, passing through the bulkhead as if it were not there.

Zephon spoke for the first time, instructing them to buckle up, and produced two small boxes fitted with thin, clear plastic tubes. "You don't have to use them," he said, "but I think the oxygen will make you more comfortable during the ride."

Zephon sat on the bench next to Chris, while one of the other messengers took a seat next to John. Their silver suits slowly faded, morphing into simple black T-shirts and trousers.

"It will be a quick trip," Zephon advised. Chris watched as the messenger assigned to John handed him charts and papers, which John inspected. Zephon explained there were things Chris had to know before the attempt at rescue. The briefing was concise.

Chris was flabbergasted to learn that he possessed a peculiar molecular variance capable of changing vibrations that made him uniquely able to withstand the extreme pressure he would encounter when he entered the cosmic warp. It took his breath away to discover that *he* was the one who could save Danielle!

When they left the train, Chris checked his watch. Only seventeen minutes had passed.

Overwhelmed by what he had just learned, he hurried up the steps and stepped out onto an airstrip in a broad field. The door they had just exited transformed into a giant oak tree.

A Learjet awaited them. *Where are we?* Chris wondered.

"Colorado," answered Zephon, having divined Chris's question.

"But—"

"No one knows the field is here. One of our concealed locations," answered the messenger.

Chris had, by now, accepted that much of what went on in this world remained invisible to the mortal eye. They boarded the jet, and it soared into the sky.

In Rome, John boarded a helicopter that took him directly to the Vatican gardens, past the huge "Closed for renovation" signs. A number of people monitored big black boxes that emitted intermittent flashes of light, while technicians made a multitude of adjustments. An ambulance and a medical team stood by. Computers, monitors, and TV screens were placed about the grounds. Chris spotted Cardinal Santis, who acknowledged him immediately and walked briskly toward him. They barely had time to say hello before a man from the medical team interrupted to alert Chris that everything was in order and set to go. Chris was administered blood pressure and oxygen capacity tests and reminded once more of the dangers and precautions that Zephon had outlined. A change in the atmosphere had caused the mission to be moved up forty-eight hours, hence the rush. Chris tried to focus his attention on his specific instructions but could not help overhearing other precautions given to those who were to assist him.

He tried not to dwell on the danger. He undressed and pulled on tights made from a specialized material. He had just learned the weight and non-conductivity of some fabrics could interfere with his mobility inside the warp. His feet remained bare, and his watch was exchanged for one so thin and weightless; it looked as if it were painted on his wrist. A medical technician placed patches near his heart, neck, lungs, and left temple.

"Remember, you only have four minutes, thirty-eight seconds to attempt the rescue," said one of the engineers. "Half of that time must be used to get out. Your watch will sound a warning when it is time to turn back. If you don't have her by then, you must abort the mission, or you will both be crushed."

Chris felt it was imperative to tell them that Kjell was inside with Danielle.

"We know," replied the *Foundation* engineer. "We are counting on his strength to get himself out."

"You will experience dizziness during the descent," continued the doctor. "Close your eyes to avoid vertigo. There will be utter silence. When you detect the faintest sound, slow down. At that point, you will be approaching them."

"We are moving you through time and space into another dimension," said another engineer. "There is no margin for error. Are you ready?"

Chris took a deep breath. "I am."

"All right . . . stand still." The doctors, engineers, and technicians coordinated their watches.

"The part of the current that is wrapped around the molecular wall," Zephon had told him during the tram ride, "has a point where it overlaps, and for just a few seconds, there will be a small separation. At that precise time, the *Foundation* will thrust into the crack a current of our own that will crash into theirs. On impact, the molecules will experience a momentary displacement, creating a void or an opening for you to go through. We will create an arch for you to move out."

"Go!" A voice in the background gave the order. The vision Chris took with him was that of Cardinal Santis in the distance, holding a cross and giving him his blessing.

As he had been told to expect, sounds began to fade, and as instructed, Chris began running in place. Everything went dark, and the only sound he could hear was his own heartbeat.

He was traveling through time once more—into space but not *outer space.* This time, he was heading to *inner* space.

He felt a change. The metal plate under his feet was no longer there; he was running on the ground. His bare feet felt grass, pebbles, mud, water . . . and grass once more. Sporadic flashes of light indicated a change from day to night, then back to day. Then darkness again. He heard a moan and slowed down. The sound of *constricted* breathing became more audible. He slowed down some more, looking around—nothing but darkness.

"Over here." A voice pierced the darkness.

Chris came to a stop. Standing still, he waited.

"We are here." It was unmistakably Kjell's voice.

Chris took a deep breath. *He had found them! Now he had to get them out.* "It's Chris," he spoke into the darkness.

"Move slowly," Kjell advised.

"Is Danielle with you?"

"Yes," responded the Edentian.

"Is she OK?" Chris wanted to know.

No answer.

Chris pressed the face of his watch: 1:45 . . . *just thirty-two seconds remaining!* It was pitch black. He had no idea which direction to go.

"Kjell, keep talking. Can you see me?"

"Yes, walk straight ahead. I'll reach for you. Put your hand out.

Chris did as he was told.

"Keep moving forward . . . slowly," continued Kjell.

He heard a distant moan.

"Danielle!" exclaimed Chris.

"She is not conscious. I'll try to lift her into your arms."

Chris stretched out his arms to take her and felt her weight in his arms. He had a most peculiar sensation; he could not feel the contours of her body but was aware only of its weight. He reviewed his instructions. He was to make an immediate left turn and walk quickly until he felt the metal plate under his feet, at which time he was to accelerate his pace.

"I'm ready."

"I am right behind you," responded Kjell, his breathing becoming heavier.

After just a few steps, Chris heard a thump that told him Kjell had collapsed.

"You go on," said Kjell. "The two of you can still make it."

Contrary to everyone's expectations, Chris knew that Kjell would not make it out by himself. He looked at his watch. They still had a few seconds. He knew his movements had to be slow and deliberate. He eased backward until his leg came in contact with Kjell. "Hold on to me! Try to get up." Kjell pulled himself up onto Chris's back. "Ready?"

"Let's go," replied the Edentian.

The weight of the two of them was all he could bear under such difficult conditions, but he managed to stagger forward. He felt the cold of metal under his feet when they were assailed on all sides by ear-splitting cracks of lightning, roaring thunder, and a sub-zero wind. Then came the deafening sound of the crack and crush of ice. "What is happening?" Chris yelped in horror.

"The *Group* . . ." was all Kjell could manage to say, gasping for breath. "They have unleashed a current above us. We are going to be crushed!"

Everything around them came crashing down. Chris could see a little now, but there was no place to take shelter. Danielle had begun to regain her human form when his watch beeped its warning. Time was running out, and as he had always heard happens, his entire life flashed before him.

In what was probably a nanosecond, he experienced myriad recollections and revelations. He thought of his mother and father, whom he had resented but who had chosen him and had given him the best they could offer; and for that, he felt immense gratitude. What he had wanted in life above all things was adventure, and that desire had led him to this moment. Danielle had provided the ultimate adventure, and he had surrendered his feelings to her—unfortunately, mislabeling them.

He would not get to see "The Manuscript," nor would he be able to finish his book. *Well, c'est la vie!* he thought, with unexpected humor. *Maybe next time.* Danielle said there would always be a next time. His life was ending in an all-out attempt to rescue the woman who had given him so much—his identity, a purpose for his existence, and the tools to discover the meaning of life. *It was a good trade-off,* he thought. It had been ironic to find out so close to the end that his

DNA was endowed with a special connection to the Edentians. He hoped his last act, his attempt to rescue one of their own, would be viewed with respect. A great epitaph would be, *We expected no less of him*, he thought with pride.

So I will die. It's been a short but fulfilling life. I have no regrets. Regrets? Well, I do have one . . . Kitzia O'Neil. I will not see her again. Will she be grieved by my death, or will she cry only for Danielle? There is no reason to deny it at this point. The simple truth is that I'm in love with Kitzia.

Chris closed his eyes to meet the inevitable.

From a distant point on the horizon, a faint light reached the three travelers. The weight of his burden, and the pressure of the atmosphere that had been slowly crushing him, began to lift. A passage opened before them. Chris moved forward. He still had four seconds. He saw a huge figure, like Atlas, holding up the arch. Summoning every bit of his remaining strength, he lunged forward. A loud boom behind him signaled that the fissure had snapped shut. They had made it out!

The medical team rushed forward and took Danielle from his arms. Kjell was lifted off Chris's back and onto a stretcher. Chris was numb. His eyelids drooped and his eyes closed, but he knew he was still alive. He was merely fainting from exhaustion.

Syrian Desert

News of the Edentians' escape infuriated Cirel, but not wanting to admit defeat to his associates, he pretended to be undisturbed by the event. He even went so far as to tell Mohammed Riezk, who he was visiting in the Middle East, that the escape had been his idea. Cirel stated his certainty that the Edentians would head straight for the *Foundation* headquarters, and thus the *Group* would be able to track them down.

The two men were standing outside a tent in the desert. The Arab, wearing his white turban, pointed proudly at his newest recruits—the new Terror Brigade being prepared to infiltrate the United States. The multi-racial recruits, wearing their khakis, stood in perfect formation under the blazing mid-afternoon sun. Cirel nodded his approval, now anxious to depart, and was glad to see his helicopter arrive. Patting the Arab on the back, he signaled to his men that it was time to go. Mohammed saluted his troops and followed Cirel to the helicopter. Before climbing aboard, Cirel looked around to scrutinize the landscape. Everything was tranquil. There was nothing to be seen but sand and barren dunes.

The two Israelis, carrying with them a camera fitted with a powerful telescopic lens, crawled back into the bunker they had dug into the hill.

"Did you get a good shot?" asked the younger man after the helicopter took off.

"I think so," answered his much older companion, reviewing the video. He replayed it and whispered jubilantly, "There he is, the despicable murderer!"

"Hitler? I still can't believe it!"

"Do you think I could ever forget that face? He murdered my family. Why doesn't he age? I think he is the devil." The older man continued, putting away the camera equipment. "They say he has a certain tree that keeps him alive and keeps him from aging. You bet that we are going after that tree as well."

"We could have gotten him just now." The young man caressed his powerful weapon with regret.

"We can't bypass our orders. We've got the photo. That's all that matters now. We will get the son of a jackal, don't you worry. I've been tracking him for years, and I tell you one thing: the piece of garbage is getting careless. He is spending much more time out of his rat hole than he ever has. Let's send this through and wait for confirmation from the prime minister before we do anything more."

Nepal

Cirel was lost in thought, contemplating his next move, still enraged by the rescue of the Edentians. He had returned to the hideout at the *Group's* headquarters, secreted in the depths of Mount Everest.

Standing in his usual pose, with his back to his associates, he was formulating his plans.

There were three visitors. Among them was Senator Nielsen, who had never been invited to the *Group's* main headquarters, Mohammed Riezk, and Kim-Sui, the Asian associate. Nielsen surveyed the surroundings with curiosity, finding high walls and a large dome at the top that gave a view of the stars. There was nothing in the room but a round stainless steel table and eight chairs.

Mohammed, the Arab sheik, accustomed to Persian rugs, brocades, and objects of gold, found the room sterile and uninviting. In contrast, the Asian, with his impenetrable countenance, was entirely comfortable in these surroundings.

Everything about Cirel was neat, cold, and minimal. Not until this moment had the senator made the correlation between systematic order and death.

The arch-rebel turned around and walked to the head of the table but did not sit down. He never sat with his associates, making it clear they never would be his equals. He ran his fingers over the table in front of his empty chair, and a rectangular screen appeared. The others followed his lead and brought up their own screens that showed a view of distant stars. They watched Cirel glide his fingers gracefully over his monitor. One of many tiny dots flashed.

"There it is," he said, pointing to the flashing dot. "That is RA, the royal transport of the life carriers. It has just turned its course toward us." Cirel's voice dripped with disdain. But as he continued to speak, his tone became perceptively wistful. "Long ago, I traveled on RA, when there was purpose to this insanity called creation. At that time, there was discrimination in the implementation of life and rules for weeding it out. Now look around!" His tone changed; his voice rose. "Everything is out of order! The absurd belief that everything imbued with life must be fostered is rubbish!" He paced about the room. "Take notice at what has happened to this planet! The races are mingling, breaking down barriers between the superior and the inferior. Look at the aberrations emerging! I will be glad when this is over," sighed Cirel. "When order returns to the universe, when the light goes out, and when the peaceful constancy of darkness returns. . . . RA will receive no signal and will move on. The *Formation* will not take place. By the time they realize they have been tricked, this planet will be history!"

"You said the destruction would not be universal!" exclaimed the Arab. "That our kingdoms would be safe."

Cirel quickly corrected himself. "They will be, as promised. but the rest will be methodically taken apart from within. Senator Nielsen of the USA has done a magnificent job of loosening the screws of the engine that runs the nation. Theodore Edwards will know how to secure the final unification before we take over."

Cirel again tapped his screen. It projected a view of the planet, trailing long ribbons of color like the tails of comets. "Those are our currents," Cirel announced with pride. "Those beautiful bands of energy, invisible to the human eye, are capable of unbelievable destruction. Aren't they beautiful?"

Running his fingers over the streaks of light, Cirel continued, "I have already scheduled the time frame for destruction. It is to be as soon as RA passes and turns its back on us."

Cirel looked up as a man dressed in a gray suit entered the room and stood by the door. The men at the table saw Cirel's face go red as he glared at the man responsible for preventing Danielle's escape.

"The walls, my lord, collapsed as we intended, but somehow, an arch was created that allowed the writer to carry the Edentians out," said the man in gray.

"You know how I detest incompetence!" After a pause, Cirel continued, "It had to be an Edentian who saved them. Robert Powers!" Cirel made every attempt to remain calm in front of his associates. "Ah, inefficiency and betrayal . . . intolerable!"

The man in gray perspired profusely. Cirel snapped his fingers and a section of the steel wall went up, revealing a cage housing two cheetahs. The cage door opened, and the animals tentatively slunk into the room.

Everyone froze. Cirel addressed the beasts. "A treat for you, my darlings." He motioned in the direction of the man in gray, and the cheetahs pounced. The man's screams were drowned out by the beasts' competitive roars as the animals tore at him and dragged him into their cage. The gate closed and the steel wall came down. Cirel stared for a moment at the garnet pool on the floor. For some reason, the sight of human blood had always afforded him a special thrill.

Nielsen loosened the collar of his shirt. The two other men attempted a show of indifference. Cirel was energized. His next act was to change the frequency of the tele-transmission to project the progression of the 747 flying the Edentians and members of the *Foundation* over the Atlantic.

"Let's try not to lose them this time," said Cirel sardonically, addressing his technicians through the speakers."

He then addressed the three visitors. "I will fulfill my promise to you and make you immortal. I will transport the Tree of Life to a place where we can all eat from it. We will rule long after this present civilization ceases to exist."

Cirel now addressed Nielsen, "Tell me, has Edwards agreed?"

"Well, of course. He'll play the martyr, the messiah . . . whatever you ask, he'll do. An attempt on his life would be dramatic, indeed. Imagine an assassination followed by a resurrection. It would be indisputable that he is the Messiah."

Cirel laughed mirthlessly. "Now, Damian, why don't you show our visitors to our hospitality area? Food, drinks, and women for their pleasure. The rest of this meeting would be unbearably boring to our illustrious visitors."

Nielsen, the Arab, and the Asian got up and followed Cirel's associate out of the room.

When Cirel was alone with his most trusted associates, he inquired, "Have we been able to get through to our allies?"

"No."

Cirel asked soberly, "And the trial?"

"Still in process. Our galactic visitors believe there is little support for Luciel. The verdict appears to be leading toward conviction and annihilation."

"I swear I'll reduce this place to ashes. Can our currents be used as magnets to cause a meteor shower?"

"I don't see why not. However, you should have them placed in orbit very soon."

Cirel thought for a moment. "Now give me a quick update on Egypt," commanded the arch-rebel.

"We have not located the monolith. The medians are keeping a tight watch on the location."

"It's time we put the medians out of business," continued the diabolical Cirel. "Prepare for demolition of the entire Valley of the Kings. Do we have enough vergonium to mask the area? We will want it to look peaceful when RA approaches."

"What if RA decides to head in this direction, anyway?" asked Cirel's associate.

"No chance. The *Formation* can't occur because I have one of the key stones." Cirel pointed to the gem on the gold chain around his neck.

XXXV

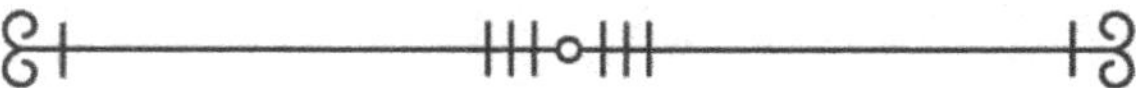

Chris could intuit that he was flying across the Atlantic in the luxury of a jumbo jet. But because he had been heavily sedated, he kept dozing off. When he opened his eyes, he saw one of the doctors from the Vatican sitting next to him. She was checking his pulse and smiling at him with satisfaction.

"How do you feel?" she asked.

"Where is Danielle?" asked Chris instead, when he saw no one else in the cabin.

The doctor pointed to the stairway behind them. "They are all still on the upper deck. She is doing fine, but it will be awhile before she can speak. Danielle and Kjell must go into a molecular adjustment chamber when we arrive at the *Foundation*. So far, their vital signs are good." She patted his hand. "You must relax. You've had an extraordinary experience."

Christian closed his eyes but tried hard not to fall asleep. He tried to review the fantastic ordeal he had just experienced and desperately wanted to be awake so he could recall every detail for when he could set it down on paper, but despite every effort, he dozed off again.

When the medication wore off, he found himself staring out the window at the ripples of water in the ocean. "Where are we?" he asked.

Putting down her magazine, the doctor answered, "We should be close to the Azores."

The mention of the Azores sent a chill down his spine as he remembered the fate of Air Force One. The presidential plane had most likely flown the same route.

"Where exactly is the *Foundation* located?" he asked.

"I really couldn't tell you. This is the first time I'll be visiting the headquarters."

"A secret island, no doubt," added Chris, with excitement.

He looked around the cabin but recognized no one. Realizing that he had awakened, a young Asian flight attendant came to him. "May I get you anything?" she asked.

"Water," answered Chris, eyeing the girl, who could be no older than sixteen.

She returned with a glass of water. "This will be the last chance for communication," said the young girl with a Chinese accent, producing a cell phone and handing it to Chris, who turned to the doctor for clarification.

"Yes," said the doctor. "I understand that all communication with the outside world stops at this point."

He took the phone and dialed the home in Los Angeles. Kit answered right away.

"Where are you?" Kit wanted to know, but all he knew to tell her was that he was somewhere over the Atlantic.

"I am so relieved to hear from you. I have been frantic . . . Danielle?"

"She is fine—still under observation. I haven't had a chance to see her yet," said Chris.

Kit let out a sigh of relief. "Thank goodness! Are you all on your way home now?"

"Not yet. I believe we are on our way to the *Foundation* headquarters," said Chris, smiling at the doctor. He felt it prudent not to mention that they were on the same route the president's plane had traveled. "How is everything there?"

"Worse than ever. Continuous blackouts, accidents on the streets, traffic lights not working, hospitals in a panic, continuing riots, and looting. It is a good thing we have everything we need here. But even our generator blinked out for a second. There was some electromagnetic disturbance that interrupted power worldwide."

"I know," replied Chris, remembering what Zephon had told him about the crashing of the currents. "Promise me that you'll stay in until I return."

"I've already promised," she answered. "When do you think you'll be back?"

"I am not sure, a few days perhaps."

"Be sure and call to let me know."

"That's the thing. I don't know if I'll be able to. Apparently, our communication with the rest of the world will be cut off in a few minutes. We'll be out of reach. But don't worry. We are all right. You be especially on guard, because Zephon is now here with us."

"I will. Give my love to Danielle. Tell her how much I miss her."

"Kit . . ."

"Yes?"

"Oh, nothing. Take care." Chris hung up, annoyed at himself. He had not had the courage to say it, even though he had sworn that if he got through the rescue alive, he would let Kit know how he felt. He redialed her number, but this time, he got a recording that said the number was out of the communications network. He looked out the window and stared at the limitless ocean.

The intercom came on and the captain's voice announced, "Ladies and gentlemen, we are beginning our descent. Please return to your seats and turn off all electronic equipment." He took a humorous tone. "We have our usual escorts."

There was laughter in the pilot's cabin. Chris turned to the doctor next to him, hoping for an explanation.

"I understand this happens every time," said the doctor. "The *Foundation's* plane is always followed by others trying to track its destination. The crew manages to lose them. The plane vanishes, disappears from radar. Fasten your seatbelt. No telling what comes next."

Chris did so, noticing the flight attendants were busy pulling down the window shades. He cast one last fleeting look at the ocean but still saw nothing but the deep blue water—not the faintest suggestion of land. When his shade came down, he noticed that all small items had been put away and tables had disappeared into the sleek white walls.

There were no unusual jolts. The flight continued smoothly for about twenty-five more minutes, but no one spoke during that time.

The flight attendants—two of them, remarkably alike in appearance—instructed the passengers on how to correctly position the oxygen masks that had popped down from the ceiling. They pointed to underneath the seats, instructing them to take out pillows and position the soft squares over their laps. The girls then took a seat and began fastening their multiple belts. Chris was still fumbling with the double chest belts when a laser-projected sign appeared on the wall. "19 seconds till impact."

The word *impact* sent chills up Chris's spine, and he held his breath, staring at the sign. The numbers flickered quickly: 17,16, 15, 14 . . . The cabin went black. A loud splash. The lights came back on. The attendants unfastened their gear and stood up. Everyone began removing the masks and unbuckling. Chris did not have to ask. The general nonchalance indicated that all was well.

"Those entering the depths for the first time may want to keep the oxygen mask on while we continue our descent," the captain added.

The window shades went up, one by one. Chris looked out the window. He could hardly believe his eyes. They were under the sea! Schools of exquisite iridescent fish were swimming all around them. Then it grew dark, and he realized they were still diving deep into the ocean.

"I haven't asked your name," he said.

"Marina Cantrelli," the doctor responded.

"Did you have any idea, Marina, that the *Foundation* was at the bottom of the ocean?"

"I suspected as much."

Chris looked out the window again. The aircraft now moved like a submarine. Running lights illuminated the waters and gave a clear view of the sea creatures.

They were all sizes, colors, and shapes—fish he had never seen, even in his books about pre-historic marine life. Here and there, he began to see broken columns and murals, marble ruins . . .

One of the attendants stood up and announced, "We will disembark shortly and will proceed in two different conveyances. The first group will include all medical personnel and technical support."

"I guess that is where you get off," said Chris to Marina.

"I've been instructed to remain with you," she answered.

"The rest of you, distinguished visiting members," continued the flight attendant, "will board the second craft."

They arrived at the terminal—a gigantic metal structure, built much like a hangar. The aircraft glided in smoothly, and a door closed behind it. The floor rose until a loud click was heard. An opening appeared in the wall, and a passageway extended out like an accordion and hooked to the plane's door with a snap. The passengers—Chris counted six of them—now began gathering their belongings. Since he had only a small bag, he remained seated, observing. After a few minutes, he got up, and, following Dr. Cantrelli, exited the cabin. They walked through the tunnel and boarded a small, sleek, futuristic submarine. The crew entered the lower part, while he and the six others assigned to this craft sat in the upper section. Four rows of two seats each under a large, clear dome made up the top section of the craft. He watched as the first vessel departed, carrying Danielle, Kjell, and the others. It was a larger watercraft and did not have a clear dome, so he was not able to see Danielle.

Five minutes later, a voice announced, "Welcome to the *Foundation*. We are now entering the ancient city of Pondera." The voice was different from anything Chris had ever heard. It was a female voice, clear and melodic. A light shone above them, almost blinding. When Chris's eyes became accustomed to the brightness, he looked around, but all he could do was gasp.

His eyes had never beheld such splendor. The structures they were passing were the remnants of ancient buildings with exquisitely carved facades, sculptures, Doric columns, and emblems, all made of gold!

Scattered and half-embedded in the ocean floor were broken pieces of marble statues that had once stood majestically above ground. There were columns of lapis and malachite, urns of rose quartz and porphyry. One statue in particular caught his attention. Chris stared at a protruding marble foot with fascination, then a broken arm, each piece standing on its own like a unique piece of art. The size of the monument must have been gigantic, Chris realized. The erect figure must have stood a hundred feet high. He spotted the broken head, its face half buried in the sand.

"The famous statue of Michael," the voice continued, "once stood guard over the entire island."

"Atlantis!" Chris whispered to himself. He admired the head as they sailed past it. He had never seen such beauty in a countenance. "That is the statue of Michael of Nebadon."

"Yes,' sighed Marina. "Isn't it the most beautiful thing you've ever seen?"

"Michael is our—"

"Creator" she said. "The Edentians say the statue falls short of his true radiance."

More broken statues and temples came into view, then gradually the signs of destruction began to lessen, and they saw more erect sculptures marking their approach to the perimeter of the city. The façade of the city retained a suggestion of the old classicism but looked solid and functional. The entrance arches were made of coral and fitted perfectly into the rock formation below. The submarines slowed down, and Chris watched the first ship separate from their little convoy and head for a structure that resembled a Greek temple. His craft reached a solid granite wall, and the blocks parted, allowing them to slip into a chamber. Once inside, the water surrounding them emptied out. The floor rose again, then closed behind them, depositing them into a room that did not in any way suggest they were deep in the ocean. The doors of their transport slid open, and they entered a room with a series of steel doors. An elderly man, accompanied by a young woman wearing a soft linen Greek chiton, welcomed them.

Chris, not knowing what to expect, walked through the portal, past a courtyard, and into a garden of unearthly delights, one lush with trees and exotic, glorious flowers. Above them, as far as he could see, was an expanse of sky dusted with puffs of clouds and dancing with colorful birds.

The new arrivals walked through an archway to see a turquoise lake ringed with marble statues representing the gods of antiquity. Inside a glass pyramid, a group of people wearing white robes sat in silence around a table. One of the guides explained that these were the *Foundation* elders, deep in meditation, which linked all their members, creating their virtual network in support of the well-being of the planet.

Chris noticed that the structures bore names: Temple Beautiful, School of Logic, and Archives. The guide stopped in front of a white house and said, "This is where you will be lodged." Four members of diverse ages and races welcomed them inside. There was a joyful reunion among some of the traveling members who apparently had been there before. Chris was greeted with high regard, due to the part he had played in Danielle's rescue, news of which had already circulated among them, and he was the first to be taken to his room.

The bedroom was an exact replica of his boyhood room in Dallas, and he was unexpectedly choked with emotion. The exact furniture, paisley sheets, and comforter, a bookshelf with his favorite books—it was all there. He moved to the desk and spotted his first cops and robbers story, the one he had written when he was twelve. There it was, with all the smudges and scribbling on the margins, and its numerous misspellings caused him to smile.

Next to it was a picture of his adoptive parents. He rested his eyes on a photograph he did not recognize. A picture of a couple with a small child, a little girl of two or three. He picked it up, recognizing his own eyes in those of the man. There was another framed photograph of a young couple holding hands at a party. The girl was the same as in the other photo but years later. Chris knew without question that it was his genealogical family.

Underneath the photos was a dossier. He opened it anxiously to find a chronological report on the Wiese family, with birth and marriage certificates, ID cards, and passports.

Chris sat on the floor as he had done in his youth. He learned that Ira Wiese, his grandfather, had been a brilliant scholar and member of the *Foundation*. Ingrid, his grandmother, had been a physicist. They had a daughter named Gabriela. Perhaps because of Ira's affiliation with the *Foundation*, he became one of the first targets of the Gestapo. The family fled Poland, and Ira became a resistance fighter. Ingrid and their daughter went into hiding. Ingrid was eventually captured and sent to a concentration camp. The daughter, at first hidden by relatives and friends, disappeared. During the years of confusion that marked the Holocaust, the *Foundation* lost track of the little girl. They did not pick up her trail again until years later, when she surfaced in America. Having spent her early years moving from hiding place to hiding place in Europe, she ended up in a detention camp in Cyprus. After the war, like many orphans, Gabriela got sent to Israel and from there, to America.

Chris experienced an immeasurable sense of grief at learning of the tragic life of his mother. The picture of the teenage couple was taken at a Jewish youth dance. The boy, most likely his father, was not mentioned again. Gabriela, an unwed teenager, placed her baby for adoption and died shortly after childbirth from complications resulting from malnutrition and chronic infection during her early childhood. Gabriela's son was adopted by Dr. and Mrs. Goodman in the United States.

The *Foundation*, having approved the adoption, closed the file. Christian Goodman was placed under the protection of the guardian Zephon.

"The *Foundation's* first and utmost responsibility," one document stated, "has always been the welfare of its members and their offspring, especially those whose lineage goes back to the colonizing period."

Christian Goodman was cataloged as a distant descendant, a *star seed* or offspring of the Edentians. Despite the immense sadness that Chris experienced upon reading the dossier, he also gained a new sense of self. He had finally found his roots.

When he woke up in the morning. The window automatically opened onto a garden; outside it was bright and sunny. The phone rang. He picked it up, hoping for news of Danielle.

"Good morning. This is Cardinal Santis. Did you sleep well?"

"Slept like a log," answered Chris.

"How about some breakfast?"

"Sure. Where are you?"

"When you walk out of your hotel, turn left and go about a hundred feet. You'll see a house with a courtyard and tables. I'll be waiting for you."

"I'm on my way."

Chris cleaned up in a few minutes and hurried down the limestone steps, humming a song. He felt unusually energetic and happy to be alive. He decided to give in to the notion that it was a sunny day. This was, after all, the ultimate high-tech make-believe.

When he came to the courtyard—a popular site for breakfast—Santis waved at him from a center table. After a cordial embrace and upon taking a seat, a tall, beautiful brunette came to greet him. She was casually dressed in cropped cotton pants and a T-shirt, but she was, nonetheless, the waitress.

"Coffee?" she asked, offering a pot in her hand.

He nodded.

"What would you like this morning, Mr. Goodman?"

He liked the personal recognition. "Don't know. May I see a menu?"

"Oh, we don't use menus, but you can order anything you want."

Chris laughed.

"What she means," Santis said, "is that you can have anything you want."

"In that case," Chris added in a droll tone, "make it waffles, fresh raspberries, one egg over easy, potatoes, two slices of bacon, orange juice, toast, with butter and jam."

"Anything else?" she asked, amused.

"That will do for starters."

"OK. Coming right up."

"I was teasing, I'll just have—" corrected Chris, but the girl had already walked away.

"Waitress or goddess?" he asked jokingly. Then, putting the jest aside, Chris asked, "Danielle?"

"She asked me to take you to her after we finish."

An expression of joy registered on Chris's face. "Really? She is OK?"

"You will see for yourself."

The waitress returned with a tray of dishes and began placing them on the table. "Do you want it all at once?" Her tone was still playful.

He shrugged his shoulders. "Why not," he answered.

She continued placing the dishes in front of him.

"You look familiar," said Chris.

"I hear that a lot," she answered, keeping a straight face.

"Really," he insisted. "I've seen you before."

"I certainly hope so. Nineteen films, two Golden Globes, one Palm d'Or, two Academy Award nominations . . ." she said with a pride devoid of arrogance.

"Suzy Lane!" he exclaimed.

She extended her hand. "How do you do, Mr. Goodman?"

"But I know you make twenty million per film. What on earth," he corrected himself, "*under the sea* are you doing serving food?"

She laughed. "Mr. Goodman, you are still so hung up on money!" She turned to Santis.

"Cardinal, may I get you anything else?" He shook his head, thanking her with a smile.

Someone was summoning her from another table, so she turned to go. Chris watched her walk up to a man and embrace him. He knew that face and that walk; it had simply thrown him off to see the movie star here, of all places.

Santis was amused by the incident. "This is the safest place for her right now—too much violence in the States."

"You are right." He suddenly remembered the two flight attendants. Shifting his perspective, he knew immediately who they were. The Chinese twins . . . the Olympic gold medal winners in figure skating.

"This is the way the world was meant to be. Different sensibilities, races, and creeds living in harmony, without conflict."

"But movie stars, famous athletes? Doing menial jobs?"

"And Nobel laureates as chefs," added the cardinal. "Your waffles were prepared by this year's recipient of the Nobel Prize for literature."

"Manuel Ramirez? I'm a genuine fan," said Chris, taking a bite of his waffle. "It's delicious!"

"You'll get to meet him. Look over there at that table. Do you recognize any of them?"

Chris looked at the group engaged in a discussion. He did recognize some faces. They were famous writers, whom he had not seen or heard of for years. Christian's attention shifted to the side entrance. President Parker, followed by his usual entourage of assistants, walked in. He looked relaxed in his golf clothes and smiled generously as he shook several hands and made his way through the garden. Parker was heading toward his table. Both he and the cardinal stood up.

"Good to see you made it! Should have brought you with me the first time," said Parker, extending his hand.

"Mr. President . . ." Chris could not find the words to express how happy he was to see Parker alive.

"No more Mr. President," Parker advised. "David, just David." He turned to Cardinal Santis and took his hand affectionately, then raised it to his lips and kissed it respectfully before sitting down at their table. Chris was touched by the sign of reverence the president showed the cardinal, despite the fact that Santis was wearing ordinary clothes, with no sign of his ecclesiastical position. Parker's assistants dispersed and joined other groups. "Can't get over the fact that you beat me last night. I assumed I was the better chess player," Parker said to the cardinal.

"One must never assume," replied Santis.

"Anyway, I'll pay up," said Parker, extracting a handful of diamonds from his pocket and extending his hand to Santis.

The cardinal selected one and slipped it into his pocket. "As a boy, it used to be marbles. I had an incredible collection. But now, the stones do more good upstairs." He pointed upward, referring to the planet's surface.

Chris was fascinated. As if guessing what he was thinking, Parker added, "Don't think all we do here is play. We work. In fact, I have never worked so hard in my life. But at least here, I go to bed with a feeling of accomplishment, not frustration."

Suzy Lane had returned. Parker got up and embraced her. "I swear, you get prettier every day!"

"What shall I bring you, David?"

"Nothing, thanks. I can't stay. Tell Manuel I'll come back for his lobster in adobo sauce—best thing I've ever eaten! Right now, I've got to meet with Rebecca Meyer, Perez Levi's representative. We've got a tricky situation to solve in Tel Aviv." He turned back to Santis and Chris, "I didn't do so well in picking out my successor, as you well know." Chris was perfectly aware of the shortcomings of Clayton McCann.

"We'll see you at dinner tonight." The president shook Santis's hand again and patted Chris on the shoulder.

"So he continues to carry on his presidential duties," commented Chris in amazement.

"Oh, sure. He says that his term is not over yet. He still has a responsibility and will do his best for the country till the end. He'll do everything in his power to try to save the nation from the spreading darkness."

"What can he do from here?" asked Chris, remembering that things were getting quite desperate throughout the nation.

"Find solutions, make wiser decisions. It really is easier to get things rolling from here."

"That is all fine," said Chris. "Conceptualize for later implementation. But let's face it. The world is desperate for help right now! Have we abandoned our friends and families to the pernicious terror overtaking their lives?"

"It may seem that way, but it is not so. In this little paradise, we all make a difference. Our positive vibrations and unwillingness to yield to dark forces crystallize with the meditations of the elders in the pyramid and are carried up to the surface where they will counteract the negative."

"And you? Will you be going back to Rome?"

"I am not sure. My presence at the Vatican right now only endangers the lives of those close to me who back up my policies."

Chris remembered the draft he had seen—the list of recommended advances and changes—the document that had sealed the pontiff's fate.

"I have recommended that you be allowed to see 'The Manuscript.' I believe you are the chosen one. 'The Manuscript' will not be given to the world for another millennium. Your interpretation is all the world will get for now." Without giving any further explanation, Santis stood up. "If you have finished, we can go. You must be anxious to see Danielle, and I would like to show you something."

The meadows were thick and deep green, and the water in the lake was a rich turquoise. Santis walked in silence, letting Chris absorb the beauty of the scenery while they made their way to the building where Danielle awaited them. Chris looked into the distance and could not help asking, "How large is this place?"

"Not as large as it seems," responded the cardinal. "I guess the entire complex is no larger than two miles in diameter." Santis pointed to the building. "We are here."

"Treasures" was carved on a plate on the door.

The word *treasures* invoked in Chris mental images of coffers laden with gold and precious stones, but instead, Christian walked into a gallery covered with paintings. Santis walked up to a fragment of a large fresco and said proudly, "*The Angel Musician*, by Melozzo Da Forli, executed in 1480." Chris understood. His eyes had also found one of the pieces he had been sent to purchase.

"How did you know of the terrorists' plans to blow up the repositories of these works?"

"The *Foundation* guessed. When there is a plot to subjugate a civilization, the first offense is aimed at its art and literature. The *Foundation* was not going to allow these works of gifted artists and writers to be destroyed. It is, after all, they who are the dream makers; without them, our civilization would perish."

"The books?"

"They are all here. There is a copy of every single book that was destroyed in the Library of Congress or set aflame by the henchmen of that madman Edwards." After a pause, he added, "Well, we must really get going. You'll have plenty of time to inspect it all."

XXXVI

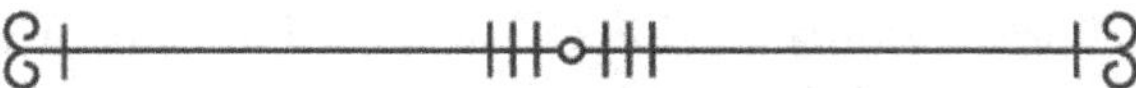

A "Temple of Health" did not in any way resemble a hospital. Chris had the impression of entering the cozy lobby of a five-star hotel. A harpist strummed soothing melodies to the delight of listeners relaxing in comfortable sofas grouped throughout the space.

John Larkin stood up and walked to greet Chris and the cardinal. Chris's eyes went straight to the sofa where Danielle was sitting with Angela. He barely shook hands with John but walked directly to Danielle, who stood up and took him in her arms.

"Thank you," she whispered. Reluctantly, he released her. She stepped back and sat down again.

"You must have things to discuss," said the cardinal. "We'll leave and meet again for dinner."

Danielle smiled at his tact. Chris barely heard the words; he was staring at Danielle, who was dressed in a simple white tunic. It was then he realized that she seemed frail, her skin pale and her jade eyes just a shade less brilliant.

"Danielle," he said, with a throbbing pain in his chest.

She knew that he understood. "This body has taken quite a beating." Then, to alleviate the fear in his eyes, she continued, "but I am not ready to shed it yet."

He took her in his arms again. "You can't! What would we do without you?"

She smiled kindly. She liked the way he had said *we* and not *I*.

"I still have trouble sorting out what is real," said Chris. "I had a beautiful dream."

She removed herself from his embrace and looked directly into his eyes. "And that is what it should remain, nothing but a dream."

"But—"

Danielle put her fingers to his lips to prevent him from continuing. "Christian, you are the future. You will accomplish—finalize—what we, the Edentians, started. You and those like you will make Earth what it was intended to be. You will find the right mate, and your descendants will inhabit a better place. If we get through the present darkness, the way will be paved for the next leap of consciousness in the human race. That is why I pled before the Council of the Most High to let you retain your right to choose. We must conclude our mission successfully.

"Danielle, things are so bad out there, and I left Kitzia alone. She wanted to come, and I prevented her. Had she come, she would now be safe. I continue to make the wrong decisions."

"It was not your decision at all. Deep down, she knows her place is out there, where she can be of service."

Danielle stared at Chris. "You love her."

Chris hesitated. *How silly that confession would ring in Danielle's ears. Not that long ago, I was professing my love for her.*

Danielle took his hand, letting him know she understood.

"You once told me that what I envisioned about you and me could never be," said Chris. "I must have seemed quite foolish to you. I was reaching for the stars."

"No, never foolish. I was very flattered by your affection, misguided though it was."

"I do love you."

"I know. But I also said to you once that we were different and had to eventually realign ourselves with those of our kind—with our soul groups. I think you can comprehend that now."

"I can. You knew . . . you always knew about Kit and me."

"I knew the moment I saw you that you two were of the same vibration and physiological make-up. My greatest joy would be to see the two of you walk the path of life together."

"I will always take care of Kit." Still looking into her eyes, he said, "Danielle, in my human and most imperfect way, I do love you and always will."

Danielle understood his feelings perfectly, even better than Chris did. "Do you want to know what I was thinking during my darkest moments, while trapped in the warp?" she asked him. "I had loved two men, and it seemed that in both instances, I had made errors in judgment. I had robbed my best friend of the love that should have been only hers and had not been able to save the other one from the enemy's grasp. I began to question the ability of love to triumph. But I was wrong. Both of you risked your lives to save me."

At that moment, Chris realized the figure holding up the arch to allow him through was none other than Robert Powers.

She touched his cheek. "Both of you have restored my vision and revitalized my faith. When I return home to Edentia, I can do so with pride, comforted to know that you will be fine and that Robert is with us. Kjell and I must now begin to prepare for our departure."

"Where and how is Kjell?"

"Doing well—much better than I am. He has been in conference with the elders." She stood up and took his hand. "There is still so much you have to see; I don't even know where to start."

They headed for the door. A woman with short silver hair, dressed in a tailored white pantsuit, intercepted them and handed Danielle a pill and a glass of water. Danielle took the medication from the nurse, and left the temple, holding Chris' arm.

They began walking past his lodgings and onto a path at the edge of a golf course. In the distance were multi-colored carts and players engaged in the game. Joggers dashed past them. "Will I be able to communicate with Kit?" asked Chris. "I promised I'd try."

"We are trying to open some channels, but we are reluctant to leave the channels open for two-way communication. Would it at least appease you to see that she is OK?"

"Yes, of course."

"Then let's do that first."

She guided him off the track, and, after crossing the street, they entered an unmarked building with a small reception room, its walls lined with master paintings; a soft piano concerto played in the background. *How glorious to exist surrounded by art and music*, Chris thought.

The receptionist looked up from the desk. "Danielle, I have a channel open for Mr. Goodman. Take booth number four."

There was no need for introductions. Everyone seemed to know who Chris was. Danielle opened the door, and they went into the narrow booth with a screen on the wall and an oblong table with a surface keypad. Danielle entered coordinates, time zones, and a series of numbers. The screen asked for depth level, resolution, resonance, and manometer type. When the codes had been entered, the screen produced an image of the area outside the Peschard estate. Danielle entered more digits, and the screen became a video camera, which she maneuvered through the house, past the living areas, halls, and kitchen to the wine cellar. It slowed when she encountered the house staff and Deborah writing something on a notepad. They stood in front of an underground cellar. Kitzia appeared, wearing blue jeans and a T-shirt. Taking the flashlight from Mai Li and followed by the staff, she led the way into the underground room.

"She has found it!" Danielle exclaimed with satisfaction. The camera followed them. It was an enormous room with small, furnished cubicles. Kitzia discovered doors that led to more rooms stocked with supplies, food, and bottled water.

Another room was equipped with large freezers, microwaves, and another type of appliance that Kit and the staff were having trouble identifying.

"Hydroponics tanks," offered Danielle, "to grow vegetables and fruit."

"It's a nuclear shelter!" exclaimed Chris.

"Yes, if the need arises," said Danielle.

The camera continued following Kit and her staff, while Chris and Danielle watched them in silence. The group came across a series of huge water tanks. Kit had grasped that those were intended to be fish farms in times of famine.

"I feel somehow that I should be there with her."

"Zephon will return to her side soon. You are here to gather information and continue your writing, and very soon, I will want you to travel with me to Mexico to help me retrieve one of the stones."

"Are you up to it?" Chris asked.

"I can do it if you are with me. Now let's see if we can get a visual of Jean-Christophe." She entered another set of numbers into the keypad. Within seconds, the screen transported them to the Valley of the Kings. The camera located the Frenchman, alone in the dark cave as he made himself ready to make his descent into the underground tombs, checking his rope and equipment by flashlight. He had located the place where the ground had collapsed during his earlier exploration. He positioned his infrared goggles and began to descend. The camera dropped precipitously as he sent it in ahead of him, dispelling the illusion that the ground was solid. Danielle spotted the medians waiting and ready to assist him. Because of their translucence, Chris could barely make them out. Danielle typed in more numbers to move the camera up to ground level and found what she suspected: a group of men in combat gear scouting out the area. They were walking around tomb KV5 with electronic equipment and metal detectors and were closing in on the opening occupied by Jean-Christophe.

"Looking for the same thing?" inquired Chris.

"I am afraid so," answered Danielle. "Jean-Christophe doesn't have much time. He has to find the headpiece and recover the stone with all haste. Then the medians must move the monolith to a place where we can take hold of it." She once again scanned the area where Jean-Christophe had gone in. It now looked solid and undisturbed. The medians had sealed it permanently. Danielle and Chris watched as two men arrived on the scene. Seeing no opening into the tomb, they positioned a few metal boxes on the ground and proceeded to program them electronically.

"What are they doing?" asked Chris.

"They are going to blow up the area."

The bomb went off, shredding tons of rock and debris over the entrance to the cave. The camera followed as Jean-Christophe arrived safely at his destination, and Danielle turned the screen off. "He is OK for the moment; but has to move quickly. Let me catch up with some of the world news." She typed almost as fast as the screen shifted. Apparently, a few seconds of each situation was all she needed. Chris caught glimpses of suicide bombings and retaliatory attacks in the Middle East, aerial attacks in Ukraine, demonstrations in Paris, Neo-Nazi marches in Germany, and the slaughtering of cattle in Europe. She slowed down for the BBC broadcasts. Images alternated from reporters in London to cardinals in the Vatican, and to scholars in Oxford, then back to reporters.

Danielle explained the reports. "An ancient papyrus has been found during the renovation of an underground cellar in an abbey. It prophesies the coming of a second messiah in the distant future, a man, who will be named Theodorus, or perhaps Eduardus."

"A fake!" said Chris as he noticed the smile on her face.

"Of course," she responded.

Danielle switched to American television news, where an interview with Theodore Edwards was in progress. The preacher had changed his image drastically, having adopted a new form of dress—a loose, white linen shirt with an open collar. His diction had also undergone a transformation, and both appearance and speech were an all too obvious attempt at portraying himself in the likeness of Jesus. It was a worldwide broadcast, with hundreds of flashes popping in Theodore's face. He wore his new humility with a self-righteous air, his fingers interlaced as if in prayer, and he responded with feigned religious fervor to the questions of the multitudes.

The lack of audio did not prevent Chris from guessing at the preacher's responses. The bowing of the head and periodic elevation of his clasped hands spoke louder than words.

Danielle switched the channel and moved the camera as fast as could to prevent Chris from seeing the worsening state of affairs in the US.

"What will happen now?" he asked.

"He'll be elected," she answered calmly. "Edwards shows support for people of all creeds and races. Let him play out his drama. We must start preparing for the *Formation*. Unfortunately, due to my state of health, I must take long rests."

"I'll take you back."

"I can manage. Keep exploring. All that exists here is at your disposal. We want you to take a wealth of information back with you."

When they stepped out of the cubicle, the receptionist came to them. "It has all been set. 'The Manuscript' is being prepared for viewing."

She turned to Chris. "You will soon have the knowledge of your universe in your hands. Once you begin, you will not wish to stop. So I suggest you use the rest of the day to visit the galleries, archives, laboratories, and universities. There are some spectacular things going on."

"May I call for an escort?" inquired the receptionist, suspecting Danielle was not well.

"No, I need the exercise," answered Danielle, regaining her smile. She kissed Chris on the cheek when they were outside. "See you tonight for dinner. You'll meet some of the elders, as well as the new head of the *Foundation*, who, by the way, is most anxious to see you again."

"Again? I've never met—"

"You have; you just didn't know it." She started to walk in the direction of the Temple of Health.

After walking the streets and paths for a while to grasp the configuration of the complex, Chris went into the different buildings. Most were no more than two stories high, but all were occupied and functional. He visited different laboratories and came across the one that manufactured the wafers Tom had sent. He found out that, aside from the abundant seafood and fresh hydroponic fruits and vegetables, the rest of the food prepared in the restaurants and resembled meat was no more than a variation of a certain type of seaweed in different textures. He visited the desalination plant and the university, to which many of the great scholars of the world had returned. At the astronomy institute, he caught a glimpse of the power of the Edenic currents. He observed the visual re-enactment of the energy streaks and listened to the scientists explain the power of such phenomena.

At the University of Theology, he had the opportunity to listen to the debates about the ongoing trial of Luciel versus Gabriel. The arch-rebel stated that his complaint was never with Michael, the Creator Son; what Luciel questioned was the right of the Almighty to retain total control of the galaxies.

The unanimous belief was that such a concept was rooted in treason, and the debate was focused on analyzing the circumstances that created the resentment toward the Almighty and led to Luciel's abdication. *Had Luciel ever seen God?* was a point of heated discussion. Some scholars felt he had, which made the treason all the more vile, for Luciel stated that the Almighty did not exist but continued to be a fabrication of the universal Fathers. Others felt Luciel had probably never seen Him. It was the questioning of the existence of the Almighty that had been one of the primary catalysts for the rebellion.

The name of the traitor, Cirel, came up. They spoke of his fury and the destruction he was implementing, the likes of which had seldom been seen in any galaxy. They called him the mad arch-rebel, for only a crazy being would wish to spread such destruction.

As soon as a guilty verdict for Luciel was passed down, all of his associates and supporters would be tracked down, apprehended, and brought back to one of the celestial courts for trial.

Of everything Chris saw or heard that day, those debates would remain forever ingrained in his mind, giving him a grasp of the feeling that prevailed in the universe.

The tuxedo fit Chris perfectly. When he had returned to his room, he'd found it lying on his bed, along with everything else he would need for the evening. There was an invitation from the elders and the head of the *Foundation* to a cocktail dinner party that would be held that evening in his honor. It included directions and a time.

Since it was already getting dark, Chris quickly showered, dressed, and headed out. In his excitement, the exhaustion from the day's activities faded. Out of the hundreds of black-tie dinner parties he had attended, none had ever been given in his honor, and the gesture touched him deeply.

It was the only house on the block that twinkled in the night. The trees sparkled with hundreds of tiny blinking lights. The other guests had already arrived. The rooms were lively with music and laughter. A piano was playing a beautiful melody by Liszt, which he had always loved. He reveled in the music for a few seconds before the door opened and Suzy Lane came out to welcome him, done up in all her Hollywood glamour. After kissing him lightly on both cheeks, she took his arm and escorted him inside to join the party.

Everyone turned to see them come in and smiled in greeting. Chris recalled the party given for Jean-Christophe at the Peschard estate, in honor of his discovery in Egypt. He saw many of the same faces again gathered in one room. He caught sight of Cardinal Santis, President Parker, John, Angela, Zephon and Camiel, whom he had not seen since they flew together on Air Force One.

In the center of the room stood four of the elders, two of them wearing white tunics and gold girdles. Kjell, looking as strong and formidable as he had during their Roman adventure and a small, gray-haired woman—who looked faintly familiar—and Danielle were there. Beautiful Danielle. Tonight, she looked stronger and more rested than she had that morning, yet Chris was troubled to notice the signs that told him the spark of life was fading from her eyes.

Danielle walked toward him and, taking him from Suzy's arm, guided him over to introduce him to the elders, representatives of the Council of Edentia, and to the new head of the *Foundation*, the woman who had assumed the position after the departure of His Holiness. Chris recognized the lovely Martine from the Auberge St. Michel, the one who had prepared the delicious paupiettes. The memory made him feel less intimidated by her presence, and he took her hand and raised it to his lips.

He recognized some of the other guests too—the young assistants who had traveled with David Parker on Air Force One, as well as Mark Ferguson, the military advisor to the president. He spotted Manuel Ramirez, Poet Laureate, Marina Cantrelli, and some of the other doctors and technicians from the Vatican gardens.

The room was not large, for the group was select and intimate. Only Kit was missing, thought Chris with regret. On the walls were more of the art masterpieces that had been spirited out of the US. One buffet table was masterfully decorated in a Poseidon theme; another table displayed a seven-tier cake adorned with flowers and exotic fruits. Not until that moment did Chris remember that today was his birthday. Once again, he wished for Kit.

The elders thanked him for his extreme efforts on their behalf and for his dedication to their cause. Martine expressed her joy that he had become part of the *Foundation*. Kjell embraced him in gratitude and whispered, "I won't forget it." Manuel Ramirez, the writer Chris much admired, congratulated him on his forthcoming book.

After a couple of glasses of champagne, Chris felt a little lightheaded.

"Alcohol does the same thing here as when you are flying. Perhaps you should slow down," said Danielle, who had now separated from the others.

His eyes fell upon a sculpture he had not seen when he'd entered the room. He approached it, not understanding how he could have missed this glorious piece—modern, minimal, and perfect.

The translucent sphere contained a pristine cube of what appeared to be clear-cut crystal that shone with the brilliance of a diamond and rested on a quartz pedestal.

"'The Manuscript' . . ." said Danielle. Chris did not understand.

Martine approached them. "An attestation to our existence, our civilization, and how we've been cataloged in the celestial archives."

Chris stared at the sphere, still not understanding.

Martine continued, "Recorded in this sphere is our entire history, from the moment the life carriers granted authorization for the implementation of life on Earth. While it has shown us the guidelines the Celestials set down for our existence, it has also encoded our recorded experiences. It is the compilation of every phase of the Urantia 606 project up to this day. It holds the records of every triumph and downfall of our evolution."

The others had been listening to Martine, and as she finished speaking, one of the elders stepped forward and addressed Chris. "It is with great honor, Christian, that the *Foundation* of Urantia bestows upon you the rarest of gifts. Today, on your forty-second birthday, we present to you the key that opens 'The Manuscript,' a repository of all knowledge and wisdom gained since the beginning of time." The elder took Chris's hand and placed it between his palms. "It was written by the Celestials and handed to us to serve as a blueprint for life and as a map to get back home."

When the elder released his hand, Chris saw the imprint of a symbol on his palm. "In the distant past, 'The Manuscript' was given to other civilizations for the advancement of the human race. But it was misused. Therefore, the Edentian Council advised that we withhold 'The Manuscript.' Today, you will be permitted to see this information, and in time, disclose it to the world in whatever manner you see fit."

Danielle took his hand and placed it on the sphere. At the touch of his palm, the sphere opened. Like the petals of a flower, it fell away to allow the crystal cube to rise and rotate. Everyone stood in awe at the revolving crystalline cube.

"It's very simple to retrieve its data once it is open," said Danielle. "Ask any question."

A large abstract painting had risen to disappear into the ceiling, giving way to a large screen. Simultaneously, wall panels slid away to expose a complex set of electronics that Chris found easily identifiable, although in comparison to the highly sophisticated technology he had seen in other parts of the complex, these seemed almost primitive.

"We have arranged this house to be a workplace for you, where you can do research and write. We have procured computers, copying machines, and other equipment familiar to you. 'The Manuscript' is composed of infinitesimal sheets of light that will open at your command. You have also been chosen to record the events in your world that will close and seal this stage of man's evolution."

Chris was overwhelmed.

"When such time comes, they will be entered by one of the messengers and become a permanent part of 'The Manuscript.' Your contribution will look like one of those tiny bubbles floating on the surface."

Chris had not noticed them until now.

"Let's try it," she said. "What would you like to know?"

Thousands of questions popped into his mind. However, there was one that he wanted most to have explained to him in full. He asked, "Who are the Edentians?"

XXXVII

"The Edentians are the connection between the higher order of celestial beings and mortals. They inhabit the largest of the translucent spheres in the constellation of Norlatiadek, a system of Satania in the local Universe of Nebadon—a world one hundred times larger than Earth and the seat of the Constellation's government. Edentia is considered a training ground. The Seraphim, the third order of angels of the local universe, is assigned to its service.

"Edentia is almost perfect in every way; it abounds in fascinating highlands with thousands of sparkling lakes and connecting streams. The luminous crystal sea, an enormous body of sparkling water, is used as the landing and departing field for all seraphic transports.

"The Edentians assist the life carriers in the advancement of newly created life forms in various galaxies. The Edentians are also called the "Immortals," for they were the first race of evolved beings in the history of the universe to achieve that status—as opposed to other forms of celestial beings that had been created with the legacy of immortality. Although the Edentians are immortal, their offspring born on an evolutionary planet are not. Edentians have a full understanding of the trials and tribulations of the human race, for they had seen it emerge and thrive from its beginning stages.

"Project Urantia 606, established to oversee and foster life on planet Earth, was assigned to Orsef—an illustrious member of the Edentian Council of Sages. Thus began the advancement and modification of life on the planet. The planet was still in its prehistoric stages—having just completed its era of extreme polar shifts. The land masses had reached a degree of stability; vegetation was flourishing, and its higher life forms had reached human status.

"Orsef accompanied the life carriers and, after a thorough inspection of the planet and an analysis of the mental evolution of its inhabitants, submitted a recommendation to the Council of the Most High, requesting permission to accelerate evolution. A planetary prince was sent to monitor the planet, while Orsef and his staff back in Edentia continued to engineer the direction of the evolution of Urantia.

"The next step was to find the pair of biological uplifters, who, together with the ruling planetary prince, were to remain on the planet throughout the primary evolutionary stages and foster its development. When the planet attained Stage V, they would depart, leaving a planet to choose its own path and write its own destiny.

"Orsef assembled the most brilliant of the Edentian candidates for the mission. The Lucifer rebellion continued to flare up among the galaxies. At this inopportune time, Edentia received news that Urantia's planetary prince had allied himself to the rebellion. Labeled a rebel planet, Urantia was cut off from the celestial communication network.

"Orsef pleaded with the Most High of Edentia for permission to go forward with the colonization project. He considered the mission the most challenging adventure ever undertaken: the colonization and re-conditioning of a fallen planet.

"Adam and Eva were chosen as magisterial parents. One hundred Edentians accompanied them. Orsef designated Kjell, a formidable engineer and architect, to design and construct The Garden of Eden—a close replica of Edentia. Kjell brought with him the *Tree of Life* and planted it in the garden. He also brought with him the first monolith to establish direct communication with Edentia.

"Next, Orsef chose Trebor for his outstanding organizational skills to design the social and economic structure under which the newly populated planet was to function.

"Lilith was chosen to act as liaison between the Edentians and groups of volunteers coming from neighboring galaxies to assist in the Edenic Mission for rehabilitation. This was the beginning of her association with Cirel of Brann.

"Daniela was the youngest of the six major Edentians that were to head the Urantia 606 project. She was to act as a monitor and recorder. She began her assignment by observing the planet from a neighboring satellite and forwarded periodic reports to the celestial archives.

"When Adam and Eva arrived on Urantia, they were shocked to find that outside their garden, the condition of the planet was quite primitive. Eva had brought with her the sphere containing 'The Manuscript' with detailed instructions and set out to rehabilitate and uplift the fallen souls they had been sent to save.

"Conditions improved somewhat, but the results were minimal.

"Eva bypassed many of the steps outlined in 'The Manuscript' and began a widespread program of genetic acceleration. Within a short time, the negative effects of such tampering became clear. The magisterial parents were charged with default and instructed to remain on the planet until a time of dispensation was issued." *(The Urantia Book)*

Chris continued his learning and discovered that when the time came for their departure, a large seraphic transport arrived to take Adam and Eva, uplifters of the human race, back to their planet of citizenship. Along with them, they took souls that had been reconditioned and returned to grace. The rest of the Edentian team chose to continue with their assignments.

In time, Trebor and Lilith disassociated from the mission and chose to make the planet their temporary home.

Christian stopped reading after finishing the early accounts of the Edentians. He tried to imagine Danielle during the time of the planetary events she had witnessed and the ones in which she had perhaps participated. He tried to imagine Lili as she had once been. Surely, somewhere within her, she had retained some of the inherent brilliance that had been hers before the mission.

There was so much he wanted to share with Kitzia.

XXXVIII

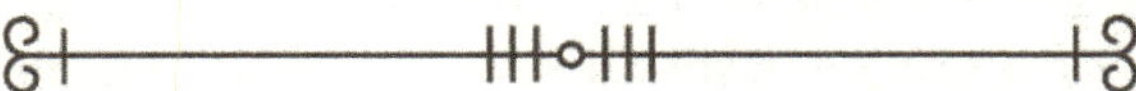

Washington, DC

The town car stopped in front of a brownstone on one of the most affluent streets in Georgetown. Lili Keller stepped out of the car, not waiting for her chauffeur to open the door for her. She tried to avoid the two vagrants sleeping on the sidewalk. One of them opened his eyes and reached out to grab at her sable coat. Whether out of sympathy or disgust, she opened her purse and threw a handful of money at him. She rang the doorbell, her annoyance increasing with each second she had to wait. She watched the two vagrants wrestling on the sidewalk for the bills.

When the uniformed housekeeper opened the door, Lili pushed her aside and stormed into the house. The housekeeper tried to regain her balance before she spoke. "The Senator is not—"

Lili did not let her finish. "Where is Edwards?"

"The Reverend Edwards is in the library, but he asked not to be distur—"

Lili headed for the library and shoved the wood-paneled door open. Theodore Edwards had heard the commotion but had not stirred from his seat behind Nielsen's desk. He feigned surprise to see Lili entering the room.

"Lili, my dear. What on earth are you doing here?"

"You know perfectly well what I'm doing here, you piece of garbage!"

"You seem upset. Sit down; let me order some tea." Edwards started to ring the intercom but changed his mind. Lili remained standing, looking at him defiantly. "You should have called," he said, "It's probably not a good idea for you to be seen here, with the reporters and all."

Lili had begun to calm down. Seeing the transformation in her onetime lover amused her infinitely. Edwards's arrogance led him to believe that it was the tone of his voice that had calmed her mood. Lili's anger was overtaken by a fit of laughter. After a few moments, she regained control, took off her coat, and tossed it over a chair before dropping onto the sofa.

"That is good . . . very good," she said, pointing to his robes. She still couldn't stop laughing.

Theodore began to feel uncomfortable. "I was saying that it would not be favorable for either one of us if the reporters saw us together." His tone was serious. "It would mar the image that—"

"The image they have created for you, that pathetic, ridiculous image that fits you so well! Look at yourself in the mirror, you stupid fool! I helped put you where you are, and now you turn on me like the double-crossing louse that you are."

"No, I have never turned on you, my dear. I am following the instructions outlined for me during Phase II."

"Not minding if I get crushed in the process. You have destroyed my business! Do you have any idea how long it took to build the empire I had? You stupid, pompous puppet."

"If you are referring to the cosmetics business, I thought you were in agreement that it had to be phased out."

"I said I would do it in my time and on my terms. The way you spoke against the industry, knowing perfectly well I was the principal manufacturer in the country. You knew that whatever actions were taken would be aimed at me . . . and yet you didn't care. My factories were bombed by the militia that calls itself your avenging army, and you didn't even warn me!"

Not knowing what else to say, Edwards added, "You know there was no way to save the cosmetics companies when their existence interfered with our ideology. We wanted you to retain the clothing industry, though."

"The sacks of burned denim! I gave you that look to place you in power. What made you think I'd permanently trade my fashion empire for that garbage? You know what, Ted? I was a fool but not nearly as big a fool as you are. You think you have gotten so big that even I can't taint your image? You think Cirel is impressed with you? He must despise you. He must laugh at you, as we all have . . . yes, I, Nielsen, and the others. Or were you really stupid enough to think that I would fall for someone like you? You clown! That is what we used to call you . . . the evangelist clown, the-catch-the-fish clown, the get-on-the-circus-bus clown, the chairman-of-the-church-clown!"

Theodore Edwards had never hit a woman, but as the anger rose in him, he involuntarily raised his hand to her. Lili blocked it, sending the six-foot-two man flying across the room.

Edwards staggered against a wall in utter shock at the force with which the slender woman had struck him.

"If you have an ounce of brain left in that big hollow head of yours, you would run while you can because, before you know it, you will have sacrificed what's left to this absurd cause."

Something in Lili's voice alarmed Edwards more than her actual words. Her tone of voice and the bitter twist of her lips had revealed in no uncertain terms her contempt for Cirel, for whom he had developed a deep admiration.

Theodore regained his balance and tried hard to reclaim his composure. Lili was putting on her coat. She took a compact out of her bag to check her appearance before departing. Despite the ugliness of the scene and her insults, Edwards did not want her to go. He knew he would not see her again and suddenly yearned for her body.

"I can understand that you are angry," he said. "Giving up material possessions is not easy. But when we enter Phase III, we will all have to do it. The promises that have been made reach a much more elevated level than the material things of this world."

"Promises?" asked Lili before walking out the door. "You think Cirel will keep his promises? What were they . . . kingdoms, power, immortality?"

"Precisely," answered Edwards.

"What do you know of immortality? Cirel will dispose of you as soon as you have accomplished what he wants."

"You don't understand, Lili. Whatever promises come from him really proceed from a higher power."

Lili looked at him with scorn, then turned to go. "You are a fool, Edwards—a vain, stupid fool."

Africa

The jungle was dense and rich with foliage. The few outsiders that had ever reached this spot had been greeted by the lethal pang of a poisoned lance. The tribe did what they were supposed to do—what they had been doing for generations, what they had been ordered by the elders of the tribe to do.

The members of the small tribe of displaced Zulus had long ago been designated as keepers of the *Tree* and had been watching over that tree for as long as they could remember. The natives were not to leave their tiny village or fraternize with other tribes, for they were never to disclose the existence of the *Tree*. That was how it had always been, and no one questioned why.

About once a year, the representative of the gods, the man with the white skin and pale blue eyes, came and took cuttings from the *Tree*. He would give them gifts and assure them of the continuing protection of the gods, as long as the tribe continued to be vigilant in protection of the *Tree*.

This time, the white man came, but he was accompanied by others. The men brought giant equipment—great machines the tribe could never have imagined, machines that made loud noises. The members of the tribe were terrified.

They hid in the jungle and watched as Cirel directed the engineers in positioning posts within a ten-foot radius around the *Tree*. Arborists were on hand to make sure the roots were not disturbed when they sliced into the ground to ready it for removal. The small tree, no more than seven feet tall and looking more like a bush than a tree, was to be lifted from the earth and transferred with extreme care into a climate-controlled box that would be airlifted from the jungle. The men synchronized their efforts and moved on cue.

The earth around the *Tree* was cut, and the *Tree* was prepared for transfer. Cirel, standing nearby, held a pistol in his hand and advised the team that he would fire the weapon at the precise moment the *Tree* had been hoisted and was ready to be placed in the box. The tribe crept in from the jungle and gathered in a tight circle, and the children cried upon seeing the sacred tree being uprooted from their village.

Cirel fired into the sky; his team quickly slipped the *Tree* into the waiting box, and misters sprayed its foliage. Suddenly, a blinding burst of light exploded from the center of the *Tree*, glowed blood red, then slowly extinguished like dying embers as its leaves withered and turned brown.

"NO!!!" screamed Cirel. His voice pierced the jungle, echoing among the hills, finally muffled to death by the thick foliage. The sound of his pistol burst through the stunned silence as he feverishly fired at everything and everyone in sight, killing not only the natives but also shooting down the men he had brought with him. Only the flapping wings of frightened jungle birds were left to be heard.

Egypt

The presence of the medians once again created a dream-like reality for Jean-Christophe, but now, aware of who they were, he was not intimidated. The archeologist could see their silhouettes perfectly and all but forgot about their insubstantial makeup until he tried to pat one of them on the back. His hand passed right through Ka's diaphanous form.

Ka and Elan laughed, and Jean-Christophe chuckled with them. He finished removing his gear before he looked around. He had arrived at the depth of the tomb he had reached on his last trip, but the atmosphere had changed. The chambers and passages were now open but still lit with the torches bearing the cool, bluish fire. But there were piles of ashes and rubble everywhere now.

Before Jean-Christophe asked, Elan volunteered, "We are being evicted."

The Frenchman looked at Ka. "We told you before that the others had found us," the Median replied. "They have been back, looking for the same thing you are after. It's a good thing you came now. We would not be able to put them off much longer. They know the chamber is here, and since we won't give them the code, nor access to our library, they're going to blow us out. That's why we have been busy destroying our records."

"If you make it out," Elan told Jean-Christophe, "we'll send something with you to take to the *Foundation*."

"Where will you two be going?" asked the archeologist. "Why don't you come with me?"

"Thank you for the gracious invitation," said Elan. "But unfortunately, we can't accept. We could not exist on the outside—not with the current conditions of your atmosphere. We were assigned to guard the records and the chambers and have done so faithfully for a long time. I think the time has come to relinquish our post. We were simply waiting for you to return and for our passports to come in. You see, we are finally going home."

They heard a thunderous explosion high above them, and Ka and Elan looked at each other with disgust. Turning back to Jean-Christophe, Ka said, "Brutes! There is no other way to describe them. They have no compunction about destroying the relics that speak of the thousands of years of your recorded history." The Median waved his hand in the air, and a vision of what was taking place above them became visible.

The men on the surface continued to set dynamite and blow up the recently discovered tombs. Jean-Christophe watched them move deeper into the tunnels of the tombs that would lead them to the chambers of the pharaoh's daughters.

"We are going to be buried alive!" exclaimed Jean-Christophe.

"Not if we hurry," said Ka, motioning him to follow while he and Elan rushed in a childlike trot down a hallway. "We decided to help you. You have the insignia, and we saw your name."

The archeologist, being so much taller than the medians, was having trouble getting through the narrow corridors with their low ceilings. And he couldn't understand what they were saying. They reached the halls the archeologist had crawled through when his ankle was broken in the fall and entered a spacious room. There were several bonfires blazing with blue flames, dissolving the metal sheets that once had constituted the medians' libraries.

"But that was the most valuable of information!" exclaimed Jean-Christophe.

"We know, but we don't need it anymore. We are finally going home."

"When . . . how?" Jean-Christophe wanted to know.

"There is a conveyance preparing for our departure. At the time of the *Formation*, we will be able to advise the carriers that we are ready to leave. It is crucial to us the *Formation* takes place," continued Ka. "So we have gone ahead and cleared the way for you to enter the chamber of Sharah."

The archeologist was still aghast at the abundance of information that would be lost forever. "But your library . . . I wish I had had the opportunity to—"

The echo of another explosion resonated in the distance.

"What is it you wish to know?" asked Elan.

"You just mentioned something about my name," said the Frenchman.

"When we cut into the monolith, we saw your name and knew you were the one, the only one, who could enter the chamber, and you will have enough insight to figure out the proper exit."

"Me?" asked Jean-Christophe, astonished.

"Yes, you are of the star seed."

Despite the echo of continuous explosions, the archeologist had to know more. "There are a million questions I could ask."

"We can only answer a few," said Ka, taking the Frenchman literally.

Any other time, Jean-Christophe would have laughed. Instead, he said, "The monolith . . . I was instructed to ask you to move it to a place—"

"It is already done," said Elan, becoming increasingly agitated by the continual shaking of the ground above. "We have cut out the center where the heart piece is, where you must insert the disk and stones."

Not having seen the famous monolith, Jean-Christophe had trouble following what the Median was saying.

"Think of the monolith as one of your present-day computers," said Ka. "Equivalent to the hard drive and motherboard. The stones will make the monolith functional and capable of interstellar communication. Each tiny part is essential to establish contact."

"And you say I am of the star seed? *Q'est-ce que c'est* [what exactly does that mean]?"

"It means you can enter other dimensions. You are one of the elite few who accept the existence of the collective consciousness and ultimately acknowledge its absence of ego. But you really must get going if you are to retrieve the piece from the chamber and get out of here alive. We have precious little time to give you instructions. We trust you will rely on your intuition and remember all that Daniela has taught you."

"We will use the last of our resources to beam you up to the level of the chamber."

"Up?" asked Jean-Christophe in surprise.

"Yes, up. It is very hard to explain. You will enter the invisible pyramid. Be wise and careful of your every move and thought. Once in the chamber, take what you came to get and nothing else. Then you must use your wits to find your way out."

"Our thoughts will be with you every step of the way. It may not be an easy journey. You will most likely have to face the Dragon."

Something in the air was changing and making it difficult to breathe. Jean-Christophe began to cough.

"Ready?" Ka asked, ignoring the Frenchman's cough.

Jean-Christophe had no choice but to nod in affirmation.

"Goodbye, my friend. We are counting on you; without you, the *Formation* cannot take place. Remember that when you encounter the Dragon," said Elan.

Ka waved to him and produced a vapor that lifted him upward. When the mist evaporated, he found himself in a dark hall and turned on his flashlight to see what was in front of him—nothing but the dark tunnel itself.

He walked straight ahead for what seemed like endless minutes until he came to a turn that opened into a wider passage. He continued walking forward. He felt something running down his nose and used his sleeve to wipe it away. When he put the flashlight to it, he realized it was blood. He could not get rid of the sporadic cough, and he began to feel dizzy. For the first time that he could remember, Jean-Christophe felt true fear. He questioned his decision to pursue this quest. He could hardly breathe and thought he would surely die of suffocation before he reached the chamber. He felt his skin tighten across his body, a feeling he had never experienced, even during his travels in the searing heat of the desert. He was aware that gas in the tunnel was playing havoc with his system. He glanced at the tightening skin on his hands and wrists and stopped in horror to see that they were inflamed and blistered, and the skin was peeling. He would have turned around and run back, except that in the darkness and maze of the corridors, he had no idea in which direction lay his escape.

He imagined what he would look like if he managed to get out of the tomb alive, centerpiece or not. He would be grossly disfigured. He touched his face, only to find it peeling, as well. His youthful appearance and his fit body were the only weapons he had against his most feared enemy—old age.

When he turned forty, he had accepted that he would likely no longer be referred to as the attractive young Frenchman, but if he stayed fit and energetic, he reasoned, he could play mentor to handsome young men. And how hard he had tried to appear attractive! No one could have suspected how tired he felt at times, feigning energy he did not feel. Then he had met Tom—that brilliant, handsome man, who looked at him as his equal, who saw through his layers of arrogance and reached into his soul. In Tom, Jean-Christophe had finally been able to end the search for understanding and companionship. He had found a friend, a brother . . . a soul-mate. But to think that Tom could see past his physical deterioration . . .

The sound of moaning distracted him, and he quickly realized it was a human cry of distress. As if in a trance, he walked in the direction of the moaning. He saw an old man crouching on the floor, writhing in agony. "Help me. Please, help me," cried the old man.

Jean-Christophe rushed to his side. The man whimpered, "I never reached the chamber." The man pointed to his shriveled, burnt skin. "Please put me out of my misery; hold me for a minute . . . kiss me before I die."

Jean-Christophe was at once confused and repulsed. He was running out of time and had to find the chamber, but how could he leave the wretched man? Despite his fear that the man might be a leper, Jean-Christophe knelt down. This was his worst nightmare, but he tried to hide his repulsion and kissed the man's forehead. At that moment, the man lifted his face and searched for Jean-Christophe's lips. The Frenchman sprang back in shock, seeing that the old man was himself! The hallucination only served to prove that he was losing his mind too. But the medians' warning flashed into his mind, the warning that he must be brave and wise upon encountering . . .

I've just met the Dragon!

He pulled himself together. Danielle had prepared him for this critical moment. Whatever shape the Dragon took, it had to be conquered before it destroyed him. He tried to regain his senses, as Danielle's face appeared in his consciousness to remind him that no one enters the heaven within until he has conquered the dragon of negative energy inherited from the collective consciousness. The hallucination vanished; the bleeding from his nose stopped, and the burning of his skin diminished. He felt himself returning to normal.

A door appeared. A metal door divided into four panels upon which were figures sculpted in relief—a bird, a bull, a lion, and a man. While looking at the images, the face of an Egyptian queen materialized, crowned with a gold headpiece and adorned with interwoven serpents. The one he had seen on his first venture into the tomb.

"You have reached the Chamber of Sharah, mistress of the West, keeper of the Truth," spoke the face on the door. "State your name and millennium from the date of arrival."

"Jean-Christophe Girard." He had to think quickly and guessed that the date in question must be the arrival of the Edentians. Remembering what Danielle had told him, he replied, "Approximately the fortieth millennium."

The queen seemed pleased. "State exact location of dimension between you and the stars that you wish to enter." She was asking for coordinates that Jean-Christophe did not know. He then remembered something Danielle had told him was vital information, and he replied, "Those do not exist but within the inner worlds of our inner journey."

The door opened, and he was inside the Chamber of Sharah. It was not a chamber laden with treasures; it contained a single open sarcophagus. He saw what he was looking for, a greenish stone encircled with gold jewels. Jean-Christophe removed it from the scepter without any difficulty and secured it in the leather pouch at his waist.

The room was no longer empty. Coffers filled with gold had magically appeared to fill the chamber. But remembering that he was to take nothing but the headpiece, he exited the room, and the door shut behind him. The face faded from view.

Now he was faced with the problem of how to get out of the tomb with his treasure. He had no idea where to start and suspected he would be presented with more roadblocks before he concluded this harrowing adventure. The medians had told him to rely on his wits to find his way out, but he could find no indication of any openings in the walls of the tomb. *Trapped again!*

The air grew thick once more, but he knew he couldn't allow himself to yield to the fear that had struck him earlier. He prayed for guidance, imploring all the deities he could think of, when a sensation, something like earliest dawn, washed over him, replacing the darkness with indefinable color. He waited, but nothing else happened.

Then he had the sensation of being suspended in time and space. His body was helpless, and he had to struggle to will his mind to work. He searched memory and experience for an answer but could find no frame of reference. He knew the key to his extrication had to be somewhere in the ruins. He tried to call up every detail of what he had seen or experienced from the time he had entered the tombs . . . the round rock, the Egyptian hieroglyphics, the Zodiac, and the Otz Chiim—the *Tree of Life*—in the center.

"That has to be it!" exclaimed Jean-Christophe. "I must follow the paths of the *Tree*."

He had spent long years studying the ancient and stoical writings of the Kabbalah but had never imagined that his understanding of the *Tree of Life* and the ten Sephiroh, or emanations, would be put to the test. He knew the first step was to give thanks to Kether—the first and highest emanation of the Almighty, whose name, EHEIEH, is not to be uttered—for the guidance that had led him this far.

Kether

As Jean-Christophe meditated on the first Sephirah, he came across one of the secrets of the invisible pyramid, which was the understanding of Kether—the nucleus of pure spirit that emanates into all dimensions but never manifests as form. He understood that the rest of his journey though the *Tree of Life* could only be attained through abstract thinking and symbols, for words would be ineffectual. He concentrated on the point, the crown, the swastika, and the color white, all attributed to Kether. He also remembered that the virtue assigned to Kether is that of attainment. Jean-Christophe took pride in his personal accomplishment; he had retrieved the disk and the stone, but his work was not complete until got it to the *Foundation*. Once again, he prayed for assistance.

Chokmah

Light swirled around him and pushed him forward into what Jean-Christophe recognized as Chokmah, the second emanation, or first crystallization of the limitless light—a force brought about through dynamic energy and power.

Here, he was to experience the primordial force without form. He offered no resistance to the force that pushed him forward into the unknown. He was sure it would take him safely to the third emanation of the supernal triangle, the essence of form without which force could not be complete.

Binah

Next, Jean-Christophe experienced the archetypal manifestation of polarization and gender. He knew he was in Binah when he experienced the potent female energy of creation. As he continued his descent through the Sephiroh, he had to keep in mind that the emanations he was experiencing were not places but states of the subconscious. Binah, the spirit mother and giver of life, binds force into the discipline of form.

Having traveled the paths of the first trinity, the French archeologist became aware that it was separated from the rest of the Sephiroth by the terrifying bridge of *Daath,* or the abyss, as it was also called. Here was the separation of the essential spirit and the mind. He had the sensation of falling into the bottomless abyss, but did not give in to the terror.

Chesed

He arrived safely in *Chesed,* the Sephiroth described in the book of Genesis, as the "power," the manifestation of form and light created by the former emanations. He saw a vision of *Chesed*—the king, seated upon his throne—the majestic white-haired god so beautifully portrayed by Michelangelo in the Sistine Chapel.

His journey down the paths of the *Tree of Life* was a mirror image of the path of his soul and of his own personal evolution. Jean-Christophe knew he must shed his attitudes of arrogance and elitism—attitudes so often attributed to the French. For so many years, he had foolishly hidden his insecurities behind a shield of intellectual superiority.

He thought of the people whom he had wronged. Surprisingly, it wasn't too many. Yet, unintentional as it was, he had hurt Mustafa, his loyal companion of the last few years. Jean-Christophe knew he should have been more tactful in breaking off the relationship. After meeting Tom O'Neil, Jean-Christophe thought of nothing else but his desire to be with him. He would make it up to him, Jean-Christophe decided determinedly. Now that Ali, Mustafa's youngest brother was in America, he would make sure the boy got the best education.

The archeologist felt confident that he would overcome whatever challenges still faced him in the Otz Chiim, as well as in his lifetime journey. He understood clearly the importance of the *Formation*.

Yet he also knew the *Formation* would close an era of planetary development, and when things came to an end, there were always separations. The medians spoke of a conveyance awaiting them; that only meant that the Edentians were getting ready to depart. Danielle was going home too.

What if everything that he had accomplished and come to understand through her was lost? The atmosphere surrounding him turned red. His newfound confidence and wisdom began to falter, as his fears took possession of him.

He had just entered the fifth and most frightening sephirah.

Geburah

Jean-Christophe stared at Geburah the Destroyer; the wise king had morphed into the warrior king riding his chariot. This sephirah was often called "Strength and Severity." The vision of Geburah was terrifying, but it was the necessary pull of Geburah against Chesed that brought equilibrium to creation—the proper mixture of cohesive and radical intelligence. This fifth emanation, so poorly understood by Christianity, had often been labeled as the force of evil. Geburah was the destroyer, but also the avenger, the dragon slayer. It is Geburah that leads the children of God into battle against their oppressors. He is also the emissary who carries out the orders of Binah, the mother spirit, to weed out what has outlived its usefulness.

It was in the plane of Geburah where the *Foundation* and the *Group* came into conflict.

All five-sided symbols were associated with Geburah. It was no coincidence that the seat of the American government was a pentagon, Jean-Christophe realized.

He continued to meditate on the power of this warrior king who leads his followers to battle. Geburah was Aries and Mars of the ancient civilizations, the vengeful hand of God that men still feared.

Tipareth

Deep in thought, the archeologist hardly noticed that he had been caught up by the chariot and whisked on swift, flaming wheels to the brilliant golden light of Tipareth, the sixth sephirah. The Hebrew word meant "beauty." Here, peace, beauty, and harmony reigned, for the sephirah was the location for the pillar of equilibrium and balanced the forces between Chesed and Geburah. This was the center of Christianity.

The light around Jean-Christophe became almost blinding. The splendor of such a golden-yellow light had, throughout history, been attributed to the sun god. Here, the radiance took human form. This was the plane of incarnation as well as redemption.

All incomprehensible abstract principles of creation were here, translated into a single vision of love—the one concept within the scope of human comprehension.

Jean-Christophe finally understood what Danielle had tried to explain to him for years. All the religions of the world were, in essence, different versions of the same truth. The Kabbalah, Judeo-Christian, and Muslim beliefs, with their trinities and three pillars of consciousness, paralleled the three channels of Prana described by the yogis. The Yin and Yang of the Tao, or the Way, in the Chinese belief system, represented the equilibrium between those forces. Thus, no matter how different the beliefs in individual religions appeared, they were actually all in agreement in principle.

From this point on, the pace of Jean-Christophe's descent accelerated. The next sephiroth were emanations that Jean-Christophe, as a lifetime scholar of the mysteries, better understood. Therefore, he peacefully contemplated the flow of energy from Tipareth into the seventh sephirah.

Netzach

Here was the manifestation of perfect physical beauty. *Netzach* also stood for "Victory and the Potency of the Female." Unlike *Binah*, the giver of life, *Netzach*, was the mother of humankind. She was the goddess of love, Aphrodite, lover of Mars, and representative of intuitive instincts. The order of angels assigned to Netzach was the Elohim, also referred to as the gods and rulers of nature.

Netzach was as deeply connected with Geburah as she was with Hod, her opposing sephirah. Netzach was often misunderstood and expressed through the misuse of sex. Thus, the sin of lust, one of the disturbing influences on the world, had often been attributed to Aphrodite.

Hod

The sephirah of "Splendor," stood at the opposing pillar, the lord of Science, Intellect, and individual Mind. He commands language and the visual arts. Here, the power of the mind is capable of producing miracles. This is the sphere of magic, where the forces of nature and intellect take on recognizable form.

The planes shifted and took Jean-Christophe to his next destination. For the first time since this odyssey began, he was able to move on his own.

Yesod

Here, Jean-Christophe walked about, making a mental correlation of the forces he had experienced since his descent.

Shimmering lights of cobalt blue and purple danced around Jean-Christophe, creating a misty atmosphere of deep violet. He became aware that he was in the realm of illusion—the trickiest of all sephiroth. The violet light, a magnetic and electrical force, to which the *Group* had somehow gained access and used to influence the Edenic currents. From Yesod, the four elements—fire, earth, water and air—could be manipulated.

When Jean-Christophe saw the vision of the serpent—the astral energy called Kundalini in the East—coiled up the middle of the pillar that supported the plane where he was standing, he recalled the esoteric interpretation of the deceitful serpent in the Garden of Eden.

Malkuth

Not wanting to remain long in this realm of tricky illusions, he made ready to take the final jump into *Malkuth*, the tenth and final sephirah—the material world. He came to the edge of the plane and looked down past the serpent that now threatened his descent and into a gulf of fire. It was a frightful sight.

He hesitated. These flames appeared to be real, but bravery, faith, and wisdom were strong weapons that would serve him well. The descent had been an extraordinary experience. Jean-Christophe needed to retain the wisdom gained and not be fooled by the illusion created by fear.

Summoning his courage, Jean-Christophe jumped into the dark void.

Jean-Christophe landed in the exact spot at the dig where he had initiated his journey. He checked his leather pouch and felt for his flashlight. Before he was able to retrieve it, he felt something hard and cold at his temple. Even before the lights of a dozen flashlights were aimed at him, he recognized the metal circle of a revolver.

All has been for nothing! A number of men in khakis were pointing guns and flashing lights in his face.

"I will take that now," said a man, making his way through the ranks and pointing to the pouch.

Jean-Christophe hesitated, even though he knew he was cornered. An immediate and intense animosity arose in his chest toward the individual coming toward him, with his theatrical accent and resemblance to Hitler.

The Frenchman started to unbuckle the belt of the pouch, when, to his surprise, the man stopped. He signaled his men to put down their weapons as he stepped backward. Jean-Christophe, now accustomed to the darkness, looked behind him. There, in the midst of the rubble, stood a group of magnificent figures—tall, imposing, and, one could say, *luminous.* It took him a second to recognize Danielle next to a fair man. Behind them, among the other figures, he recognized Camiel and instantly knew it to be a band of Edentian warriors.

The men in khakis, as well as their leader, had now taken flight. Camiel and some of the messengers went after them. Danielle came to Jean-Christophe and embraced him; then, taking the pouch from him, handed it to her companion, whom she introduced as Kjell. The rest of the messengers, who had now taken full human form, picked up the large stone in a corner of the cave.

"The monolith!" exclaimed Jean-Christophe. At that moment, two blue spiral coils of light burst from the stone walls and moved upward and out of the tomb.

Danielle and Kjell waved to the escaping streams of light. Jean-Christophe understood that he had witnessed the separation of the medians from the material plane, now heading toward the spot where they would await the conveyance that would take them home.

"There is a helicopter waiting for you," Danielle said to Jean-Christophe. "We will join you shortly. One of the messengers will ride with you."

Not used to taking orders without explanations, Jean-Christophe asked, "*Qu'est- que c'est?*"

"We are sealing the invisible pyramid permanently. Go on, you are finally going to the *Foundation.*"

The Frenchman did as he was told. He exited the tomb and headed toward the helicopter. The man and his army in khakis were gone. He could still make out their jeeps in the distance. As he walked toward the helicopter, he saw the messengers place the monolith on the ground. Two of them stood in front of it, and a shining arch formed behind them, stretching horizontally, making them look like angels but with wings of light. The arch closed around the stone, and the figures and the stone became one vertical ray, which was immediately shot toward the sky. The rest of the messengers followed and became bright dots, disappearing into the firmament.

Jean-Christophe realized the accounts of winged angels were not so far-fetched. To unknowing onlookers, the beams, which had transported the medians to a spot to wait for their starship, must have looked like angel wings as they took to the sky.

XXXIX

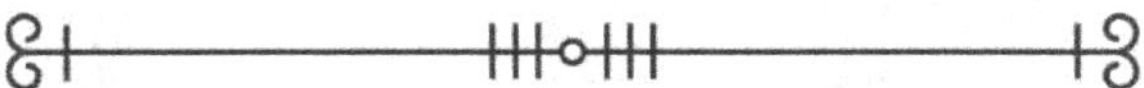

Los Angeles

The days continued to go by with no word from Chris. Tom had left the clinic in San Francisco and continued his research privately, mostly at his weekend home in Sausalito. Packed and ready to head for LA, Tom and Ali anxiously waited for Jean-Christophe to arrive.

Kit found herself comforting Tom and trying to be optimistic, trying very hard to keep life as normal as she could while preparations at the shelter went on unabated.

When Officer Jones called to inform her of the partial destruction of Hoover Dam, Kit felt her fears were justified. She had followed the instructions Tom had given her and had placed in Jones's hands a number of vials whose contents were to be poured into the water supply at key locations to prevent the contamination of irrigation waters to nearby farmlands. But something else had happened to Hoover's turbines, which caused a serious shortage of energy. The turbines had been designed to generate low-cost hydroelectric power for use in Nevada, Arizona, and California, and the dam was set up to provide four billion kilowatt-hours of electricity to half a million homes. After the initial panic, people had to institute a more judicious use of electrical power. But contamination of the drinking water would have caused havoc, had the *Foundation* not prepared for the situation.

Danielle's Aspen home, the Colorado compound, was equipped with an underground shelter and a water-bottling facility. For months now, the facility had been working nonstop, bottling water from two main springs. Millions of warehoused bottles were immediately distributed to the most affected areas.

By now, Kit had learned she would have to anticipate and meet whatever disaster might come next. In the evenings, after a full day's work, she sat with Deborah in the den and watched the news.

Tonight, Clayton McCann was to appear on television and deliver a speech expressing his full support for Theodore Edwards as the next presidential candidate of the United States.

Houston

Theodore Edwards's big day had finally arrived. Today, President Clayton McCann would publicly endorse his candidacy for the presidency.

The Brown Convention Center was packed. The streets in downtown Houston were lined with crowds, hoping to get a glimpse of the evangelist-turned-politician.

Edwards sat in front of the make-up mirror in a large hall while a number of stylists got him ready for the press conference. He was thinking through his life and the series of events that had brought him to this day. *President Edwards . . . President Theodore Edwards.* These stunning words that made up his name kept repeating in his head.

Nielsen had accompanied Edwards, as he often did these days. *I'm getting tired of this arrogant senator!* thought Edwards. *Well, it won't be long before he is out of the picture. Oh yes, there will be some serious changes in the country!* His stomach felt a little queasy. He noticed the senator appeared a little more on edge than usual. *Natural,* he thought. *It would be a day that will change the world.* So far, the *Group* had provided him with excellent exposure through meticulously planned campaigns that had proved effective, and he was secure in his position.

There is no reason for anything to go wrong, Edwards kept telling himself. He looked around the room—at the secret service, the producer, the director, cameramen, the advisors, and the technicians. Everyone was engaged in checking on each detail to make a resounding success of the day. He looked again at his reflection in the mirror and was pleased with what he saw. He went on to review in his head the speech he was about to deliver—the prayer, followed by reference to the recent disasters, including the contamination at the Hoover Dam. He would then remind the world of the prediction he had made a few weeks earlier. He had spoken about God's retribution and anger.

"The Lord will cut off that which is most precious to you . . . water," Edwards had warned. "I will not be surprised if such an important facility as Hoover Dam should burst or become contaminated with flaming rocks from Heaven." That was precisely what had happened.

"Perfect!" The stylist expressed his delight, putting the finishing touches on Theodore's hair.

"Is McCann's make-up done?" inquired Edwards.

The stylist touched up the blush on the evangelist's cheek. "Apparently, the president refused to be made-up. In contrast, you will look strong and energetic."

Nielsen walked up to them. He observed Theodore without saying a word and then dismissed the stylist with a glance. "All the major TV anchors are on-air right now, discussing what you might say. They all are getting excellent ratings."

Instead of calming Theodore, the news made him break into a sweat. The stylist returned to blot the perspiration from Theodore's forehead. Nielsen became quiet until the stylist walked away.

"You must be calm," said the senator in a friendly tone, hiding his scorn. "Everything is in position. The whole thing will be over before you know it."

"Are you sure?" Edwards could not control his apprehension.

"I am sure. Give a great speech, and we'll handle the rest. Remember the keywords that we are using for synchronization. Deliver them in a timely manner. That's all."

The plan was simple enough, Theodore had been told. This was to be a time of reconciliation. The president would introduce Edwards, thank him for his service, and acknowledge him as the spokesman of Christ on Earth. He would refer to the recent world events, as foretold in the biblical apocalypse. Theodore would then join him and offer a prayer for the country.

When President McCann took the microphone again, it would be Theodore's cue. Someone in the crowd would fire at the president. Theodore, being closest to McCann, was to throw himself over the president to shield him. The secret service would be slow to act, and the camera would get a clear shot of Edwards protecting the president. This selfless act, to be viewed by millions, would make a martyr of him. The world would watch Theodore Edwards being shot to death by the assailants—all make-believe, of course.

There would be fake bullets and pre-positioned blood bags that would burst upon activation. Edwards would be rushed to the hospital, the way Kennedy had been. This would be a replay with better close-ups. Theodore Edwards would supposedly be in a coma for several days, die, and then come back to life. McCann's injuries would prevent him from continuing his term, and he would step down. The vice-president—under control of the *Group*—would take over until the forthcoming elections and Edwards's recovery.

Edwards's bodyguard, a tall, muscular man, walked up, indicating that it was time to go. Edwards followed him toward the auditorium, with Nielsen following a few steps behind. His entrance coincided with that of President McCann, who came from an adjacent back door. Yet Edwards was sure the cheering was for him. The president took the podium and delivered his speech, as planned. More cheering. He then introduced Theodore Edwards. McCann spoke of the need to return the country to its former greatness, the need to reinstate family values and order and the need for listening to the man who was doing God's work.

Edwards was becoming anxious. *Now, what is the word?* he wondered nervously. *Have I missed my cue? No, it hasn't been uttered yet.* Nielsen remained immobile, facing the stage. Edwards looked up, wondering where the assailants were hiding. Then he remembered he was not supposed to look around. So he concentrated once more on the speech. *No sign of firearms yet.* Then, without seeing, he suddenly knew. His eyes shifted to a corner of the room where he saw a man putting on a mask, a gas mask. Before Edwards could move or even think straight, secret service men jumped out of the background and grabbed President McCann. Slipping something over his head, they pulled him off the podium, and pushed him toward the exit. The audience cried out in terror! Edwards jumped up from his seat, even as his bodyguard tried to protect him.

"Poison gas . . . that is not how it was supposed to happen!" muttered Edwards with fury. *The camera! I have to get at least one good close-up before I run out.* He slipped from the arm of the bodyguard and whipped around to face the camera in a theatrical display of despair. In a panic, he knew that nothing else mattered but his life. *Forget the plans of the* Group! he thought. *I've got to get out of here!* Fairly close to the exit, he felt it—the shot into his back.

He knew, though there was no pain. A second impact to his neck made him stagger. He saw Senator Nielsen on the ground at his feet, blood gushing out of his mouth. Edwards still registered no pain. Then a sudden rush of heat flushed through his body. He tumbled to the ground in slow-motion and fell next to Senator Nielsen.

There was screaming and pandemonium in the room, but Edwards could no longer hear. Sight and sound were slowly shutting down, but he was still conscious when he was put on the stretcher. As silence loomed within his head, he kept repeating to himself. "I am alive. God is my shepherd; I shall not perish."

Los Angeles

Despite the antipathy Kit had always felt for the minister, she could feel only compassion for him and all those killed and injured during the attack. Holding on to Deborah's hand, Kit continued to watch the live broadcast from Houston—Theodore Edwards and Senator Nielsen had been shot. The gas had been confirmed to be a potent poison. There had been numerous casualties, mostly secret service agents and members of the press. As of yet, it had not been determined who was responsible for the attack.

"How were the guns smuggled past security?" asked Deborah. She had come into the room to join the others.

"And the gas . . . it is incomprehensible," muttered Kit.

Houston

Leaning on the counter of the bar and holding a glass of scotch in his hand, Cirel watched the news of the attack. He listened to the report of the aftermath, feeling no emotion. Senator Nielsen had been pronounced dead upon arrival at the hospital. Theodore Edwards, besides suffering from gas inhalation, had been critically wounded; he was undergoing surgery at Hermann Hospital. President McCann had managed to get away, presumably unharmed, and had headed back to Washington, DC. The number of casualties continued to rise. So far, ninety-four were dead and 137 injured. The gas had been identified as sarin (GB).

Cirel refilled his glass, shifting his eyes to the screen, monitoring the entrance gate. A smile crossed his face when he saw the car pull up. As Lili stepped from the automobile, the staff greeted her courteously. Cirel remembered that this was—or had been—one of Lili's homes. He opened a bottle of champagne and poured a glass for her. A couple of minutes later, she walked into the room.

"*Ciao,* Caro." She looked carefree and as lovely as ever.

He handed her the flute. "*Ciao*, Bella."

She noticed he had been watching the news. "Why would you want to kill Edwards?" she asked casually, taking off her sunglasses and setting down her purse. "He is your most faithful servant."

"And he rose on the third day, according to the Scriptures," he whispered ironically, kissing her on both cheeks.

"Ah," sighed Lili.

"And to what shall I attribute the honor of your visit?" asked Cirel.

"This is also my home, or have you forgotten?"

"Oh, yes, forgive me, my dear. Sometimes I do forget I am the visitor. It's just that I did not expect to see you here. I thought you hated Houston."

"I do. But you insisted that I should have a home in Houston because of its being an energy center or whatever."

"I did, indeed. It's no coincidence that NASA was built here. We can tap into more unused energy here than just about anywhere else."

"I see. That is why you were adamant about having the debates and the press conference here." She had made herself comfortable on the sofa. "You must be delighted. Everything seems to be going your way. You even have me where you want me, ruined and unemployed."

Cirel laughed. “I seriously doubt that. You have more wealth than anyone can imagine.”

“I did like my rejuvenating business . . . and my fashion empire, you know.”

“What good would it all be now? This place is finished. The planet is all but dead.”

“You are right,” said Lili. “And I’m ready to leave whenever you want.”

Cirel looked amused. “So you have made up your mind? You are coming with me?”

Lili took off her jacket to appear even more comfortable. Then, loosening the top button of her silk blouse, walked up to the bar and refilled her glass. “Did you have any doubts?”

“Actually, yes. I did.”

“Cirel, you are such a pessimist. You and I have always returned to each other. We are all we have.”

“That’s what I say. So why this infatuation with the boy?” asked Cirel, referring to Jeff.

Lili smiled coquettishly. “Darling, you sound like a jilted lover. Now, do I question each and every one of your flings?”

“I don’t have time for flings,” he said emphatically.

“Well, perhaps you should make time, now and then. You would not be so tense.”

Cirel dismissed the remark. “What can you tell me about your sudden alliance to Trebor?” asked Cirel. “Now there is a traitor if I ever saw one!”

“There is no alliance. I was just trying to figure out what he was up to.”

“And?”

“The usual. He doesn’t know to which side to turn. He is leaning towards the *Foundation*. They must have treated him better than you, dear.”

“Or perhaps that is where his love interest lies,” said Cirel, toying with Lili’s feelings.

“She has left him, though,” she said indifferently. “He has no idea where she is.”

“At the *Foundation*. Where else?” Cirel seemed annoyed. “We know where it is, but we still can’t figure out where the bloody entrance is located. It keeps shifting. So we’ll just take it all with the meteor storm.”

“You are still set on demolishing the planet?”

He shrugged indifferently.

“You are right. Why should we care? Isn’t it time for us to leave?” added Lili.

“It is, my dear. But be patient. I’ve got another surprise in store for you.”

“Do tell me. Where are we going?”

“All in due time.” Cirel was amused by the charade.

She feigned disappointment. “Do you have my potion and herbs?”

“Well, of course,” he smiled maliciously and opened a malachite box, retrieving a vial and a plastic bag with dried leaves. “I knew you’d be coming for them.”

Lili took them and immediately put them in her purse, as she had done in the past. Except this time, she did not look at the contents, fearing he would notice her awareness of his deceit. Lili knew Cirel was keen and extremely hard to deceive.

"I am bored, darling," said Lili, moving close to him.

"So am I. Bored . . . very bored." His voice was weary.

"It will be nice to start somewhere else," added Lili in a more jovial tone.

"The next place could be as dull as this one."

"Perhaps. Perhaps not." She was running her fingernail around his ear. "I have realized that the only fun I ever had was with you."

He laughed. "We had some interesting times!"

He was letting down his defenses, and Lili had a glimpse of Cirel as he used to be. "I used to get angry with you because you enjoyed killing so much."

"And you found it distasteful . . ."

"I didn't get the concept that they were merely animals," said Lili.

"Animals in human cover. They resemble Edentians, but they are animals, nonetheless. Infinitely inferior to us." Cirel casually classified himself as an Edentian. Lili pretended not to notice. "No matter how much we tried, we could never make them as perfect as we are; it just couldn't be done," he concluded.

"We gave them our language, our alphabet, our thought process, even our feelings," added Lili.

"But all were beyond their capabilities. The human race is a botched experiment." Cirel continued, "They make good slaves and excellent physiological hosts. Any attempt to make them out to be more than that is futile."

"You once wanted to rule them and the planet."

"I would have weeded out the race and implemented a new way of life. Tell me, Lilith, how did you like me best? As Genghis Khan, perhaps Caligula or Ivan the terrible . . . or as Hitler? Those have certainly been my most impressive roles, where my performances were at their highest caliber."

Lili did not answer right away. She remembered the cruelty each inflicted on the human race.

"As Hitler, no doubt," prompted Cirel. "Am I right?"

"Your personality was certainly fine-tuned and finally aligned with your ego. Although, I will never understand the reason for all the destruction."

"To prove a point, my dear. To prove a point. I demonstrated that masses can be maneuvered if given the right dream. A man can be driven to do anything if guided step by step. You can take an ordinary man, the worst nitwit, and turn him into a ruthless warrior; hand him a lavish uniform, give him a tiny taste of power, and he will do the unimaginable. Reward him for his ingenuity, and he is ready to annihilate a race."

Lili forced a smile. It became more and more difficult for her to hide her contempt for the madman. Cirel continued speaking—evidence that he was in love with his own voice.

"You know action follows thought. There was murder in the heart of every man who allowed me to kill. Here and there, I found exemplary disciples who risked it all for the taste of power. I offered them immortality!"

"Such as Lucius and Edwards?"

"Such as Lucius Catilina," said Cirel, not wanting to discuss Edwards. "Had I been wrong about the human race, my experiment would have failed! You think my contempt for the *Foundation* includes hate for the Edentians, but you are wrong. I like you all. But I cannot allow my personal feelings to interfere with my plans."

"I know we all have been let down by the human race," said Lili, trying to sound sympathetic. "We had such dreams for them!"

"Believe it or not, I had the highest hopes for the planet as Hitler. I wanted to save the purest and finest of the human species, build a city of white marble for them, surround them with art and the music of Wagner. I outlined my projects. Did anyone listen? No!"

"Like I said before," added Lili, wanting to return him to a more romantic mood. "Perhaps it is not too late for us." Her face was close to his now, and he could smell the scent of her breath. Yet, he could not pass up the opportunity to ask sarcastically, "So now I am good enough for you?"

"Oh, you were always good enough for any Edentian. The problem was with me, with my restlessness. But I'm with you now. Nothing else matters."

"Not your good friend Trebor?"

She gently shook her head in denial.

"Not your boy toy?"

Her lips were now on his. He whispered before succumbing to her kiss, "You may have to kill him now."

"I will," she whispered and proceeded to kiss Cirel ardently while he tore off her clothes.

Lili gave herself freely and passionately to Cirel, like she had done numerous times in millennia past.

Cirel woke up in the morning to find her gone. He had enjoyed her. Oh, how he had enjoyed her! At one time, he had been in awe of her. But to his surprise, he now found her gullible. How could an Edentian be fooled so easily? He continued to laugh. He got up and walked up to a mirror. He ran his hands through his jet-black hair in amusement. Then he noticed the medallion with the stone was missing from the chain around his neck.

Cirel screamed and furiously began smashing the fragile porcelains and laying waste to the paintings in the beautifully decorated room of the River Oaks mansion.

Hermann Hospital, Houston

Theodore Edwards slowly regained consciousness and gradually became aware of his surroundings. He could hear the distant echo of voices he did not recognize.

"A miracle!" a female voice expressed. *Yes, his being alive is a miracle—that is what they are saying.* Little by little, Theodore could make out more of their conversation.

It all started coming back to him. He relived the whole episode over and over again, like a silent movie rolling nonstop inside his brain. He knew for certain, now, that he had been shot and rationalized that to be the reason he was so heavily sedated. He could hardly wake up, let alone move. Then he became aware of something in his throat—a tube of some sort—and tried to chew on it but couldn't.

"He is awake," the female voice said. Edwards kept struggling with the tube that was choking him. The rhythmic pace of his breathing let him know he was on a ventilator. He tried to open his eyes again. He was able to keep them open for a second, long enough to confirm that he was in a hospital bed, surrounded by IV stands, monitors, tubes, metal boxes, and voices he still did not recognize.

The ICU nurse approached the bed, and Theodore could hear her voice again. She was talking about him as if he were not in the room. "He is coming around, Doctor. Should I give him the sedative?"

A masculine voice responded, "Yes, let's give him another dose."

No, no! Theodore wanted to protest. *No more medication!* He wished he could scream past the intruding tube. He felt no physical pain; he just wanted to wake up. Again, he tried to get the awful tube out, but immediately, he realized his hands did not obey his brain's commands. It was a frustrating and desperate feeling to issue a command and have the limbs ignore it. In this awful manner, he came to the realization that he was paralyzed. He closed his eyes, refusing to accept the horror of that implication.

It's all a bad dream, he thought in despair. *When I wake up, it all will be as before.*

XL

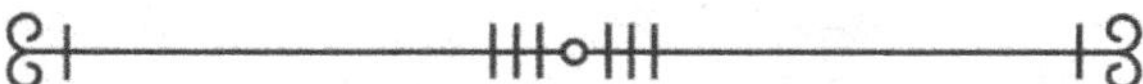

Guanajuato, Mexico

The white colonial house, just outside of the town of Guanajuato, Mexico, was charming and unpretentious. Because of its simplicity and remoteness, Lili had chosen it to be her safe house.

Lili seldom visited it but kept it ready, should she ever have to go into hiding. The overseers of the property were a devoted elderly couple, who had been in her service for over fifty years. In this place, Lili chose to dress in casual linen and sandals and wore no make-up. Jeff was fascinated by the sudden transformation in Lili, who was addressed by the servants as Miss Duran.

"What makes you so sure that we will go unnoticed indefinitely?" Jeff asked, stripping the white cotton dust covers from the furniture.

"Not indefinitely." She was arranging a bunch of wild flowers into a blue vase. "Just until a certain event takes place, which should occur in a fortnight." After a brief pause, she added, "Why don't we go into town and get some supplies?"

She started to write on a piece of paper.

"How about some tequila for margaritas," he said to her.

"Yeah, let's get drunk."

They laughed blissfully, and for the first time, Jeff noticed tiny lines around her eyes. Once again, he became aware of the age difference between them. Though, he did not care.

"Anything else?"

"Well, I know you mentioned not using the phone, but shouldn't we ask for Wi-Fi so you can at least connect your laptop?"

"No, absolutely not. Only electricity. We are not to use any other sort of service that could place us here." She put the list in her purse and picked up the car keys. "Ready? I also have a couple of things to mail." She picked up the envelopes from the credenza, and he took them from her.

"One of them is addressed to me," he said with surprise. "Can't I save you the postage?"

"If you promise not to open it until the need arises."

They spent the day in town, alternating between shopping and sight-seeing. They bought housewares and magazines and visited the opera house and the cathedral. On the plaza, they drank micheladas while they listened to the local orchestra play a Dvorak concert. The annual Cervantes Festival was in progress. Young poets from the university, wearing long black capes, stood on the steps of the cathedral and recited passages from Don Quixote. The accustomed tension in Lili's face softened. Their last stop was at the shop of *artesanias,* where they selected baskets, candles, and glassware. The attendant, wrapping up their purchases, smiled, taking them for newlyweds.

"Oh, I forgot to pick up fresh vanilla beans from the store," said Lili.

"I'll go get them," offered Jeff.

"No. I'd rather go myself. You wait for the packages. I'll be right back."

Jeff followed her with his eyes as she crossed the street. Heads turned as she walked, her white linen skirt flowing gracefully with every step. When she disappeared into the shop across the street, Jeff moved to the jewelry counter. He wanted to have a little gift for her when they arrived home. He admired some crosses but decided against them. A little further down the case, he spied the perfect piece: a necklace made with large silver beads. A young boy, noticing his interest, took the piece from the glass case and laid it on the counter. Jeff held it up and thought how lovely it would look on Lili's long, porcelain neck.

"Sterling silver, mister," said the boy. "Two hundred, fifty dollar."

"Two hundred," replied Jeff, remembering one should always bargain.

"OK," said the boy with a smile.

Jeff handed him his Visa card. The girls signaled that his packages were ready, and the boy rang up the silver. Suddenly, it dawned on Jeff that he should not be using a credit card.

"Stop! Don't charge it."

The boy stopped. "You don't like?" he asked, confused.

"I do like it," said Jeff, "but do not want to charge it." He pulled out his wallet but, looking at his depleted cash, added, "I'm sorry, I only have sixty dollars left."

The boy voided the transaction.

"I tell you what. I'll be back in the morning." He noticed the disappointed look on the boy's face and smiled. "I'm sure you've heard that before." He handed him the cash. "Here, take this, and keep it as a deposit."

The store owner walked up to assist.

"I was just telling Pedro," said Jeff, reading the young boy's name tag, "that I'll leave a deposit and return tomorrow."

The man smiled. "I could have it sent to you at your hotel. Where are you staying?"

Jeff hesitated. "That won't be necessary. I'll be back in the morning."

The store owner smiled politely. Noticing that Lili was approaching, the manager placed the jewelry in a velvet pouch. "You look like an honest man," he added. "Here, take it and you can pay the rest tomorrow." Jeff thanked him and placed the pouch in the pocket of his jacket, picked up his packages, and turned around to meet Lili.

"The electricity will be turned on tomorrow," said Lili. She was lighting candles in the pewter candlesticks.

Jeff threw another log on the fire. "I kind of like this, though."

"It is cozy," agreed Lili. "Tomorrow, I'll go down to the wine cellar. I remember sending down a case of Dom Perignon. Tonight, this Chilean Caliterra will have to do if you want some wine," she said, looking at the wine bottles.

Jeff walked behind her and clasped the silver necklace around her neck. She touched it and looked up at him, then into the mirror.

"It's beautiful."

Lili, who possessed the most beautiful jewels in the world, found the necklace particularly charming, and Jeff knew it. It was the first time Jeff had seen genuine love in her eyes. He prayed their stay in this house could be eternal—away from the world gone mad, away from greed and intrigue.

Lili kissed his lips lightly. "Thank you, my love." She tried to hide the exhaustion stemming from the lack of nutrients that had nourished her for so many years. There was a tinge of regret for having listened to Robert and closing up the research labs in Switzerland. The IPS shots had worked well for many years. The whole thing was not as diabolical as it seemed, she reasoned. A little unethical, perhaps, but after all, those embryos were engineered to manufacture plasma and exhibited almost no brain activity. They were never considered to have human potential. She could not help wondering how much Jeff knew. Not too much, she hoped.

In the morning, after a long night's sleep, Lili felt better. They ate a light breakfast and went hiking.

Lili spoke of a dream she once had. As Lili described life in Edentia, Jeff was astonished by the creativity of her imagination, having no clue she was simply relating the circumstances of her past life.

After a pause, Lili suddenly said, "I am afraid . . ."

"Why?" asked Jeff. "What frightens you?"

"I don't know exactly. Tell me, Jeff, if I were on trial and you came to my defense, what would you say about me to validate my existence?"

Jeff answered truthfully. "I would say you were the embodiment of beauty, that you possess a sincere lust for life, the gift of laughter, and a unique sense of humor. You have given the world beauty through your unerring fashion sense. Well, until recently . . ." he added with a sly grin. "You despise mediocrity. But most of all, I experience love because of you."

"You never gave up on me, even when you came across my darkest secrets."

"Because I knew that was not the real you."

There was a tear running down her face. She brushed it away with her finger.

"Oh, Lili, you are such an enigma. I loved you from the moment I first saw you. I saw the most beautiful of jewels, mired in a valley of corruption."

"That is good," said Lili. "Not entirely true but good." She tried to smile. "Knowing that I loved and was loved in return justifies my existence."

"We've got plenty of time to live and love together. The world will straighten itself."

"I hope so, my love," she said. "I need to be alone for a while. I'll walk back to the hills and gather some herbs I saw on our hike."

"OK," said Jeff, understanding her need for privacy. "I'm going to run to town for a little while. I will be back at the house for lunch." He kissed her and clutched her in his arms. He knew now that they belonged together, and nothing could tear them apart.

"How much do I owe you?" asked Jeff, pulling out a roll of hundred-dollar bills.

"One hundred, forty dollars," said Pedro, the young attendant in the *artesanias* store.

The store owner walked up and took over, sending Pedro away to wait on another customer. Jeff noticed he was less friendly than he had been the day before. His movements were sharp and his smile forced.

"Thanks," said Jeff, taking the package and putting away his change.

"Thank you," replied the man. "Here is my card if I can be of future service."

Jeff took the card and noticed there was something written on it.

Leave town immediately. They know you are here.

Jeff looked up at the man; then, without saying a word, he rushed out the door. He jumped into the Jeep and drove off. He rounded the plaza, his heart pounding. Sitting at a table outside a café, he saw them. He knew it was *them,* not so much by their appearance, but by their demeanor. He recognized one of the men in the group. He looked somewhat like Theodore Edwards, but not. On second glance, the man with the ultra-black hair and sunglasses was the one Jeff had seen speaking to the *Group* in Switzerland.

Jeff drove out of town like a maniac. The twenty-minute drive to the house seemed like an eternity. *The* Group *has found us!* He hated himself for his stupidity. *The credit card charge must have gone through before it was voided.* He cursed the efficiency of the electronic world.

He passed trucks and busses on the shoulder of the road and almost hit a fruit vendor. He had to get to Lili! He would get her, and they would head out. He was not sure where they would go, but they would lose themselves in the jungle if necessary.

When he pulled onto the dirt road that lead to the house, he saw Lili walking toward the front door. She opened it and stopped when she saw Jeff racing toward her so recklessly. He was honking and waving frantically for her to come to the car. She smiled and waved back but walked inside the house to put down the basket of herbs. She heard him call out her name then started out the door, but before stepping out, she decided to switch on the light to check and see whether the electricity had been turned on.

It was instantaneous. The house blew up with the force of an atomic bomb. And just as the Met's wing had exploded before Jeff's eyes, the red-tiled house dispersed into a million pieces.

In a state of shock, Jeff ran toward the house, bathed in soot from the falling ashes. Nothing was left—neither of the house nor of beautiful Lili. Jeff threw himself on the ground in despair and shook with sobs that wracked his body and soul.

A few minutes later, still in shock, he drove aimlessly for hours. Or days. He really couldn't tell. When he came to his senses, he found himself standing at the ticket counter at the airport in Mexico City, ready to return to New York.

Because of my stupidity, I've lost Lili. He handed the ticket agent the same Visa card. He no longer cared what happened to him. He hoped the card would bring him a fate that would reunite him with Lili. He no longer wished to live.

The agent handed Jeff his boarding pass. The look on her face reminded him of how dirty he looked. He glanced around. Here, in the big city, the trash look was taking over. Though he didn't stand out in the crowd, he decided to get some clean clothes and headed for the nearest boutique. On his way there, something caught his attention. At the magazine stand, in both Spanish and English newspapers, there were featured pictures of Theodore Edwards. The headlines read, "Miraculous recovery of the man of God—Theodore Edwards to be the next president of the United States."

Houston

"You have a visitor," announced a soft female voice.

Theodore Edwards refused to open his eyes. If he kept them closed, he could pretend he was still asleep and would be left alone. All he wanted was to be left alone. *Why can't they just do that?*

He had lost track of time and desperately wanted to lose touch with reality. The hospital, with its endless procedures, had been a stay in a torture chamber, and he was sure it had affected his mind. The tube in his mouth had come out, only to be replaced by a tracheotomy tube in his throat. It was evident that he would not be able to breathe on his own ever again. He was totally paralyzed. Only his eyes retained movement and sensitivity, and he preferred to keep them closed, choosing to remain in the darkness and depths of this hell.

"You have a visitor, Mr. Collins," the voice persisted.

It seems they won't leave me alone, thought Edwards. *And are they calling me Mr. Collins?* That annoying name change had come when they had moved him out of the hospital and into that shabby convalescence home.

Long days of solitude and immobility had sharpened his perception. Even with his eyes closed, he could divine the number of people who entered the room. Right now, there were three. Two had stayed by the door, and one was approaching the bed.

"Hello, Theodore. I know you can hear me," said the man with the familiar, deep voice.

Edwards had no recourse but to open his eyes. The voice was that of Cirel. It took Edwards a few seconds to sort out what he was seeing. Standing there before him was the image of himself, Theodore Edwards, as he had been before the accident. Theodore stared in disbelief and horror, and Cirel burst out laughing.

When Cirel had composed himself, he looked at the paralytic with disdain, saying, "Pretty good, isn't it? Everyone was convinced it was you when I gave a statement to the press. But I was curious to get your reaction. I can see that you approve." Cirel was now using Edwards's tone and diction.

Edwards's eyes shifted frantically, trying to signal his disapproval.

"Oh, you don't? It really doesn't matter, one way or another. The world will be overjoyed. I'll take over where you left off," he added sardonically. "This country cannot be ruled by a paralytic. But I assure you that I will continue your good works in the name of God." His vicious laughter echoed around the room. "Goodbye, Mr. Collins. I don't think we'll meet again." Cirel continued to laugh as he took off his wig and put on his sunglasses. He left the room, followed by his bodyguards.

Outside the nursing home located on the outskirts of Houston, everything looked normal. Two deliverymen carrying boxes stepped aside to let Cirel and his men through. They watched the three men walk arrogantly toward the black Mercedes parked by the front door. As soon as the car drove off, the men put down the boxes, and one of them spoke into the microphone concealed inside the pocket of his white uniform. He spoke in Hebrew. "It's him. Don't lose him."

The white van left the parking lot, following Cirel's car at a distance.

Teotihuacan, Mexico

"Danielle held the cellular in her hand. She had just dialed Kitzia but had to disconnect immediately. She turned to Chris, who anxiously awaited her response. "The house is bugged. I had to abort."

"I can't believe it," said Christian. "I've been waiting for the opportunity to communicate with her, and now that we are out, we can't get through?"

She leaned on a pyramid stone at Teotihuacan. Next to them was a stone block Kjell had removed, and he and Jean-Christophe had gone in to clear the way. It was early in the morning, and no tourists had yet arrived. Camiel, standing a few feet away from them, kept watch.

"I'm sorry," said Danielle. "We can't risk it. Someone with the *Group* is inside, which means Kitzia is no longer safe." She turned to Cam. "As soon as we finish here, you'll have to return to her and stay by her side." Then back to Christian. "Right now, we have to concentrate on completing our mission. The *Formation* is to take place in seven days, and we must have all the components in our possession."

"Does she sound all right?" Christian pressed on, but Danielle appeared disconcerted and did not hear him.

"Something is wrong," she said finally. "I feel the emptiness, the pain. One of us has exited."

Kjell emerged from the opening and walked straight to Danielle. Her suspicion was confirmed by the look in his eyes. They embraced.

"What is it?" Chris could not contain his apprehension. Neither one answered.

Cam came up to them, and only then did they break the embrace. The three of them held hands in silence, as if in prayer. When they spoke, it was in a language Chris could not understand. After a few minutes, the trance broke, and

Danielle answered his question.

"We lost a sister. She was part of Kjell's trinity," said Danielle.

Chris' eyes registered puzzlement.

Kjell spoke, making a great effort not to show his pain. "We Edentians operate under a Master Soul who assigns a group of three spirits to work together for at least fifty thousand years."

Chris knew they were speaking of Lili Keller. "But I thought she had betrayed you," he said. "She left you both to die in that cosmic prison, didn't she?" Chris was suddenly outraged by the memory. Neither Danielle nor Kjell showed any resentment toward Lili—only grief was in their eyes.

"Lili was astute in her moves and would always find the most creative ways to bewilder us," added Kjell.

"She could have been with us, it's true," continued Danielle, "but she chose to do things differently. But in the end, she was an Edentian, one of us, and would not wrong us to the point where we'd perish."

Chris didn't know what to say or what to think. He remembered risking his life for something that now his Edentian friends considered trivial.

"Back then, she knew we would be rescued," Danielle said, trying to alleviate Chris's confusion. "Anyway, she recovered the stone that was taken from the statue at the Vatican." Danielle pointed to the stones that were now mounted on the medallion she was wearing. There were four of them, including the one of Kjell's that Chris had been allowed to wear. "Adam, Eva, Kjell, and I . . ." She pointed to each stone separately. "We need to recover Robert's and Lili's. Robert has given us a precise map of their location."

"When you said *exited*, I thought you meant Lili had died." Chris was not sure he had understood.

"She has exited this plane and has gone through a transition. We've requested that she be detained at the vortex and not sent through until we arrive."

Chris listened to Danielle with a sense of anxiety, understanding that the Edentians were planning on departing.

"If there is to be a trial," said Kjell, addressing Danielle, "she should travel back with us. The way she came here."

"I agree," she said. Then, in a pensive tone, added, "I've always wondered what made her change."

Chris had the impression they were forgetting he was there.

"Lili wanted to experience humanity in all its fullness and still remain celestial," said Kjell.

"I am sorry . . . so sorry." Danielle touched his hand. Only she could understand the immense sorrow of his soul. "We will not abandon her."

At that moment, Jean-Christophe emerged from the pyramid, signaling for them to hurry inside. The archeologist had found the switch that controlled the opening. The large blocks of stone supporting the serpent's head rolled aside, widening the entrance. The stones were positioned at a slant, and Danielle jumped in to show Chris that there was an immediate drop once they entered. The blocks closed after the three of them were inside. They slid down a polished stone, turned on their flashlights, and put on their night-vision goggles.

The pyramid of Teotihuacan was lower in height but larger in perimeter than the Egyptian. Therefore, the tunnels and chambers stood in a more horizontal formation. When they reached the chamber they were searching for, they found it to be a circular room, with painted murals in primary colors representing the ancient legends of the plumed serpent.

Danielle explained to Chris the meaning of the murals. "The ancient legends of Mexico demonstrated that the world of matter and spirit were coexistent, each possessing what the other one needed."

Kjell's radar device emitted a faint sound, implying they were closing in on the stone they were seeking.

"Where there was neither heaven nor earth, sounded the first word of God." Jean-Christophe quoted from the sacred books of Chilam Balam of Chumayel, of the Mayan and Nahua peoples. "And He loosened Himself from the stone and declared His divinity, and all the vastness of eternity shuddered."

Chris processed Jean-Christophe's recitation with interest, for he continued to find many similarities of thought and concept in all ancient religions. He noticed Danielle and Kjell were somewhat amused by the representation of the gods.

"Here, Quetzalcoatl, who represents spirit, dances with Tezcatlipoca, who represents matter," continued Jean-Christophe. "Quetzalcoatl was the fair, blue-eyed god of the wind, represented by the multicolored plumed serpent, who came from the sea to live among the people and taught them everything they knew."

Chris could not fail to notice that Kjell felt a little awkward at the eloquent description of the role he had once played. *Oh, my!* thought Chris, *So, he was the one that gave birth to all the Mexican myths!*

"Over here is a painting of Tlaloc, the rain god," Jean-Christophe continued his discourse, not yet having made the connection.

Kjell began pounding around the image. "This is where the stone and the conductor must be!"

"*Voila!*" Jean-Christophe suddenly exclaimed. His hand rested on a tiny square that was not painted, but inlaid with mosaics. He pried at the square, and the stone popped out.

Danielle rushed to take it from him. "That's it! Now we have Lili's."

Kjell was busy trying to figure out what was making his radar detector beep nonstop. Jean-Christophe was chipping at the rock. When he made a hole in the wall, he reached inside. "I feel something," said the archeologist. "Feels like wire . . ."

"Pull," ordered Kjell. "That must be the conductor."

Jean-Christophe extracted a small wire frame consisting of two overlaid triangles in the shape of the Star of David. He handed it to Kjell, who in turn, gave it to Danielle.

"We have almost everything. We need just one more stone and, of course, the centerpiece," Danielle exclaimed with joy. But the sound in the radar box had stopped.

"I'm afraid nothing else is here," said Kjell.

"But they've got to be!" insisted Danielle. "Robert told me my search would end here. That I'd have all the stones."

"Except his?" Kjell asked. "Think, Danielle, if he implied that you would have them all, that means that you have his already."

"But when . . . how?" After a moment she knew. "Robert gave me a coin once—a very rare coin. Then he gave me a Roman medallion, a Bulgari piece. He knew I'd replace the coin and wear it and that it would not attract attention. That's got to be it. The stone is in the coin. You are right. I've had it all along without knowing it!"

"Look!" exclaimed Jean-Christophe. He had come across an empty circular space in the mural.

Kjell examined the mural and said, "Now we know where the centerpiece was." He took a few steps in meditation. "OK. It all makes sense. Lili kept a secret place in Mexico, no doubt to keep some connection with the stone that she was unable to retrieve. So she must have known about the centerpiece."

"Well, we are on our own now. We've nothing else to do here. Cam can go back to retrieve the medallion from the safe in California. Let's go back to the *Foundation* and rework our calculations. We've got seven days left," she muttered. "Only seven days."

Los Angeles

Having heard Danielle's voice both encouraged and frightened Kit. "Why would she click off?" Kit asked Deborah.

"She will try again."

"The land line phone rang. Deborah, who was the closest, picked it up. Kit knew by her mother's face that it wasn't the call from Danielle.

"It's your lawyer," said Deborah. "He sounds alarmed."

What now? thought Kit as she reached for the receiver. "Hi Kenny, how are—" Kitzia turned pale and signaled Deborah to turn on the news.

The report was halfway in progress. A gruesome murder had been discovered in a home in San Francisco. The body of a young boy, approximately thirteen years old, had been discovered wrapped in linen bands like an Egyptian mummy. Cuts and bruises on his body indicated that he had also been tortured. The house in Sausalito belonged to a prominent physician, Dr. Thomas O'Neil, once nominated for the Nobel Prize. The reporter went on to mention the long list of O'Neil's accomplishments, including his extensive research on the brain and methods for looking into the subconscious. The renowned doctor had been taken into custody as the primary suspect in the murder. The cameras then turned to the front of the house, where Tom was shown handcuffed and being escorted by several policemen who shoved him into a police car.

"No!" screamed Kitzia. She did not know which hurt more, Ali's murder or the ridiculous accusation of Tom. Kit was shaking but made an effort to remain calm and simply whispered, "I'll be ready."

Her mother took her into her arms. Kit whispered, "No, not this!"

"It is a grave mistake. It will be cleared up in no time."

"They have framed him! And they have killed Ali . . ." She could no longer control her tears. Kenneth Levin, her attorney, was flying her to San Francisco.

"Kenny and I are leaving immediately to post bond and get Tom released. He is meeting me at the hangar in forty-five minutes. I'm going up to get my purse. Please tell Eddy to have the car ready in five minutes."

Halfway up the stairs, she turned around. "Mom, go through everything Danielle has in this house and search for a contact number. There must be a way to contact the *Foundation*."

"I will find it." Deborah watched Kit run upstairs to prepare to leave the protection of the compound. It would do no good to try to stop her.

San Francisco

After six hours of aggressive negotiating, Kenneth Levin was finally permitted to see Tom, but Kitzia had to remain in the crowded waiting room. Signs of frustration were deeply set in the brow of the attorney when he emerged.

"What is happening?" Kit asked anxiously. "How is Tom holding up?"

Her attorney shook his head. "I don't like this, Kit. Don't like it at all! Everything that is going on in there is unprecedented and highly irregular. I was not allowed to confer with Tom in private."

"That's unconstitutional!" exclaimed Kit.

"You're telling me . . . plus, we were not allowed to post bond at this time."

Kenneth, walking in front of Kitzia, was opening the way for her. She stopped and pulled at his arm. "What do you mean? We can't and won't leave Tom in there!"

"We've got no choice," he said, turning to face Kit. "The arraignment date is set for three days from now. To be perfectly honest, I fear for Tom."

"I'm not moving from here until I see Tom," said Kit.

"You are wasting precious time." He put his arm around her and continued to walk out.

"Was he able to tell you what happened?" she wanted to know.

"He is not sure. Tom went into the city to meet with someone. Ali was left behind, packing. They were to leave the following day. When Tom got back, there were cops all over the place and television crews . . . and he was arrested." Levin took a deep breath before continuing. "They have more garbage on him than you could imagine. Even if we can clear him, he is finished as a physician. His sexual deviations will make for a horrendous scandal." He looked at Kitzia in the eyes. "Did you have any idea?"

Kitzia nodded. "I know about Tom, but that doesn't make him a murderer."

"Tell that to the press. They are going to have a field day with the story."

"What about Ali's body?"

"They won't release it yet. But I'll take care of that tomorrow. Did the boy have any relatives in this country?"

"Not that I know of. Jean-Christophe, our friend, is our only link to his family. I have no idea who to contact. We could look at his passport."

"I'll handle it," said Levin. "Our priority right now is to get Tom out. We are going to use any and all of our contacts. Today is the day when we cash in on any outstanding favors."

Kit thought for a moment, realizing that all of her friends with any power at all were unreachable. She had no idea whom to call.

When they reached the street, Kenneth Levin pulled out his cellular and called his driver, who was probably nearby. A town car turned the corner and came in their direction. Ken and Kit stepped out into the street and signaled for the driver to stop. The car sped up and raced toward them. Kenneth pushed Kitzia out of the way with so much force that she fell, but he kept her from being run over as it sped by.

"Wow!" exclaimed Kit as Kenneth helped her up. "That was close! What do you think that was about?"

Their car pulled up, and the driver got out to open the door for Kit.

"I suppose it's a warning to stay away," said Kenneth, assisting Kit with her damp trench coat as they got into the car.

He was quiet and preoccupied. Kit broke the silence. "What on earth are we going to do?" she asked.

"You get back home. What just happened is proof that you won't be safe here. I'm going right now to speak to Judge Henderson."

"I'll be careful, Kenny. But I think that I should remain close, just in case."

He took her hand. "Trust me on this one. There is nothing you can do here. I'd rather not have to worry about you and totally concentrate on Tom. What you need to do is contact anyone who can help."

"OK. I'll do that." After a pause, she spoke again. "Ken, I don't know if Tom told you. He has a number of enemies."

"He did mention a group of individuals who were violently opposed to what he was doing. He also said they were dangerous. In fact, earlier this month, he gave me documents and certain formulas for safekeeping. I wonder if that is what they want. They could have killed him, and us, for that matter. I think what they want is to make an example out of him. Did he tell you what he was doing?" Kenneth asked.

Kit shook her head.

"That makes two of us. We need to watch our backs. I'll drive you to the airport. My pilot will fly you back"

Kit knew Kenneth was right. Her being there was pointless. She should get back and find a way to reach the *Foundation*. Only they could help now.

Tom O'Neil was in a cell by himself, and for that, he was thankful. It was shocking to see the incredible number of prisoners and the condition of the cells. He had no idea there were so many drug addicts. The majority of the men around him should have been in hospitals or rehab centers, not in jail cells.

He couldn't help wondering if the *Group* had wanted him to see these conditions to flaunt the success of their tactics and rub in his face his failure to prevent it. The heroin addiction had come not only from needles, he remembered. *How many of these individuals started on this road with over-the-counter-medications?*

There was much he wanted to tell Kenneth but was not allowed to speak with him. He hoped his longtime attorney had grasped the situation. This was a major set-up, and working the ropes of the law was not going to get them anywhere. He had told Kenneth to protect Kitzia, and the best way to do it was to send her away and make her stay in the compound. The *Group* would probably do away with him, but it would not be immediately; that he knew. Or they would have done it by now. The elaborate scheme to frame him was a ploy directed at the *Foundation*.

They were using him as a pawn. Yet they had killed an innocent boy in the process, and for that, he hoped they'd all burn.

Why had he delayed his trip to LA? Only a few days before the *Formation* . . .

Tom understood that the *Formation* was a world event that would put a stop to the madness unraveling the country. He well knew that if the members of the *Foundation* could manage to stay alive until that day, things would be OK.

XLI

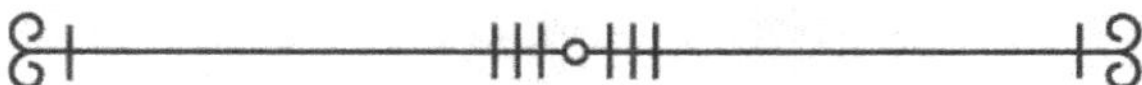

New York

When Jeff punched in the numbers 206976 on the lock pad, the door to the apartment opened, just as Jeff had expected it would. He had memorized the sequence from the note Lili had given him at her cabin some time ago. He had come to understand that she always communicated in numbers. Now, following the same numbers and rearranging them, he would find his way to where she ultimately wanted to take him.

The address on the Upper East Side of New York was the last location in the treasure hunt. Jeff had no idea what he would find but was sure it would be the culmination of all she wanted him to understand. News of Lili's death in a house fire had reached New York. Oddly enough, there had been no mention of him in any of the news reports.

There was no longer any reason for him to remain in New York. He had lost everyone he cared for, and the situation in the city kept worsening. The former Keller building now resembled a military facility; it was heavily protected by armed guards. He had not been able to contact Robert Powers. Jeff was glad he had put away money in the last couple of years. He would put his life back together somewhere else; but first, he had to finish the business that had to do with Lili.

The simplicity of the windowless apartment surprised him. It was minimally furnished but had Lili's touch. The scant furnishings consisted of a desk and chair, a recessed bookcase, a piece of modern art, and a narrow bed. He sat at the desk with a tortoiseshell finish and pulled out the envelope Lili had given him in Guanajuato. Inside he found a small disk and the oddest of objects: a translucent round shaped stone about two centimeters in diameter. He had no idea what it was but knew that it was something important.

Jeff let the contents of the envelope spill over the desktop, and to his surprise, when the disk touched the desk, its surface transformed into a computer screen. Different colored lines crossed to indicate positioning for the disk.

Lili's voice began to speak . . .

> *My dear, if you are listening to this, it only means one thing . . . that I did not return with you and that you are alone. You have in your possession a crystal chip. It is an important component of a configuration necessary for interstellar communication. It has been in my possession for centuries, and that is what we came to retrieve in Mexico and give to Robert. It belongs to and must be returned to the Foundation. If the package reached you, and the stone is inside, then I can only conclude that Robert has disappeared, as well. So now you will have to do it for us.*
>
> *If my calculations are correct, the Formation will take place around October 19th. You must reach the Foundation before that. Use this terminal to enter the numbers I have given you, to determine where to find the entrance to the Foundation's headquarters.*
>
> *Go to them now. They are the only ones who can help you.*

Jeff entered the co-ordinates, and the screen responded with the locations. A flashing symbol corresponded to a spot close to the Azores. The close-up image showed the rippling ocean, and Jeff stared at the screen in confusion. Then a circle formed, and out of the ocean, a small island could be seen. The computer guided him to a selection for points of departure: Bermuda, Lisbon, Madeira . . .

The phone rang. Jeff looked around the room. He did not see a phone. After a couple of rings, he realized the sound came from the desk itself. On the upper left-hand corner, two buttons had appeared on the screen. He punched one of them but did not speak.

"Jeff?" a familiar voice asked.

Jeff still did not answer.

"Jeff, answer me. This is Tracy Jackson."

Jeff froze at the sound of Lili's former attorney.

"I know it's you," continued Tracy.

Jeff looked around the room for a camera and wondered if Tracy could see him.

"It is OK," continued Tracy, "All I know is that this line goes to one of Lili's secret locations . . . and trust me, I have no idea where that is. It lights up when the line is in use. So I took a gamble that it might be you."

Jeff realized then that he must have accidentally pressed the phone line.

Tracy cleared his throat. "I know about Lili."

"Yes, tragic accident," answered Jeff, his voice full of irony.

"I know it was no accident," said Tracy in a grave tone. "I still can't believe they did it!"

"They are *you.*"

"No. I would never have hurt her. Not Lili. She was the only person I truly cared about."

The genuine sadness in Tracy's voice prompted Jeff to question him. "Why are you telling me this?"

"Because I know you'd understand. You loved her too."

Jeff felt the wound in his heart reopen. But Tracy was the last person in the world with whom he wanted to share his grief.

"Jeff, I understand the animosity you feel toward me. It is well-founded. Yes, I have been loyal to the *Group*. It has fed my greed, and I would continue to serve them but never at the expense of Lili." Tracy took a deep breath before continuing. "The least I can do now is what she would have done—that is, to try to keep you alive, now that you hold so many cards."

"What are you talking about?"

"As executor of Lili's will, I hereby inform you that you are the sole beneficiary of her estate."

Jeff was dumbstruck. Too many thoughts raced through his head. *Is Tracy mocking me? Is he trying to keep me on the line to pinpoint my location? What in the world is this fiendish attorney up to?*

"I thought Keller DeWinter had gone under and that the *Group* had appropriated Lili's assets."

"Well, that is partly true. The *Group* believes it has seized a large portion of her assets. But that is not so. Lili was a lot smarter than they realized." He laughed derisively. "She moved her assets around at the beginning of Phase I. Hardly anything remains in the computer technology industry, which will collapse any day now. Her fortune is unimaginable and well diversified . . . gold, steel, oil and gas, solar and wind energy, nanotechnology—the basic stuff that will be needed to rebuild this economy, and now it is all yours."

Jeff could not believe what he was hearing.

"I will do whatever you want me to do," continued Tracy. "My only recommendation is that we transfer the assets as expeditiously as possible. I don't want to be around when the other members find out what is going on."

Jeff was speechless.

"Do you realize that, aside from Robert Powers, you are probably the richest man in the world?" Tracy told him.

"Where is Robert?" was all Jeff managed to ask.

"I honestly don't know. Neither does anyone in the *Group*. He'll do well to stay in hiding." This time Tracy let out a voluminous chortle. "How he tricked them!" He continued to laugh. "Made them put all their money in an industry that was doomed to collapse—Powers Digital! The world is about to take a drastic turn."

"And you?"

"I'll hurt a little," said Tracy, in a more serious tone. "Fortunately, I caught on to what was coming when I saw Lili begin to pull out. Anyway, get back to me as soon as you can with your instructions if they differ from what I have outlined for you. And watch your back. It'd be wise if you stayed away from your apartment. Remain where you are."

"I don't know," said Jeff, rubbing his forehead. "I just don't know about this whole thing."

"It's all yours. She wanted you to have it." After a pause, he said, "I know you still have trouble trusting me. Hey, I don't blame you. The incident with Penelope kind of messed up things between us. But I see no reason why I shouldn't tell you the truth now. Yeah, Penelope was my girl. She happened at a time when things were not going well with my wife, which coincided with a time when several members of the *Group* were feeling resentment toward Lili. Penelope cashed in on both situations. She used me to get ahead. Then, when she started seeing one of the members who had more power, she picked up on the fact that he wanted to ruin Lili. She decided to do the dirty work for him, stole some secret information, twisted it, and tried to hand it off to the press. I couldn't let her do that. I had become aware of the animosity for Lili, perhaps due to her lack of interest in the *Group's* activities. Right then, I made it my mission to protect her interests. I was one of the few who really liked her. I tried to reason with Penelope, hoping she'd see just how dangerous the *Group* could be. The rest, you know. My concern was for Lili, always Lili."

Whatever might really have happened, Jeff felt the sincerity in Tracy's voice when he expressed his feelings for Lili. Jeff was rather amused. He would have never guessed that, all along, Tracy was in love with Lili.

"Tracy, I need a little time to think about all this. It's a lot to take in. I have to give serious thought to whether I want to be in any situation that would get me involved with the *Group* again."

"But unfortunately, you are involved, whether you like it or not."

"I was just thinking of leaving New York. But before I do, I have to accomplish one more request of Lili's."

"Is there anything I can do?"

"I don't think so. It is something that I have to figure out by myself."

"If it involves numbers, I recall that Lili had a preference for the number six."

That caught Jeff's attention. "Say again?"

"You know how Lili recorded everything in numerical sequences. I thought it very peculiar. But some people have a keen aptitude for those things. Anyway, whenever she wanted to keep something confidential, she would add or withhold the number six, and that threw everything out of sequence for anyone who might pry. Hope that helps you. I will leave a set of documents for you to review and sign at Vargo's, the coffee shop around the corner from the Keller building. Ask for Donna, the manager. The contents of the packet will be self-explanatory. I trust that Lili placed in your hands the numbers to the Swiss accounts and safety deposit boxes. Most likely, we'll never meet again. Good luck, Jeff."

The connection cut off. Jeff cast a glance at the rows of numbers on the paper Lili had mailed him and stared at the number six placed at exact intervals among the digits.

The Foundation

Entering the *Foundation's* headquarters on a regular basis was less dramatic than when Chris entered it for the first time. Upon returning from Mexico, the jet headed for a tiny isolated island in the vicinity of the Azores. This was another location the *Foundation* kept camouflaged under a shield of the extra-terrestrial element, veregonium.

Kjell and Danielle flew the plane. Christian, sitting across from Jean-Christophe, was silent, immersed in his own thoughts. He kept looking out the window. Camiel had gone ahead of them. It was obvious the messenger didn't need to make use of an aircraft.

From the air, the ripples of the ocean's waters appeared to be uninterrupted. Descending to a certain altitude, an island became visible. Chris understood that only those with precise co-ordinates knew where to begin the descent. The landing strip appeared at the moment before the aircraft touched the ground. The perimeter of the island remained protected by the currents that maintained the shield and diverted any approaching vessel.

Christian lived in a state of amazement. It was hard to believe he inhabited a world that existed parallel to other realities, that there were fantastic places that remained concealed from ordinary view. He had learned that different dimensions co-existed and time travel was possible. The physicists at the *Foundation* had demonstrated to him how negative energy could hold wormholes open long enough to make traveling to the past possible, which was how Danielle had taken him to ancient Rome, to a time that existed in a space parallel to his time. He had come to accept the fantastic properties of negative space. He realized that accepting only the reality of positive space offered limited vision. The universe was mostly composed of negative energy and negative space, where most other multidimensional realities unfolded.

He was aware of his personal limitations but did not feel in any way hindered by his humanity. He liked being the observer, the recorder, the future rememberer. *Will the world believe me when I write of beings of a higher vibration living among us? Of communication to other galaxies?*

He continued to miss Kitzia, but with each passing day, she became more abstract.

The plane landed and taxied down the runway and into the mouth of a cave. After exiting the aircraft, the Edentians and the two men took an elevator to an underground transport, and from there, to the *Foundation*.

The elders and a medical team from the Temple of Health were there to greet them. Chris had temporarily forgotten Danielle's delicate condition, for she always played down her discomfort. Danielle and Kjell conferred with the elders for a few minutes before the medical team escorted Danielle back to the Temple to let her re-energize.

Kjell returned to Christian and Jean-Christophe and said, getting right to the point, "Something dreadful has occurred. The *Group* has Tom and has murdered Ali." He proceeded to give a short version of what had taken place in San Francisco.

"No!" exclaimed Jean-Christophe, clenching his fists, screaming a string of profanities in French. Tears rolling down his cheeks, he invoked the names of his departed friends, the medians, "Ka . . . Elan, my dear friends, guide our dear Ali through the steps of the transitional world, that he may not walk alone."

Putting their arms around Jean-Christophe, Kjell and Chris walked him out of the station and into the paradise of the underwater world.

For the next two days, the scientists worked non-stop at assembling the communicator. The *Foundation* had recruited the brightest minds from the outside world to work on preparations for the *Formation*. Chris watched with fascination from a distance.

The section of the monolith that had been transported to the *Foundation* was a block of stone about three feet square. In its center was an indentation that indicated the exact placement for the conductor and the metal frame, which was fashioned in the shape of the Star of David. Metal sheets containing infinite chips and wires were fitted into each of the triangular slots. In the center of each of the six sections, a multicolored stone was placed. Then the entire block was placed on a dolly and rolled into a metal box with connections to a giant computer. In total, the components made up a whole that would test the proportions of a giant airport hangar.

Chris counted about fifty scientists working on the set-up, and when Kjell was ready to deposit the final stone, ten others came to assist. A number of *Foundation* members watched with interest from a glassed-in observation room and stood ready to assist in any way they might be needed. Having been officially declared to be the rememberer and recorder of these events, Christian was allowed to watch the project from a closer spot.

In the meantime, the Council of Elders had reached the decision that Camiel and Zephon would be sent out again, this time to rescue Tom from prison. Kjell came out to inform Chris that the wormholes would be put to use again, creating a momentary slot of unaccountable time, during which Tom would be freed. Kitzia O'Neil would be brought to the *Foundation,* as well. How this would be accomplished was explained in detail to Chris and Jean-Christophe. Though neither of them could fully grasp the concept, both were thrilled and relieved to know about the rescue.

Los Angeles

Kitzia returned home to as much pandemonium as she had witnessed outside the jail in San Francisco. She was astounded to see the high-security electrical gates standing wide open. *And why in the world are police cars and ambulances on the grounds?* As Kit's taxi reached the front door, the siren of an ambulance blared and drove away at a clip. She feared the worst.

Kitzia jumped out of the cab and ran past officers who tried to stop her.

"I live here!" she shouted, pushing her way into the house. She spotted some of the staff, but could not see her mother, and her stomach twisted into knots. A second stretcher was being brought out, bearing a body covered by a sheet. Kit could see the edges of a plastic bag. "Mom!" her voice cracked.

"It's Enrique," said Eddy behind her.

"And my mother?" asked Kit, anxiously watching the stretcher being put in the ambulance.

"She is OK. Mai Li tried to shoot her."

Her policeman friend, Officer Jones, hurried over. "Your mother is all right. A bullet brushed her shoulder; she fell and suffered a small concussion, but she refuses to go to the hospi—"

Kitzia did not let him finish. She ran into the house toward the library where several people stood outside the door. Deborah was sitting on the sofa, her blouse halfway removed and a bandage across her upper arm and shoulder.

"Mother?"

The paramedic, closing his medical bag, was the first to speak. "Lady, I think your mom should go to the hospital and have that checked," he said, pointing to the bump on Deborah's forehead.

Deborah waved her hand in the air. "It's OK, really. My daughter is a doctor."

Kitzia nodded without taking her eyes off her mother. The young medic and his crew took their exit.

Eddy and Officer Jones had now reached the room.

"It seems your housekeeper and driver broke into the safe; both had guns and their argument turned deadly. Your mom happened to walk in on them," said Jones. He paused, giving Kitzia time to digest the news. "They shot each other. One of the bullets brushed Deborah's shoulder, and she fell and hit her head."

Kit shot a glance at Deborah for confirmation.

"Eddy called Officer Jones, and he got here within minutes."

"I'm glad I was nearby."

"Thank you, Jones."

He took that as his cue and added, "Well, I guess I'd better wrap this up." Bowing his head to Deborah, he shook Kitzia's hand.

"I'll go lock up," added Eddy. "I've corrected the glitch in the system."

Kit waited until they were alone to ask her mother. "How did you know?"

"I have suspected them for a while." Kit sat down as Deborah continued. "I've been keeping an eye on those two. Tonight, Mai Li broke into Danielle's safe and was sorting through the contents. I confronted her, and she shot me. I fell and think I hit the corner of the table. I must have been out for a few minutes. When I came to, Mai Li was dead, holding Danielle's necklace, and Enrique's body was shot and lying next to hers." Deborah took the Roman medallion from her skirt pocket and handed into Kit.

"So it was this medallion in particular?"

"Yes." said Deborah. "We trusted Mai Li for so many years!"

"I wonder when they turned on us? Was she planted to spy on us from the beginning?" Looking at the piece of jewelry, she added, "I'll have to figure out why this medallion—"

"Now, tell me," said Deborah. "What happened with Tom?"

"It's bad. They wouldn't let me see him. It's a big frame-up, and we have to get him out."

Kit looked exhausted, and Deborah was sure that Kit had not eaten all day. "Why don't you go change? I'll have some food prepared, and we'll figure things out."

Kit did not have the energy to protest. She headed upstairs, holding the medallion in her hand. In her closet, still clutching the medallion, she reached for a pair of flats. She felt the stir of a breeze in the room behind her and was startled. She slowly stepped out of the closet and saw them. Standing on each side of the window were Camiel and Zephon. The erect figures were almost ethereal.

Kit stared at them for a moment. The unrelenting apprehension and fear regarding the fate of Danielle, Chris, and Tom began to diminish. The knots in her shoulders and stomach simply melted away. And she knew that these two elite messengers would be the salvation Tom needed.

Her mind was about to explode with questions, so many that she was unable to articulate any one of them. Zephon's smile assured her that they understood. He reached out to take the medallion. And Kit burst into tears.

San Francisco

How long can I go without eating? Thomas O'Neill wondered. He knew better than to eat the food at the prison. That would be the easiest way to be poisoned. Tom had not missed the scornful look in the guard's eyes. He knew something Tom didn't. If he had to die now, so be it. Tom felt exhausted.

Will it happen tonight? Tom resigned himself to the inevitable. He had provided the *Foundation* with valuable information that had saved millions of lives. It was just a few days until the *Formation* was to take place.

"The *Formation . . .*" repeated Tom to himself while sitting on his bed, holding his head in his hands. *Communication with celestial monitors, an exchange of information with the carriers of life! An event that occurs only every so many thousand years.* Robert had told him this *Formation* was a particularly important one. Humanity would be seen as a successful experiment of Project Urantia 606 and capable of choosing its own destiny. There might be hard times ahead, Robert explained. Rectification of the existing planetary imbalance would bring about what would be perceived as catastrophic occurrences. He hoped Kitzia had prepared the shelters.

His only unforgivable mistake had been to compromise the safety of Ali, the child that had been entrusted to his care; and for that act of negligence, *he deserved to die,* he reasoned.

He wished he could have seen Jean-Christophe one more time.

His thoughts came to a stop when he realized it was almost ten o'clock. The lights would be turned off in seconds. He had come to hate the dark. He heard a loud click, as if the generator had stopped. The lights dimmed but didn't go out. He saw the guard coming toward his cell, still wearing the sneer on his face. Tom took a deep breath and prepared for what was coming. The guard never reached his cell. His steps slowed, and he stopped mid-stride. Guards and prisoners, alike, began to resemble toys with dying batteries. Tom was perplexed. His cell door slid open, and he heard a voice coming from the dim hallway. "Tom . . . come on out."

It was the voice of Camiel.

Los Angeles

Zephon had stayed behind to take Kitzia to the ranch in Colorado where she would join Tom, who had been freed from prison. From there, they would be taken to the *Foundation.* Kit could hardly contain her excitement, but it was tinged with apprehension, and she could not get rid of the knot in her stomach.

"Are you all right? You look pale," said Deborah.

"I'm fine." Kit kissed her mother, who would await Ali's body and give him a proper burial.

"Darling, from now on, your life will be such a wonderful adventure!" sighed Deborah.

Kit understood that she was referring to the wasted years—the years of emotional paralysis when she had determined that she could not live without Tom.

Zephon stood by. The pilot flying the helicopter was named Jeffery. Somewhere outside of LA, they were to switch to an airplane and then go on to Colorado.

The ranch in Aspen was a veritable fortress, with armed guards at the entrance and others posted as lookouts on the roof of the house. Tom came out to greet her. Kit, in her jubilation, tried hard to control her nausea. The changing of planes and flying at lower than normal altitudes had made her motion sick.

Tom stared at her, then broke into a gentle smile.

"I'll get you get something to eat. Let's go in the house and relax."

She was touched by his concern over her discomfort. "Oh, Tom, I was so frightened for you!"

He took her hand and kissed it. "I know, but everything is going to be fine now. I promise."

They talked for hours. She tried to alleviate his guilt over Ali's death, and he related everything he knew about the *Foundation.* He spoke about the importance of the upcoming *Formation.*

At this point, he saw no reason to withhold the fact that he had been doing genetic research for Danielle. That she had asked him to help her find those carrying the Edentian genetic code, the extra gene in the DNA helix.

She recalled the bloodwork Tom had insisted on, and she suddenly knew. She knew everything. She knew about Chris and herself. Her eyes focused on Tom, with a suppliant glance, in hopes that he would confirm what she already suspected.

"How could Danielle have guessed that we would find one another?" asked Kit.

"It wouldn't have mattered to her where your happiness was concerned, but the fact that you did find each other confirmed her suspicions. With each of you carrying the extra gene, your offspring would have the opportunity to reclaim some of the lost Edentian traits. The race will, in time, get back on track and expand its quest for perfection, as was once intended."

The excitement had made her nausea bearable. She smiled incredulously at Tom, who upon seeing her, had immediately guessed what she had failed to realize—that she was carrying Chris's child.

Kit mentally relived the one night of lovemaking before Chris had departed.

"I suspect Danielle was one of the Edentians entrusted with the mission of bringing together a couple that could unite the genes again," said Tom. "You have no idea, my dear, the destiny that awaits you."

While Tom was explaining to her about the gene research, the TV caught their attention. This was Theodore Edwards's first television appearance since the accident that almost took his life. Leaning on a cane, the minister looked stronger and more determined than ever. He addressed the nation, thanking the populace for the faith they had shown during his ordeal.

"And now the time has come for me to carry the Lord's Word and take action to protect His kingdom," said the minister. "As president, I will return this country to its former glory. I need every one of you who believes in Jesus Christ to stand with me in support of the retaliation for the aggression of the Israelis against the Islamic citizens in Gaza . . ."

"That is not possible," said Tom, watching the broadcast.

"With the current oil shortage, it's no surprise that he's speaking for the Arab countries now."

"No," corrected Tom. "It is not possible that Edwards would recover after the type of spinal injury he suffered. His X-rays were sent to our staff for neurological evaluation."

"He looks perfectly strong."

"I am telling you," insisted Tom. "There is something wrong here."

The transmission was viewed in its entirety at the *Foundation's* headquarters. They had no trouble identifying Cirel in the guise of the preacher.

"He feels cornered," said one of the elders in the viewing room. "Therefore, he is launching the attack."

"Can we run those tapes again, the ones in the Gaza Strip?" asked Parker. "We had Perez Levi's word that he would refrain from retaliation until after the *Formation*."

"And he is trying," said the elder. "But what can he do when there are rockets and daily suicide bombings against his people?"

The tapes ran back, and they watched in silence. Members of Hamas drove trucks laden with explosives toward the Israeli Army post in the Gaza Strip. None of the seven trucks reached their destination. One after the other evaporated in huge explosions as the Israeli Army fired back.

"People around the world don't understand the difference between official Islam and the radical Islamic who screams for the destruction of Israel," concluded Parker.

The next news report showed the anti-Israel demonstration in the West Bank town of Ramallah. Youth, women, and children carrying green Hamas flags chanted slogans.

"Roll that back," said Kjell. "The background—zoom in. I see Cirel and . . ."

In the crowd, next to the Cirel stood a handsome man. "That is no other than Lucius Catilina! He has brought the depraved villain into this time!" exclaimed Kjell in a rage.

"We did not do a very good job of sealing the crack," whispered Danielle in the background.

"We did!" Kjell objected. "He must have sneaked him in right before the miniscule polar shift."

"What do you suppose they are really up to?" asked one of the elders.

Danielle, feeling out of breath, allowed Kjell to answer. "The plan is clear. With the launch of violence against the Israelis, they will start fulfilling the prophecies and begin World War III. With worldwide support, they'll annihilate as many Jews as possible. Cirel is still convinced they are hiding the center piece needed for the *Formation*."

"Cirel and Catilina will destroy the planet!" said one of the elders.

"We have a very serious problem. Do we use the energy of the current we control to protect Israel, or do we use them to help launch our signal? Without the center stone, we absolutely cannot do both!" said one of the lead scientists.

"We still have thirty-six hours," said Kjell. "I say we use the current to create the weather conditions to protect Israel and continue trying to launch our signal with our technology and the remaining current."

"I'm afraid we won't make it work without the center stone," replied John Larkin. "We simply can't hold the wormhole open long enough to send our transmission."

"How far are we reaching?"

"Out of our galaxy but barely out of our sector," replied Larkin.

"Keep trying. This situation changes everything, including our departure," said Danielle. "If the Urantia 606 project fails, then we have failed as well. We will remain here with you to face the outcome . . ." It was becoming harder and harder for her to keep up her oxygen level.

"If we miss our *Formation*, how much time do we have?" Martine asked Kjell.

"Before the hail?"

"Yes."

"The meteor shower is an electromagnetic shower that will hit in a matter of weeks. The first hit will cover a radius of 300 miles over the Atlantic."

"The *Foundation* will be destroyed," declared Martine.

The *Foundation* elders exchanged a glance. "We have always prepared for a time such as this," said one of the elders. "We will not allow our treasure, the accumulation of knowledge, to fall into the wrong hands. Once again, we must wipe the slate clean. I propose we initiate the operation to self-destruct. We will begin evacuation in seventy-two hours."

XLII

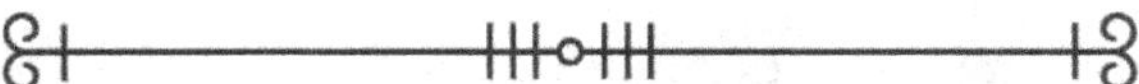

New York

Jeff was not fully aware of the urgency of delivering the crystal chip to the *Foundation*. He thought he was acting expeditiously when he made arrangements to lease a SableLiner and hired a flight crew. To him, the most important thing was to check the background of the crew, and he did so in painstaking detail. After much deliberation, he headed for the Bahamas and then for Bermuda; once there, he would inform the crew of his final destination.

It was late morning when the plane landed in Bermuda. Jeff was asked to deplane to clear customs. The pilot informed him that customs agents would be boarding the plane to conduct a routine drug search. In the meantime, he would supervise the refueling. Jeff started back toward the plane when the pilot raised his thumb to let him know the aircraft had checked out. Then, two customs officials boarded the plane, accompanied by a German shepherd. The pilot climbed aboard behind them. In a few moments, the dog and only one of the inspectors left the plane. Jeff was alarmed and hurried aboard to see what the problem could be.

"Is everything all right?" he asked the pilot.

The engines revved. "It is now." The senior pilot turned around. It was Robert Powers.

"But . . ." At that moment, Jeff saw the former pilot gagged and bound in the farthest back seat. "What is going on?" Jeff asked.

"Don't have time to explain right now," answered Robert. "You've got something to deliver to the *Foundation*. Take a seat and prepare for the fastest flight of your life."

Jeff did as he was told, casting a glance at the man tied to the seat who, resigned to his fate, had stopped struggling. When they approached the *Founda-*

tion, Jeff experienced the same apprehension all first-time visitors felt when the aircraft began its descent and no land could be seen from the air. Like those before him, he nervously watched the endless ripples of the ocean. Robert's voice came through the intercom. "It's OK, Jeff. Sit tight."

It was a smooth landing. The island emerged from nowhere with its long, wide landing strip. The co-pilot took over. Before the plane came to a full stop, Jeff got up and walked to the cockpit. Robert was already out of his seat, ready to jump out as soon as the plane came to a stop. He patted Jeff on the back. "C'mon," he said urgently.

A number of men in fatigues met them. There were no greetings or exchanges of any kind. Robert merely pointed to the back of the plane, and the men climbed aboard to get the interloper. Someone signaled to Robert to hurry and yelled something in a foreign language. Robert began to run, urging Jeff to follow him into a camouflaged opening in the ground.

Robert responded in Hebrew and turned to Jeff. "They want us out of sight before the next plane lands."

"What plane?"

"The one that has been tailing us from Bermuda. The one that has been right behind you since you left New York."

Jeff looked genuinely startled. He had been so careful, plotting his course. The second plane arrived just a few minutes later. Cirel was the first to descend, followed by Lucius Catilina and four bodyguards. Behind them, the pilots and four men in camouflage, the toughest of Cirel's new terror brigade, stepped off the plane.

Catilina looked around and exclaimed, "Fantastic! What I admire most about your time is this . . . what do you call it?"

"Technology," responded Cirel, amused.

"Yes. How you can keep places such as this hidden from sight. You say the enemy is here and underneath the water?" He tapped the ground with the heel of his foot. "That is even more remarkable!"

"And there they will die like trapped rats," said Cirel.

Catilina looked disappointed, so Cirel added. "Don't worry. I'll give you some hand-to-hand combat. I am told you enjoy tasting the blood of your victims."

"That is an exaggeration," said Catilina casually. Then, changing the subject, he added, "But I have to admit that I have found the majority of the men in your time to be lacking in determination and valor. They are complacent, and your women are unfeminine and sloppy."

"I told you this is a pathetic race."

One of his men pointed to a nearby opening. Cirel smiled maliciously and headed in that direction. "Might be one of the exits. We will blast them to pieces.

Without its headquarters, the *Foundation* will crumble. You'll see some unforgettable action; then you can go back to your time and rule, rule the whole Roman Empire!"

"I thought you said history can't be changed," commented Catilina.

"Who said anything about changing? Don't you know who you are, Caro? The true ruler of Rome!"

"Don't mock me, Cirel!" There was sudden fury in Catilina's eyes. "I have seen the historical documents. None of them list me but as ruler of the underworld."

"They will, I assure you. They will!"

Something rose in Catalina's throat, and his voice began to quiver. "You told me that nature would not allow paradoxes."

"Only when they are inconsistent. You are meant to rule, and you may do so in a Rome parallel to the one you left behind."

"What are you talking about?"

"Let me explain. Reality does not consist of a single universe. When you travel forward or backward, you do not reach the same universe you departed from. You enter a multidimensional reality. In this time, the method of rearranging the world at a sub-atomic level is called Quantum Theory, and is ruled by probability and chance. Therefore, nature will only allow those behaviors that are consistent. One cannot be a pauper and a ruler simultaneously."

When Cirel saw the look in Catilina's eyes, he smiled, thinking that he should know better than to deceive a ruffian. He sought to amend his statement.

"Words of current technology seem empty; instead, let me show you." Cirel took out a device, a square metal box that fit in the palm of his hand. He aimed it at the sky. The white clouds began moving in a circular motion, turned gray, and were followed by a rumble of thunder. Cirel reversed the movement, and the sky became as blue as it was before.

"You see. I control the skies and the weather. I can control the world—demolish it if I want to."

Catilina's eyes were fixed on the gadget. His mind filled with the infinite number of applications for such power. The arch-rebel did not miss the look of desire in his eyes and knew he now had something Catilina desperately coveted. He signaled his men to go ahead of them, and when they were a far enough away not to overhear, he turned toward Catilina. "So, my friend, are we together?"

Catilina looked Cirel in the eye and gave him an enigmatic smile. "Caro, it has been such fun and all . . ." He pulled a short gold dagger and lunged at Cirel.

The arch-rebel, always aware of a possible double-cross, never failed to wear a protective vest under his clothing. The dagger encountered resistance, and before Catilina understood what had happened, Cirel shot him in the stomach with a laser gun.

Catilina fell backward, his eyes wide open. Cirel watched the body hit the ground and then knelt next to it. Cirel's men had turned around and stood at a distance, afraid to get closer.

"Sergius Lucius Catilina . . ." Cirel articulated every word slowly, as if savoring it for the last time. "Beautiful Catilina, what a pity! We could have had some good times before the end."

He raised the wounded man's head. His breath was irregular; his eyes remained open and fixed. Cirel leaned to kiss his lips, then removed the ring carved with the coiled serpent and placed it on his own finger. He ran his finger over the wound and raised the bloody finger to his lips. Catilina took his last breath, and only then did Cirel acknowledge the obsessive attraction he had always felt toward the young patrician.

Concentrating on his ritual, neither Cirel nor his men saw the Israeli soldiers until it was too late. The terror brigade tried to shoot but were gunned down by the band of Israeli soldiers that sprang from the numerous openings on the ground where they had hidden themselves. When Cirel saw the men advancing toward him, he jumped up and reached for his laser gun but knew immediately the laser would be useless against what he recognized to be clear veregonium shields, which they were carrying. He tossed the gun and pulled out his metal gadget—the one that had made Catilina so envious—and pointed it to the sky. To his horrified surprise, nothing happened. It would not activate the current, for he had locked into the command to activate a geomagnetic shower!

He tossed the gadget to the ground and stepped back, but when he turned, he saw he was surrounded. He saw the unremitting stream of fatigues coming at him from all directions. Cirel felt like a cornered beast. He stopped, stood still, and his last effort was to raise his arms to the sky. His body shook violently and, to the surprise of the soldiers, sparks of electricity flew from his fingers.

The Israelis halted. Their orders were to get him dead or alive. They would have preferred to bring him back alive, but confronted with the freakiness of his nature, they realized they would have to kill him. With guns at the ready, the soldiers awaited the order to shoot. Electric currents continued to blast from his hands. The color of his skin turned crimson red, and shockingly, the body of Cirel of Brann, whom they recognized as the personification of Adolf Hitler, self-ignited. Flames engulfed his body for several minutes, consuming it almost instantly.

"What the heck was that?" the Israeli colonel uttered.

The soldiers moved cautiously closer to watch the gruesome spectacle, some thinking it was a trick, others a hallucination. But little by little, they were convinced they were witnessing a true incidence of spontaneous human combustion.

Within minutes, it was over. The body incinerated faster than if it had been in a crematorium. Shards of bone and ashes were all that was left of Cirel of Brann, a.k.a., der Führer.

"We were told to be prepared for anything, but this—" said the Israeli colonel, shaking his head in disbelief.

"The main thing is that he is gone. Let's gather the bones and take them with us as proof," said another Israeli officer.

Some of the men had now gathered around the spot where Lucius Catilina had fallen. The Israeli colonel pushed his way through his men, who stood stupefied and speechless. The body of Catilina was slowly disappearing, at first losing its solidity, then fading out, as if it had been no more than a hologram. Circles of light rose from the ground, fainter and fainter, until the body had completely vanished.

"Incredible!" said the colonel, unable to say another word.

The Foundation

The transmission room was abuzz with activity. Scientists and technicians were working frantically alongside John Larkin and Kjell to set in motion the operation of the now intact monolith.

Danielle observed from a distance. Marina Cantrelli continuously monitored her vitals. Despite Danielle's frequent reassurances that she was all right, everyone knew better.

"We have a visitor," announced Kjell through his headset, "and trouble on land."

"Would you like me to switch on the monitor to oversee the ground?" asked a technician at the station.

"No," responded Kjell. "Right now, we need every ounce of energy focused on our transmission."

One of the elders wearing a headset intervened. "It is Robert Powers. I have asked him to return to us."

Martine turned and addressed Danielle. "His job on the outside is finished. He needs to stand with us again."

A smile registered on Danielle's face. How silly she must have seemed to the Edentian Council, stating that she could not leave without him, when they knew perfectly well that Robert was with them to the end.

Martine's hand rested on Danielle's. "Amazing! Robert managed to maintain the confidence of the *Group* until only recently."

"Stand by . . ." announced John Larkin through the loudspeaker. "We'll run the sequence again."

One by one, the numerical series appeared, filling a portion of the huge screen. After all six sequences were locked, there was static, then a blur.

"It is hopeless," announced John Larkin. "We can't keep the sequence locked without the central piece."

A moment of silence followed. All heads turned to Danielle. As senior monitor and recorder, this was her transmission. It was her call.

"Disengage," she ordered sadly.

The metal door flung open. "No!" shouted Robert Powers in his deep, stentorian voice. "Lock it!"

Jeff Montgomery appeared behind him. The violet aura, that only Edentians could perceive, surrounded the young man, letting them know he was carrying the crucial missing piece.

Danielle, Robert, and Kjell exchanged a smile of triumph. "Continue the sequence!" ordered Kjell.

All the scientists and technicians jumped into action. Robert guided Jeff to the monolith, where John took the piece from him and placed it in the vacant slot in the center of the medallion. Quick computations were made on the computers, and the main terminal acknowledged the insertion. Within seconds, the whole sequence of numbers appeared on the screen, and the progression continued to its ultimate conclusion. One of the elders switched on an auxiliary screen on one side of the room and moved toward Danielle.

"It is over," he announced. "Cirel, the arch-rebel, is no more. We will begin the dissolution of his operation."

Danielle nodded.

The connection was ready. Within fifteen minutes, they would commence lockdown for the *Formation.* The atmosphere was electric. Danielle, the official monitor, was to transmit the message. Christian and Jean-Christophe helped Danielle up and then Robert picked her up in his arms and carried her to the platform. The scientists yielded their seats to the two Edentians. Danielle pushed buttons and turned knobs with agility. She spoke in the Andonic tongue, as frequently used by the Edentians.

"Andos Rashin hjun brac . . . Urantia 606 00101100 7800 606." When she finished, she signaled Kjell that she had recorded the message in its entirety, and it was ready for transmission.

John Larkin advised them the final stone had more than tripled the potency of the conductor, and there was an indication they would have plenty of time to deliver the signal exactly when it should connect with RA.

"With Lili gone, we are going to have a vacant spot at our end."

"I think we'll manage," John said.

"I was thinking that Christian and Kitzia, given the fact they are both star seeds, could fill in for us."

Robert waved at Camiel and Zephon, who stood on the other side of the room. "How long will it take to bring Kitzia O'Neil here?" the Edentian asked telepathically.

"About three hours," responded the messengers.

Robert signaled them to go ahead, and the messengers disappeared through the walls.

"This is very exciting," said Danielle, filled with a burst of energy. "We will make contact with our brothers and sisters on Earth." she said, referring to the other Edentians stationed on the planet.

Robert signaled to Kjell, who activated the synchronization that would communicate simultaneously with their fellows throughout the world. After the message was sent, the screens switched to a map of the globe, and Robert went to assist Danielle back to her seat. But his time, she chose to walk. Marina checked her pulse.

"I've never felt better," said Danielle.

Christian watched with anticipation. He had observed with minute interest every step of the process, as had President Parker, Ferguson, and the staff. On the screen, a blue light popped up in a couple of locations in Europe, then a third one in South Africa. Chris could not contain his curiosity. "What is happening?" he asked.

"You are watching the synchronization of the *Formation*," answered Danielle. "There are other Edentians on Urantia, lining up for the event, some of whom we have been unable to contact. They are awaiting our signal that they have been recognized. When RA receives our signal, it will view the *Formation* as a sign of order in the U-606 project. Each sector will then transmit its message. An evaluation of the world situation will be made by the life carriers on RA, who will send a response to each of our sectors within thirty-six hours. We have decided that you and Kit should represent the evolving race on the *Formation*."

Danielle looked at the expression of surprise on Christian's face.

"I think our mission will be well represented by you," she said.

Robert joined them, accompanied by Jeff.

Danielle looked at the young man and said, "I know that you were very special to one of us. I can truly say that she chose well."

Jeff kissed her hand, remembering it was Danielle who had once saved his life.

"Let me introduce you," added Danielle. "This is Jeff Montgomery . . . Martine DuChamp, head of the *Foundation*, and Dr. Marina Cantrelli." When she finished all the introductions, Jeff shook everyone's hand with respect and nodded to Kjell at a distance.

"Marina will be glad to show you around the premises, which unfortunately will soon shut down."

The elders standing by a monitor signaled them to approach.

"But right now," said Danielle, acknowledging their signal, "we all should go and see what just took place upstairs. I think you will be most interested." She was speaking to Jeff, in particular.

The whole episode had been recorded—from the moment Cirel's plane landed until his extinction. They also got to watch the dismantling of the arch-rebel's hunting operation. The two Israeli commanding officers walked about in consternation while the rest of the men gathered the ashes of the former arch-rebel.

"I did not think it would end like this," one of the Israeli men was saying. "I always thought there would be the right kind of closure, some sort of retribution. The filthy criminal still got away in his own way."

"Oh, we don't know that. There are things we'll never understand," his companion responded.

"Neither will our minister. We had a hard time convincing him it was Hitler. Now, we have nothing to verify that."

"I think Perez Levi will believe; he'll understand."

"It's still not fair, not right. The murderer took over twelve million lives and died one miserable time in a single, quick incineration." He shook his head. "Not fair, really . . ." A roach climbed onto his boot. He shook it off and stamped it repeatedly, reducing it to mush.

The other officer laughed. "Stop. I think you got it."

The officer lightened up. "It felt good, unusually good, to smash it. I don't know why. What was I saying? Oh yeah, 'retribution' . . . twelve million lives, six of them ours. I'd like to think that there would be some type of equity in retribution."

"Perhaps there is," answered the officer, swatting a mosquito on his arm.

Danielle watched Jeff, who intently watched the scene, without understanding what was going on. But when he saw the flames consuming Cirel, he felt a huge release in the knowledge that Cirel had suffered in the same way his beloved Lili had.

"Retribution," murmured Danielle. "Oh, I think there is."

Christian, watching the crushing of the insects, understood better than the officers, that there would be retribution, indeed, that justice would be served for the twelve million lives.

"May I get you anything?" Marina asked, addressing Danielle.

"I am really all right," answered Danielle. "It would make me feel better if you were to show the *Foundation* complex to our guest." She pointed at Jeff.

Marina hesitated but could not refuse. "I'd be delighted," she said.

Jeff followed Marina. He was feeling unusually upbeat, perhaps a little guilty. He did not particularly want to lose his inner pain. He wanted Lili to be part of him forever. He suddenly realized that he had not looked at another woman since the moment he had met her.

Marina turned to him and smiled. Jeff could not deny that she was indeed lovely.

The *Formation* took place as scheduled. On October 19, at 4:00 p.m., a faint spiral of light left the Earth's atmosphere and, forming two concentric circles, disappeared into the firmament.

Shortly after sending the original salute, the screen in the *Foundation's* transmission room showed signals flashing randomly around the globe, representing the positions of the many sectors. They looked like stars twinkling on the map, with Asia being the last to appear. One after the other, the sectors lined up in position to forward their salute to RA, the monitoring vessel.

Kitzia and Tom arrived at the *Foundation's* headquarters just in the nick of time, just as the alignment began. Without any formalities, she had been taken underground and hurried to the transmission room, where she was asked to stand in a glass cube next to Christian.

Neither one spoke, listening carefully to their instructions. Chris and Kitzia were asked to project a thought, formulate an evaluation of life on the planet, or simply say a prayer that would accompany their hologram to the celestial life carriers. It was during those minutes of silent meditation that Christian picked up Kitzia's thoughts and knew that she was pregnant. Her vision of infinite hope for a brighter future and a prayer for the welfare of those she loved, especially Chris and her child, broke his concentration. Not being able to contain his emotion, he put his arms around her.

It was that picture of unselfish love, joy, and hopefulness projected as an example of the human condition. Danielle was pleased.

Kitzia was able to see Danielle for only a few minutes after the transmission, barely long enough for one embrace and a few scant words to express their mutual joy. The medical team broke up their reunion to urge Danielle to accompany them at once. Kit was distressed and fraught with anxiety at how frail Danielle had become. The presence of oxygen tanks and a clearly identifiable resuscitation team indicated just how compromised her friend's heart had become.

Tom O'Neil joined the team and signaled to Kit to let Danielle go. There was nothing else she could do.

"I'll send for you shortly," Danielle whispered before she left, and Kitzia, controlling her tears, smiled back and nodded her head.

"We are losing her, aren't we, Chris?" Kit asked, watching her friend disappear through the series of glass corridors.

"Yes," answered Chris.

"Where are they taking her? I am a physician, and she is my best friend. I should be allowed to be near her."

"I'm sure she will send for you, shortly. Danielle goes into a crystal chamber much like a giant MRI machine that recharges her heart. In this manner, she will be able to go on for another twelve hours."

"For how long?" asked Kit.

"As long as she needs it."

"Of course, in here, in this high-tech facility. But will she ever be able to leave this place?"

"She is leaving; they are all leaving."

"To go where?" Kit said, alarmed.

"Come on, let me show you around," said Chris not wanting to overwhelm Kit. "There is so much to see, so much Danielle would want you to see before it is gone."

"I don't understand," said Kit.

"You will after I tell you what I have learned."

Kit followed Chris out the door. She cast an inquisitive look around the room where the *Formation* had been accomplished. The technical teams continued to work at their computers. She spotted John Larkin through a window on the second floor. He waved but returned at once to the monitors to continue programming the computers to receive the expected reply from RA. To his right, on another level, was an observation room. Through the glass panels, Kit could see several groups of people engaged in animated conversations. Among them, she saw President Parker and several other high-profile dignitaries. On another platform, in a corner of the gigantic transmission room, her eyes rested on another glass cube. Standing outside the cube was Cardinal Santis, surrounded by a group of men. Her first impulse was to go to him, but, seeing the number of people in the group, she decided to speak with him later. Besides, she needed to be alone with Chris. Taking his hand, she let him guide her through one of the exit doors.

RA

The luminous interplanetary vessel, that looked like no more than a brilliant star spinning out of orbit in the cosmos, welcomed the greeting from the monitors in charge of the Urantia 606 project.

Aboard the ship, the visiting dignitary, a member of the Edentian Council of Sages, was who opened the channels of communication. In accordance with procedures, as the series of messages began arriving from Urantia's worldwide sectors, the ship's processors decoded the incoming information.

"All is in order," announced Orsef of Edentia, and the life carriers proceeded to give the orders to turn the vessel around and head in the direction of Urantia's solar system.

The Foundation

"Of all the places down here, this one baffles me the most," said Chris when he and Kit entered the observatory—a room connected to the transmission room, outfitted with a wealth of high-tech telescopic equipment. Kit was speechless, moving almost in a daze through a world that seemed incomprehensible.

"How can an observatory be underwater?" she asked.

"It is linked to the most powerful telescopes on the planet. Carnegie Institute in Washington, Mount Stromlo Observatory in Australia, Lawrence Berkeley, Kitt Peak, the Space Telescope Science Institute . . ."

She moved to the multitude of computer screens registering the movement of the galaxies.

"I've always been interested in astronomy." She began running her finger across a screen that plotted a timeline on a logarithmic scale. "I believe these tick marks represent in seconds the immense periods of time since the creation of the universe. We are here," she asserted, pointing to the mark between the Stelliferous Era and the Degenerate Era."

"Most likely, the purpose of this time line is not only to show how the universe started, but how and when civilization will end," volunteered Chris. The *Foundation* has always known things that the world is only now beginning to grasp.

"Advanced civilizations periodically reach a certain technological level. But since the level of the spirit of the race does not keep pace with its technological progress, the advancement is eradicated. And it looks like it will happen again," said Chris.

"But I thought the *Formation* would change that."

"It will, in a way. Danielle says the monitors need to see on this pass, that the world is truly ready for that leap. Unfortunately, the *Foundation* has already given the order to seal and evacuate its headquarters, so they will be sealed and shifted to another location. Don't ask me how. Anyway, we are to evacuate this place in the next forty-eight hours."

"What about all the art and literature that was brought in from the outside world?"

"It is already being moved to a safe place."

"But what is to become of all this history and documentation?" she asked anxiously.

"I suppose it will be rediscovered one day and finally put to good use."

"With all I have seen happening in our world today, the savage way we behave, I question when we will be really ready as a civilization to take that leap? Have we evolved?" Kit placed her hand on her womb.

"Don't be afraid. Our child will be born into a better world. I am sure of that!" He stood behind her, placed his arms around her, and whispered close to her ear, "We have evolved."

"There is a global plot to make it look otherwise."

"That is why the *Group* had to be stopped; why its leader, Cirel, had to be taken out. It was Cirel that was behind the lie. It is obvious that a great number of people have begun to unravel the mystery of creation. There won't be any reason to continue hiding the truth."

"And what is the truth?"

"There are many truths. To me, the most important truth has been the understanding that we are not the center of creation, or even the most important creation in the universe, as so many religions would have us believe. In fact, we, as well as the matter that composes our world, comprise an infinitesimally small percentage of the matter that constitutes the universe—something like five percent of its entire scope. The rest is 'dark matter' and 'dark energy.' You see, it turns out that we are not even made of the same stuff the rest of the universe is made of. We, our galaxy and the rest of the galaxies we see, are merely minor creations, spinning out of control into this dark energy." He thought for a moment. "It is really beyond what we can comprehend!"

"Wasn't that one of Einstein's early theories that he abandoned as a mistake?"

"Perhaps," said Chris. "If so, it turns out he was right. The universe is saturated with some sort of anti-gravity or dark energy, and that is what is truly real. That unseen force is what is responsible for the whirling of the Milky Way, for causing our universe to expand, and for tossing the galaxies farther and farther apart. That brings us back to the big question. Are *we* even real? Do we merely exist in God's mind or that of some other deity?"

"Are you saying that we might not be God's ultimate creation, but most likely, a creation of the created?"

"I'm not sure. That has crossed my mind." Chris was glad Kit was on his same wavelength. "Furthermore, look at this." He pointed to another screen that showed positive and negative curvatures of the universe. "These happen temporarily, depending on the amount of matter the universe contains at a given time. From what I gather, after reviewing all the theories the astrophysicists at the *Foundation*'s propose, the universe is actually flat."

Kit looked at him, not quite with him on that one.

"Well, doesn't much of what Danielle has said to us make a lot of sense now?" he asked.

"I don't follow you."

"We are always dreaming of going up in space, of reaching the stars. But if the universe is actually flat," he said, pointing to the trillions of shiny dots on a screen connected to Mount Stromlo Observatory, "then our evolutionary journey is pretty much a straight line. Not into outer space. We are already out there, but inward, into *inner* space, into the center of creation. It is important that we comprehend this and become properly aligned in the right direction. If we are unworthy, we could just be left to float aimlessly until the time of oblivion."

"Oh," sighed Kit. "I so much want to understand!" She began pacing around the room. "There is a museum in Houston, Texas—a tiny chapel, the Rothko Chapel. It houses the last paintings Mark Rothko executed before his death. They are huge, dark canvases with only ever so subtle variations of hue. The simplicity and solemnity of the work makes you want to kneel down in contemplation, in utter humility. His work moved me beyond words because he understood. He unraveled the mystery. Rothko managed to capture that flick of eternity, and he passed on to us the legacy that all that is real is the dark. The light that comprises the essence of our existence is nothing but one of the infinitesimal holes in the eternal veil of the night."

Chris remembered Danielle's fascination with art. She had mentioned that so much wisdom was encoded in color and minimal lines. After a moment of silence, he continued. "I think what the Edentians are trying to do for us is secure a place of permanence for our race. Allow us to be on a course for deceleration so we can join in the slowing down our particular universe."

"If we slow down, we'll be able to remain part of the universe, and if we continue to speed up aimlessly, we'll join the galaxies headed for extinction?" she asked incredulously.

He shrugged, not sure of the answer. "Do you know what that is?" he asked, pointing at a screen.

"I am not sure. A type of explosion?"

"John Larkin told me it is known as a 1A supernova. The *Foundation* has its own cosmic background explorer satellite to track such things."

"Where does this info come from?"

"The Hubble Space telescope at Carnegie."

Kit moved to yet another monitor and read "DASI" on the screen. She turned to Chris.

"It's the microwave telescope on the grounds at the South Pole," he explained.

"Hmm . . . do you think RA has received our message?" she asked. "And will they be sympathetic?"

"I hope so."

"Do you realize that our image, the image of you and me, was projected as a prototype of the human race?" Her voice had a tone of concern.

"Yeah, I suppose that is an awfully serious responsibility," Chris added.

"What if we can't live up to it?"

"We have no choice. We've got to be our best, or we will fail Danielle."

"Why do you think she chose us?" Kit asked.

"We'll never know. But I am glad she did."

XLIII

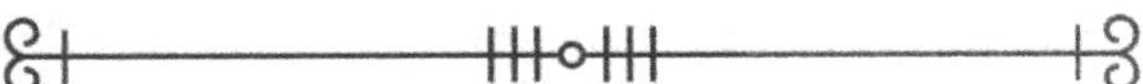

The answer from RA came thirty-six hours after transmission of the *Formation*. It entered the Earth's atmosphere as a simple beam of light, which, to the untrained eye, might have been dismissed as a passing comet. Attention was focused in other directions that night.

Deborah saw it, though, because the events of the day had rendered her sleepless, and she was standing on the terrace at the California house. It happened the same day the New York stock market crashed; anthrax was diffused throughout the country by way of an advertising pamphlet; the Dome of the Rock in Jerusalem was bombed, and intense fighting resumed between the Israelis and Palestinians, who were now backed by three other Arab countries. It was a Friday, one ever to be remembered as the darkest day of the millennium. For some mysterious reason, Deborah found the sudden appearance of a comet to be somehow reassuring.

At the *Foundation*, the majority of the members and visitors not directly connected with the technical aspects of the transmission went out onto the island to watch for a response. It was a spectacular night. Millions of stars were twinkling in shades of yellow, white, and lavender, from one side of the horizon to the other.

The signal from RA came as a salute that flashed across the heavens, bringing with it hope and optimism for the state of the world. Cheers rose up from the crowd as relief and elation carried the *Foundation* on a tide of celebration well into the early hours of the morning. Danielle, exhausted and weak from the excitement, which strained her already weakened state, remained inside in the company of Robert and Kjell and watched from the transmission room.

The reply came, as expected, partly in numerical code and partly in the Andonic language of the Edentians. And it had to be translated. The life carriers, solitary messengers, universal reconciliators, and the crew from RA acknowledged the greetings from U-606 as a sign of welcome. RA was not unaware of the conflicts and troubles plaguing Urantia. The hazy reddish aura surrounding the globe had alerted them to the concerns of its inhabitants.

RA's message continued, extending a warm salutation to the Edentians and respected members of the *Foundation* from the constellation Fathers and Most High of Norlatiadek, followed by an update of the situation in the governing constellations.

The Trial of Gabriel versus Luciel had come to a satisfactory conclusion, with a unanimous vote for the extermination of Arch-rebel Luciel. All of his followers who continued to instigate rebellion throughout the galaxies would be brought to trial and charged with treason, insurrection, and criminal intent toward the evolutionary souls.

The spirit of Cirel of Brann #30947188, a.k.a., Cirel Hansen, Hitler, Caligula, et al., had already been detained and arrested at the vortex.

As of yet, no charges had been brought against Lilith of Edentia—former intergalactic diplomat and member of the Adamic mission in the colonization of Urantia 606. Thus, members of her trinity, friends, and associates who wished to speak in her defense had to appear in front of the Celestial Judicial Courts of Edentia on the appointed date.

With that, Danielle, Kjell, and Robert saw the urgent need to accelerate their departure.

The unlawful manipulation of the Edenic currents and the meteoric debris shower scheduled to hit the Earth in twenty-four hours would be thrown off course by a gravitational acceleration, missing Urantia. As a consequence, Urantia and its surrounding system would pick up speed from energy generated by the passing asteroids. Such acceleration would go by unnoticed by the inhabitants of the planet, except for a subtle increase in the passing of time. There would be small amounts of debris hitting the Atlantic Ocean in a radius of one hundred miles around the *Foundation's* headquarters. As a matter of precaution, the area had to be immediately evacuated.

RA outlined several situations that needed to be resolved and advised on how that should be accomplished:

1. The eradication of the pall of negative energy that had settled over the planet. RA had picked up the existence of a general hopelessness that was taking root in the collective consciousness. Primarily, this feeling lay in the general lack of concern for the environment, a fear of what might come as a result of its degradation, and the belief that doomsday was inevitable. RA would create a universal wind swipe to dissipate this feeling of hopelessness. The first layer would fall apart during the first seventy-two hours. The underlying layers would fade out within a period not to exceed twenty-five years. The wind

swipe would cleanse the air, seal the ozone holes, and address global warming. This phenomenon occurred every few hundred years without causing serious damage, but this time, man's greed and continuous reliance on fossil fuel would result in the planet's degradation and irreparable damage.

2. It was noted that an excessive amount of radiation was leaking out of nuclear plants, especially in the US, where the nuclear reactors were old and had mechanical problems. The radiation seeping into the ground traveled, covering a radius of hundreds of miles from the nuclear plants. The contamination spread to grass roots and was depleting the land of elements needed for human sustenance. American children appeared to be the most affected victims of this low-grade radiation. RA presumed that high levels of Strontium 90 would be found in the blood of children. That condition would explain the reason for violence and brain dysfunction in the young—because the developing human brain mistook the Strontium for calcium. The wind swipe would maneuver the necessary atmospheric conditions to render most nuclear reactors inoperable in time.
3. The global distribution of addictive narcotic drugs would slow down drastically now that the economic conditions of the world were compromised. The attention of the western nations would now focus on rebuilding itself after its multiple national disasters and restoring the economy, instead of satisfying the greed of the powerful.
4. Vast amounts of mercury in the ocean waters were another point of concern. It was imperative to clean the waters, since those were to provide the largest part of the world's future food supply. As a means of rectification, faults in the crust of the planet would open and swallow the contaminants. The inevitable result would be earthquakes and tidal waves. Drastic precautions should be taken for such times. There was no other way of repairing the damage.
5. The air quality showed a medium to high level of contaminants: biological, chemical, as well as man- and animal-made gases—all pointing to the inevitable results of overpopulation and its carnivorous indulgence.
6. The wind swipe would annihilate the effects of all biological and chemical agents dispersed by international terrorists.
7. The eradication of disease. No condition could arise on the planet that had no remedy. Everything had been carefully planned and put on the planet by the life carriers. Therefore, every illness has a cure in one of the plants native to the planet. A single rainforest contains the cure for every possible ailment. Pharmaceuticals should stop manufacturing chemical substitutes. The AIDS epidemic, SARS, and other man-made viruses,

engineered and manipulated by the greedy to weed out unwanted groups, continue to get out of control and should stand as a reminder of how insubstantial the human race is when manipulated by stronger forces. The first step toward the eradication of world pandemics is to treat the sick soul and lead it toward the acceptance of its brother. Otherwise, more devastating, worldwide plagues will be unleashed by nature to bring balance to the planet. Hunger, poverty, hatred, and violence would diminish as soon as the collective consciousness stopped refueling them.

8. The spirit of Cirel was now in custody. The remaining leaders of his *Group* would be brought to trial. All the nations should unify and stand together in peace, should another assault emerge, and positively face the period of inevitable cleansing and restoration that is to follow.
9. A period of solar flares, meteorite showers, and planet misalignment would appear, but Urantia is to know that your Creator will not abandon you.

RA accepted the report from Daniela of Edentia and agreed to allow the planet to step into the next plane of consciousness. The carriers were touched by the image of love in the heart of the Urantian couple. Despite all the malicious efforts to keep the star seed apart, they had found one another, lending optimism for the future in the midst of the current darkness. The one trait RA found extraordinary in the human spirit was the endless effort to try again. No matter how many setbacks the spirit had, it never gave up. A race with such a strong spirit could not fail. Sooner or later, they would get it right.

Thus, the human race of Urantia was deemed ready to open a new era, a time of enlightenment. Given the planetary conditions, such enlightenment would come to them slowly, but it would ultimately find the right pace in the human spirit.

Project U-606, despite its numerous setbacks, would be on track now. There was some proof of rehabilitation of the repented rebel souls. The Edentians had done a good job. Urantia 606 was classified as an ongoing project.

RA concluded with approval for all Edentians stationed on the planet to relinquish their posts and return home. The recording and remembering should now be passed on to the humans of their choice.

A respectful salute was sent to Trebor, Kjell, and Daniela of Edentia, affirming the messengers were prepared to escort them on their journey home. The transmission closed with direct messages to the other sectors around the world, addressing their particular conflicts and concerns. It bore the signature of Orsef, member of the Council of Sages of Edentia.

Foundation Headquarters

Two hours had passed since Robert and Kjell had entered Danielle's chamber. Kitzia waited patiently in the waiting room, surrounded by Christian, Jean-Christophe, and Tom. In a separate area were Marina Cantrelli, Jeff, and Martine DuChamp. In the corner of the room, among other close friends of Danielle's, sat President Parker and Perez Levi.

There was absolute silence in the room, and an immense sadness prevailed. Kit was sure this would be the last time she would see Danielle. Her thoughts kept returning to the day when she had seen Danielle at the hospital shortly after the accident. She recalled the shock of seeing her friend's badly burned body and the sudden awareness that Danielle was vulnerable. In retrospect, Kit realized Danielle had started dying the moment the lightning hit her. Tom had explained that the mysterious brain implant had produced a glioblastoma when it was removed. And now the necrosis in the brain tissue resulting from both incidents had spread. Danielle's heart was giving up, regardless of medical intervention.

The engraved double bronze doors opened, and everyone's eyes turned anxiously in their direction. Kjell stepped out, followed by Robert, whose eyes searched for Kitzia, letting her know it was time for her to go in. Kit took small steps in the direction of the chamber, as if to prolong the inevitable.

The room inside the Temple of Health suite resembled more a royal chamber than a hospital room. The walls were covered in square blocks of gold metallic leaf and were lit by two gigantic torchiers. The medical personnel, dressed in ecru linen tunics, moved about quietly, unobtrusively administering comfort to the patient. In the center of the room stood a majestic bed with linens of a fine pale-yellow silk that rustled with every move Danielle made.

Danielle was propped up on several large, square pillows, looking like a queen in a morning conference with her advisors. The tiny oxygen tube in her nostrils was almost invisible. Nothing around her suggested illness, much less death. But Kit knew, all the same, that Danielle was expiring.

As Kit approached the bed, Danielle smiled, but it was hard for Kit to maintain her composure. Her pain overshadowed any other possible emotion.

"I see fear and sadness in your face," whispered Danielle.

"I don't want to lose you." Kit could no longer control her tears.

"You know that I'll always be with you. Be happy for me. I am finally going home."

"I know." Kit reached for Danielle's hand.

"For so long, I thought that I would remain here forever, that I had somehow failed in my mission." She sighed. "This is a magic planet indeed, and I got to experience what it is to be human."

"How many incarnations have you experienced?" asked Kit with interest.

"Too many to remember, enough to record everything over and over again." Danielle's face registered a sudden flash of the truth.

"What is it?" Kit noticed the hesitation in her friend's voice.

"Nothing." Danielle could not quite remember what her subconscious had stumbled upon.

"I'm sure you did everything perfectly," continued Kitzia. "The recording, the targeting of the traitors—you even made sure I found a mate. You didn't want me to be alone."

"It is more than that," said Danielle. "Remember when I spoke of the fragmented soul? There are different aspects of the soul in the feminine and the masculine psyches. Those must eventually unite for the soul to become whole again. So the search for a mate will continue through eternity—at least until all the split souls are reunited. Women have understood sooner the need to find their soulmates. Yet you see that men, at the peak of success, still yearn for women. They justify it as a need for sex, but it is actually that need for wholeness.

"You and Chris are of the same soul. Your evolution is nearing completion. Your children will give way to a new line—one that, in the future, will be like us. You see, Kit, your mission is a very important one for humankind. You possess the psychological traits to make the leap.

"I suppose I never made my position clear; I was seeking balance in my life." Danielle took a deep breath before continuing. "The world has existed under a patriarchal society for a long time now, almost five thousand years. But it was not always so. There was a time when society was matriarchal, when civilizations thought of God as a female entity. That concept prevailed for over twenty-five thousand years. It was a more gentle society, definitely more nurturing. The pendulum is swinging that way again. Perhaps this time, it will find balance." Danielle had to stop because she was running out of breath.

The nurses on both sides of the bed reached for Danielle. One took her pulse; the other gave her something to drink.

"I made for you a list of instructions to ensure your survival," Danielle said when she recovered.

"I've read it," said Kit. "I know what to do about the shelters. I'll keep in mind that we cannot save everyone during the wind swipe but will make sure the group designated to me survives. Chris and I will take over the California shelter; my mother the one in Colorado; Tom, until his name is cleared, will not surface. He and Jean-Christophe are heading for a place somewhere in South America."

"Tierra del Fuego," whispered Danielle.

"Jeff and Marina will take over the Keller DeWinter installation in Switzerland, and, of course, Cardinal Santis will head the one at the Vatican."

"Good," said Danielle. "The wind swipe will be brutal, but I hope short."

"I will miss you so much," said Kit. "I wish you could somehow let me know where you are and that you are all right."

"I won't be able to communicate with you, but I will speak to you through your children. They will be great receptors."

"You know that I am already carrying a child. Tell me about him."

"What can I tell you that you don't already know?" Danielle knew Kit had already figured out the genetic variance. "The most dangerous part is over; you survived. We kept you out of Cirel's reach." A smile of satisfaction appeared on the Edentian's lips before continuing. "You will continue to fulfill the promise made to Abraham and his descendants; you will continue to give light to the world.

"Cirel hated those who carried the divine spark of life. He would have destroyed you because you are to open a new era, a rebirth of Gan-Eden. Yes, your descendants will be here till the end of time. Cirel wanted to change that."

"Cirel," murmured Kit, "who was he really?"

"The representative of Luciel on Urantia. He took the place of Satan, Luciel's first lieutenant, after the imprisonment. His mission was to thwart every divine plan in existence and take out his revenge on the evolving souls. Cirel was once a high priest in Atlantis. He was the son of the pharaoh who enslaved the Jews. He was the Caesar who encouraged the crucifixion of the Christians—a sect of the Jews. He was also the Roman in power responsible for the diaspora. He was the instigator of the Inquisition because Spain had the largest settlement of Jews. As Hitler, he created the Holocaust. He appears in every page of your history that is stained with blood.

"What he was doing on the planet was nothing compared to what Luciel had in store for the universe. He was to infect the galaxies with a desire to seek death and not life. The malady was to engulf all living organisms. Even if he did not attain total annihilation of life, your planet would have been set back five-hundred thousand years, at least. During the recent *Formation*, RA received proof of that plan, the proof that every one of you helped me to assemble.

"Yes, Cirel was set on destroying what was most precious in the universe: the gift of life. Earth, or Urantia 606, was the testing ground. Cirel's plan began with the contamination of the soul. Then he imported a virus that was to kill all animal life and spread to the botanical world. Everything, and I mean everything, in the universe was to yearn for death until there would be nothing left but devastation and darkness."

"But why? What could Luciel gain by destroying everything?"

"He proclaimed a bizarre desire to return to the way it was before the creation of the universe. He wished to mar the image of the Creator, whose job is to create beauty and endow everything he touches with life and a longing for life.

"As a doctor, you saw the preliminary steps of such conditioning: severe child abuse as well as the use of certain narcotic substances, leading eventually to a wish for death. There were so many subtle ways the *Group* used to induce the death wish. The signs go undetected in most individuals: the nostalgia for the past, the excessive wish for law and order. Life itself is chaotic and unpredictable. Those infected with a death wish love technology and mechanical objects more than living organisms and will be more attracted to force than to beauty. Children's toys of choice will be powerful, destructive androids. That is the beginning of death, or self-destruction."

Kit thought of the Russian leadership, the Taliban, Al-Qaeda, and other radical terrorist groups seeking to destroy everything that was sane and noble.

"Chris will write and help you spread the awareness," added Danielle. "His writing will also erase erroneous ideas about God. Santis will lend strength to religious practices and will have the ability to abolish the myriad religions that popped up during the last centuries and free humankind of the exploitation carried out in the name of God. Perhaps in the future, there will not be a need for religion. The race will come to understand that the Divine Mind is conscious and conversant with all people, all the time, everywhere, without the need for intermediaries . . . and God is incapable of the human emotions attributed to him. Mostly, he is incapable of anger. In fact, emotions that are mean and despicable are totally foreign to the perfect nature of the Universal Father. Yes, Cardinal Santis will be an excellent representative of the Edentians on Earth."

Danielle closed her eyes and became silent. "I feel tired," she whispered.

Kit's heart beat faster. She didn't want to exhaust Danielle any further, but she also knew that if she let Danielle drift into sleep, she would be gone. Still clutching her friend's hand, Kit kept talking, trying to keep Danielle awake. "Tell me about what will happen to you next. Who will you meet? Will the other Edentians follow you? Do you have a soul mate?"

After so many questions, Danielle opened her eyes. "My departure will be followed by a journey through the giant helix of consciousness. Then I will encounter a master soul who will guide me through the transition worlds. I will turn in my mental transcripts, the compilation of my life experiences and accumulated information. The records will be evaluated, translated, and placed for safekeeping in the celestial archives. Then, if my mission is deemed complete, I will finally go home. Once there, I will resume my life as it once was, with my soul mate, with my love—with Orsef."

"Was that the reason why you and Robert . . ."

"No, no. Robert and I were not meant to be together. We . . ."

"Yes?"

"There is something I was to do. Why can't I remember?"

"It is all right," said Kit, patting her hand.

"Love . . . is to . . . transcend . . . all . . . boundaries," said Danielle. Her speech was becoming disjointed. Cardinal Santis, who Kit had not noticed was in the room, approached the bed. The cardinal was wearing the formal vestments of the Catholic Church. Having already given Danielle her last rites, he was still holding the anointing oil in one hand. He made the sign of the cross and began speaking in Latin.

"Santis, my dear Santis," murmured Danielle, "to you I entrust the intellectual unification of the planet. In your hands is placed the eternal quest for integration and . . . divine coherence."

Kjell and Robert had come into the chamber and took their places around the bed.

Danielle looked at them and asked, "Will *he* be there for me? Will he be proud of . . . my performance?"

"I think Orsef will be most proud," answered Robert.

Danielle turned to Kitzia. "My dearest Kit, I so much enjoyed being human."

Kit put her arms around Danielle, and her face, bathed in tears, pressed against that of her friend. Holding Danielle in her arms, Kit felt the spark of life slowly ebb from her mortal body.

XLIV

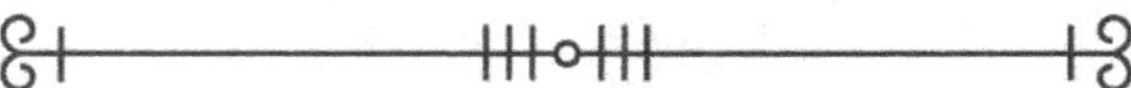

The funeral for Danielle Peschard was small and private. It was more of a formality for those close to her who felt comfortable with a religious service performed by Cardinal Santis. Robert Powers read the eulogy, and Kit scattered the ashes into the ocean.

Danielle Peschard was no more, Kit sadly realized. She tried to find comfort in Danielle's assurance that she would return to her rightful home, but the loss was no less painful.

Most of the areas at the *Foundation's* headquarters had by now been evacuated, sealed, and obscured. Kit and Chris, being among the last to exit the underwater installation, noted the interesting procedure. After each building was vacated, a metal sphere the size of a soccer ball was placed in the entry hall of each building. Within a few minutes, the contents of the building vanished—an Edentian maneuver that was incomprehensible to humans. It shrank and reassembled the molecules in another place. The astrophysicists explained that, on a smaller scale, it was the same procedure that would unfold when the universe expired. Next, the outside of the building was sprayed with a substance that caused it to appear hazy, and within minutes, the veregonium shield camouflaged the structure. Now transparent, each building separated from the others and shifted, becoming invisible and lost at the bottom of the ocean.

The evacuation of hundreds of members, personnel, and visitors had been going on non-stop. Planes landed and took off from the island continuously. Kit observed in silence. President Parker and his entourage, in the company of Martine DuChamp, were the first to depart. Perez Levi and his Middle East associates followed. Tom, with a group of scientists and physicians left next. To her surprise, Jean-Christophe boarded the plane for Europe, although there was no question in her mind that he and Tom remained a couple. Cardinal Santis and other dignitaries boarded the planes to their respective destinations.

Robert and Kjell, along with a number of the messengers, remained on the island as the arrangements for the departure of Kit and Chris continued. They were to take the last plane out, along with Marina Cantrelli and Jeff Montgomery. They would be flown to Bermuda, and from there, they would be taken to the States. Chris and Kit would reach Colorado through an underground transport—the same one Chris had traveled on earlier. The weather had turned, and the winds had the distinctive sound of an approaching storm. Kit suspected the winds announced the arrival of the wind swipe.

The Edentians would be departing shortly after Kit and Chris. Neither asked how the Edentians would exit the mortal plane. There were so many things both of them wanted to know but were fully aware that the time for questions was past. Marina and Jeff had already boarded, and Chris and Kit now made their way toward the aircraft. Robert walked next to Kit, while Kjell helped Chris carry bags full of notebooks. In his arms, Chris clutched a book he had been allowed to take from the *Foundation's* headquarters.

When they reached the stairs, Robert handed Chris a small silver USB drive. "I have put as much information on it as I could. It will help you understand what is coming in the times ahead."

"Precautions for the wind swipe?" interrupted Kit.

Robert smiled. It was a melancholy smile. "When the wind swipe arrives, you will welcome it gladly. This is to help you face the cataclysms to come. You may want to view it upon take off. But I must warn you; it is a onetime view. The contents will self-destruct after you have your look." Robert shrugged his shoulders. "I am sorry."

Chris understood. He shook Robert's hand as well as Kjell's. All of a sudden, the Edentians seemed taller and more imposing than ever. Robert held Kit in his arms. "Dearest girl, you have done, and will always do fine. You have our utmost respect and confidence."

Kit kissed him and then moved on to embrace Kjell. She was trying hard not to become emotional. The plane took off while the passengers waved at the two Edentians. Just before the jet lifted from the ground, Kit and Chris saw the Edentians and the messengers behind them vanish into thin air.

Kit and Chris looked at each other; nothing could further surprise them. Then their eyes moved to Marina and Jeff, who were silent but had not noticed the disappearance of the Edentians. Kit wondered what they were thinking. *Were they overwhelmed by what lay ahead of them?* After all, the four of them had just been informed that, along with the *Foundation*, they owned a large percentage of the wealth and resources of the world. Danielle's investments and possessions had been left in their entirety to Kit. Jeff had been left all that was Lili's, and Robert's fortune had been passed on to the *Foundation.* Kjell's interests were to be managed by the Cantrelli Medical Foundation. The dismantling of Cirel's and the *Group's* operations was sure to yield incredible wealth, which would be turned over to the Vatican.

Marina and Jeff were engaged in conversation, probably discussing what they should do first. Kit turned back to Chris, who was in the process of inserting the USB drive into his laptop. The computer screen opened, and the first page of Robert's document appeared. Kit and Chris read it carefully before proceeding to the next one, remembering that they would never have a chance to look at the document again. When it was over, Chris closed the laptop and sighed.

Kit went over her thoughts before she said, "So they stopped the deadly virus, and we get to go ahead—but into a world of pure chaos!"

"We'll survive it. It has happened countless times before. I've figured out that the universal fear of Armageddon comes from a memory imprinted in our genetic code. This time, we are prepared, and we shouldn't feel alone, even though we are not to receive any further communication from them, except through quantum cryptography. They will use the nature of the atom to encode information," added Chris. "I imagine that from time to time, we'll get messages from the *Foundation,* when the scientists decode a message."

"Do you understand what it was all about?"

Chris made an affirmative gesture. "Somewhat." He smiled before continuing. "Considering the Edentians went to such great lengths to make sure I understood. They could have just told us the truth and be done with it. But knowing my lust for the fantastic, they gave me time travel, underwater installations . . . and did not stop until I was convinced that there is more than the reality we perceive."

"So the Edentians in charge of the rehabilitating project called U-606 have been the keepers of the prison called Earth?"

"Exactly. The energy that should be used to escape the prison is put back into the system to perfect techniques for genocide and mass murder. No wonder the Celestials had become disillusioned with our race."

"One Edentian did not give up on us. Danielle fought for us till the end. She procured passage for those ready to move forward, to take the leap, and in so doing gave the planet one more chance for redemption. Chris, you are to tell the world the truth. But where will you start?"

"At the beginning, I suppose. What just transpired here is, in an infinitesimal way, part of the ongoing and eternal conflict that has afflicted our universe since the beginning of time."

"The struggle between good and evil?"

"The two forces in conflict view it differently. Each one sees its ideology as right. The best way to describe it is the struggle between autonomy and union."

"So it is autonomy versus dependence really the question?"

"I think so. It is that quest for autonomy that causes the imbalance in the universe, because of its impossibility. How can anything disconnect itself from its source? Instead of admitting its error, it seeks justification."

"Do you think this conflict is still ongoing throughout the universe?"

"No, I don't. This particular conflict has simply not been resolved down here." He took Kitzia's hand and kissed it. "We are here for such a short time . . ."

"I just can't imagine what cataclysms are to come," said Kit. "So much has been destroyed, so many landmarks, museums, libraries—"

The word *museum* caught Jeff's attention. Remembering the bombing at the Met that killed his friend Linda, he wanted to join the conversation.

Chris turned to face the couple across the cabin and included them. "Yes, it seems there has been further destruction," said Chris, condensing the report he had just viewed. "Upon hearing the news of the capture and death of Cirel, their leader, his death brigade, which had cells all over the world—especially in the US—went immediately into action, accelerating his plan for Armageddon. In the States alone, the devastation is incredible. New York was attacked first. Terrorists bombed the United Nations and several other landmarks."

"Terrorism will be stopped," Jeff added emphatically.

The voice of Jeffrey, the pilot, came on the loudspeaker. "There has been a last-minute change of plans. I have just been informed that no planes are allowed to land in the US. I will therefore fly to the Gulf of Mexico and drop you off as close to the American shore as I can. You will be picked up and taken by boat to Texas. From there, you will proceed to Colorado through underground transport."

Jeffrey connected the audio he was receiving to the loudspeaker in the cabin so they all could hear. "The unexpected terrorist infiltration, assault, and occupation of one of our country's secret military bases near San Antonio, Texas, was a catastrophic attack on American territory. It is believed American terrorists, part of the international group of terrorists known as the Death Brigade, turned on their brothers by firing two missiles from the installation. The missiles were fired within minutes of each other—the first aimed at Hoover Dam, destroying the facility that provides water and power to the West Coast. The second hit the downtown area of Chicago, killing thousands of people. The worst nightmare for the American people has become a reality. Both missiles dispersed much-feared biological agents that will take even more lives . . . the *Bacillus anthracis* bacteria, which is known to cause anthrax, and the *Brucella suis* responsible for brucellosis."

Chris took a deep breath and spoke over the transmission. "What we are facing is the culmination of many attempts to erase us from the planet. But that will not happen."

"That is absolutely correct!" replied Jeff in an outburst of defiance. "We must unite and fight."

"The wind swipe is on its way," added Kitzia. "It will arrive soon, and we will eventually learn that it is in our favor."

"The human soul suffered a setback, and we are facing the consequences," said Marina Cantrelli in a sad tone.

The voice of the pilot returned. "I have just been advised of the place where we will land. It is a small island in the Gulf near Tampico, Mexico. Representatives of the *Foundation* will be awaiting you, Dr. O'Neil and Mr. Goodman. Please take this opportunity to review the equipment that has been placed under your seats."

The four passengers reached under their seats and extracted backpacks holding booklets, bottles of antidotes, antibiotics, and, of course, Israeli-made black rubber gas masks. They read the instructions and adjusted the straps and filters on the masks, while in the background, the news transmission with its tale of terror continued.

EPILOGUE

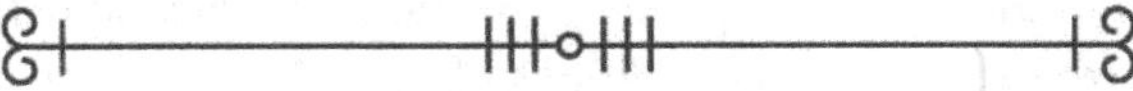

Afterlife

The reassembling of her persona was slower than Daniela had anticipated. It was to take effort and pain, enormous pain. The experiences of her last incarnation on Urantia began falling into place, but it was the others—those of the ancient past—that she had difficulty processing.

The awareness of being was what she first experienced upon awakening. She slowly savored the notion of "I am" as a formulation of her first complete thought.

I am . . .

I am Daniela . . .

I exist eternally.

The images of her life as Danielle Peschard in Urantia paraded through her consciousness in sequence, as in a dream, followed by an echo of pain that went all the way to her soul. Millions of luminescent sparks filled her memory like brush-strokes on a half-finished canvas.

Daniela experienced her new weightlessness, and the lack of form gave way to infinite freedom. But the first step, she knew, was to create a vision of herself as she had been during the last incarnation. She had to put some order to the boundless chaos and the multitude of suffocating grays that wrapped around her. She remembered the shock she had once experienced upon awakening in the limbo of the suicides, that terrible place of emptiness and desolation. But this was something different altogether. She had to project a new sense of reality.

As she formulated her wish, she found herself again in the image of Danielle Peschard. Her body was similar in shape and stature, but infinitely lighter. It was void of the circulatory, nervous and digestive systems that made mortal bodies so cumbersome. The inner structure of her body was nothing but light and air, and it generated a state of euphoria.

As soon as she opened her eyes, she projected her image onto a mirror and liked what she saw. She clothed herself in a black, tailored wool gabardine suit, like the ones she wore to corporate meetings. On her feet appeared a pair of alligator pumps. Her red hair fell smoothly to just above her shoulders, and her visage appeared perfectly groomed.

She proceeded to project a room with high walls and a coffered ceiling. But she changed her mind and ordered up polished, modern walls, and the image transformed. She continued to call up recreations of the things she loved most in her life on the planet: the statue of Aphrodite that she had excavated in Knidos, the Doric sculptures, the "Dora Marr" painting by Picasso, and the Louis XIV desk from her study. In no time, the room looked sumptuous, but Daniela changed it up by banishing half of the French-period furnishings and replacing them with less ostentatious contemporary pieces. The décor now resembled her penthouse in New York. She created large windows through which a vision of the ocean could be seen. It was a turbulent sea, with waves lashing forcefully against the glass walls of the room, and from the depths of the ocean rose a gigantic statue of Michael of Nebadon. The monument stood erect and magnificent, as it once had in the Kingdom of Atlantis.

Daniela smiled at the contradiction of styles, timeframes, and locations. After all, this was the wonderful part of the transition worlds—the freedom to create. No master soul had yet appeared to guide her; therefore, Daniela took the opportunity to review her memories in her own way.

She had passed on to Tom O'Neil part of the secret for refining DNA. He would certainly be a good keeper of the secret and would perhaps, one day, use it in the cause of humanity.

Christian and Kitzia were the perfect choices to be rememberers—being the offspring of Adam and Eva. Jean-Christophe would gradually discover sites that would reveal the hidden secrets of the planet, the lost technology of diverse alien visitors, and the relics and remnants of giants whose civilization once ruled the Earth.

Cardinal Santis would get a book that Jean-Christophe would one day discover, containing passages from the beloved manuscript. The book would reveal the true story of the sojourn of Michael of Nebadon, as Jesus of Nazareth on Urantia.

President Parker would help dismantle the terrorist cells around the world.

She had successfully completed her assignment and could finally return home with her associates. The two trinities, once again united, would stand together at Lili's hearing. Charges against Lilith would certainly be dismissed.

What made Lili go back to Urantia, anyway? Daniela wondered. She suddenly remembered a time when Lili's reconditioning was complete. Yet she had chosen to return to Earth, and because of it, had suffered a setback and had become once again seduced by the vices of the land. Had Cirel called her back? She would not have come back for *him*.

There had to be something else. She would only have returned for someone she truly loved. Kjell? He had never been seduced by the dark side. Trebor? It could not be Trebor, a.k.a., Robert, either. His recent association with the *Group* had been a cover.

Daniela soon realized there had to be another reason. The only explanation was that one of them had been unable to exit. *But who?*

"Trebor . . . Kjell," she implored. "I know you are back. Please help me remember what I have forgotten. Adam, Eva, my dearest friends, I found your children. I've done what I was supposed to do." Daniela's voice ached with pain.

The four beings stood on the threshold of her realm.

"Shall we go in?" asked Trebor. "We might be able to help."

Adam, Eva, and Kjell got ready to enter, but Orsef's voice spoke sharply.

"No!" Orsef ordered, standing behind them. "Daniela must do it alone."

"But . . ." hesitated Eva. "The Council is beginning to assemble. She may not be ready to appear before them."

"I know she will be," added Orsef, with complete confidence. "She is at the point of self-realization. I want her to appear as she is, self-sufficient!"

"You are right," agreed Trebor. "She has done it all alone. Let's not interfere in any manner that may suggest we have offered assistance."

"It is important for her to know that she undertook the complete journey back alone," concluded Orsef, and looking at each of them, asked, "Shall we join the Council?"

"What about Lili?" Kjell asked.

"Her appearance at the Council is scheduled to be right after Daniela's. The outcome of Daniela's appearance will greatly influence the Council in favor of Lilith's."

Orsef's confident stance had a reassuring effect on the others. "Shall we?" Orsef the Magnificent led the way, and the others followed.

"No one comes, not the master soul, nor my friends," whispered Daniela. "There is something of great import that I must remember!"

One more time, she reviewed the life of peace and comfort she had lived on Urantia, her altruism, the desire to be of service, the sharing of her fortune with others. Step by step, she reconstructed her life up to the moment of the attack, the lightning bolt that hit her, the momentary separation from her physical body, and her brief return to Edentia and her encounter with the Almighty. She clearly recalled His asking what she wanted to do and the vanishing of her fears the moment that she decided to return to Earth to finish her assignment. At that point, she had had the feeling that she was back in grace, that she had been forgiven.

Forgiven . . .

At that precise moment, she knew. She remembered.

Like a thunderbolt, it all came back to her. She knew why she had been on Earth so long, why her Edentian friends had returned and would not leave her behind. She understood that all along it was she who had been trapped on Earth.

It was she who was the rebel soul.

It suddenly came to her that she had created a hiding place within herself to retreat from what she wanted to forget. She began clearing away objects from the image she had created, as if discarding detritus from her soul. As her understanding unfolded, so did the memories. Urantia 606 flashed in her mind. The project was successfully underway when she applied for the assignment as recorder. Orsef was opposed at first, stating she was too young and too inexperienced.

"Urantia is a remote place, a desolate training ground for fallen souls," he insisted. "We are not even sure how the souls will respond to reconditioning." But Daniela would not yield. She was determined and wanted desperately to be given an important project at which she could succeed.

At first, she was posted on an observation satellite to record the initial steps of evolution in the human mind. She witnessed the encasement of rebel souls in matter and the beginning of the journey back to grace. She witnessed the arrival of Adam and Eva and the uplifting of the species. She watched Robert, as Trebor, lay out the grounds for civilization, and Kjell design incredible structures from dirt and stone. She saw Lili arrive and work successfully with them as part of their team.

Urantia had been cut off from the circuits of celestial communication, so it was up to Daniela to relay updates of the rebellion to her friends. The newness and excitement of the assignment began to diminish, just as it did for Eva on Urantia, because the reconditioning process of the fallen souls was unendurably slow. Two hundred years of Earth time had elapsed, and there was no advancement to be seen in the fragmented souls. As humans, they were brutish and more interested in experiencing humanity with all its vices than advancing to restore their souls.

Daniela wanted to help Eva. *Or was there an ulterior motive?*

Yes, there was. She wanted to return home. She came to realize what Orsef had foreseen: the rehabilitation process would take a very long time. She had to think of a way of moving things along. While she contemplated such thoughts, Satan, Luciel's first lieutenant, arrived at her station. Until then, the rebels had been free to roam the galaxies. The unanimous celestial belief that the rebels would repent in time never happened. They continued to seek recruits and proceeded to enlarge their ranks.

Satan entered the satellite from which she was monitoring Urantia's progress and spoke with the technical advisors and other Edentian monitors. His eloquent discourse fell on deaf ears—until he spotted Daniela. He must have read the unrest in her soul, and his words found a way into her consciousness.

Daniela listened.

The seed of doubt was sown. Unaware that her soul had been contaminated, she set out on a plan that would once and for all settle in her mind the point in question.

Autonomy . . . an interesting concept, she told herself, and the concept circled endlessly in her mind. *What could possibly be wrong with testing the concept? I will do it only for the benefit of my cause. What if I were to aid Eva in the acceleration of the species? So what if we bypassed their orders? The end result will be the same; the fallen souls will be reconditioned.*

Daniela went to Urantia and conferred with Eva. She spoke of her meeting with Satan. "He clearly insists that Luciel wants no attack on Michael, the Creator Son," she explained. "Satan simply questions the authority of the Most High to retain absolute sovereignty over our universe in the name of a god we have never seen."

"This project was assigned by Michael," said Eva.

"And comes bearing the seal of approval of the Most High. It was they who set the rules. I doubt that Michael, Himself, would mind how we accomplish the job, as long as we accomplish it."

Eva listened with interest; she admitted her frustration with the project, the impatience she was experiencing.

"What if you were to accelerate it?" asked Daniela.

"But the orders and guidelines are specific!" insisted Eva.

"They are nothing but guidelines. Nothing says they cannot be altered if a better way is found to accelerate the advancement."

"I do have the knowledge . . . and the means," whispered Eva.

"Of course you do! You have the DNA code. You can manipulate the DNA any way you wish. Perhaps you could enhance the molecules with extra-terrestrial ones. You also have access to the fruit from the *Tree of Knowledge*."

Eva was tempted but reconsidered. Although enhancing the genes was part of the plan, it was decreed that manipulation should be done gradually and under very precise conditions. It was not until Daniela reinforced Eva's suspicion that Adam had fallen under the spell of Lilith that Eva made the dread decision. She knew Lili was dabbling in some questionable activities, and she certainly didn't want to see Adam trapped in the realm, as Lili likely would be.

Eva formulated a plan. She would take it upon herself to find an alternative method to mutate the species. The results would speak for themselves. Either the race would move forward from its present stage, or it would prove to be damaged beyond repair. Daniela was right, Eva concluded. Either way, they would all go home sooner.

Tampering with the DNA at such an early stage was a grave error in judgment. Veering from the guidelines caused the project to fail. The stages of evolution were to reach a certain level before Eva should manipulate the genes and allow the transition. Nonetheless, Eva jumped the state of the human mind from level two to level four. The experiment was a disaster. Only a handful of beings were successful in reaching the next level of consciousness. The majority became excessively aggressive, their brains not yet able to assimilate the manipulation. The rest, completely unable to make the leap, went into extinction.

Adam and Eva, along with Daniela and Lilith, were relieved from their posts—demoted and ordered to finish their assignments as inhabitants of the planet. The suspicion that Adam and Lilith were involved proved to be unfounded. Actually, it was Adam's extraordinary loyalty that influenced the outcome of the verdict. The Edenic group was never charged with treason; neither was it suspected of rebellion, but it was adjudged in default.

As Daniela relived the past, she gained full recognition of what she had done. She further understood why her rehabilitation had been slower than the others, why her sin had been of more consequence. Eva had erred in her desire to help humanity. Daniela had erred because of selfishness. She recoiled at the significance of her failure and succumbed to her unknown fate. She understood, now all too well, there is no separation from the Almighty, no wisdom greater than His, and therefore, no better way of doing things than those set by His representatives. The Urantia 606 project had been dangerously compromised, and she considered herself the catalyst.

Three hundred years passed. As mortals, Adam and Eva continued to work at uplifting the species, and they did an exemplary job. The races were greatly improved by their teachings. Having successfully completed their reconditioning, they were the first to depart. Lili and Kjell departed shortly after. Trebor disappeared and Daniela assumed he had departed as well.

Daniela watched her friends' departure and the disappearance of the other Edentians, and sank into despair. As she set out alone on her pilgrimage through the ages, she experienced agonizing episodes of loneliness. She blocked her transgressions from her mind as she watched entire civilizations flourish and dissipate. As she continued to record, she tasted the pleasures of the realm. Then came the worst of her transgressions. In Rome, during the reign of Gaius Claudius Caesar, on a whim, Daniela projected herself into Messalina, Claudius's consort, and became intoxicated with power. She began to associate with Cirel and Catilina and was introduced to every vice and debauchery of that fabled time.

As Messalina, she frequented the Coliseum, and expressing a sudden contempt for the believers in Christ, she amused herself in the carnage that took place. At that point, her soul plunged into a downward spiral. Ultimately, Claudius had Messalina executed for her excesses.

It was during the period between incarnations that she reconnected with her Edentian friends, who were aware of how she had let herself be corrupted and had returned to the realm to help her save herself from ultimate disgrace. On seeing her real friends, Daniela was shaken and embarrassed to realize the scope of her transgressions. Once again, she begged the Council for forgiveness and implored her friends to help her earn one last chance to conclude her mission with honor.

Daniela sadly witnessed Lili renew her association with Cirel. It was because of her that Lili had returned to Urantia and had again allowed herself to be compromised. At that point, Daniela swore never to leave Urantia without Lili, not realizing that her journey back to grace would be much longer than Lili's. Trebor watched from a distance, and because of her shame, Daniela avoided him. Kjell's loyalty to his friends and associates assured his permanence on Earth for millennia.

Daniela once again set out on her trip toward redemption. There continued to be occasional setbacks, but she saw patterns emerge and moved forward with renewed energy and joy. In her journey back to grace, her spirit evolved through the ages, and she slowly found redemption. Through her many incarnations, Daniela experienced every race and belief. She was tempted in every possible way. But she stayed on course, reassessed her values, and never again veered from her innate sense of loyalty and obedience to the Most High of Edentia. She moved through the ages, observing, recording, and attesting to the glory of creation.

She had keenly observed the evil manipulations of Cirel, his recruiting of the weakest, most malleable souls and his institution of their conditioning for battle. She had sworn to stop him but needed to find his ultimate motive.

When she realized his desire was to implement a longing for death throughout the universe, she forwarded her warnings and selected her collaborators. She would stop Cirel.

The wish for self-destruction was endemic to the human race. This was the circumstance that the Celestials were trying to eradicate. Therefore, all the information she had forwarded through the millennia was of little consequence. There was nothing they did not know. Her assignment had been one of understanding and redemption; but it was perhaps that achievement that had gained favor with the Most High in listening to her plea in favor of humankind.

That she had assured the survival of her friends and the members of the *Foundation* was crucial. She knew they had the wherewithal to sustain the soul of positive energy in the collective consciousness. She was certain the plan of Morphic resonance would work this time. Urantia 606 would now succeed! The survivors would hold fast on Stage 8 until the portal opened to level nine, and humankind would walk into a time of enlightenment and perhaps redemption.

Her strength and confidence returned. Her thoughts returned to her friends, confident they would eventually grasp the truths she had imparted. She hoped Kit and Chris would have an awareness of the million realities existing concurrently in their universe and that every soul possesses its own space to create its personal evolution. Her only regret was being unable to disclose that life is but a rehearsal, a stage upon which man must perfect the role he chooses to play throughout eternity. Perhaps one day, they would understand.

Beyond that, there was not much more she could do. Absolute peace would never reign on Urantia; there would always be conflict. It was, after all, a rehabilitation realm for damaged souls seeking unification, and they would continue to come from all corners of the universe. Daniela realized she had just exited Urantia, *the insane asylum of the universe.*

The time had come for her to take her exit from the room her imagination had built. She knew what lay on the other side of the door: *home*, the world she had left behind in her quest for adventure. She had yearned for more and had attained infinitely less, tangled in the traps of a rehabilitation world.

She would never, never leave again.

She would present her case and felt almost certain she'd be exonerated. She cast aside the image of her mortal body, along with her proper black suit. As her transformation took place, she reclaimed her splendid Edentian presence, and without doubts or regrets, she opened the door.

The Council awaited her. In the glorious salon of translucent pillars and golden light, she spotted Trebor, her dearest friend and protector, who had never given up on her, who had always loved her, who had observed her unobtrusively throughout the ages, always watching over her. She saw Kjell, who had played the role of brother and eternal guardian. She saw Adam and Eva, who, from Edentia, had monitored her progress step by step. Between them sat His Holiness, the recently departed pope and former head of the Earth's *Foundation.*

Daniela approached the Council. With every step, her excitement and happiness grew. She saw the kind smiles and welcoming eyes of the Most High, the Melchezedeks, the entire Edentian Council.

And then she saw *him*: Orsef the Magnificent, surrounded by a resplendent aura. He walked toward her, extending his hand to take hers, and his unspoken words echoed through the galaxies.

"Welcome home, Daniela, my beloved Edentian."

ACKNOWLEDGMENTS

Gratitude flows daily to my husband, Conn, who stays the course with me in loving steerage of the process from the first to the last words on the page.

I would like to thank my dearest friend, Bet Joy, daughter of novelist Tom Ham, who took my first rough manuscript and gave it consistent and enthusiastic encouragement.

Deep thanks also goes to David Hancock, founder of Morgan James Publishing, for advising and guiding me through the process of getting my manuscript approved and ready for publication.

To Jim Howard, publisher, for his professional and focused leadership—his advice and suggestions, were essential in refining each detail from cover to cover. And for the efficiency of Emily Madison, my author relations manager and the entire MJP team.

Special thanks to my talented editor, Cortney Donelson, who took the vision of my story and, with her aptitude for detail, made it better.

I feel indebted to the *Urania Book* and the Urania Foundation for opening doors of thought about the universe, after which I felt a channel of inspiration and information flow from unknown sources.

My path for publication included experienced encouragement from my friends, Kathy and Victor Brook, who had also found success with Morgan James Publishing.

And finally, I would also like to recognize my children, Lynn and Sean Zeid, whose creativity and love for life inspired me to write.

ABOUT THE AUTHOR

Gissele Trussell was born in Mexico City, the daughter of a successful fiction publisher. Her childhood was full of writers and artists. This atmosphere stimulated her imagination, and at an early age, she began writing short stories.

She attended Trinity University, became fluent in four languages, and worked as a legal and technical translator, language teacher, and illustrator. She continues her research in Hermetics, comparative religion, philosophy, and Kabbalah.

The upsurge of public consciousness that "we are not alone in the universe" motivated Gissele to write her first novel, *The Edentians*, a metaphysical adventure about the connection between humankind and cosmic forces.

When not writing fiction, Gissele paints and travels the world with her husband, Conn Trussell. She lives in Houston, Texas.

Printed in the USA
CPSIA information can be obtained
at www.ICGtesting.com
JSHW022312271023
51011JS00002B/9